WHAT'S BECOME OF HER

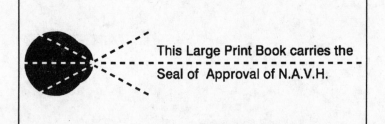

WHAT'S BECOME OF HER

DEB CALETTI

WHEELER PUBLISHING
A part of Gale, a Cengage Company

Farmington Hills, Mich • San Francisco • New York • Waterville, Maine
Meriden, Conn • Mason, Ohio • Chicago

LIBRARY OF CONGRESS CATALOGING-IN-PUBLICATION DATA

Names: Caletti, Deb, author.
Title: What's become of her / by Deb Caletti.
Description: Large print edition. | Waterville, Maine : Wheeler Publishing, a part of Gale, a Cengage company, 2017. | Series: Wheeler Publishing large print hardcover
Identifiers: LCCN 2017019100| ISBN 9781432842390 (hardcover) | ISBN 1432842390 (hardcover)
Subjects: LCSH: Large type books. | BISAC: FICTION / Contemporary Women. | FICTION / Romance / Contemporary. | FICTION / Mystery & Detective / Women Sleuths. | GSAFD: Mystery fiction. | Suspense fiction.
Classification: LCC PS3603.A4386 W48 2017b | DDC 813/.6—dc23
LC record available at https://lccn.loc.gov/2017019100

Published in 2017 by arrangement with Bantam Books, an imprint of Random House, a division of Penguin Random House LLC

Printed in the United States of America
1 2 3 4 5 6 7 21 20 19 18 17

For my family

Thou wast all that to me, love,
For which my soul did pine —
A green isle in the sea, love,
A fountain and a shrine . . .

— EDGAR ALLAN POE,
To One in Paradise

Back to the land of freedom. Back to breaking the law with her sisters to make sure justice got served. God, just the thought had her tingling all over.

— FERN MICHAELS,
Blindsided

CHAPTER 1

In about twelve minutes, Isabelle Austen's old life will be gone forever. Right now, though, the seaplane is still in the air, out of her sight, a few miles off the coast of Parrish Island. When it finally arrives and splashes down, and when Henry North ducks out of the doorway, that'll be it. Done. Over. She has no idea. Not a clue. Dear God, it'd be easy, if you could read the future. But you can't, so she just stands there on that dock as the air currents shift, and wings tilt, and change jets her direction from across the sea. It'll all be very good and very bad, quite necessary and disastrous, because love plus tragedy plus fury is a potent but untidy mix. Now she only waits, surrounded by gray, choppy waters.

There's a sudden commotion in the sky. She looks up. No, it's not the plane yet. It's those birds. The flock of crows is overhead, midway in their evening commute. She watches and can't help but shiver, because there are hundreds of them. *Hundreds.* The sky almost turns black. It could be a Hitchcock film, even if it's just nature, being weird and creepy and magnificent. She has seen this too many times to count, but she never fails to be awestruck.

Isabelle holds still and listens; she hears the *whiff whiff* of wings as they pass. A *murder of crows,* it's called. No one is exactly sure why. Perhaps it's due to all those years with a bad rap, with the mean reputation as creatures of terror and loathing. Or it could be because of that old, frightening folktale, which says that crows gather to decide the capital fate of the criminal among them. A death-sentence jury in wings and black satin.

Look, they come and they come and they come, and it's like some freak event, only it happens every morning and every night, every single day of the week. If they are harbingers of danger, then there is a lot of danger coming. If they are portents of retribution, the guilty better watch out.

Then:

The plane arrives. Isabelle ties it down to the moorings, with big ropes wound in figure eights onto iron cleats. She wipes her hands on her jeans. Eddie Groove, the pilot, cuts the engine of the four-seater Cessna. When he does, there is an abrupt silence. At least, the only sounds are the waves sloshing against the plane's pontoons, and a far-off radio on a boat, and the whisper-flap of those crows overhead. The propeller slowly spins to a stop.

Inside, Eddie and the passenger exchange a few last words. The door of the plane opens, and a man appears. He has tousled hair and a quiet confidence and bright eyes with smile crinkles.

"Welcome, Mr. North," Isabelle says.

"Isabelle? Nice to meet you in person."

Henry North takes her offered hand and steps onto the dock. Why this handsome man — an innocent-looking man, carrying a leather case and wearing a sweater with soft elbow patches — chose this far-off corner of the world, well, it's not a question that occurs to her until much later. The *too late* kind of later. She doesn't think about what his plans are, or what his history might be, probably because her own history is shouting and crashing so loudly in her head right then. She recently left Evan after eight years together — two married, six not — and her mother's just died, so she's as unanchored as a ship from its shore. History jammed with history is always where the trouble starts, even without all the suspicions that shadow Henry North.

"Beautiful," he says, as he looks around before settling his gaze back on her.

The word seems to refer to the harbor, the cove, the island, to the fact that he's arrived, and even to Isabelle herself. For a second, this makes her feel something lately unfamiliar: happy. Isabelle doesn't spot the dark circles, which tell the truth of his haunted, sleepless nights. She doesn't think about crow metaphors and doomed foreshadowing, or what your own wrecked self brings to a situation. Instead, the positive and grateful word *beautiful* reminds Isabelle that she's always been a positive and grateful person, and all at once she smells that great gasoline-and-saltwater smell, and notices the way the waves sparkle, and how do you explain a swift turn of mood, anyway? Her emotions have been all over the place. It's just maybe a good day for once, a good day during a bad time.

He grins at her, and she smiles back, and right there, *zing,* something sort of aligns with something else. It's not the huge, tectonic shift of love at first sight. It's just a crickle of energy. Still, a grin can be enough to set things in motion, same as a loose rock can start a landslide, same as a burble of lava begins a blast. Things have to start somewhere. Because, what a great grin. It's the kind that makes you like a person instantly.

"Did you have a pleasant trip?"

"I definitely did."

He stares straight into her eyes. It's a trick of both lovers and predators, she realizes, but so what? Blame the fact that she's brokenhearted (but ready to be done being brokenhearted), recently uprooted, and orphaned (if you can call a thirty-seven-year-old with dead parents an orphan). Blame fate, or the semi-evolved parts of a human brain, whatever. But her heart flops like a newborn. The fingers she'd just grasped were warm and solid, so it's understandable.

He shields his view, takes in the eerie flock above. The dock rocks a little. The sky has turned dusky pink. The crows are a multitude of stark shadow puppets flap-flapping behind the sunset screen.

"Wow."

Henry North watches for a while. As he does, Isabelle checks out his nice leather shoes. She takes in the rest of him, too: his left ringless hand holding a briefcase, a maroon bag slung over his shoulder, and

Oh, no, Isabelle — the way he smells. He smells like outside, sun plus wind, an open-air largeness that makes her remember old, great summers.

" 'With many a flirt and flutter . . .' " Henry North finally says. To Isabelle's confused squinch, he clarifies. "Poe. 'The Raven.' "

"Ah."

Intriguing, she thinks.

Actually, slightly thrilling. *A poem!* (Though her hiding, cynical side, the dream squasher she ignores, scoffs. *A poem?*) Evan, the reluctant husband, the cruel heartbreaker, was in pharmaceutical sales. He could quote the highest prescribing physicians in a tristate region, but that was all. Oh, the number of missteps already! She's completely forgotten that past lovers and future ones are sometimes like dogs. They can look so different from each other, but they're still the same animal.

"Does this . . ." He indicates upward.

"Every night. Every morning at sunrise, too."

"I've never seen anything like it. What are they doing?"

"Coming home. They go to Friday Harbor for the day and then return here to their roost."

These are common questions. Most of Island Air's flights leave in the early hours and arrive at dusk, a schedule that nearly matches that of the crows, so the unrushed tourist will often ask. Right then, Isabelle can see another one of their pilots, Liz Rajani, off in the sky-distance. She's in the tiny yellow-and-white Beaver, bringing six passengers for a family reunion on Parrish. Out their left-side windows, they'll glimpse the swath of black, looking like the long, trailing scarf of a widow.

If they even notice. If they're not too busy chatting about so-and-so's new boyfriend and Aunt Someone's heart attack and whether they've ordered enough chicken for the barbecue. Who ever notices omens, anyway.

Pilot Eddie salutes Isabelle with two fingers, indicating he's done, that's all, no more help needed. All the pleasantries with the customer are finished — the *Thank you* and the *You're welcome* and the *Have a great time.* Henry North walks up the dock with the intoxicated-looking gait of one unaccustomed to the bumping and rocking of water. It makes him appear humble and vulnerable, and so do those soft elbow patches. With his briefcase, he seems like a

15

too-serious child, the ill-fated sort, on the way to a school full of bullies.

Isabelle feels a gust of concern for this stranger, the sort of compassionate goodwill that gets a thoughtful person into trouble. On a whim, she follows him, trots to catch up, not something she would generally do. It's unusual enough that she feels Eddie Groove's eyes boring into her back, or maybe that's just her good sense jabbing her between her shoulder blades.

It's not Eddie's business, anyway. He's known her since she was small, but she's his boss now. Since her mother died and she came back here five months ago, Island Air is hers until she decides what she wants next. What she wants next is a question that gapes like the dark mouth of a cave. All she knows so far is that she wants things to be easier than they have been. It's been effort, effort, effort trying to make things work with Evan; she'd put the coins in that particular slot machine for years hoping for the sweet jackpot of a happy marriage and children, and instead, the slot machine just stopped taking coins one day. That dream is gone, but she maybe still wants the regular good stuff a life can offer — love, a little happiness, peace.

But maybe she wants to take chances, too.

She's always been so ridiculously careful. She kind of hates herself for it. Come on — be bold! Life is short, right? Hers is a complicated legacy — might as well get some pleasure out of it. For all the mess and hassle, she can at least have a pleasant conversation with a good-looking man. Why not? She's a grown woman, for God's sake. Sometimes grown women must remind themselves that they are grown women.

I sign your paycheck, Eddie, so stop looking at me like that, she thinks, while Eddie is only peering at the distant sky, gauging the change in weather. Isabelle gets angry with the wrong people and not angry enough with the right ones. It's silent anger, besides; all stomachaches and insomnia, because anger is nuclear. Her acts of rebellion occur mostly in her head, which has been a big problem. Another problem: It can be hard to tell if your best traits are actually your worst ones. *You've got a kind heart, Isabelle,* her friend Anne used to say, and it's the common refrain. Her entire life, from the first grade on, when Mrs. Baxter paired her with Tony Jasper to be a good influence, it's been *You're so helpful! You're always smiling! You're so* nice! Nice can feel like being shoved in a trunk with your wrists bound and your mouth taped shut.

17

Her mother is gone, so there's no hovering threat, no forceful presence or hand about to smack. Evan is gone, too, so there's no moody baby-man to tiptoe around. She can be anyone she wants. Do whatever she wants. She can rewrite her own history, starting today. She has always wanted to travel, to be a part of a wider world, so how about it, huh? She can be spontaneous, learn to scuba dive, climb Everest (okay, maybe not climb Everest).

She finds Henry North waiting just outside the small white bungalow that serves as Island Air's office. He faces the street that's rapidly filling with ferry traffic.

"You have a ride?" Isabelle is out of breath from the jog. She should exercise more. Grief makes you eat too much. She needs to start swimming again.

He slings the bag from his shoulder, but before he sets it down, he eyes the ground as if checking for other people's impoliteness — chewed gum or cigarette butts. Maybe it's a detail she should take note of. Maybe it hardly matters in the grand scheme of things. Henry takes his wallet out of his pocket, fishes inside. "I do. Remy Wilson? Coming to pick me up."

Isabelle's surprised. Remy's got a few vacation properties, but she rents only long-term now. This one bag — it's a bag for a weekend, not for a year. He hands her a folded slip of paper with an address on it — the address of Remy's house off Deception Loop, near Isabelle's own.

"You have my cell already, right? Now you know where you can find me."

He smiles again. Suddenly, she can't speak. It's like a pair of hands are on her throat, squeezing. One could get all self-helpy and say she's never had a voice, and while it might be true, this is an actual, physical happening. Her body is likely shouting things, but who can hear over the rumble and roar of Liz's plane coming close, ready to splash down. Isabelle better hurry back to secure the Beaver, but she doesn't move. The last of the crows have passed. Isabelle sees Remy Wilson's old VW coming up the road. Remy is about a million years old. Isabelle wouldn't get into a car with her unless it was dark and she was being chased and she was out of options. Even then, even with her life in danger, they'd chug along at twenty miles an hour, tops.

The VW spurts and splutters and Remy pulls up, rolls down her window. She pops her head out, her hair a white dandelion poof. "Isabelle, sweetie. Glad I caught you.

I wanted to say sorry about your mom."

"Thanks, Remy."

"That old bitch. People like that, you think they'll live forever. Get in," she says to Henry North.

Henry and Isabelle meet eyes. Isabelle shrugs, and Henry smiles. "See you soon," he says, and this is how it starts. Or ends, depending on whether you're Henry North or poor Isabelle Austen herself.

CHAPTER 2

Six thousand miles away, as Isabelle closes the bedroom window of her mother's house and takes a last look at the hypnotic spin of the Point Perpetua lighthouse before turning in, Professor M. Weary shuts off his computer.

Henry North has been on Parrish Island for exactly six hours.

The professor knows this, and much, much more. He knows when Henry left, and how much his ticket cost. He even knows where Henry sat on the Island Air flight from Seattle: seat C, which on that model of Cessna is behind and to the right of the pilot. At least, that was the assigned seat on North's ticket, paid for with his Visa card.

It's all so easy! People will keep on being who they are, for starters, and on the Internet you can find out anything. The glorious, ever-flowing, ever-providing Internet. Even when the Wi-Fi goes in and out and in and out, a little perseverance and patience will pay off. Professor Weary loves, loves, loves the Internet. It's technological magic, information gratification. What did we ever do before? How did we spy, stalk, and scheme? How did we look up the answers to crucial, nagging questions, like the name of that actor on the tip of your tongue or the whereabouts of one's enemy?

It's 4:45 P.M. in New Caledonia, eighteen hours ahead of Parrish Island. It's almost like seeing into Henry North's future.

Professor Weary sighs, satisfied. If he were the type to rub his hands together in glee, he'd do that, too, but it's overkill. Now that the cyclone season is nearly over and the strong winds have stopped, a swim sounds nice. A swim before a lovely dinner of the leftover cassoulet with maybe a glass of wine. (Maybe? Who is he kidding.) The pool looks so inviting. In this hillside cottage with a view of the Coral Sea and Mont Dore, only the mynahs will see him in his swim-suit. He may be aging, but aren't we all? In spite of everything, he's fighting the good fight, damn it. He still tries to stay in great shape. Vanity is a curse.

Professor Weary drops his robe on the wooden deck of the pool. Birds twitter, as birds always do in Grande Terre. It is humid and warm. On Parrish, Isabelle climbs into the cool sheets that smell of her mother's linen closet. She settles in to that complicated time before sleep, when competing thoughts crash and battle, when good sense and future mistakes fight each other using the jagged pieces of your sorry psyche. She tries to talk herself out of the everlasting thought of the overly responsible and anxiety-ridden — that she needs to pee again — as Professor Weary takes the plunge. This sounds like the title of a children's book, which pleases him.

He pops up, slicks his hair back. He keeps it a little too long, long enough for one of those inadvisable yet somehow alluring ponytails streaked with gray, a concession to his younger self and the longed-for days of the past. After a few easy laps, he gets out and quickly wraps a towel around himself. He's starving. It's the exercise, and the excitement.

It's the *anticipation.*

After these hard, hard years, this time of loss and heartbreak, his luck may be changing at long last. Henry North is on the move. He's *migrating.* And while birds migrate to find better climates and avoid predators, they also change locations to *feed*

23

and *breed.* Now Weary will just have to wait, which is the hard part. Wait and watch, just as he watches Grande Terre's *Corvus moneduloides.*

Weary does not yet know about Isabelle, finally drowsing before the lurch that comes with dreams of falling. He is still only wondering who it will be — who Henry North will choose this time. If she'll be a blonde, or another brunette. If she'll be delicate, like Virginia, or more sturdy and broad, like Sarah. Either way, it'll be tragic. Either way, it'll be the thing he most wants, finally happening.

CHAPTER 3

On Isabelle's desk — no, correct that, on *her mother's* desk — there is a stack of death certificates. Who knew you'd have to order them practically in bulk? She never had to settle anyone's estate before. *Settle* sounds like flannel pajamas and a cup of tea. *Settle* sounds like a permanent landing spot. All of these papers and bills and accounts feel more like a treacherous pile of tasks and questions building to a mountainous migraine.

She crunches a triangle of toast. Yes, a few moments before, she cut it on the neat diagonal. Triangle toast makes her feel like she's in a hotel. You should take in every small pleasure, Isabelle believes, the first jab of a knife into peanut butter, warm laundry out of the dryer held against your face, new PJs. Life is rough enough without these little rewards.

She sips her coffee. After she "settles" the

end of her mother's life, she'll have to focus on hers. The questions feel as stacked as that paperwork — what she wants, and where she wants it. Who to be, now that the plan's changed. God, beginning again is exhausting. It's unfair how many beginnings a life sometimes requires.

The view out that window is familiar, but even so, it compels her. After all this time, she's still drawn to the curved bay of Point Perpetua, the lighthouse, and the waters of the sound. Orcas and porpoises have been leaving and coming back home here for hundreds of years. Right this minute, as she gazes outside, they're slumbering beneath the smooth surface. The water is as still as a mirror, reflecting evergreen trees and the pewter sky of early hours. She's slept through the morning crow commute, but no matter. Nature is still spread out before her, doing its astonishing business of eating and warring and procreating.

It's quieter here than it is on the other side of the island. Over there, there's the ferry terminal, and the seaplane landing strip, and the restaurants and shops of town. But here it's almost dead silent. There's the call of a gull, and a clock ticking downstairs, but that's all. Tourists occasionally come to climb along the beach, but the wind gets cold and you need a sure step on the rocks. The sound waters are calm only in the bay. Beyond that, they are notoriously rough, rough enough for terrible old stories of shipwrecks. There are terrible old stories that took place on shore, too. Some years ago, a man shot himself out there by the lighthouse, and you can still see the blood on the rocks if you look close enough.

The fog is slowly clearing, a tidy fog metaphor. Isabelle brushes the crumbs from her lap, from the silk robe embroidered with a crane that she found in a box in her mother's closet, a gift for Isabelle's now-passed birthday, judging from the card inside. *Happy 37th, Izzy!* Well, she loves it, so thank you. The horrible undertow of grief Isabelle thought for sure was permanent has eased a little in recent days. Enough that she notices what else is on the desk, right next to the remnants of her mother's life — that small piece of folded paper, the one with Henry North's address on it. Remy's house. One of Remy's houses. Of course she knows which house it is. You grow up here, and you know every house. Clyde Belle lived with his wife there, before he walked down to the beach and put that gun to his head.

It doesn't say some big, bad thing about

the place. It's not like Clyde Belle did it in the bedroom. Louella Belle, his wife, what a sweetheart, what a great woman — she stayed on for a while after, and then came the Greggory family with their two little daughters, and then that rich guy who lived alone with his guitars until Remy booted him out when he painted the porch black. Houses, like humans, have long histories, and they're never all bad.

If she leans far enough over, Isabelle can see a corner of that house's flat roof, and a sliver of its east side. It lies low and long, a mostly glass house, with a few salt-grayed shingles. After the rich musician, Remy started to get a little haphazard with her upkeep. She's eighty, for God's sake, she's allowed. But people complain. Henry North should be careful out on that deck.

Enough! What's gotten into her? She stops sneaking looks at that place, but honestly, this is not the first time she's done it. There was that midnight peek to see if the light was still on in Clyde and Louella Belle's old bedroom, too. After Evan, come on! It's ridiculous. A little argument ensues in her head. Words get thrown around. The chorus says mean stuff, like *What are you, one of those women who go from one relationship to the next?* and *Why did you even stay with*

Evan so long? A guy that doesn't want to get married after six years is a guy that doesn't want to get married, period and *You shouldn't trust yourself when it comes to men.* It's all the righteous and judgy things usually said by people with a different childhood than hers. People with well-adjusted, happily married parents, who grow up thinking that anyone who makes bad relationship choices is stupid and annoying besides, beyond comprehension, same as irritating third world inhabitants who just keep having more babies.

Wait — no.

She recognizes that tone. That particular taunting lilt, it's her *mother's* voice. Maggie, not dead after all; very much alive, in Isabelle's head, anyway.

The voice shames her. Well, Maggie was good at that, whether with her words, her silence, or her unpredictable fury. A smacking hand is always shaming and never forgotten, just ask any family dog.

Isabelle stares at that desk, and for a moment, a weird moment, her blood pumps hard and she imagines setting the whole thing on fire. Or, God, smashing it to smithereens with a sledgehammer. Isabelle is a thoughtful, gentle person. She was a be-seen-and-not-heard child, a straight-A student, an English major! She has lovely flats in all colors, and swerves to avoid hitting animals already dead on the road. Her cleavage is demure; she has never worn a white bathing suit, after her mother's warnings of what happens when they get wet. She has enough backbone to say no to band students collecting money for foreign trips she herself has never been on, but she still feels guilty about it. And she had enough backbone to hire a tough lawyer for her divorce, which only meant she paid a lot of money to get her half of the furniture. It means something to her to be a good person in the world, so she overlooks cranky old people who say biting things, and she never glares at screaming children in grocery stores the way her mother would. She did not slash Evan's tires or write him a hundred furious emails. There was some raw weeping alone in the car after her solo appearance in court, but luckily, she had that handy package of Kleenex that she keeps in her purse for emergencies.

And yet lately . . . lately. Offshore currents of anger have been appearing in her own distant weather system. They feel like a haboob, a mistral, a monsoon, mysterious and sudden storms of dust, wind, or water. The spinning cloud of white on the map is far off. Possibly, it will change direction entirely, not hit the shore at all. Still, something is building out there. It's not just Evan, and the ways her trust was splattered. It's every Evan in the world, and every superior Nordstrom saleswoman, and every creepy guy who hits on her, and every parent she sees gripping a child's arm too hard. It feels like her heart or her soul or some other unknown piece of her is rumbling, coming loose. Maybe she's just stuck in the fury part of grief, or maybe, now that her mother is dead, she can finally strike a match without bending ten of them first.

She's on her way to Island Air when she sees him, this stranger who's been making the occasional appearance in her head. There he is — right by the side of the road, off of Deception Loop. This is how it generally works on an island this size. A couple flies in from Canada, and you see them on the weekend in the Front Street Market choosing a bottle of wine. You welcome a young family, and there they are at Honey B's Bakery, ordering croissants and hot chocolate, or at the beach, hunched and shivering because they imagined California. Now, here's Henry North. He's standing in front of an old Thunderbird with the hood up, looking inside at the engine as if he's started the surgery but doesn't know where to go from here.

Isabelle was never late for work at Evergreen Publishing in Seattle, where she used to sift through submissions and handle difficult authors and proof manuscripts about boat building and bird watching and the Northwest's best hikes. But she can be late now. She pulls over.

That Thunderbird . . . She'd laugh, but it wouldn't be nice.

Isabelle's tires crunch in the gravel. She parks, gets out.

"Need help?"

"I thought that was you." Henry North is casually dressed this morning. He wears a nice-fitting pair of jeans and a soft, tucked-in T-shirt. The running shoes are clean enough that they might be newly bought. He looks relaxed, in spite of the car trouble. It makes him seem familiar.

"Don't tell me you bought that from Kale Kramer."

"I did. There was a sign in —"

"The window of Boss Donuts."

"The window of Boss Donuts," he says. "I've been had?"

"You and, like, a hundred other people."

"Shit."

"I think he buys it back from Ron at the tow truck place for a case of beer." Kale Kramer was a sleaze in high school, and he's still a sleaze. "It's not specifically illegal. The police have been trying for years to catch him doing something they can actually arrest him for, but . . ." She gestures with a flat hand, scooting it beneath an imagined fence.

"He slips under the radar."

"He slips under the radar. And, wait. Police? What am I saying? We basically have Tiny Policeman, who's five-foot-five, and a couple of deputies. Welcome to Parrish?"

"Oh, wow." Henry runs his hand through his hair. "I thought it was too good of a deal."

"How much did you give him?"

"I shouldn't even tell you. Two hundred?"

"That's it? Two hundred? I think he usually asks five," Isabelle says. "My mother always said you get what you pay for."

"Guilty," he says, and holds up his hands. "I thought it was a steal. And I was right." He laughs. She sees a flash of a filling, from the time they used to be silver. She wonders how old he is. Older than her by a good five or ten years, which she admits she finds attractive, especially after Evan, the man-child. Isabelle likely has mother issues *and* father issues, and if she had any siblings, she'd probably have issues with them, too. Honestly, who doesn't?

He folds his arms, appraising the situation. "I guess I'm too trusting."

"It was a good-looking car in 1986," she says.

"You're right," he says and sighs. "Gold is for retirees, anyway."

"Can I give you a lift somewhere?"

"That'd be great. The library?"

"Sure. No problem."

The library! Isabelle's holds are always maxed, she's a book person, and so this seems sweetly promising. She could like Henry North. Maybe she could like him a lot. Those who fault her for her naïveté, who roll their eyes at her hope, can go back to their ice-cold cave to eat more nails, in her opinion, because it's the people who destroy hope that should be blamed, not the ones who have it.

"I thought I'd try a new place to work. The house is pretty isolated."

"Oh, I hear you. You're basically alone out there. It takes some getting used to."

"Let me get my valise."

As he does, she gets back in her car, leans over to unlock the passenger door. He slides in beside her.

"Valise?" She grins. Maybe it's his upright demeanor, the clean hands and slightly accented voice (From where, though? Somewhere east? Somewhere coastal?), but teasing him comes easy. It never came easy with the athletic and concrete Evan. You don't tease a brick pile.

"Briefcase? I don't know. I think those are for bankers."

"I guess you have a point. Who's a valise for?"

"Poets. Poets and dashing men of mystery."

Nice. She likes this, too. The only time the word *dashing* left Evan's lips was when he got drunk at holiday parties and sang that Christmas song.

Of course she hears it. That voice in her head again. The mean one. The cutting one. The cynical, dream-squashing, shame-inducing one. The one she never fought back against and now never would. *Don't be stupid, Isabelle,* her mother says.

Isabelle turns onto Horseshoe Loop, heads into town. "What kind of work do you do?" She almost doesn't ask. There's something about the way he sits there with that *valise* on his lap that makes him seem like a private person, but they've passed Rufaru

School of Marimba, and Bud's Tavern, and the police station, and no one's said anything in a while, and she feels uncomfortable. It's a bad habit, filling silence with chatter and ill-advised confessions just to ease her anxiety.

"Me? I'm a professor. On sabbatical. Boston University? I decided to take some time off. Finish a book I've been working on."

"Wow."

The *wow* is not actually a true expression of astonishment or admiration. It's caution. Her former job at the small press taught her one thing: Everyone is either writing a book or wants to, and when you hear that claim, it can mean anything. It can mean a children's story with images of scary, badly painted teddy bears, or a Story of Survival about one's grandfather in the war, which sounds like everyone else's Story of Survival of their grandfather in the war. It can mean three pages of an already awkward mystery heading for the glut of self-publishing, or six hundred pages of self-aggrandizing holding forth. *Wow* is Isabelle's professionally trained response, a deflection. It's also a test. If nothing more is said, the writer just might be serious enough to keep his work to himself until it is good. That's a rarity.

36

But Henry North says nothing more.

She waits, but there is still only nothing and more nothing. *Maybe he's the real deal,* she thinks. It gives her a little shiver. Also, it makes sense, in some fateful-universe way. She spent years searching for the real deal at her old job, and now one just shows up when she isn't even looking.

She pulls over to the curb in front of the library steps. "Here we are."

"Really appreciate it," he says. "But, before you go . . . Know where I can get a car that actually works?"

"Well, if you don't want to take the ferry into Anacortes, I'd ask over at Eugene's. The gas station? Two blocks over, one block up."

Then it hits her. "Wait. What am I saying? I've got an almost new Acura that I need to get rid of, sitting right in my driveway."

It's out before she can take it back. Regret washes in, with a nice undertow of guilt. The political analysts in her head debate the issues. She'll have to sell it sometime, so why not now, when the solution is right here in front of her? Yes, but she shouldn't forget the old cake plate. It had so many bad, sad birthday memories that Isabelle threw it away. *Tried* to throw it away — she had to fetch it back out of the garbage because she could hear that cake plate shouting what a bad daughter she was from underneath the coffee grounds and browning lettuce. She's not at the getting-rid-of stage yet. If she'll ever be at the getting-rid-of stage. Probably, she should just figure it out now, how to strap all of her mother's stuff on her back so she can carry it around for the rest of her life.

Henry is out of the car, leaning in the open door. "Perfect. I'll take it."

"Wait, though. It's way more than two hundred dollars."

"You get what you pay for." He smiles. Behind him, a girl chains her bike to a lamppost and heads up the library stairs, and a good dog sits outside, waiting patiently. "How about if we have dinner? Then we can discuss the details."

Perhaps she *could* just sell the car. Her mother barely had it a year. Mom would have just kept her old clunker if she knew she was going to have a heart attack and die. The Acura holds no memories for Isabelle. She never even saw her mother drive it, so it could be anyone's. It's not the cake plate, or the records, or the clothes, or the shampoo bottles, or the garden gloves.

"Okay," she says. "That'd be great."

"Tomorrow night?" he asks.

"The Bayshore?"

"Oh, no. Come over! I'll cook."

She barely knows him. He's a stranger. But right then the girl goes into the library, and the dog's owner (Nathan, the artist — he's gotten older, but who hasn't?) comes out, and a fat, white cloud passes across the sun and moves on. It's a beautiful day. Someone has recently mowed a lawn. The air smells like grass. It's spring, and strangers are friends you haven't met yet, et cetera, et cetera.

"Terrific."

After her second wedding anniversary, when Evan told her he thought they should see other people, Isabelle briefly saw a counselor. The counselor mostly sat back in her chair and listened, but she did say one thing that Isabelle hasn't forgotten: *It's all about who you choose to bring into your life.* And while this is no doubt true, it implies the wisdom of foresight. How is a person supposed to know? Sometimes the wolf looks enough like Granny that you let him in. You don't notice the teeth until he's close enough to bite down on your neck. You have to trust. You have to have faith — even if your trust/faith control panel has been known to throw sparks and even catch fire.

Henry reaches in, squeezes her hand. Isabelle's heart thuds. Her stomach flips. Of course, these are the ways a body shouts about both the best things and the worst ones.

CHAPTER 4

It's too early. He knows it is. But Professor Weary checks anyway. He's curious. Fine, all right! He's obsessed. The click-refresh is soothing and anxiety-provoking and hope-filled and disappointing, and he's helpless against it. Who isn't, with our phones and tablets and laptops? We're all crows, tapping at the levers for the reward.

With a few strikes of the keys he's there, at his favorite first stop. It's called ShutR, and it's a small and hardly used photo-sharing site. Henry North generally stays off social media, but he cannot resist the narcissistic joys of the Web entirely. How could he, Renaissance man that he is? Poet, intellectual, chef, photographer . . . Ugh. Please. He's the kind of person who learns how to play the piano and speak several languages just to demonstrate that he can play the piano and speak several languages. The problem with narcissists is that it can be hard to see past the glare at first. Honestly, they're sort of glorious and fun and magical until the deep and abiding assholery begins to show through.

Weary scrolls through the familiar images, the photos of forests and North's solo trip to the desert, subpar sunset shots, blooming flowers, the usual fare for amateurs. Sarah is even in a few of the old ones. Professor Weary gazes at those longingly. Sometimes he misses Sarah so badly, his heart feels entirely absent; his chest is the dark and empty bottom of a ship still moving through the sea.

Henry North does not use his real name on ShutR. He uses an alias, *Mr. Aperture.* Cute, no? How adorable, though if Professor Weary were to choose, he'd pick another photographic term, like *Mr. Aberration,* or *Mr. Distortion,* or, wait, *Blowup.* Yes, how about that one! *Blowup:* Weary loves it. He chuckles. It matches his intent. It matches the rage that rises, rises, rises when the professor opens ShutR to check (too soon) and sees Sarah again, her long, dark hair blowing across her wide, hopeful smile. She and Henry are on a bluff on Spectacle Island, he thinks. They used to like to go out there, he remembers. Sarah wears a blue windbreaker. If he closes his eyes, he can almost be that wind, brushing her soft cheek. The edge of Henry's finger is on the lens, so it's bad as far as the photo goes, Mr. Aperture, but a lovely image of her. She looks so happy.

Anyway, there is nothing new on ShutR. The last photo is still that lavender crocus blossom, tender and open. Weary's pretty sure the flower is from Sarah's garden, taken just before that asshole sold the house and gathered up his money and left town. He had every legal right to do it, too. This makes Professor Weary furious. Sarah's garden has been left behind, and so has her kitchen, and the bedroom she painted. Weary remembers the way her hands looked at work the next day, still splattered with yellow. She's gone, and meanwhile, North tromps around on his merry way.

Someone needs to do something.

Someone *is.*

The professor first found Mr. Aperture on ShutR after searching for *HNorthpoe,* which by luck was his user name on the account. It's the same moniker North sported for both a review of a kitchen knife on a shopping site and the one he had used for his old university email address. So, now, the professor types *HNorthpoe* into the search bar. Same old same old. Nothing new.

Weary leans back in his chair in his office on lush Mount Khogi. He likes to think his "office" extends all the way to Parc Provincial de la Rivière Bleue, even if the research facility is here. The windows are open and so is the door, because there is no air-conditioning. He takes a pluck of his shirt and waves it in and out for relief. A gecko shoots up the wall and disappears into a crack. The crack in the wall, the beautiful gecko that disappears — it makes him think of Sarah and Henry North, but what doesn't? Think of how it all might have been different if they'd never met at that holiday party at the department head's house. He lured her with his broken arm, his weakness, Weary is sure of it. Compassionate people are such vulnerable marks. He's sick about it. She was completely gaga for North after that. Her own work in the lab suffered. It wasn't a priority anymore. Professor Weary thought she had a passion, and not for British literature, nineteenth century, either. For *birds*. For *Corvus,* specifically. But look what happened.

He hates to admit it, but he was disappointed in her, letting her passions slide for love. He still is, a little. Those passions were a lot more loyal to her than Henry North ever was.

Weary thinks about how Virginia and Henry met, too, paddling in the bay in Sausalito, with two groups of friends. He lost an oar. Surprise, surprise, weakness again. Ginnie (this is what her friends called her) helped tow him back in. That tiny thing! She looks like she weighed maybe a hundred pounds. How powerful she must have felt for a short while, saving him on that first day.

See the theme? Get it? Well, there are only two instances, so it's merely conjecture. Still, when Grande Terre's *Corvus moneduloides* twice picked up a twig, stripped it of its bark, nibbled its end to make a tiny hook, everyone immediately understood it was no coincidence. Helplessness is Henry North's hook, his modus operandi. Along with everything else, this theory would never hold up in court; Weary has no real proof. The broken arm was real, to be fair. But why be fair? He's a hundred steps beyond fair. The best predictor of future behavior is past behavior.

Professor Weary can still see North on campus with his arm in that sling, knocking over a stack of cups in the cafeteria, fumbling with his silverware. Broken wing display. Most often seen in shorebirds and waterfowl and plovers, the bird will cock his wing and feign injury to distract a predator from a nest. The most dramatic and conspicuous displays come when the investment is greatest. Great potential loss means it all gets as bad as high school theater. Hobbling and dragging, exaggerated shows of pathetic plights . . . It's all about tricking the predator, making him look away from the hidden thing.

One can forget, though, that this behavior is aggressive, too. It says, *Come and get me*. It says, *You just wait*.

It can get confusing in the great big game of life, who is predator, who is prey, who initiates the standoff. Who contributes to their own demise, seals their own fate with passivity.

At any moment, one of Weary's research assistants will be arriving. They'll take the Jeep up the mountain to the *Corvus* roost. They'll spend the long, thrilling day doing what Weary does best: waiting and watching.

So, now, he hurries. He checks the credit card bill, his final hope of the day, or at least, his final hope until he can get back here and check again. How he's able to look at that credit card — he's not telling! He shouldn't tell anyway — my God, he certainly wouldn't want anyone to be able to see his. *Tip-tip-tip, tap-tap-tap,* and there it is.

He scrolls.

Mundane, mundane, mundane.

Gas. Ferry terminal. Coffee shop. Whatever, whatever.

Bookstore, pharmacy, who cares.

But, then . . . What?

What is *that*?

His heart drops. His hands actually start to tremble.

Can it be?

A grocery store. *Front Street Market.*

He feels a little sick. This is not usual, not at all. Oh, wow. Wow, wow, wow. Weary feels giddy, true, but also suddenly anxious. Look at that. Look at it! He wants to shove back his chair and pace around with nerves and worry and the magnetic energy of possibility. Because this is no regular grocery bill. This is not the cereal and four-roll pack of TP and the single pink chicken breast of the lonely. This is not even the amount of a new arrival stocking his cupboard. It's an extravagant figure, and knowing Henry North, it can only mean one thing.

Dinner for two.

CHAPTER 5

It smells fantastic in that house, garlic and butter and wine, the holy culinary trinity, in Isabelle's opinion. She'd eat that smell if she could. She can't remember the last time someone cooked for her. Maybe Jessa, back in Seattle, who was the last in a long line of friends who drifted off after having a baby. The only thing Evan could make was Kraft macaroni and cheese from a box, though truthfully, Isabelle loves the stuff.

Henry wears a denim shirt, and his brown hair is ruffled and relaxed, and he hasn't shaven, and Isabelle likes that look. He's all Sunday morning, but wearing cologne or some clean-smelling soap.

"Can I take your purse?"

She hands it to him along with her sweater. He sets them on the couch right next to where he stands and gives an apologetic grin. "The former renter turned the coat closet into some strange storage unit with long hooks."

"For guitars, maybe? He was a musician."

"Guitars! Well, if you'd brought one of those, I could hang it up."

Isabelle forgot what a view this place had. She used to come here to babysit the Greggory girls when she was in college and home for summer break. It's still light out, and she can see the waters of the sound stretching to forever. The house is glass and more glass, and its wide deck extends out over the bluff. There's a trail, too, which hugs the hill, but you can't see it from there. It's all coming back, though — how exposed you could feel with all those windows, in spite of how secluded the house is.

"That view," she says.

"Right?"

"Everything looks so great. I can't believe you're all unpacked already."

"Oh, I barely had anything to do. Put my clothes in a drawer. Plugged in my laptop. The house came furnished. Previous tenant left all this, apparently. Can you imagine?"

"I think he was a musician-slash-dot-com guy. Lots of money. He painted the porch black and Remy kicked him out, and so he just left."

"Does everyone know everything here?" He grimaces, but he's joking.

"Island? Small?" She laughs. "So, tell me. You just popped a few clothes in a bag and took off? That sounds amazing."

"Well, I got rid of a lot before I moved, and then I stuck the rest in storage. Why drag your old life behind you?"

"Ah. I envy that. Just picking up and *going.* It sounds heavenly." Isabelle's old stuff and her mother's old stuff live together like spinsters. Most of her former life is now jammed into her mother's garage. She wishes she could be free of all of it. Imagine how weightless you'd feel, ditching refrigerators and old outfits, small appliances and Christmas decorations. Things, she suddenly realizes, that have all been merely *of use,* or else burdened with false sentimentality. "You'll be returning, though? Sabbatical, you said."

"Well, *sabbatical* loosely used. I quit."

"Oh, wow. Were you tenured?"

"Tenured, unhappy . . . So, why stay, right? Life is short."

"Bold move."

"Bold moves are necessary sometimes, don't you think? I'm sure you get a lot of that — people starting a new life in a place like this? People flying in with a bag and a credit card . . ."

"Not really. We get families with multiple

suitcases and guys with romantic intentions who forget their wallets."

"Are you a pilot, too?"

"I'm not, but my mother was. It's funny — I've been around the planes all my life, but I never really got to the point in my thinking where I understood they'd be mine one day."

"Lucky you."

"I guess so. The jury is still out. I may need my own bold move."

"Wait. I have wine," he says.

In spite of the black porch incident and the guitar coat closet, the musician had done great things with the house. His furniture looks beautiful. Remy's floors are aged oak, and there's a white rug and a black leather couch in a stylish, comfortable L. It's sparse and contemporary, more mature than she'd expect from the guy, with his ripped jeans and retro Nirvana T-shirts.

Henry North hands her a glass of red wine. Music is playing at a tender volume, and the singer has the sort of raspy, moody voice that makes Isabelle feel as if she's unfurling, like a fern in a thicket of moss. Well, it's the wine now, too. Henry's eyes are a little sad, yet he's confident, and it's the lethal combination. Why is that? Just one without the other would be too much of the thing, but like this — protector, needing protection — it entices. *Kinda like Evan?* her mother pipes in. Isabelle shuts her up with another sip of cabernet.

"It's a little warm in here." Henry slides open one of the large glass doors. She hopes he doesn't go out on that deck, though. It looks like you could step right through the rot in some places, plunge to your death, or at least break an ankle.

"It smells amazing. What are you making?"

He sits beside her. The life-is-good, deep-water smell of the ocean wafts in and takes a spin with the garlic and butter. "Mesclun salad with burst tomatoes? Lobster capellini with leek sauce?"

"Oh, my God, really? I may just give you the car."

"The car! I forgot all about it."

"I drove it over, so you can see it and decide."

"Wonderful."

He rises again to bring them a cheese-and-charcuterie plate. The meats are laid out like a mosaic, and the wine loosens everything, and the sun begins to set, turning the sky gold and then pink. Isabelle has barely cooked for herself since she's been back. The time spent on feeding her — it shows a kind of care, she thinks, a care she's unfamiliar with.

"I think I may be in shock," she says, gazing at the plate. "I was married before, briefly, and my former husband . . . He could throw together a tuna sandwich on a good day."

"I'm glad this is a new experience. Wait. Something else I forgot." Henry lifts his glass to hers. They clink a toast. "To us," he says.

He has a great sense of humor. It almost surprises her, because he's a little reserved. Maybe it's the wine, but they laugh to the point of doubling over at his story about the first time he tried to ski. She confesses her general lack of athletic ability, bravely shares the incident with the hockey stick during high school PE. He tells her about his brothers and lacrosse; she tells him about her mother chasing her father down the street with a golf club. He laughs so hard that he slaps the table in hilarity, causing the silverware to jump and the lit candles to flicker. It's an unexpected gesture, a regular-guy thing, and she likes him more because of it.

Isabelle knows this is a funny story. She uses it at parties and changes the details for effect (a nine iron, a rainstorm), and hauls it out during first meetings like this, because it's old and reliable, but also because it says something about her. Something important, if anyone notices.

It's not just a funny story for Isabelle, of course. She remembers the door slamming and the windows rattling, and her mother yelling, although she doesn't recall exactly what was yelled. She remembers being afraid. Very afraid. She was scared that the golf club might do the same thing to her father's head that Justin Frankle's baseball bat did to their jack-o'-lantern the day after Halloween. Those slick pieces of pumpkin skidded across the asphalt of their cul-de-sac and splatted against the curb, and right then, her father gripped the sides of his own skull as he ran, in a feeble effort at protection. As soon as her parents' fight began that day, Isabelle fled to her room. But when she heard the garage door slam and the screaming outside, she peeked through her venetian blinds. At the sight of the raised golf club, she actually hid in her closet and sat on the toy box and plugged her ears. She rocked and tried to name the fifty states. A few months later, her father moved to Florida. He'd finally had enough, because, of course, if a person threatens with a golf club, it isn't their first time being threatening. She didn't see her father much after he left. He fled. And then he died when she was in college.

Henry senses the layers, it seems, because he quiets. He stands then, and squeezes her shoulder and says, "How about dessert?"

It's another good sign, this astute empathy. And now he brings in the dessert, presents it, as if they are celebrating a special occasion. It's a chocolate torte, and it's gorgeous, a perfect chocolate hat for a chocolate queen. "Tell me you didn't make this, too," Isabelle says. "Or I'll have to slink home in shame. I can make brownies out of a box."

"Front Street Market. I had it specially made."

"Oh, thank goodness." He offers her coffee, and when she declines, he empties the last of the wine into both of their glasses. "So." She pretends to count. "You're a professor of nineteenth-century literature. You're writing a book. You took classes at Le Cordon Bleu, and you play the piano. What else?"

He slides the cake from the knife onto her plate. "Don't kill me, promise? Photography. It's a hobby."

"Aargh! I read novels. I used to swim. I

indulge in bad TV."

"You run a business. You were an editor."

"That sounds grander than it is. I mostly shoveled the slush pile. What do you write? Fiction? Let me guess. Something intelligent and historical."

"Ha, no. Poetry. Clearly, I am not in the writing game for the bucks."

"Hmm. Probably not."

"I am . . . How should I say it? Somewhat of an expert on American Romanticism? I've spent years studying the life and work of Edgar Allan Poe. Teaching it, writing about it. Quite a lot of critical essays on *Pym,* Poe's only novel . . . Dare I admit? Proud member of the Poe Studies Society." He cringes for effect.

"So, who're your influences?" She laughs. "Okay, I'm not going to tell you I edited *Best Places to Bring a Date in Seattle.*"

"Nonsense. I'm sure you edited many kinds of books."

"I just realized I should probably call you *Dr.* North."

He sits across from her again. "Such a beautiful, intelligent woman, and she gives herself no credit," he says. He barely takes two bites of his dessert — no wonder he's in such great shape. He reaches for her hand. Rubs her skin with his thumb.

Oh, God, that's nice. It's gentle and lovely, and his eyes are incredible, actually. They stare right through her. *Beautiful* — though people have called her this before, it's not a word she connects to herself, with her prominent nose and all her mediums: medium height, medium-length brown hair, medium-brown eyes. But perhaps she could be beautiful, the way he's looking at her. She remembers her old confidence — at least, she recalls when she didn't feel as vulnerable as she's felt lately. Okay, maybe that was a long, long time ago. She felt brazen and sure maybe for a few months of summer back when she was seventeen. Most people, she supposes, feel brazen and sure during those exact same months.

It's gotten dark out. So dark. It's a deep dark, sea dark, endless. There's only the slow, far-off turn of the lighthouse beam, and the twinkle of boat lights across the bay. It could be just the two of them all alone out here.

The candles flicker. Isabelle swallows the last of her wine. Clyde Belle, with his torrid thoughts, who once lived in this very house, has been gone for years. The space between Henry and Isabelle has gotten soft and quiet. Intimate. She realizes how much she doesn't know about him. Old adages about love taking time and things being too good to be true just seem stingy and scared when hope swirls and hums in your bloodstream. "So."

"Another *so,*" he teases.

"Tell me. You're here on your own? No wife, no kids visiting on the weekends?"

"And we were having such a nice time."

"I'm sorry."

"No, no. I just hate to talk about all that, don't you? Who came before, what happened. How it all went wrong."

"I do. I hate it."

"Especially now. First date and all."

She feels a jab of misstep. A hit of wrongdoing. It's her old baggage, this sensitivity to criticism, coming from a childhood requiring perfect moves and vigilance. She's also surprised. *First date.* Well, of course it's one. She hadn't exactly called it that, so it's somehow strangely shocking to realize what this is. "I apologize. For leaping into the deep end."

"It's fine. How about the abridged version? I was married. Not long. No children. But she left me. Just a few years ago. And that's enough for now, right?" He laughs. "That's *plenty.*"

"Oh, heartbreak," Isabelle says.

"Well, look, if it hadn't happened, I

58

wouldn't be here."

He takes her hand.

"And I am liking here very, very much."

The music has long since stopped and the house is silent. The night is. There's not a car engine, or a wind through a tree, or a plink of rain on the roof. Just the silence of that house out there on the bluff. Energy begins to fill the space between them, and this energy is so real it could be a sound. First, it's a low hum, and then it builds to something more, something large. Dear God, she feels it. The big thing waiting, needing only one small move to tip it over to ravage-energy, the teeth-clacking, hair-pulling kind. She feels it right there, and he must, too, because he clears his throat and pushes his chair back, and Isabelle decides it's time to collect her purse and head home.

"It's been such a lovely evening," she says. Her voice is hoarse. *Lovely* — it seems wrongly prim and gentle after what she just felt.

"It has," he says, and the moment is gone. "And we forgot all about the car."

"The car!"

"I'll come out and see it."

"It's pitch-black out."

"Let's go."

The Acura is parked in the gravel spot in

front of Remy's house, and it's too dark to see a thing. They need a flashlight, at least.

His hand is cupped against the glass as he peers in. "I'll take it," he says.

"You can't take it! You can't even see it. I haven't even opened the door."

He reaches in the pocket of his jeans. He removes a check, which he unfolds and then hands to her. It's not so dark that she can't see the figure written there. "Oh, my God, no. This is too much."

"Not at all. It's fair. *Blue Book.* I've done my research. Sold! Quit shortchanging yourself."

"You can't do this."

"I can and I did. Now get in, and I'll drive you home."

She likes it all — she likes his age, forty-six, and his decisiveness, and his broken heart, and his Ph.D. She likes the way he can handle this unknown car without accidentally flipping on the windshield wipers or popping the hood. She really liked that dinner, but who wouldn't, after meals of cereal and Marie Callender's frozen lasagna? She's nervous, though, because it's very dark, and far off, there's the creeping sense that she's in over her head. She thinks it's because of the discrepancies in their experience: He knows wine, and she picks whatever's on sale and has the best label. He's got the assurance of a man who's been with fabulous, accomplished women. She's just her regular self, who spent much of her adult life with Evan, whose finest points, truthfully, were his great sisters and his ass in jeans.

She's just being insecure. And when he reaches her street and parks and pulls her to him, Henry North's experience instead becomes a proven asset, because, holy hell, that kiss. Well, damn. That right there is what a kiss should be. Her first thought is how much she's missed kisses like that. But her next thought is wondering if she ever really had them.

Her breath is gone, stolen. He pulls away. Her mouth is wet.

"Where did you come from?" she whispers. It's a lover's question, asked when a person can't believe their sudden good fortune. But it's a better question than she knows right then.

"See you soon," he says.

She hopes so. Already, she badly hopes so.

The car pulls away, and she watches the red brake lights disappear down the road. There's not even a small bit of regret about selling it. Her heart is doing that rising, soaring thing. It's all wings and liftoff. She's taken flight. Regrets are for later, anyway.

CHAPTER 6

When he wakes, Professor Weary's sheets are on the floor, kicked off from his thrashing. It's hard to sleep when it's this hot. Maybe it's that cramp that's woken him. It's there in his calf — the tightening that comes after long hours crouched on damp jungle ground, waiting for corvids to take their bait of cat food and hard-boiled eggs. The birds need to be caught, tagged, and identified, in order to be studied. One corvid is not like the next. Each is an individual and needs to be understood as an individual. But catching them is very, very difficult. They are rightly wary. They are incredibly smart. They will watch the food for weeks on end, sensing a trap.

They are much smarter than many humans, who'll plop right in, even when the net is practically in full view. In the middle of the night, that's when Weary gets most angry with himself. He's angry because his love and care for Sarah was too little, too late. He should have *seen*. He should have *acted*.

He rubs his calf as he lies in bed, and then it starts. A sound — a scritching and scratching. Maybe that's what woke him. He gets up to see what the noise is, and no, it's not some bird, some raven messaging with its beak. It'd be a nice touch of the fates, a raven, but no. It's just the sharp tip of a palm frond, bent from wind, scraping the shutter. He opens the window, yanks and pulls, yanks and pulls, until the frond breaks.

He tosses it, and it falls, falls, falls.

How can he sleep after that? Even though the branch lands with only a soft plink, how can he possibly drift off now?

Limbs break and bones crush. Skulls do.

He comforts himself with thoughts of Raven, who made the world. Not Poe's annoying bird, but *Raven,* capital *R,* honored by so many ancient people — Greeks, Hindus, Natives, Celtics, Norse, more . . . Raven created the world, but he created humans, too, and through trickery and seduction and honest concern — yes, actual care — provided them with fire and rivers and food, and even taught them how to make love. He created death, but he also

64

carried their souls to the land of the dead.

And sometimes, when something so terrible happened that sadness traveled onward with that soul, Raven would bring the soul back to earth to right the wrong.

How can you not respect *that,* huh? Seduction, sex, death, retribution? Weary does. Plus, for such a powerful creature, Raven's misdeeds were so wryly hilarious, and his frailties so humble. People should remember when hearing such tales, when narrowing their eyes at the slick black wings and sharp beak and craftiness, how complicated the situation was. You could judge him for the bad things he did. And, oh, he did do bad things. But he had his reasons. He had good reasons. What a weight Raven carried.

Making things right is a tough business. A haunting business. You worry; you worry a great deal. You hope nothing bad happens, before you can get in and save the day. Nothing *else* bad, nothing more, because too, too much has already happened. Maybe even Raven had sleepless nights such as this, Weary thinks, as he turns his pillow to the cool side for what feels like the hundredth time. What're you going to do? Darkness is always the dance floor where anxiety spins with regret until you finally drop from exhaustion.

Chapter 7

Isabelle swirls her coffee in its white mug. It's the best stuff, thick as chocolate. One swallow makes you sure your luck has changed. Nicky Talbott, the barista at Java Java Java, still has that beard he had when they graduated, but now he also has hemp bracelets and a twinkle in his eyes that must come from either strong beans or finding his passion. Isabelle remembers how shocking it was that someone their age could grow a beard like that. She always liked Nicky, even if he was high their entire senior year.

"You look happy, Iz," Jane Mason says. She takes her reading glasses off, sets them on the table, and nods. "Yeah. You look better than I've seen you in weeks."

"I do?"

Isabelle feels better than she has in a long while, too. Since she met Henry, since they've been spending time together after that dinner at Remy's house, everything looks different. She feels like a teenager. She's all "Wonderwall" and "Fever" and "Love Potion No. 9." When she wakes up, she's excited for the future, and she hasn't felt that in ages. She wants to go places and see new things and allow her heart to be blown wide open. And those flares of anger — they've gone right out. Poof! Extinguished. Why be angry? Why spend time on the negative, when life is beautiful and way too short? Anger isn't healthy, anyway.

"More than weeks, Iz. Years? Years! You look like the weight of the world is off your shoulders. I mean, first you're free of that douchebag Evan . . . And you must be finally getting through all this shit . . ." Jane waves her hand across the table, where statements and spreadsheets are fanned out like a tarot deck. Jane has managed the office at Island Air for thirty years, ever since Isabelle's mother, Maggie Austen, inherited the place from *her* mother when she died. Jane has been there through everything, every malfunction and season of bad weather and disaster; the increase in boat population; the noise complaints; the mandatory safety changes. Yet she's still going strong. Her flannel shirt looks like it's been around the block, because it has. Isabelle has never seen Jane in anything but flannel shirts and jeans, with her long, gray hair pulled back in a braid and her eyes a soft, tired blue. Jane spent more time with Isabelle's mother than anyone else on earth, including Isabelle, which is maybe the thing Isabelle finds most miraculous.

"I don't know how you did it," Isabelle says.

"It all looks harder than it is. Everything was already organized in the computer. Basically, all I had to do was push a button, print it out."

"I mean Mom. Dealing with her all those years."

"Ah."

"What do they say? You have the patience of a saint. I wonder about those saints. If they didn't just go in their rooms and scream into their pillows."

"I admit, there were a few days where I had Jack Daniel's to thank."

More than a few, Isabelle guesses. Jane has a drinker's face. Then again, Jane lost her partner, Eva, to cancer a few years ago, and that plus a life of Maggie Austen may have caused the additional wear and tear.

"I feel like I should apologize to you."

"To me?"

"I sort of . . . Ran off. Left you holding

the bag. You were here, so I didn't have to be."

"Oh, no. No! This is my life. This is my home. I love it here. You *should* have gone out in the world and had other experiences. You still should! Your mom and I — okay. She was tough on a person. When she didn't like you, she could get petty and cruel as a junior high school girl. She could make you feel two inches tall. When she loved you, though — it was complicated, but she was loyal as hell."

"She was. She'd do anything for you, if you were on her side. Her generosity was boundless then."

"And, God, she could make you blush like a virgin, the things she'd come out with! Right? If I had a quarter for every *dick* and *cunt* . . ."

"That's not something a person says every day."

"The Sisters of Mercy of my old high school would have washed out my mouth. But I miss her. We all do. We haven't heard a good tit joke in months. Don't tell Kit I said that, or else he'll make twelve of them before his first flight of the day."

"She was hilarious, wasn't she? One of the funniest people I know. Knew. The past tense is weird."

"It is. It always is. But without a doubt, Isabelle, she had a heart of gold, at times."

"Definitely. I'm glad to hear you say this, though, because I felt bad. I heard how she talked to you sometimes. I mean, I know how that feels."

"Most of the stuff she'd aim my way, I just . . . *Whffft.*" Jane zips her hand over her head. "And, well, we understood each other. Her own mother — do you remember much about her? You were pretty young."

"She had a cookie drawer, and a coat with lots of pockets, and a little dog I loved."

"Maggie was a pussycat next to her."

"Oh, wow. I can't imagine."

"*I* can. You grow up like that and you're always on the offensive. You watch out for what might hurt you. You strike first. Either that or you learn to step carefully, like I did. Like you did."

The bells that hang on the door of Java Java Java ring, and Isabelle startles. She half expects Maggie to walk right in then, furious at her betrayal, but it's just a tourist couple holding hands and looking up at the chalkboard menu. Isabelle loved her mother. *Loves.* But she was always scared of her, and she still is, even now that she's dead. Powerful people — truly dead doesn't even seem possible.

Oh, for Christ's sake, Isabelle, Maggie says. *Stop being such a pussy.*

"Remember the whole thing with Phil?" Jane chuckles.

Phil owned Lake Union Air in Seattle, and their reliance on each other's ports meant they needed a smooth-running partnership. "War of the Roses," Isabelle says.

"She hated him. He looked like your father, that was the real problem."

"Whatever happened with that? I stopped asking."

"I forbid her to talk to him."

"He's been really nice to me since I've been here."

"He's a nice guy, he just didn't tiptoe around her, which was against her rules."

"Remember *Harv?*"

Jane winces.

"I still feel bad about Harv's kids." Maggie and Harv had a relationship for a few years. Harv's daughters hated Maggie, and the feeling was mutual. When Harv died, Maggie left them out of the obituary she wrote for *The Parrish Chronicle.*

"Yeah. Well, she was a child inside. That's the thing you have to remember."

Isabelle does remember. She can still hear Maggie's small voice on the phone, telling Isabelle how much she missed her. Maggie would clutch Isabelle's jacket sleeve when they had to say goodbye. This was such a different mother than the one who gripped a young Isabelle's wrist hard enough to leave marks, saying, *Stop hanging on me! Stop being such a whiner!*

"You know what, Isabelle? Every person is complicated. Every single one. Even me, even you."

"That's for sure."

"And you know, about your life in Seattle . . . I've been wanting to ask you something. While we're here, sitting in front of these numbers."

"Go for it."

Jane leans forward. Her eyes aren't tired anymore, and, Isabelle swears, her gray hair enlivens to a bright silver. "All this . . . I mean, I understand, this is a family legacy. Island Air, daughter to daughter, whether that's your plan or not. But you've been saying you're not sure about it. I want to tell you, you've got options."

There's a surge of steam from the espresso machine, and then the bells bang against the door again. Officer Ricky Beaker saunters in. They call him Tiny Policeman because of his height, sure, but also because his attitude makes you want to take him down a notch. Still, attitude or no, he raises his hand to Jane in a wave, and she does the same back, because everyone here has known one another forever, and that's just what you do. Bud from Bud's Tavern is placing his order at the counter, and Tiny gets in line behind him. In recent years, Tiny has traded his usual coffee at Boss Donuts for the good stuff, and who hasn't. Memory flash: her mother's ever-present cans of Folgers on the kitchen counter, which disappeared sometime in the 1980s, although one still survives, full of nails and screws, in the garage.

Out the window, Isabelle can see Cora Lee from the Theosophical Society taking a hundred years to cross the street. She sees the spot where she hit Clive Weaver's mail truck during her driver's test. Whenever she's visited Parrish as an adult, Isabelle feels like time had stopped, like she's still fifteen years old, still hiding in her room, plotting escape, kissing the occasional boy underneath the stadium bleachers. Only now, these last few weeks since she's been seeing Henry — the place looks old and new, too. It could maybe hold her past plus her future. She could maybe change and grow and move forward *here,* which never seemed possible before.

The point is — Jane's blue eyes piercing

hers, the excitement in them, the papers, the talk of all the years of understanding — Isabelle knows where this is heading. She's not sure it's somewhere she wants to go.

"You want to buy the business."

"I do. I have for a while. Your mother talked of retiring . . . I don't want to retire. I told her then that I'd be —"

"God, Jane . . . I don't know! I mean, if you'd asked me a few weeks ago . . ."

Jane leans back in her chair. She folds her hands together. Her excitement jets off to a safer place. "So you've decided to stay?"

"For now."

"Okay. I understand. And, I mean, I'm disappointed, but I get it. Look at this place. Is this the most gorgeous place on earth? You go anywhere else, and when you come back here, you feel so damn grateful."

It's more complicated than that for Isabelle. Sure, Parrish is beautiful. It's stunning, with its moody beaches and towering evergreens majestically keeping nature's secrets; with its shimmering water turning steely gray when the weather comes in and the sky darkens. A place that melodramatic and rich takes your breath away on a regular basis. But her child-self was formed here, and that child-self is a troublemaker and a sneak, a brat with yellowing bruises who still draws Isabelle into dark corners. It might be better, honestly, not to keep her on this temperamental island where she thrives. But what if Isabelle could actually get rid of that scared, problematic child-self for good? Fling her from the rocks of this very island, so she's never seen again? Start anew, maybe even with Henry? There's power in the idea. A full-circle rightness. "I'm just not through here, I guess."

Jane gathers up the papers. "We've agreed, though, we should pay off the loan for the 185? If she'd gone to the bank, the interest would be half that . . ."

"Do it."

"If you change your mind . . ."

"Better believe it. If I change my mind, there's only one person I'd ever sell to."

They are outside now, standing on the street in front of Nick's place. Isabelle is sad to have let Jane down, because she loves Jane and she owes her, and Jane is a great, solid person, and a dear friend. A rare person, the kind who actually deserves the word *deserves*. Jane hunts for her car keys, finds them in her pocket. "Before you go. I gotta ask. Is this about Joe?"

"Joe?"

"The reason for the glowing face? The new desire to stay? Our Joe? Eva used to

75

make me feel like that."

"God, no, Jane. That was eons ago. Plus, we work together now."

"I just thought . . . I don't know. Who else? There's no one here! And I remember you two in high school, both in those overalls you guys always wore. You were adorable."

Joe is one of their pilots. Joe was also one of the boys Isabelle kissed underneath the bleachers. The best one — the most important one. She adores Joe. He's still got the same lean frame and dark curls as he had years ago, and they still have the easy back-and-forth they've had since they were fifteen. But Isabelle is clear about past loves. After she met Dan, her old college sweetheart, for drinks, and found out he still raced his ATV every weekend and wrestled on an over-thirty team, she understood that it was only her younger, trusting self that she really wanted back.

"Overalls! I miss overalls. And Joe is a great guy, but we're just friends."

"Too bad. I love Joe."

Jane blows a kiss, gets into her car, and slams the door shut. She drives off, gives a little wave.

"Someone else," Isabelle says then.

No one hears. The words are a whisper. It's all she says, too, because she's in that time when you first meet a person, when it feels possible to break a spell with only a name, with the wrong move, with the truth about yourself, edging in.

After work, he's there waiting. She's hardly been able to concentrate all day. They've already had many phone conversations late into the night, a few beach walks, and another dinner, at The Bayshore this time. She's confirmed that Henry is smart, funny, generous, and elusive enough to be interesting. There have been only a few, dropped details about his wife and marriage: His wife's name was Sarah Banks. They did a lot of outdoorsy things together. She worked at the same university as he did. There have been hints of a betrayal before the leaving. They were married for three years; he apparently had a fiancée before that. That leaves a lot of history, a lot of time, unaccounted for, but he's not the sort of man who likes to live in the past. *Elusive* only means a person has secrets, but it's easy to forget that when you're drawn into the delicious mystery of a person. What's secret-keeping and what's discretion when you first meet, anyway?

What's he doing way out here? her mother says. *Have you noticed? Parrish Island is the farthest point on the map from Boston.* God, the Maggie voice is a pain in the ass. And the real Maggie — she *would* have found out exactly why Henry chose to come to this distant spot. She would have done all she could — googling, stalking, lurking — to unearth every dirty detail about him, anything to avoid the slight chance of being had. When Isabelle first fell for Evan, her mother bought an online background check of him, something Isabelle found out only afterward. Maggie discovered Evan's arrest for a minuscule amount of pot and a small-claims court dispute over a bill for a storage unit and that was all, but Isabelle had been furious with her. And she refuses to be anything like her. She will not google, stalk, and lurk. Isabelle wants to trust, to relax, to let things unfold naturally. Plus, Henry's shine is so bright she has to shield her eyes, and even then he's still all glow and warm rays coming down.

Now: She runs to the car, her mother's Acura, and gets in. She isn't sure what it is — the spring day, the run to the car — but it all feels familiar, like school is out and summer is starting and time is wide and generous. Henry kisses her, and then she doesn't feel like a girl anymore. She remembers quite clearly that she's a woman who wants things.

"Where are we headed? A surprise, you said." Henry starts the engine.

"A place only the locals know."

"Nice. A secret."

"You got that right."

The key ring is still her mother's — it's a pair of outstretched silver wings, and it clacks against the dash when he hits a bump. Isabelle looks away. Also, she realizes that she forgot to clean out the glove box, and so it's still likely filled with the fast-food napkins and the Latin music CD *Corazon* that her mother had in there. Does it matter? It doesn't matter. Even if she can picture Maggie with the windows down, shimmying her big, cushy chest to the beat.

Isabelle directs Henry to the far north side of the island, the Delgado Strait, with its harbor docks packed with sailboats and cruisers that come to tie up for the night or weekend. The Hotel Delgado is perched on a small hilltop and overlooks the scene. Teddy Roosevelt supposedly once stayed there. The hotel is one of those places that has been so present throughout your life that you don't even really see it anymore. She hasn't really taken a good look at it in years, but now, with Henry beside her, she sees it through his eyes. It's gotten a little dilapidated. Maybe it's just because this season's ivy hasn't grown in yet, but the paint looks chipped and faded. It's tired. Seen with some generosity, though, the hotel has charm, with its white clapboard with shutters and a big rocking-chair porch. The staff sets tables outside in the summer for lingering, candlelit dinners.

As always, the harbor is busy. It's worse on the weekends, when it gets packed and there are parties aboard the boats. After any San Juan Island regatta, this is the spot to be. The alcohol flows, the music thumps. Now the boats only rock and clank, and a fisherman appraises his catch. A huge sailboat swoops in, and the two men on board navigate the maneuver. There's muffled shouting, and then a clear "Fuck you, Captain Ed," and a laugh. It smells like seaweed and deep water out there, beachy dead stuff (Isabelle loves that smell), and onions frying from the hotel restaurant.

Isabelle takes Henry's hand. They're having a regular day together, outside in the real world, and his face is feeling so familiar lately, too, and so is that hand in hers. His camera hangs from his neck and bumps against his chest as they walk. It's the old kind of camera with the huge, professional lens. There are no quick shots from his phone for Henry. She's learned this about him, plus more. The way he expects quality. The way he likes things done right. It's admirable. She respects that.

He smiles at her eagerness, at the way she pulls him toward the trail marked with the wooden sign HISTORIC SITE. Sometimes she has the sense that he's indulging her, and it feels both shameful and fantastic. She wants to feel both big and small with a person, powerful and powerless. Clearly, it's a doomed desire.

"Come on!" she calls.

"Here?" He's understandably skeptical. The trail is damp and dark. It's the pathway of fairy tales involving talking trees and menacing stepmothers. Of course, he might just be worried about wrecking those new running shoes.

"I should have warned you it might be muddy."

"You should have warned me it might be muddy."

She pays no attention to the small jab. Actually, her brain shoots the words down its complicated machine of turns and flippers, transforms them to something harmless, a joke. Her brain has performed this trick all her life. She barely notices Henry's critical edge. With Evan she didn't notice the critical edge until he was shoving her off of it, but this is what happens when you've been raised to fall short. Isabelle drank criticism from her baby bottle. It's got to be pretty strong stuff before she even tastes it.

She punches his arm playfully. "Hurry up, old man."

"Old man, huh? Where are you taking me? Can I trust you, or are you going to bring me out in the middle of nowhere and take advantage of me?"

"Henry North, Henry North," she sings.

It's dark in there, and the woods close in; the evergreen trees spread their wide boughs overhead. She forgot this part. It's a little creepy, and that's why high school stoners and people doing things they shouldn't were the only ones who ever came here.

"Are we there yet, Mom?"

"It's a lot farther than I remembered."

They're speaking low and quiet. The path is thick with rotting leaves and pine needles, and it is now the sort of dark-alone that requires hushed tones and soft steps. A branch cracks. Isabelle looks over her shoulder. It's time for the knife-wielding rapist to run out and for the audience to scream.

"Come on," she says.

Henry stops as if he, too, has heard something. He pulls her in close and kisses her. Isabelle moves her hands up the back of his shirt and feels his bare skin, slick with sweat from the walk. It's getting crazy with him, the want. After the beach walks and dinners, how much more waiting can a person stand? She breaks away and tugs his sleeve. They're almost there.

And now . . . Here they are. It's always sudden and surreal even when she's seen it many times before: that stone table with the stone chairs around it, all set on a high wooden platform turned a forever-green from moss. Each chair has the name of a dead McKinnon etched on it, and each has a dead McKinnon buried beneath it. The scene looks like something from the time of knights and ancient kings. It's a mystical place; dreamlike, and strange enough that you can believe you've stepped into another era. But it's a tomb from only a hundred years ago. McKinnon family mourners would walk that same trail while carrying a coffin on their shoulders.

"Ta-da," she says.

"Incredible."

Henry removes his lens cap and begins to snap photos. He walks a slow circle, bends low to get the entire table in the frame, steps up to capture the name *Walter* on the back of one stone chair.

It's damp out there, though, and getting cold as late afternoon turns to evening. Isabelle rubs her bare arms.

"Chilly?" he asks. "I wish I had a jacket for you."

"I forgot how eerie it is here."

" 'Each separate dying ember wrought its ghost upon the floor . . .' "

"Poe?" Of course, Poe. Lately, she knows more about the poet than she ever could have imagined she would. How he lost both parents before he was three. How he was once so poor he had to burn his furniture. How he had his heart broken by a fickle fiancée and a dying wife, whom he married when she was fourteen. Not the most cheerful guy to spend your life on, if you ask Isabelle. Still, she respects this, too, his knowledge and experience and passion.

"Mmm-hmmm. Indeed."

"I wonder if the McKinnons even come anymore."

"Great spot for a family reunion!"

Isabelle laughs at Henry's joke and is rewarded. "You are much too far away," he says.

She goes to him. He wraps his arms around her. God, it feels good. He has the kind of big hands she likes. "You know, this place is very, very odd but amazing."

"Strange, right? In high school, this was where you went if you wanted to do something and not get caught."

"Stop giving me ideas."

He lifts her chin and kisses her. Wow, she's attracted to him. The kiss is so sweet and soft and quiet, but then the key is in the lock and the lock clicks and the door swings open, and finally, finally, after that frustrating make-out session last time in front of The Bayshore with the diners watching from their padded banquette seats, he's shoving his hands roughly up her blouse and her hands are under his T-shirt, and nothing is sweet and soft anymore. It's hard and fast and who can stand to do anything but shove and pull until you're closer and closer still.

He pulls her to that platform. "We don't have a blanket," she says.

"Shh. No one's here." He doesn't care about mess or propriety now. He only lifts his shirt and lays that down, and it's enough, it's fine, because finally there's no more waiting. He's above her, and so are the wing-branches of trees and the geometric pieces of blue sky. She unbuttons his jeans and yanks the zipper and shoves them down, and he's got her jeans off, and he's inside her and she's moving with him and crying out and he's crying out before she even realizes the pain in her elbows and tailbone.

"Oh, God," he says. His weight is on top of her, his breath hot on her neck. "I couldn't wait."

"Oh, Henry," Isabelle says. And then, "Ow, ow, I have to get up."

There's that twisting and adjusting of clothes. "Look where we are," he says. "This is all your fault. All that 'not getting caught' talk."

"We are weird! We are so weird!"

She is laughing, and so is he. "Let's go," he says. He takes her hand. They run. It's time to do that again more slowly, and in the crisp, clean sheets of Henry's bed.

In his room, she wakes with a startle — something has its hands around her neck. Jesus, she's suffocating! She tries to bolt upright, but she's tangled in a sheet, which has wound tight around her. It's just dream-truth, the choking.

He stirs. The moon shines through the big windows. She wishes the room had blinds to close — you can feel watched with all that glass. She notices that his nightstands are nearly empty. There are no photos, no personal history, no telling bottles of aspirin or tubes of ChapStick. There's only a clock, which probably belonged to the musician. "I better go," she says when she sees the time.

He kisses her forehead, so sweet. "I'll miss you."

Back in her own bed later that night, Isabelle feels the sharp bruise on her tailbone, a reminder now of their first time together by the stone table. She replays the intensity of the moment, the urgency. A crass thought pops into her head. Her head is the only place she's crass. She thinks: *The dead watched us fuck.*

Right there in the woods at *Walter's* feet. It's the crazy kind of thing you do when you're not thinking rationally. When love makes you totally lose yourself.

That bruise — it hurts whenever she moves wrong.

CHAPTER 8

Weary's assistant, Lotto, names the new crow Roussette. Rouss, for short. It's what the locals call the flying fox, a species of fruit bat. Lotto's mother used to cook roussette, and that's what Lotto said he felt like doing to the bird when they finally captured him after all those weeks. Mama Yeiwene would take the creature and boil it, strip its skin off, and then cook the flesh again in coconut cream.

Their Rouss is too smart to be boiled, though, Weary knows, almost too smart to be caught at all. *Corvus* is one of the most intelligent creatures on earth, and Rouss was pissed, oh, boy, when it happened. When the mist net came down over the top of him, he flapped and cawed in fury. *Damn it!* he seemed to say. *Damn it, damn it!* A person could almost feel bad about the yellow plastic tags newly around his foot and the satellite transmitter, which now mark him as a prisoner, never to be completely free again.

When the net comes down on Henry North, though, Weary will not feel bad. Not for a second.

The thing about Henry — he's not just smart, he's evil. Evil enough to both avoid the trap and lay the trap. He's not some wild-eyed, knife-wielding psychopath, leading some high-speed police chase. And he doesn't twirl a villainous mustache, imagining the gleeful demise of some poor woman. It's what makes evil so evil, the everydayness of it. It's as regular as the boiled egg or the cat food set under the net, the things that draw you forward so you don't notice the other things. Evil is a clinking teaspoon against the teacup, the good manners, the worldly hobbies and the passionate kiss.

Evil is two women, gone forever. One down a cliff, one lost at sea. Going on your merry way afterward.

But evil is Henry North just being Henry North in his daily life, too, Weary believes. Henry being his superior self, first sitting above a person, and then observing and calculating, peck, peck, peck. He's like *Corvus* with a shiny object, turning it around, investigating, playing with it for a while until it gets boring, and then burying it. Whatever the object is, the point is that it's an object, a thing that loses its shine the more he looks at it. It's dull, it's plastic, it's subpar, it's not as shiny as he thought, and so he jabs and turns it and jabs from another side, and then discards. At first, the object is the shiniest and most special object on earth until, look, just as he suspected, it's only a gum wrapper, a piece of garbage.

What or who could be up to the standards of such greatness? No one. Every single person is an inevitable disappointment next to his own hungry, beautiful self. Weary remembers Sarah's slow decline. You could see it right on her face, like the air being let out of a party balloon that was once bouncing, full, celebratory. No matter how you make a person disappear — it's wrong. It's a misuse of power. But evil doesn't necessarily even know it's evil. It can't see *other,* so its effect on other is meaningless. The self is king, and any damage, well, who cares? Move along! Objects are all in service of the glorious non-self, the shadow self, the empty vessel self of Henry North and others like him. Round of applause for the amazing, incredible Mr. Marvelous! Sweep the trash out of the way, so he can find more shiny things that please him.

Push the once-shiny object off a fucking

cliff if you have to.

Lotto is a young Kanak, the original inhabitants of New Caledonia, and he wears a *paseo* in retro homage to some relative who supposedly first led the revolts in 1878. He also wears an American T-shirt on top, which sports an image of Bazooka Joe. Weary likes Lotto. He's affable, and he cares about the birds. Something else Weary likes about Lotto — he does what he is told. And what Weary tells him to do after the trap is dismantled and the distressed Rouss set loose again is to go home. It's early, but they've done good work, Weary tells him. Every crow adds to their understanding of the species at large, and of the human-animal world as a whole.

Blah, blah, blah.

Not that Weary doesn't truly care about the research. Oh, he does. Very much. But since he lost Sarah, he's lived with a divided mind. A divided life. Secret obsessions have a way of drowning out everything else. They pound a drumbeat that gets louder and louder and closer and closer. It can sound like a haunting, taunting heartbeat, or the thump of stone upon stone as the wall of a cave is closed up. Weary dislikes Poe by association, but Poe was right about one aspect of revenge. One must punish, but punish with impunity.

That is the tricky part, yes? Weary drives the Jeep back down the mud-and-crater road of Mount Khogi. As he rumbles past the black trees and the banyans and the coconut palms, navigates through the diminishing sandalwoods stripped by hunters, he thinks about the way oppressed animals have the last word. Those lions, the ones made to jump through humiliating hoops and stand on their back legs like silly lap dogs, they get their moment, don't they? The dolphins, too, after one too many cute wave and forced high five with a flipper — they finally snap.

And the crows, *Corvus,* perhaps most of all — well, they will remember a dangerous human or a kind one. If you are evil or malevolent, beware. They will spread the word about you, they will describe you in detail to one another, and they will even tell their children, who will tell their children's children. And then they'll plot bloody revenge.

Enough is enough, that's the thing. For an animal, for anyone.

Objects, well, they become enraged eventually.

Is respect so hard, Mr. Marvelous? Though, Weary supposes, a creature with a cold reptile heart and beady little reptile eyes will only slither and victimize and then lie on a warm rock, being who he is. A snake doesn't think about that rodent or bird. He just thinks about being a snake, and what a snake needs.

God, it fills him with fury. Finally back home, in his silent compound overlooking the sea (well, *compound* is generous, but it is spacious and cool with those lovely tile floors and walls and sliding doors and shutters made from the wood of the breadfruit tree and the coconut), Weary showers. It's weird, maybe, but in private, he uses a lavender shampoo because Sarah did, and he uses a soap that smells like orange blossom on his own firm body, because that's what she smelled like. And the smells bring her back like nothing else, as smells do. They make her come alive. It makes his heart ache.

He sobs right there in the shower. He sobs so hard that he bends in half. And then he recovers. He regroups. He remembers what is still good, as lavender and orange blossom washes down the drain.

He ties a robe around himself. Pads in his bare feet to the desk. He closes his eyes in a brief prayer that is not quite a prayer, because after everything that happened and is about to happen, he's not entirely sure how he feels or should be allowed to feel about God.

Please, he says, in a general way.

He has, after all, been anticipating this all day. All week. Much, much longer.

ShutR opens like a dream.

There are three new photos. Weary's heart is thumping so hard it's almost a wild animal there in his chest. He tries to breathe — in, out. The anxiety and excitement is too much. If those photos are just Henry's usual ho-hum flowers and sunset beach shots, the disappointment may be more than he can bear.

But. You can *feel* when all your time and efforts and patience are about to pay off. Just like *Corvus* and the mist net, you can sense it about to happen.

All right.

Well, he doesn't understand what he's seeing. There are new images, all right, but what is this? It's a word, carved into stone. *Walter.* Walter? It makes no sense, and there are no other clues. It's not a headstone, although it looks like one. There are no dates or even a last name. It's a frustrating mystery.

Next image, useless. One of Henry's typical nature shots, dime a dozen, tree branches shot skyward. God rays of sun shining down, as if Henry North has more right to claim God than Weary himself does.

Onward. Number three.

Oh, it's strange. So, so strange.

It's a table of sorts, a stone table in the woods. Weary will have to look this up. He will type in *table* and *stone* and *Parrish Island*. He will look up *trail* and *woods* and *Parrish* and *Walter*. His mind is clicking along, speeding down all the possibilities of his next move. He will find out what it is, and where it is, and then he'll search for all recent photos anywhere by anyone. Maybe there's a crowd of people there, not in that image. Maybe someone else snapped a photo that will —

In all his leaping ahead and scheming his next move, he almost misses what's right here in front of him this very second. But perhaps God (or fate, or whatever Weary manages to believe in on a given day) is tap, tap, tapping on his chamber door, urging, because he spots it.

What is that?

What is that *there*? Something almost out of the frame, but not quite.

Enlarge, enlarge — zoom, zoom, zoom.

It's a hand, on the back of one of the stone chairs. There's the bump of wrist bone, and a woven bracelet. Small, delicate fingers.

A hand that Henry North, the great photographer (Mr. Marvelous is never as great as he is in his own mind), has neglected to crop out. And the most important thing about this hand (*Calm down!* Weary tells himself) is the bracelet and the shiny pink-orange polish on the fingers.

It's like he's in the forest, crouched on his haunches with the binoculars pressed to his eyes. It's like he's spotted a singular and long-awaited specimen. Blood whooshes through Weary's veins in the same pulsing way. He was right about the grocery bill, and later, that Visa charge at a restaurant. The Bayshore. He was absolutely right. Henry is seeing someone.

There she is, he thinks.

Oh, the color of that polish — it's so hopeful, so open.

It hurts to see it. And it hurts to see that bracelet, too. It reminds Weary of Virginia's watch, things ripped and torn in moments of anger. He's crushed. And now the anxiety, the fear, really shoves forward, because how did he not anticipate this, the responsibility he'd have to this girl? Dear God! He's been waiting, he's been wishing, and suddenly, she's here, and his plan is in motion. But he hadn't thought this through. He should have helped Sarah sooner, and he didn't, and it's the biggest regret of his life. He now realizes he has timing issues. He now realizes he has even larger worries than he first thought. Because a plan is fine. But another dead woman is not.

CHAPTER 9

Isabelle has the weekend free, since Taylor Han comes in to do all the secondary tasks that Island Air doesn't really need Isabelle for anyway. Kit had a kidney stone and had to take a few days off, but Jane already arranged for a contract pilot from Anacortes to keep their schedule on track. Phones get answered; payments get made. The planes go in and the planes go out as they have for years, splashing down, lifting off, right on time. Really, Isabelle feels as useless at Island Air as she did in college working at Nordstrom's Brass Plum, where she'd hang back shyly as the other "sales associates" boldly approached shoppers looking for the right sweaters to go with certain jeans. Isabelle is not passive; she hates that word. Just, if people are larger and louder, she tends to let them go ahead being larger and louder.

But, hey, it's great, because Saturday is

hers. And it's the kind of spring day that gives spring its reputation. You can smell that summer is coming with just a few more twirls of the planet. The air is warm, and dewy arrowheads of bulbs have recently edged up. Isabelle should be going through all her mother's stuff, she should at least have a conversation with Jenny Sedgewick, who's called more than once, saying her son, Thomas, wants to buy the house if she's selling. She should maybe mow the little lawn in the back; the small patch where the two lounge chairs overlooking the sound now resemble a pair of cats crouched in long grass. She should *maybe* do a hundred different things. But this is a day she wants to greet.

And Henry has called, as he does now every morning and every night. They've both decided that it's too beautiful a day to waste. *They,* meaning the two of them, making decisions together. *Waste,* meaning every have-to on her list. It's true, though — in the Northwest, days like this are ones you should take advantage of. The weather of the San Juan Islands is mercurial, stormy. It's as moody as Isabelle's mother was. The clouds can go from plump and angelic one minute to dark and vengeful the next, spitting a fury of hard rain. Blue sky days make everyone a little euphoric. The convertible tops come down and the shorts go on, even if it's sixty degrees out.

And now that the endless, dull metal-gray of winter is mostly over, tourists are starting their annual migration, so it's good that she and Henry had decided to meet over by the harbor rather than in town. It'll be quieter, without ferries dumping traffic onto small streets.

Let's go out, Henry had said.

Out?

Out-out, like on the water.

There's a couple of boats you can —

Just come. I'll handle it. We can pretend we're away from all this.

There isn't much of *all this* that Isabelle wants to be away from lately. Look at the old hotel, sprawling like an aging actress managing to keep her graces, look at the green lawn rolling down to the docks, look at the blue water and the perfect white V of a seagull propped in a postcard sky. It all makes Isabelle feel glad. It makes her want every bit of it, and more. And here comes Henry, his hands in the pockets of his cargo shorts, his shirt untucked, his brown hair loose, and an overlooked dot of sun lotion on his nose. A dog trots beside him.

"You made a new friend," she says, as they

kiss hello.

"This is Rocko, who'll unfortunately be returning to The Windswept." Rocko's ear twitches at his name. Henry scruffs the dog's neck. Even Isabelle's mom would have approved. *Good guys like dogs,* she always said. Isabelle's father (no wonder she hates the word *passive*) liked cats, and Harv didn't like anything, even Maggie, it often seemed.

"Pleased to meet you, Rocko."

"I rented us a boat. The *Red Pearl.*"

"Oh, wow. Yeah. I know the boat." She wants to laugh, because the *Red Pearl* is a cabin cruiser that's been docked at Delgado Harbor forever. Isabelle didn't even know the motor actually ran. A couple of sleazy former divers, Jan and Dave, own it, and there always used to be high school parties on it, with young girls in bikinis aboard. Now, Jan and Dave are at the age of Viagra and bad knees. Back then, though, the *Red Pearl* was for losing both your virginity and your common sense.

"Come on. I got us all set up."

There it is, the *Red Pearl,* same as it ever was. "Fantastic old wooden boat, don't you think? What a beauty." Henry hops on board. He holds out his hand, even though Isabelle doesn't need it. She's been stepping onto rocking vessels since she was a toddler, and can drive a boat like a captain. When you grow up on Parrish, water is your element.

"Oh, it is. It's lovely," she says. She doesn't know why she's lying. All she sees when she looks at the wood cabin and brass rails is Kale Kramer puking up too much tequila over the side. She smells the faint pee-tang of beer, too, but maybe it's just her memory adding details.

"This right here is history. Imagine the stories."

Well, she doesn't exactly have to imagine. And she doesn't tell him this, either. She's doing that thing, the thing she swore she would never do again, the hiding, the pleasing, the polishing. If she can't be herself entirely now, if she can't say what she really thinks, when will she? When she's ninety?

Henry ducks into the chartroom. "Hey, look!" he calls. He's sitting on the wooden stool mounted in front of the desk, one hand cupping an old brass compass. "This probably brought the old girl in from rough waters many a time."

If anyone was in rough waters, it was *young* girls. Young girls in rough *underage* waters, and the captain didn't so much sit on that stool navigating high-sea adventure

102

as sit on that stool getting blow jobs he should have been arrested for.

"I'm sure it has," Isabelle says. A person could misunderstand and think that all the careful steps and mini-evasions are about keeping herself perfect in his eyes, but they're really about keeping him perfect in his own. If she tells him the truth about the boat now, he'll feel like a fool, and she perhaps already senses that Henry's ego is a fragile thing that must be held carefully, lest it break. Isabelle performs this self-saving service for everyone, not just the men in her life. She buffs up the esteem of repairmen and grocery clerks, fellow passengers on airplanes, and waitresses. It's a tough job, helping everyone feel good about themselves. An exhausting job.

And to all the strong women in her head who judge her for performing this endless service, especially for the men in her life, women like her friend Alice, who'd never dance around a person's mood or flagging self-image, she says, *Shut up.* She says, *You have no idea,* and Alice doesn't. Alice was raised with the right to speak her mind and not be smacked for it. Alice got her MFA because she wanted to. Alice doesn't take shit from anyone. But Alice had not spent her formative years making nice to avoid being *in trouble, in big trouble.* Alice had not been a little child weatherman, watching the sky, bolting for shelter, holding the kite with the key in the lightning storm. Alice will never get the way childhood fear can lead to paralysis and perpetual anxious tending, so shut your mouth, Alice! Isabelle knows full well what she does and why. She just can't get to the next part, where she stops.

"They don't make boats like this anymore," Henry says, outside again. "Don't you hate those big Bayliners with the cup holders and the giant speakers pumping music?"

"Evan loved those," she says.

"And we won't go hungry." He nudges a cooler with his toe. She looks inside. Cheese and wine and fruit, stuff the *Red Pearl*'s never seen before. Its usual fare was Budweiser, maybe. Bean dip in a can.

"Wow. That looks amazing."

Henry sits in the driver's seat outside, turns the engine, which coughs and then spits black noxious gas before clearing, like an old smoker with emphysema. Isabelle lifts the top of a bench and tucks her bag inside. She could back this boat out of this marina with her eyes closed, and she knows just how far they can go out on the sound before the water gets too rough. But she tosses her sweatshirt on the padded chair next to the captain. It's okay. For now, he can drive. "Where are we heading?"

"A little trip around the island?"

"Let's do it."

Isabelle is untying the floats when Jan himself comes jogging up the dock with a few life jackets under his arm. They're the retro orange kind, the sort you used to wear as a kid, that strap around your waist and buck your chin high.

"I just remembered that these were on the *Sunsurfer*! Coast Guard regulations." Jan's got a big gray beard now, and booze eyes. He can still see clearly, though, because he says, "Isabelle Austen, is that you?"

"Hi, Jan."

"Hey, sorry about your mom."

"I appreciate it."

"Tough old broad. She used to scare the crap out of me, to tell you the truth. But I respected her."

"I hear you."

Jan tosses the jackets and Isabelle catches them, and then they wave as Henry backs the boat out of the slip and eases away.

"That's the life, huh?" Henry shouts over the motor. "Live on your boat, have a small rental business. Keep it all simple . . ."

"I don't know how simple. Supposedly, he and Dave have been hiding here for years after some drug trouble in the Bahamas."

Henry shakes his head as if he can't believe what goes on in the world. The boat putters past the slips. It's early, but the racers have already left, and only the weekend fishermen are up, settling in to their favorite spots. The rest of the boats are still tucked in tight, their residents sleeping off Friday-night fun. Later, it'll be a madhouse out here.

Henry picks up speed, heads to open water. Isabelle stands beside him, holds on as the bow smacks the waves.

"You can be my Dirk Peters," he shouts, grinning.

"Oh, no. If this is Poe, I'm worried."

"The *Pym* novel. Pym and Dirk sailed to the South Pole together." From this elevation, she can see a sprinkling of gray in Henry's hair as it shines in the sun. It makes her feel tender toward him, and she kisses the top of his head. The wind whips past them.

"I love this," Isabelle shouts. And, hey, after all the misuse, the *Red Pearl* is getting a second chance, same as she is. Here's who they both were meant to be. God, it all fills her with the glory of being alive. She *wants* to sail to the South Pole. She wants to sail to everywhere.

The island gets farther away, and the marina retreats into the distance. Isabelle can see how magnificent it is, the mighty Northwest, with that rocky shore against the deep green waters, with the nearby islands rising from the sea like a pod of killer whales.

Henry heads east. From there, Isabelle can see a ferry heading to Orcas, and one of their own planes rising northward. The beauty is ridiculously abundant, and yet all of the San Juans feel like a secret, with their tiny harbors and clapboard main streets, hidden arcs of rocky, windswept beaches, everything painted in ancient, watery hues. The scenery sweeps by. Isabelle leans over the side, lets the cold saltwater spray against her arm.

"Look," Henry calls. It's a team of sailboats speeding toward a buoy. He heads in their direction, and the tiny triangles grow to full-sized spinnakers shouting colors.

"Spring Series Regatta," Isabelle says.

He cuts the engine. "I've got to get some photos. This is stunning out here."

They bob and slosh for a while as Henry snaps. "Let me take one of you," she says. "You can send it to your brothers."

"No, no. I should tell you, I hate getting

my picture taken. *Hate.*"

"Really? All right. How about one of both of us? Would that help? Do you have a timer on that thing?"

"Nope. Nice try. I'll take you, how about that? If there has to be some recorded proof that we were here."

His tone is teasing, but his words are a little sharp. It's probably not how he means it. Before she can object, he focuses, clicks, and then checks the results.

"Pretty nice, actually." He shows her. It's an art shot, the way the sun shines down behind her in streaks, lighting her blowing hair. The spinnakers of the boats fill the back of the frame.

"I could win a prize with that," he says.

"I have missed this." Henry brought real plates and real white napkins, too, not the Chinet and roll of paper towels of Isabelle's boating life until now. There's a fine, chewy loaf of sourdough that Henry tears into artful chunks.

"You did this a lot with Sarah, you said, when you were married?"

"Well, I don't know about *a lot.* When I was growing up, my father fancied himself a sailor. He mostly went alone, though. I think he just did it to get away from my mother. She was afraid of water, so it was the one place she'd never follow him to."

Isabelle notices it, the way he slides the conversation away from Sarah. He *always* slides the conversation away from Sarah, as if it's too unbearable to have nearby. She has to piece the woman together from tiny bits of information. Wealthy family. Catholic school. Brilliant but troubled. She wishes Henry would talk about his marriage and what went wrong. There've been hints of another man, some flirtation or maybe something more, so this may be why his ego is so tender. Still, she'd like to talk about where *her* marriage went wrong. She wants to really know him, and have him know her. The angers and disappointments, the loneliness of life with Evan, the loss of all the years with no true partnership and children and family to show for it — she wants to share this. She needs to, so she can move forward.

"You said your dad was an attorney?"

"High-powered attorney and asshole of the highest magnitude."

"Why is *high-powered* always used with attorneys? You never hear high-powered dentist or high-powered teacher."

"Easy answer. Most attorneys are assholes. He was, anyway."

"Is this why your brothers and you all became, let's see if I get this right, a potter, a pediatrician, and a poet? Every gentle profession imaginable?"

"Hoping to give him the heart attack he eventually had."

"That's awful." She socks him.

"He deserved worse. All right, this is Roncal, a Spanish cheese. Meaty, lightly nutty. This is a Grayson. Lively, bold . . . made from the raw milk of Jerseys on a Virginian farm."

"I've never eaten this good in my life."

"This *well*?"

"Henry, if you correct my grammar again I may have to stab you with this knife."

"I stand warned."

The moment is there and gone, and you could call it a red flag, only it's not an alarming color, and it does not even wave in warning. It's small and quiet, easily ignored as a whisper. And why not ignore it? Does what he said matter? No. Does the fact that he said it matter? Not really. It wasn't very sensitive, but Isabelle has her own faults. Love requires generosity. Love requires giving someone the benefit of the doubt.

Love requires not being an asshole, Maggie says. *Tell him where he can stick his "well."*

Maggie needs to shut it. Maggie couldn't maintain a relationship to save her life. See what good anger brings you? It's a poison that kills off whatever is nearby. Maggie is clearly trying to toss gasoline onto a little flare of irritation, which Isabelle douses. Henry hands her a plate of food, and Isabelle is otherwise having one of the best days she's had in a long while. She wants this. Who he is and who she is are complicated variables in *this*. Love always involves an identity crisis; at least, it involves the small shifts of self that make room for another person.

"And what's cheese without wine?" Henry says.

His feet are planted, balancing on the rocking boat as he hunts through a cloth shopping bag. He finds the bottle and grabs it around its neck, holds it in the air with a flourish.

"Perfect," she says. He tucks the bottle between his knees and twists in the corkscrew. "Don't hurt anyone with that."

"You're in good hands, Isabelle Austen. Don't you forget it."

With that, any small criticisms are gone. *Good hands* — such beautiful words. Pretty much the thing anyone really wants.

He pops the cork from the bottle. "Voilà!"

he says, like he's just pulled a rabbit from a hat.

He pours the wine into two glasses, and they clink. They feast on the bread and cheese and fruit — thin slices of apple and pear, small boughs heavy with grapes. They sip; they eat. They gaze out. The boat is sloshing and rocking, though. Isabelle's stomach sloshes and rocks, too.

She is watching his face as he sits beside her on that wooden bench seat, and so she sees it, all at once, the way his face changes. It goes slack. He suddenly looks his age. He stares at the scarlet wave inside his glass, as if it's a miniature ocean in a faraway land. The cheese on his plate has lost its magic, and only looks like any cheese, flat and finished.

"Henry? Are you okay? When we're not moving like this, it gets pretty rocky out here."

"No, it's fine."

"I'm feeling a little seasick myself."

"I'm fine, I said."

She doesn't say anything more, and neither does he. There's just the slop of waves against the side of the boat and the awkward shouting of silence. She begins the accounting, scrolls through the ledger of what might have gone wrong.

"I'm sorry," he says finally. "I thought I could do it. All this . . ." He sweeps his hand out toward the sea. "The boat, the wine, the outing . . . I wanted to . . . I don't know. Erase. Do over! Foolish. *Crazy.* One of the last times with my wife, Sarah? A boat, a bottle of wine . . ."

"Jesus."

"We'd gone out to Rockport, rented a cruiser . . ."

"Jesus, Henry."

"Had a big fight. And after that . . ."

Oh, he's crushed. Destroyed by Sarah leaving him, that seems clear. Who can resist such heartache? Who can turn away from the chance to make everything right? Not Isabelle. She reaches over, takes his hand. She brings it to her mouth, kisses it softly. His skin smells like wind and sun and boat gasoline, and something that's just Henry. She wants to smell that and smell that and smell that.

"And then she was gone. It was done." His voice is hoarse. He looks like he might cry. "It's impossible to understand, someone just taking off . . ."

Isabelle can't, that's for sure. In a way, she wished Evan had left that way years before, rather than the protracted distancing and returning he did, like the lion coming back to pick at the carcass. God, what is crueler? She has no idea.

"What did she say, Henry? How did she explain herself?"

"She didn't."

"She didn't give any explanation?"

"Well, we'd been fighting. There'd been problems. But, then, after that night, nothing. Not another word."

Not another word? Maggie says. *Not one single one? What the hell, Isabelle. What the hell!* "You mean, like after that, you just communicated through lawyers and such?"

"Pretty much. Look, Isabelle. I'm done talking about this. I'm sorry, I . . . I just wanted to have a great day doing something I love to do with you."

"Of course, Henry. Of course. And we did. It is a great day. I'm so sorry that happened to you. No one deserves that. Especially not you."

He gives her a squeeze, but he's clearly shaking her off, shaking off the demoralizing memory. Rejection, well — it always turns you right back into the nine-year-old no one wanted to eat lunch with, even when it doesn't turn your whole life upside down.

"How about I drive us to the marina?" Isabelle says. "These waves . . ."

"Let's not let her ruin everything. Come here."

Henry pulls Isabelle to his lap. He takes her face in his hands. He kisses her hard. Her face, that kiss — she doesn't want to just be a thing that erases another thing, but it's a good kiss. A great, if complicated, one.

"Let's start back," he says.

Kiss or no kiss, it seems that Sarah has ruined their day after all. At least, when they return to the harbor, Henry is terse and short-tempered. The marina has filled with weekend boaters coming in and going out, and the sailboats from the regatta are arriving, too, and it's as crazy there as Isabelle predicted. Henry nearly clips a catamaran, and when Isabelle urges (strenuously urges!) he not use the wheel to dock, just the throttle and shift, he snaps an "I *know.*" He follows that up with a curt *Watch the bow.* Docking tiffs or all-out arguments — threats of divorce, even — they're a common occurrence in boating, she knows, given the stress of the task and the added embarrassment of onlookers. Isabelle's glad, though, when they're in and all tied down. They gather up their bags. They drop the keys off with Jan, who's already half tanked over on

Hideaway, his liveaboard.

That night, though, in Henry's bed, in the room where Clyde Belle likely tumbled with the despair of his life, the day's tensions fall away. They reconnect, with skin on skin and mouths on mouths and bodies that are still new to each other. As much as Isabelle hates tension like that (her childhood made nearly any upset feel cringing and unbearable), something feels more real now. It's not just tra la la, roses and flower petals and lots of sex between them. He's a person with a past and she's a person with a past, and she felt some of his hard memories with him today, navigated a few difficult moments as a couple, literally and figuratively.

"Thank you for the boat ride and everything else," Isabelle whispers after they've made love. Her head is on his chest. Her arm crooks around him like he's shelter or like she is.

"Look at this tiny wrist," he says.

"Small but mighty."

"I'm falling for you, Isabelle Austen," Henry North says into her hair.

She smiles. She kisses him. "And I'm falling for you, Henry North."

They've gotten through something. Her heart is so full. He's weathered stuff, and she's weathered stuff, and this makes her think they can weather stuff together. She forgets that stuff plus stuff plus weather leads to crushed buildings and drowned ships and broken glass everywhere.

"It's very possible I love you already," Henry says, and somewhere, maybe somewhere like the South Pacific, a cold, unstable wind gathers. Isabelle's life, honestly, has been a collection of generic troubles until now. A distant, cheating partner, an unfocused identity, an overbearing mother turned into an overbearing ghost. But all of that can change when a wind circles around a center, when spirals of rain join the party, when gusts pick up, and the newly formed beast travels over the water to the most convenient shore.

CHAPTER 10

Weary's fridge is nearly empty, save for a few eggs, a carton of milk, and half a dish of that blasted Kanak casserole, *bougna*. He eats a few cold, miserable bites straight from the container, slaps the door shut. Checking Henry North's Visa while hungry is a bad idea. He's tired of seeing all that food. All those pricey charges at grocery stores that certainly must mean fancy wine and meats and cheeses. He misses cheese, the good kind of cheese. Since he came here, he misses large stores with shining delicacies. Here, it's mostly fish, rice, coconut, banana, taro, yams. Root vegetables and meat cooked in banana leaves. Sure, Weary indulges in the occasional French meal at Le Saint Hubert or Café de la Paix — it's not like they live entirely in the boondocks. Still, fruit . . . even fruit! There isn't the delightful tropical abundance you'd imagine. Most everything is imported, except a handful of things — mangos, coconut, pawpaw. Those fucking Visa charges can make him get that familiar, unhelpful longing for the States. It's a great life here, a beautiful life, but a person can't have everything, and not having everything means always missing something.

Perhaps he's just in a bad mood. It hasn't helped that his assistants, Aimée and Yann, French and Melanesian, have begun an affair, fueled by once-warring cultures and long hours doing counts together. Today, Weary spotted them kissing passionately, Aimée's skirt hiked up against the far outdoor wall of the research facility, Yann's hips grinding to hers. It made him think of Sarah, and stolen moments, and the fire at her center. Jesus, he misses passion and grinding and fire. It made him ache and then feel sad and then furious at every large and small thing, including cheese.

Oh, yes, he is furious, but he also feels the mountain of his task, casting its shadow. God, patience is tiring.

It's been a disappointing week, with the Visa bill consistently netting him only the grocery charges and the blip of activity at another clichéd-sounding seaside restaurant. He expects nothing from ShutR, either. Nothing from life in general. It's the kind of day where you could just give it all up, sweep away every goal and dream and vision with one tantrum-swoop, like a child losing at a board game.

Still, he must go through the motions. Eventually, something will happen, some small piece will arrive, giving him the information he needs about the woman with the bracelet. All of those grocery bills tell him she's still around. He just needs her name. One name! One something!

He settles at the computer, which sits on the desk in his bedroom in front of the shuttered windows. The sounds and smells of night falling come in through the screens. He opens the site. Types *Mr. Aperture* into the search box. If there's only another fucking picture of a fucking beach, he'll lose his fucking mind. Yes, that's a lot of *fuck*s, an overkill of them, but that's the kind of mood he's in. Plug your ears if it bothers you, because this is not the time for him to be his best self.

ShutR needs a serious redesign. Maybe he should write a letter of complaint. The oldest photos are posted first, so you must scroll, scroll, scroll to see what's new. He can't believe this hasn't been addressed before. Then again, who even uses ShutR? Probably just the friends and family of the app's designers, plus one wife killer.

The forest, the desert; sunsets, flowers, the garden, Walter's chair. The beach, beach, beach.

Sailboats.

Sailboats!

Oh, God. Dear God. When he sees the final new image, he's not even gleeful. He's not filled with fresh hope, or with the joy of new leads. His stomach falls like a ruin. Next, his already bubbling fury turns to rage. *That fucker,* he thinks. *A fucking boat!* Henry North can just go have a fucking day on a fucking boat with another woman after Sarah! Excuse his mouth. You would understand if you knew everything he does.

Look at that. Look at Mr. Marvelous now. There's the watery horizon, and the group of racers. There's a lame close-up of a red-and-white spinnaker, and a heeling vessel with the crew sitting in a row along its portside. And then there she is. There's the woman with the bracelet. Her face. Her actual self.

Weary doesn't jump and leap; his heart doesn't even soar. He feels quite sick, actually. He could vomit. His head begins to throb. He closes the shutters of the windows, as if in protection. Because Henry just can't resist, can he? Weary sees the ego in the shot — the way Henry is in love with the idea of his own talent. That light on her hair, that captured glow — Henry can't help himself. He's got to boast that her beauty in this shot is all due to some skill and special gift of his. Nothing can make you madder than when you guess what a person will do and then they do it, because he's with a woman, all right. And whoever she is, she is beautiful all on her own, and the way he claims that is criminal.

Already criminal.

Weary turns on his desk light, and the bulb hums like an insect. He leans forward, squinches; takes her in. So, here she is. His nose practically touches hers on the screen. He's wondered who it will be, and now he knows. She's lovely. She weirdly and wrongly looks happy, even if she also looks slightly perplexed. She looks too happy to *know.*

What comes to Weary's mind, what fills his battered spirit (which only moments before was ready to surrender but which now begins to flicker with new life), is the story of the virgin princess in *The Metamorphoses.* As she walks by the sea, that creep Neptune, the God of the ocean, leers at her. He tries to flatter her and get her attention, and then, rebuffed, he attempts to take her by force. When he tries to rape her, though, the crafty, determined Minerva — always the one with a great idea — turns the princess into a crow. Her arms darken with soft plumage, her shoulders turn to feathers, and she lifts from the ground and sails high into the air, up and away from that asshole.

Round of applause for Minerva. Go, Princess Crow! It's inspiring, come to think of it.

Very inspiring. He gets up, invigorated, once again ready for battle. He makes some coffee. He gets to work. First, he combs those Visa charges again. Had he missed something? A boat charter? An unusual expense to a new company?

No. Of course he hasn't missed anything! You don't check a Visa bill fifty times a day and overlook a *boat charter.*

All right. So, Henry paid cash. Or *she* chartered the boat. Or she *owns* the boat. He must find out who the boat belongs to.

He just needs the woman's *name.* Now that he's seen her picture, it feels like she's only inches away.

He studies the images on ShutR. Those sailboats. It's a race, which means race photos, and race photos mean there's the slight possibility that Henry's boat is in one of them, too, floating in the background. *Regatta, Parrish,* he tip-taps. Three regattas in the San Juans in one weekend? Good God. Which regatta? Enlarge, enlarge. All right. Very good. A part of a name on one of the boats. *Val* on one side of the sailors' legs, *rie* peering from between two others.

He works into the night. Who can sleep now? He checks the lists of registered boats for all three races. *Valkyrie.* Class B, Spring Series Regatta in the San Juans the previous weekend.

Next. Search for *Spring Series Regatta.* He hunts for the photos taken by the race boat photographers, and any other participants. There are hundreds. Hundreds! He rubs his forehead. He urges himself on. He tells himself to remember Minerva and the Crow Princess. He pours more coffee. After a few hours, he switches to wine, because his head is spinning from caffeine and his hands have started to tremble.

In each photo he finds, Weary clicks and enlarges and searches the horizon. He's looking for a boat out there, one with a woman in an orange T-shirt on board, and a man . . . Well, Weary knows what he looks like. Can you spot smugness in the pinpoint dots of a photo? Can you spot ego, blown large and tight to the point where a burst is easy and inevitable?

Hours pass. His neck aches, and the damn cramps start up in his legs. He stretches. He walks a loop around the room. Rolls his shoulders. At this hour, it's him and the *papillons de nuit,* the hundreds of species of moths that come out only at night. He can hear the click of their wings against the screens.

The bottle of wine is almost gone. He's exhausted. He should have gone to bed long ago. His eyes are bleary, but not too bleary to see that *Radical Rapture* (who came in third overall, by the way) posted photos of the race, important photos, critical photos, because there it is, the flash of orange on a boat just off of *Radical Rapture*'s starboard side. It's a beautiful shot. Well, the shot itself is just okay, but it's a perfect capture of a wooden vessel with two particular passengers aboard. Weary can't see faces. They are both hunched over something, maybe a cooler. But he sees something more valuable.

The boat's name.

The *Red Pearl.* It sounds like the name of a Chinese restaurant, if you ask him, the old kind of Chinese restaurant with red leather booths and murky aquariums and menus with pictures that resemble crime-scene photos. The boat looks like a piece of shit. If Henry chartered that thing, what was he thinking? Clearly, his standards have plummeted, or maybe he's just being careful not to blow through the house money and his cashed-in pension. Either way, Henry North would praise his dilapidated choice. He'd declare it vintage or an antique — a classic. He'd call it *The Grampus* or something. *Jane Guy,* something from *The Narrative of Arthur Gordon Pym of Nantucket.* He'd hit it with a little Poe legitimacy, lame but handy. Then, he'd privately sigh with relief the minute he was able to ditch it. People like Henry, that's what they do with everything and everyone in their life.

The Red Pearl, he types. *Charter. Parrish Island.*

It's so easy. All you need is one right piece, and bam. *Sail the beautiful waters of the San Juans on the beautiful Red Pearl!* Clearly, the boat's owners are weak in the adjective department, but why quibble? *Jan Stephenson and Dave Lovell,* plus a phone number, thank you very much.

Weary is so close to her now.

He checks his watch. It's eight in the evening there, too late for a charter office to be open. Then again, the *Red Pearl* doesn't exactly look like it is part of a business with a receptionist and a 401(k) plan. What's there to lose?

Weary dials. The phone *brrrr, brrrr*s across the miles. No answer.

He hangs up. Tries one more time. Why not?

More ringing. Weary is about to call it a night when, much to his surprise, there's a voice on the other end.

"I told you not to fucking call anymore."

"Jan? Dave? I'm looking to rent one of your boats . . ." Weary asks.

"Oh, hey, man, I'm sorry. Yeah, it's Jan. I thought you were my girlfriend."

"I'm afraid not."

"She just threw my goddamn keys off the dock!"

"That's awful. What a shame! I'm sorry."

"Blond, twenty-five, and crazy, what're you gonna do."

Weary hates this man. He's a bargain-version asshole from the asshole catalog, Weary guesses, lacking a Ph.D. and Italian leather shoes. *Honestly,* he wants to tell the twenty-five-year-old, *If you're going to spend time with assholes, at least they should take you out to nice dinners and pretend to have manners.* "I was calling about your boat. The *Red Pearl*?"

"Yeah, sure. I got that, but the *Sunsurfer* has a little more speed, if you want to ski."

The guy sounds drunk. His *S*'s spin out and crash like a bad day at the racetrack.

"No, a buddy of mine just took out the *Red Pearl* and loved it. Henry North?"

"Oh, yeah."

"He went with . . . Damn. I can't drink like I used to," Weary says.

"Tell me about it."

"Totally forgot her name."

"Isabelle? I never seen him before, but she's a local."

"Isabelle, that's right."

"When do you want it? Are you from around here? You sound, like, a million miles away . . ."

Weary hangs up. Really, why waste another second? That guy won't even remember the call in the morning. Weary has what he needs anyway. There won't be too many Isabelles on an island that size.

He shuts down his computer. He feels like he's just survived a typhoon. Like the windows shimmied hard and the roof threatened to blow off, but he's okay. He's better than okay, because, while there may be a mess out there, he's less frightened now, and he's alive.

Isabelle.

He undresses, gets into bed. After *Virginia* and *Sarah,* the name *Isabelle* is as gentle as a flower petal. This is a worry. He hopes she's stronger than she sounds. Tomorrow, he'll find out everything about her that he can, starting with her last name.

He is so exhausted, he expects to conk out the second his head hits the pillow. But this does not happen. Stupid coffee, plus wine — uppers and downers, how do the rock stars do it? Fears lurk in, performance anxiety, the weight of the world. He should have eaten a proper dinner.

All blueprints need flexibility, and no strategy can predict every potential problem, especially from this distance. He is working in the dark. How to go forward, yet exercise due diligence? As he lies in his bed, he tries to think like a careful physician. What is the best way to cure the cancer without killing the patient?

Watchful waiting — isn't that what it's called? It's too early for step one, his first contact; he knows that. But he will observe every move as best he can for now and act accordingly. Any huge change or terrible danger on the horizon, any tumor encroaching on a vital organ, well, like it or not, ready or not, he'll have no choice but to tip the whole thing over, alert the authorities, if they haven't been alerted already. Weary doubts that's even happened. He has to do everyone's job. That's why he's here to begin with. He's rock star, physician, researcher, destroyer. Lover, fighter, seeker of justice, too high from coffee and suddenly starving.

CHAPTER 11

They've been seeing so much of each other that they've established a routine. After work, after taking phone reservations, and tying down planes, and greeting new arrivals, and after her daily meeting with Jane, who keeps Isabelle in the loop out of sheer politeness while Isabelle keeps herself in the loop out of sheer duty, Isabelle heads straight over to Henry's house. When she arrives, he is cooking something fabulous. They eat and drink and talk as the sky turns shades of sherbet, as the sun drops below the horizon and the lighthouse begins its slow, endless arc across the sea of black.

There are late-night confessions about hard childhoods, personal failures, life's disappointments; there are morning chats about the big dreams that still shine away in spite of it all. Occasionally, they might read or watch television — entwined or cozily side by side — interrupting their reading or their television watching to have sex. She stays the whole weekend, and now that it's early summer and Parrish is perfect, they do something outdoorsy in the day. Henry likes to hike. Isabelle needs the exercise. He appreciates the chance to see things from a high, craggy distance, and she wants the butt firming, so they hike a lot.

Maggie's last birthday gift, the silk robe embroidered with the crane, is now at Henry's, and so are some of Isabelle's clothes, which spill from an old suitcase. An extra toothbrush stands alongside his in a cup by the bathroom sink, like a pair of dental soldiers. She's barely at her mother's house anymore. At Maggie's, there's a bottle of catsup in the fridge and pancake syrup left over from her mother's own never-to-be-made breakfasts. There are a few eggs and real butter and English muffins from the one time Henry stayed the night. There's a container of peanut butter, and a tin of tuna, and two or three Marie Callender's in the freezer for those rare nights she and Henry have some squabble or need a little space from each other.

Her mother's house is feeling ghostly. Without Isabelle or her mother living in it, it's all dust and echoes. It's past tense. No new memories are being made, and, weirdly, there, her mother seems to be getting farther and farther away. In her head, it's another matter. You should hear Maggie, going on and on. She's pissed that Isabelle is disappearing into another relationship. She doesn't believe men can be trusted. Isabelle never uses her good sense. Does she even have good sense? And what's with that haircut? It's unflattering. It makes her face look round. She looks like she's gained weight.

Actually, Maggie's just pissed because Isabelle has abandoned her. That's what Isabelle thinks.

The lounge chairs on the back lawn have really disappeared now, to the point that getting a mower through there will be a chore. The house is starting to have a shut-in smell when Isabelle returns to locate a certain belt or pair of shoes. *Why are you the one to live out of a suitcase and not Henry?* Maggie asks. God, she's a bitch! Sure, the arrangement is more convenient for Henry, but Isabelle doesn't really mind. It's sort of a pretend life at Henry's. There, her worries are suspended, like a sick body frozen until the time a cure is found. At Henry's, they're a couple, and she's cared for, and the view is better, anyway. *Cared for* is a crooked finger, summoning you to tempting, delicious inertia.

She's learned so much about him: the crisp way he turns pages, his generous laugh, his strong opinions on electronic books, the secret ways to make him come. He adds spices with a flourish, as if he's making up the recipe as he goes. He handles tickling with strong wrestling moves. He spends his day at the library, working on his poems or reading, or hiking dunes with his camera. He gets sunburned when he's not careful.

Yet there's much that is still unknown. Why does he feel like a mystery? How can he be so available and so held back at the same time? She's sure this is mostly her own, skewed perception. She's not used to mature men, who exercise boundaries and discretion. Evan would burp as loudly as he could. He revealed every tidbit from every former girlfriend, from their small breasts to their lesbian interludes. No secret was safe with him. Henry likes his own corners. He doesn't even show her his poems. She caught a glimpse of a few of them on his desk once, and even his writing was unre-vealing — it was full of Poe flourishes, bells tolling, cities by the sea, but no baring of the soul, no spilling of painful romantic his-tory. To Henry, the past is the past. He'd like it kept there. Let sleeping dogs lie, and all that.

The dogs, though — they don't seem to be sleeping. That's the problem. The absence of the past makes the past loom. Or maybe Isabelle is just reading too much into everything. Silence can do that. You fill it. Your imagination does. She catches him gazing out at the sound, his face troubled, and she thinks, *Sarah.* On beach walks, he climbs the cliffs away from her, stands atop some ledge as if considering a plunge, and she thinks, *Sarah.* He switches off the television at any mention of Boston or the nearby cities he lived in, as if it's too painful to hear.

There is still nothing of him here — no favorite books or photo albums, no shirts from college he can't get rid of or sentimental cards from his family. He takes calls from his brothers in private, walking down the street in front of Remy's house with his phone pressed to his ear. He's slammed the lid of his laptop shut when she's unexpectedly entered a room, as if he's been caught attempting to stalk his ex. At least, this is what Isabelle guesses he was doing. She understands, because she only recently cut Evan free from her cyberlife after finally tiring of that game.

But what about his restless sleep? Isabelle notices him lying awake, staring at the moon-cast shadows on the ceiling, or else twisting, turning, giving the quilt an occasional punch as if he's been buried alive. She once woke and saw him standing by the bed, his dark outline as startling as an intruder's. Another time, realizing the bed was vacant, she got up and there he was, curled into a fetal ball in the corner of the couch.

I have bad dreams, he said.

Come to bed, she said.

I don't ever want to hurt you.

God, it was awful. But the mattress at Remy's house is hard, and the room gets stuffy, and occasionally the foghorn moans and moans like a slowly dying man, none of which contributes to a peaceful night's rest.

And here's another worry, something stupid, because she has zero evidence, really, but she suspects that Henry never liked his mother. He's dismissive when he speaks of Ellie North, as if she were the housekeeper, a person he never really saw. Isabelle can't get a feel for who Ellie was; there are no funny stories or favorite foods or forgivable quirks. Instead, Henry's mother is lumped into generic piles — simpleminded, naïve, uneducated.

You've always overlooked the obvious, Isabelle, Maggie scolds. *Disdainful-asshole comments about the deceased Mrs. North are not to be ignored! Men and mothers, girl. Come on! Haven't you been reading your* Cosmo Psych 101? *Your* Huff Post *Ten Things That Tell You Everything? Pretty basic stuff, sweetheart.*

Clearly, Isabelle has no right to talk about people and their mothers.

And regardless of these small, nagging concerns, these unsettled rumblings, Isabelle is crazy for Henry. It's his *command*. She has completely forgotten that what most draws you will be your biggest problem later. She likes his strong shoulders and decided jawline, and the way he holds himself in the world. He is sure of his opinions, confident in nearly every situation. He was important at the university where he worked, too, she can tell, and while it's perhaps a shallow thing to like, it underscores his calm authority. Clearly, his students adored him and his colleagues respected him. She'd love to read one of his many articles on Poe or American Romanticism, but until he gives her a copy as promised, she won't. She'd have to find them online, and he looks down on all the searching and investigating and delving that goes on anymore. He has made this clear. He wants an old-fashioned love affair based on trust, and after the Maggie-Evan background-check disaster, Isabelle agrees. There's a purity to it. And after all the recent snooping and prying in the life of pre- and post-divorce Evan, a *relief*.

It's *all* a relief. His command, his confidence, his surety — the relationship itself, which seems to be a decision of some kind, made. It's a relief, and it feels like safety to Isabelle, too. Safety is such a beautiful lure. It's the only thing she craves. She's a desert traveler, so thirsty that there are mirages all around.

Safety — is it even possible? Does she dare believe? It seems possible. There are signs that it is. She feels more at peace already. Her anger at Evan feels distant, and already the story editors are on board, erasing, tweaking, making meaning. Evan, their marriage, that pain — it was all supposed to be, all leg-bone's-connected-to-the-thigh-bone, all if-that-hadn't-happened-this-wouldn't-have-happened. She could even feel generous toward Evan, the poor, lost soul. And the more ancient fury at her mother, the acid flowing in the deep, unexplored aqueducts, well, that's mostly gone, too. She feels softer lately, sexier, jazzed up with hope and not pointless resentment. She's looking up, not down. She thinks *mountain,* not *iceberg.* She thinks of all the hope rising above yet to be discovered, not all of the bad stuff hidden below where she can't see it.

They are lying in bed, legs curved with legs, when he says it.

"You're spending more time here than you are there."

She's not sure how to take this. She can't read his face the way they are positioned. She pops her head up, chin on his chest. He looks like a monster from that angle.

"Should I get my purse?"

"No! I mean, aren't you tired of having to go back and forth? Just to water some plant or find a certain shirt?"

"That ficus is a lost cause."

"Move in with me," he says.

The house sells before a sign even goes up. Maggie's old friend, Jenny Sedgewick, had already expressed an interest in buying it, so it's as easy as making a phone call. Isabelle squinches her eyes shut, makes the decision, and before she knows it, it's done.

You what? Jane says, when Isabelle tells her. Eddie Groove says, *Jesus, Isabelle, what'd you do that for?* In line at the Front Street Market, Remy grasps Isabelle's arm.

Sweetie! I heard about you selling your mother's house. That was stupid.

They're acting like she lit all her money on fire or married a convict. It's silly. And she can tell that Jane and Eddie don't like Henry anyway, though she can't understand why. When he comes to pick her up, they meet his effusive charm with frostiness and distrust. She attributes this to protectiveness, and to the territorial outsider/insider tribal impasse common on the island. They love her and care about her; she gets it. But she won't participate in these worn ways of thinking, and she's not a child anymore. She does not want to be burdened with the past, living in her mother's house while running her mother's business.

This is big, Iz. I mean, selling the house? *What about having* options? Jane says. *How well do you even know this guy?* Eddie says. *You could have rented it. I make a bundle on rentals,* Remy says. *But you can't unring a bell.*

For God's sake! You'd think this was a fatal choice, by the way they cluck like alarmed chickens. But Isabelle is glad to be rid of a house full of such mixed emotions. It's a bold but necessary decision.

It helps to have all the chaos of moving, the boxes going to the new place, the junk ready to be picked up by Old Shit Hauling, the last-minute runs to Red Apple for more packing tape. All of the motion quiets (but does not silence) the self-doubt that descended as soon as she signed the final papers, and the guilt, guilt, guilt, the curling shame, of boxing up the last of her mother's things, vacuuming out the old rooms, and cleaning the crumbs from the back of the cupboards before Jenny Sedgewick's son, Thomas, moves in.

Isabelle tries to calm herself with logic. What, she's supposed to hunker down in the dark corners of history? She and Henry are in love, and love is a risk. She can't keep holding on to this stuff forever. It's like ripping off a Band-Aid, and she should be grateful the opportunity arose to be free of it. Besides, Thomas has a college-aged daughter who will come to visit and stay in Isabelle's old room. The house will have new life. Thomas has already come over to mow the lawn and ditch the rusty lawn chairs. He's brought a few tomato plants, which he's set on the back deck. They have promising little starbursts of yellow flowers. She is leaving the place in excellent hands.

How could you? Maggie says again and again. *How could you, how could you? Bad daughter, bad daughter, bad daughter.*

Most of Isabelle's stuff — her and Evan's old furniture, boxes of college papers and photos, once-hopeful holiday decorations, books and more books, outdated-but-once-expensive electronics she can't bear to dump — is now in a storage garage at Island Air. Also there: cartons of her mother's clothes and kitchen items Isabelle remembers from her childhood — serving platters and a cookie jar and silverware, a mixer that her mother likely hadn't used since Isabelle was small. There's an entire box of records and a pair of nightstands and an elaborate floor lamp that belonged to someone's grandmother. (Her own? Her dad's? Her mom's? No idea.)

And more. There is much more now crammed into that storage space, which Isabelle tells herself is sort of like Maggie's own home, once removed. At first Isabelle vowed to keep only things that she actually remembered or could look at with love and fondness, but this proved impossible. Every item had complications. Each pair of shoes or salad tongs vibrated with bad feelings, or some memory, or just the mere fact that Maggie herself had kept it so long. How do people do it? Isabelle envies anyone who can separate a certain blue coat from the person who wore it. She understands the basics here — when a loved one is gone, these objects are all that's left, and tossing the object is like throwing away the person. Yes, she also understands that she needs to get to that Hallmark-card place that says a person is always there in your memory, but there is no Hallmark card that talks about the way a brush entwined with a mother's hair can haunt you.

She doesn't pack away everything, of course. Some things are going with her to Henry's. They've rented a U-Haul at Eugene's Gas and Garage. Now, in the back, there's a rocker that's been on Maggie's covered porch forever, one Isabelle always loved, and there's a painting a friend made for Maggie, depicting the exact view of the sound from her property. There are a few boxes of Isabelle's clothes and personal effects. Henry and Isabelle have also decided to take the better mattress from her mother's house to replace the hard one the musician left. There's a box of quilts and blankets, too, ones that Isabelle remembers from childhood illnesses and cold winters, and, finally, there's Maggie's desk. Isabelle can remember both her mother and her own younger self working there — laboring with crunched and serious penmanship over school reports on earthquakes and Chile and the three branches of government.

The door of the U-Haul rolls down with a slam. Isabelle hides her last keys under her mother's faded welcome mat. She tries not to look in the windows, at the empty and accusing rooms. Her stomach hurts. She might cry. She climbs up into the cavernous cab of the truck and sits next to Henry. She lies to herself, saying she can come back whenever she wants to.

Henry drives. His face looks tired. Isabelle guesses this is from all the endings and beginnings his life has brought, or maybe that's the source of her own fatigue. Probably, no one is in the best mood, after the heavy boxes, and the drawers sliding out of the desk as they inched it up the truck ramp, and after the days of packing and cleaning.

If a couple can get through moving without some tension, they are either medicated or fictional, so Isabelle isn't too bothered by the joint snappishness that occurs when, back at Remy's, they navigate the wobbly mattress out of the truck and across the front lawn. She's glad when everything is out of the U-Haul, though. It means the whole ordeal is almost over. They've unloaded quickly so that Henry can return the rental before Eugene's closes, so except for the mattress now inside, the rest of the stuff is in the driveway. Maggie's desk sits there as if waiting for the job applicant to arrive, and boxes are strewn around, and that painting with the view of Isabelle's old life leans against a tree trunk, looking somewhat baffled.

Henry kisses her cheek. "I'll be right back, and then we'll carry that desk and open a bottle of wine."

"I'm cooking tonight, after all this help."

"Well, I had my own motivations for that help. It'll be great to remember what all of this is for. And we'll just order in, are you kidding?"

He grabs her ass. She grabs his. They're a little giddy with exhaustion. After the headaches and tensions of moving, they can now remember that they like each other. She tugs the tail of his shirt in a goodbye.

He opens the truck door. He's just about to step up into the cab when the police car cruises down Possession Loop toward Remy's house. The light on top of the car spins, but the siren is off. Henry stops cold. He watches the vehicle as if it's a thug about to jump him.

"What'd you do, rob a bank?" Isabelle jokes, but Henry is frozen in place. It's weird. It's like that tag game they used to play when they were kids. His hand is still on the truck door handle. The car slows in front of Remy's house and then comes to a stop.

It's Tiny Policeman, of course. Officer Ricky Beaker. The whole department is made up of Tiny, a couple of deputies, office staff, and the occasional committed Parrish High intern who's watched too many crime dramas on TV. Parrish doesn't need anything more. There hasn't been a significant crime here for years, not since Vince MacKenzie offed what's-her-name's husband and stuffed him in the trunk of his Triumph. It was some sordid love triangle, and Tiny P. was in his glory back then. Lately, though, all Tiny has to strut about are loud parties or some shoplifting tourist or trying without luck to catch Kale Kramer doing something actually illegal. Tiny's body is small, but his dreams are big. Henry parked the truck in a loading zone, she guesses.

She guesses wrong.

Ricky Beaker steps from his car. He hitches up his little pants. He has his hand on his gun. Wow, imagine if Henry had parked in a handicapped spot. There might be an actual shoot-out.

"Can I help you with something?" Henry says.

"I thought I'd come by and say hello, Mr. North. Since we hadn't yet met. Check in, so to speak. You moving again?"

Isabelle steps toward them. She — local, longtime islander, knower of the ropes — will sort this out.

But then she stops. She stops because an odd shimmer is starting. Officer Beaker knows Henry's name, knows he's recently moved once before, and the tone of his voice is strange. Stranger than a wrongly parked truck deserves. Something is happening. She has no idea what is going on, but something is happening, and it's bad. Henry and Officer Beaker have locked eyes, and this, this whatever that's playing out in front of her, has nothing to do with her at all; she doesn't even exist in this scene. An understanding — no, not an understanding, more like a small, eerie dawning — creeps in, and she shuts her mouth fast, not just because she's forgotten what she was going to say, but because some horrible feeling is arriving in her stomach.

"I'm not moving. A friend is moving in."

Ricky Beaker raises an eyebrow. He's so intent on Henry, he doesn't even glance Isabelle's way. The little man actually looks tough. The days of donut eating and shooing away teenagers lingering on street corners have been stacking up, boredom upon boredom, waiting for a moment like this. "Well, we got a call."

"A call." Henry looks disgusted.

"A tip. An anonymous tip."

"Oh, really."

"Then we had a chat with our friends in Boston."

"This is harassment," Henry says.

"No harassment. Call it a friendly stop to say hello. To say, you know, we *see* you."

"If there are any more stops by to say hello, you'll be hearing from my attorney."

The last few months of her life and their result, this imagined and longed-for future, are maybe over. A part of Isabelle realizes this. It's the part that is squeezing her so that she can't breathe. Henry doesn't look right. Not at all. His jaw is clenched and his face has turned red. She didn't even know he could look like this, this furious. Curves of sweat are starting under his arms.

"Henry?" Isabelle says. Or, at least, she may have said that. Some sound escapes her throat, anyway. She's having one of those experiences where she feels out of her own body. She's watching this woman on the lawn, the poor thing — her mouth is hanging open in what is clearly shock and disbelief. Isabelle has felt this watery distance before. When she was nine, as her mother dragged her by her ponytail down the hall of their house, she looked at the girl with her shorts sliding low and the shirt scrunched high from the motion, and thought about the rug burn the girl was sure to get. And she felt this same odd separation the time she drove away from their apartment after she saw the emails Evan sent that woman. Then, her disembodied hands on the wheel and the surreal swirl in her head caused her to miss a merging car, and she ended up in a small crash against a guardrail.

"Isabelle Austen? Is that you? I haven't seen you around since your mom's funeral. What are you doing here?"

Tiny Policeman is talking to that woman on the lawn, but she only stares at him. She can't seem to talk.

"You're not *the friend,* are you?"

"I'm . . ." the woman on the lawn says.

"Jesus Christ! Your mother would be furious! You better make sure you're not number three."

"I swear to God . . ." Henry says. He clenches his teeth hard. His hands are fists at his sides.

149

"Number three?" Isabelle is momentarily convinced she's dreaming. You can have dreams like this. They upset you into the next day because they seem so real.

"She doesn't know?" Officer Beaker actually chuckles. "Well, aren't you two going to have an interesting evening."

"This is against the law," Henry snarls.

"Against *the law*?" Officer Beaker makes an incredulous face, a dramatic and theatrical face, one pronounced enough to be seen by the audience in the back row. He shakes his head. He walks back to his car, inconsequential chatter blaring from the radio on his hip. He gets into the cruiser, settles into the seat. He sits right there for a while, writing something down. He makes it clear he's not going anywhere until he chooses to. He taps his pen against the pad, as if he's composing a poem and is stuck on a line.

"Henry?" Isabelle says.

Isabelle's old life is all around her in pieces. Her new life is through the door of that house. But dread has cemented her feet, and horror settles so heavy in her stomach, she thinks she's about to be sick. And it feels quite clear, quite clear indeed, that the wobbly mattress they just muscled inside will not do a damn thing to fix what keeps Henry up at night.

CHAPTER 12

As he sits at his desk at the New Caledonia Corvus Research Facility and Sanctuary on Mount Khogi, Weary is trying to keep it together.

Ever since he made that call to the Parrish Island Police Department and spoke to the detective with the little clown voice, there has been nothing online. No Visa charges, nothing on ShutR, nothing nowhere in all the places he looks, except big fat echoes of zero, which his imagination is happy to fill with endless and varied disasters.

It's all been one looming, terrifying, cavernous zilch.

He can't work. He can't concentrate. He can barely eat; he's become a danger on the road, and he keeps walking into rooms and forgetting why he's there. He found his car keys in the refrigerator, and left the coffeepot on to burn. *Think!* he begs. *Focus!* he cajoles. *Get it together! Use your God-given strengths!* Not happening. It's impossible.

The silence is making him *nuts.*

After those glory days, too! Information, pouring down like the rain in the Mount Khogi jungle. It had been so easy to find her. *Isabelle* plus *Parrish Island,* and, bam, there she was. *Island Air* appeared first, and then it all made sense. That's how Henry must have met her. That first day. The story always makes sense. Weary opened the Island Air website, and her photo was right there on the About Us page. *Isabelle Austen,* the same glowing young woman on the boat.

Isabelle Austen. A treasure trove! Old swim meet results from the local high school. Yearbook photo. A LinkedIn résumé including her experience working at a small publisher in Seattle. Wouldn't Henry love that? Egomaniac would assume she'd have an in to get those maudlin, knockoff Poe poems published.

And more, so much more! Isabelle Austen receives a scholarship from the Rotary Club! She graduates from the University of Washington with a degree in English! She lives in an apartment for a long while in the U-district (small, drab). She marries! She divorces! (That was quick.) The ex's name is Evan Donaldson, works for GenCrest Pharmaceuticals, looks like a glory-days-are-over jock turned sales guy. His Facebook page shows him raising lots of beer mugs with the boys like he's still nineteen. Jerk. She deserves better.

For days, Weary is satiated. He gazes at the photo in *Seattle Magazine: Roger Thurston, founder of Evergreen Publishing, and Isabelle Austen, editor, celebrate the release of Mark Elliott's* Trout Summers. He surveys Isabelle's last address in the Seattle neighborhood of Queen Anne, where she lived with Evan Donaldson. It's a building with a brick façade; a similar apartment currently for sale shows bright windows and a small kitchen and an inner courtyard with garden space. Next door: a park, and on the other side, a Mexican restaurant called El Toreador. Weary reads the menu. He walks along the street via Google Maps, turns down unfocused corners by clicking wide arrows. He checks out her old workplace, Evergreen Publishing. (Nice views. Right in front of a bus stop, though.) He reads Isabelle's well-written five-star Amazon review for *The Princess Bride.*

And then he speeds forward in time, moves with Isabelle to Parrish Island. Change of address: 52 Possession Loop. The house is small and charming, with graying shingles. It overlooks the sound. It's hard to see any more than that, as it's protected on all sides by large trees. But look there — 52 Possession Loop, owned by the now dead mother, Margaret Austen.

He puts together the picture, comprehends the personal storyline of poor Isabelle. A brief marriage to that dweeb, a divorce, returning home after the mother dies to run the business that — according to the Our History page — had been handed down from grandmother to mother to daughter. Weary spends time on Margaret, too. He scours the Web for information about the tiny airline, peruses the photos of the pilots on the site, reads about the planes, scrutinizes the annual profits, smaller than you'd think. There is Maggie's hundred-dollar contribution to the Democratic Party, and her bitchy quote about Fourth of July fireworks in the *San Juan Islander.* On the more personal end, he discovers that Margaret was divorced from Edward Young Austen, who passed away (*the family requests no flowers*) shortly after. There's little to be found about Isabelle's father, except a brief line in the *Puget Sound Business Journal* about a new job at Chambers Insurance, St. Petersburg branch.

Daily, Weary types in the address: *52 Possession Loop.* He map-strolls down the road, curvy and looming with evergreens, one that must be hell at night. He investigates all the houses along it, "drives" the roads that lead to town. He "walks" the streets of the island, explores the stores and the waterfront, treads the wide swaths of pastures speckled with private homes and B&B's.

Henry North is there somewhere.

It's the same thing every day until suddenly it isn't. It happens. He types *52 Possession Loop* and something unexpected occurs. A blip. A change.

A Record of Sale! Holy hell! She sold the place! Meaning: She's moving. Meaning — he knows it, he feels it in his bones — she's *moving in* with Henry.

It pops right up like a friendly toasted waffle, Isabelle's change of address: 58 Possession Loop.

Henry, Henry, Henry. Right down the street the whole time.

He panicked, he admits. Well, shit! It was the big shift he feared, and so soon, too. He remembers quite clearly what happened to Sarah after she moved in with Henry and then married him — how that commitment started the downward slide of Henry's insecurity and paranoia and general bad behavior, which Sarah tried to manage but could never manage. Weary saw the house sale and was flooded with alarm. He could think only of the terror of Sarah's last days on that boat, and Virginia's last moments, standing on that cliff. He had to do something. Someone had to know what was going on over there, if they didn't already. The phone was in his hand before he realized it, the number dialed. He paced the room, heart thundering, jungle heat adding to nerves and sweat as he spoke to the clown-voiced officer before abruptly hanging up. Then he ran to the toilet, retched up his horror and regret.

And now, silence.

The last Visa charge was a U-Haul rental from Eugene's Gas and Garage, on Front Street.

Maybe Isabelle's ditched him, and the silence is only the lovely sound of Henry's ruined heart.

Maybe they've barricaded themselves inside his house, together, against a common enemy, the police . . . They're in a standoff, so to speak, using up rations of fancy cheese and fine wines, expensive, bland crackers.

Maybe Henry is in a deep depression. Maybe the stress has taken its toll, and he's in bed with the covers over his head. He hasn't showered for days. He's contemplating suicide. (One can wish.)

Maybe he's sick. A terrible flu. Summer pneumonia. Something vicious that could kill him (more wishing). Maybe Isabelle — still blissfully ignorant due to police who don't do their jobs — is making him soup and fetching him glasses of ginger ale. Maybe she's caught it, too, and they've been staying in, eating what's left in the cupboards because they're both too wan and frail to shop and cook.

This has to stop. Weary's losing it. He must try to stay busy. Honestly, he doesn't need to *try*. Weary *is* busy. He doesn't just sit around thinking about Henry. Running a research facility is no walk in the park. He is swamped — counting birds, watching birds, catching birds, banding birds. Managing assistants. Attempting to discover the effects of temporal change in design of tools, and quantifying what appears to be the aiming of candlenuts onto rocks to extract kernels. Providing proof for newly found wonders: the way *Corvus* use their beaks for the equivalent of human hand gestures; the way they will name their captors. He also supervises the work of Matias Vargas, a Ph.D. student from the University of Auckland — research topic: Cognition and Neuroanatomy in New Caldonian Crows.

Do you see? He is not just plotting the downfall of Mr. Marvelous. He has a staff, and donors, and students, and lots and lots of winged charges. Right this minute, Lotto is waiting for him in the field. But after a morning of click-tap-nothing, Weary needs something to satisfy him. One small wired reward, one benevolent screen tidbit to quench and temporarily gratify. After his recent technological frustrations, he needs his go-to, his teddy bear in a lightning storm. He's seen the video a hundred times or more. He taps the sideways triangle and it begins to play. There's Gavin Gray's voice. Professor Gavin Gray, dearest friend, deceased mentor. Pancreatic cancer, he didn't have a chance. It's an old video. North was still in Weary's future when it was filmed. This research facility was. Gavin Gray was years away from his own death. But it's comforting to hear Gavin Gray's voice. It fills Weary with sweet nostalgia, gratitude. Weary has Gavin Gray to thank for this position now. Everyone needs someone like Gavin Gray in their life, someone who believes in you, who reaches out a hand, who keeps your secrets, even.

Sarah deserved that, too, damn it.

"We're in the jungle of Mount Khogi," Gavin Gray says. He's offscreen, speaking in hushed tones. "We're observing *Corvus moneduloides.*"

The bird hops about on a tree branch. In the background, there is the twitter and chirp of the Mount Khogi forest. *Corvus* squawks a friendly *awp* before setting to work. First, he locates a forked twig. Next, he removes and discards one side of the fork. The camera zooms in on his black velvet head, his long, determined beak, snipping and snapping, removing leaves, tidying and perfecting. Making a tool. Light filters through the thick forest cover.

"Beautiful," Gavin Gray whispers.

It's the word *beautiful* that gets Weary every time. Also, the fixed, almost tender determination of *Corvus.* The bird does not care about the research assistant's camera. It does not care about Gavin Gray's wonder-filled eyes and pad full of notes. It does not care about inclement weather or a spring day or a stubborn strip of fleshy bark or the amount of hours it all takes. It cares only about its solitary mission. Weary admires this to no end.

"That's all for now," Gavin Gray says from another time. The video ends. Weary's heart fills — with love and appreciation and respect. With sadness. With loss.

There is a soft knock at the door. "Yes?" Weary calls.

Lotto pops his head in. "You're still here, Professor? I was getting worried."

"You came all the way back. Apologies, Lot. I got hung up with these evaluations."

"It's raining like a bastard out there," Lotto says, and it must be, because his hair is splattered to his head, and his boots are dripping.

"Let's go." Weary snags his rain jacket from the coat tree on the way out.

It *is* raining like a bastard, as Lotto says. Their heads are down. They hunch their shoulders as they tromp up the trail.

Maybe Henry North has gotten a job and is now too busy to cook or date. (Ha.)

Maybe he's had a family crisis.

Maybe Henry North himself has been pushed off a cliff. Maybe he is swimming for his life, choking on seawater and his own terror.

Weary knows, he does, that his mind is trying to be kind with these vivid scenarios. They keep him occupied. They shield his vision from the *maybes* he can't bear to imagine: Maybe it's over, and all of this has been for nothing. Or worse. Much worse.

Maybe she's still with him, and the clock is ticking.

CHAPTER 13

Somewhere during this horrible night, it has begun to rain, hard, and Isabelle's wipers are *cha-chunk cha-chunk*ing madly. She can barely see. She wipes the fog off her windshield in a circle with her palm. She knows this island so well, and yet she thinks she might be lost. Well, of course she's lost, psychically, emotionally, and otherwise, as far gone and stunned as a human can get, but she also just can't find the street, either, and she's taking those turns too fast.

Who is this woman, she thinks, who has made another disastrous decision, who has just lost her home and is driving late at night with a painting and a silk robe in the passenger seat? Who is this person who pushes the accelerator down against all good sense? Look, she's even wearing flip-flops in the pouring rain, the fool.

Something to notice: Isabelle is not angry, not blazingly furious, as one might expect.

The new baby anger she'd begun to feel after her mother's death had been tossed like a useless appliance into a trash heap, and so it is not only absent, but rusty and buried. Her anger is just a disorderly huddle. It's pieces and parts, lying under bent bicycle frames and carburetors, waiting for the magical day when they locate one another and weld into some new, magnificent monster.

More than anything, she's confused. So unbelievably confused and shaken and in the strangest spinning fog of disbelief. Disbelief requires you to find belief, but right now there is only this grasping around in the dark and this mad driving, as she searches for Jane Mason's house. Fight or flight? No, she's fight *and* flight. She hasn't been to Jane's house in many years, and in this part of the island, where there are miles of yellow fields turned black, black, black in the night, she could be anywhere. She could be in a foreign country. What is making all of this worse is that she has no home herself. No home in Seattle, no home here, no home on this whirling planet. After what just happened, and with the sea of black out her rain-dripping windows, she feels like an astronaut sucked from the spaceship. There's only the endless, dangerous universe she floats in.

Her mother's desk is still in front of Henry North's house. Now it's raining. She should call Henry and ask him to bring it in, at least. No, Henry would have done that already. He's careful like that, always the one to think about expiring yogurts and pipes freezing. Wait. Is he? Because *who* is he? Everything she knows about him hasn't just disappeared, has it? Is he, in any way, the man she knows?

Wow. This makes Evan look like a prince.

Isabelle shuts Maggie right up. She jams a pillow over Maggie's face to keep her quiet. That voice is the last thing she needs.

The road is skiddy with motor oil after the sudden shower, and a gust of wind whips down the empty road and rattles the car. This is how storms work on the island and in life, coming out of nowhere, downing tree branches and flooding basements. Isabelle grips the wheel. *Help me,* she pleads to whoever might be listening, though it seems no one is listening, and no one has been for a good long while.

The reply? Silence and pouring rain.

But wait. Way far off in that pasture, two squares of light appear in this dark night. They look familiar. It's a long-ago familiarity — she used to ride her bike way, way out here when she was young, after dinner when the sun was setting. She's sure that they're the lights of Asher House. Beyond them, that dot of orange is the porch light of Osprey Inn. These are the two B&B's right near Little Cranberry Farm, the name of Jane's residence, with its small, charming house. It's a farm if you count Jane's two dogs, her patch of blueberry bushes, and all this land.

Isabelle spots the tilting mailbox next to that wide, wild swath of blackberry scrub that separates Jane's property from the one next door. The car crunches up the gravel road, splashes in potholes that have filled up fast. When she gets out of the car, Isabelle clutches the painting to her chest, and the silk robe. There are no stars visible in the sky, only dramatic, fast-moving clouds. Beyond Little Cranberry Farm, Isabelle can hear the whoosh and swirl of the sea shouting *madness, madness.*

The old dogs are finally barking. They're falling down on the job, because they didn't hear the car drive up; after Isabelle rings the doorbell, though, they go crazy with the thrill and anxiety of a late-hours visitor on a night like this. Isabelle is shivering. She is still in her moving clothes: shorts and a

165

T-shirt, those flip-flops. She hears the rustle and scuffle behind the door that means Jane is coming, accompanied by a small canine cyclone.

"Rosie. Button. Enough."

Jane only cracks the door. She's no wilting flower, but she's still cautious.

"Isabelle? What in God's name are you doing here?" Jane's clad in her chenille robe, and Isabelle can hear TV sounds coming from the other room. When Jane opens the door wide, Isabelle sees that Jane holds a baseball bat.

"I didn't know where else to go."

"Jesus, you scared me."

Isabelle is wrapped in a quilt on Jane's worn leather couch. Jane sits across from her in a mission-style rocker. Two empty glasses of Jack Daniel's are on the coffee table in front of them. Rosie lays on one side of Isabelle and Button on the other, Button with his chin on Isabelle's lap. The goldens are like two old ladies in the church basement after the funeral, hovering and providing what comfort they can.

"I have to remember he might be innocent."

"Two dead women, Isabelle? *Two.*"

"*One* dead. One is missing. He says they

166

don't know for sure. She just took a boat that night . . . If he's innocent, Jesus."

"What, she ran off? I doubt that's what the police think. Come on! Dear God. Has anyone gone missing in your life? Has anyone died tragically while you watched? Have *both* of those things happened? No, Isabelle. The answer is no."

"But they couldn't arrest him! There wasn't enough evidence. There wasn't enough *proof . . .*"

Isabelle sounds like she's defending him. Is she defending him? Maybe she's just defending herself and her choices. Her judgment. Her decision to *trust.* Belief is as vulnerable and tender as a flower bud, blooming away in good hearts, stupid, naïve hearts, hearts that should have barbed wire around them. Jane is right.

My God, my God, my God, my God . . .

I swear to you, Isabelle. We were just hiking, and we were standing over a lookout, and she was emotional, gesturing. She said, "I don't even know what I want," and that's when it happened. Her foot — it's like the ground crumbled. She either slid or did it on purpose . . . I don't know which, but Virginia was like that. Sensitive. Always so sensitive! And, Sarah, I give you my word, Isabelle. I woke up and she was gone. The dinghy was gone.

I never heard a splash, never heard the motor, nothing. They found it washed up on the beach, but anything could have happened. She was pissed. She could have taken a tanker out of there, for all I know. I swear to God, I just went to bed and I never saw her again.

You never saw her again? You have no idea what happened? With two women, Henry? Two?

I swear on my life. I swear on anything, everything . . . Do you know what I've been through? Park Service investigation, and then the FBI, *Isabelle! It was a national park! The fucking FBI cleared me! Two other people fell right nearby in the previous two years! They put up warning signs after that. And, Sarah — I have been hounded! I have been hunted! I am an innocent man. You have no idea how badly they wanted to find me guilty. They didn't have anything. Nothing! They questioned me repeatedly, searched my house, followed me . . .*

You lied to me!

Isabelle, try to understand. Please! I just wanted to live *again. I am so sorry. I was going to tell you!*

"Proof," Jane scoffs.

"I don't understand this," Isabelle says. "I don't understand how this can be happening. This isn't anyone's real life. I don't even know where I am right now. This doesn't feel real." She starts to cry again. This is how it works — tears, shock, and questions, talking in circles, tears again.

"I know, sweetie." Jane scoots the dogs off the couch, sits by Isabelle. She rubs Isabelle's back like a mother would.

"I don't get why this is happening to me."

"I know," Jane croons. The painting is propped against Jane's end table. What a day it's had. "I'll tell you, though. Something felt off about that man. I didn't trust him. I didn't trust him for two seconds."

This pisses Isabelle off. It's the kind of thing her mother would say. This superior, after-the-fact knowledge makes her feel like an idiot.

She is such an idiot. Does she need reminding? She lacks this piece other people have, this instinct that senses danger. Say she's stupid, say whatever you want, but danger is a concept she can't seem to grasp.

"He was good to me, Jane. How was I supposed to know? He was successful, competent. He knows how to cook! He likes *dogs*."

Button's ear twitches.

"He lied to you."

"God. Why did he let me find out like this?

After I sold my *house*? I thought we were so close. I thought we loved each other! If he's innocent, why didn't he *tell* me?"

How could I tell you? How? he cried.

You were just going to let me go on, not knowing the biggest fact of your life? Now, the biggest fact of mine?

Of course I knew this day would come!

And this is how you let me find out?

I was going to tell you, I swear —

After the last piece of furniture was in? After I, what, married *you? I don't even know what to think! I don't know who you are. You're a stranger.*

I'm not a stranger. I'm the man you know. The man you love! Why do you think I didn't tell you? If I told you from the start, would you have even given me a chance? Gotten to know me? Without ever knowing me, would I ever have had a prayer that you'd believe *me?*

How can I believe you now when you lied to me like this? The man I love would not have kept this a secret.

We wouldn't have had a chance. Not if I'd told you earlier. You'd have never seen that I'm not that man.

We don't have a chance now.

Don't say that! Please don't persecute me like everyone else! Please don't condemn an innocent person. Try to understand! You do *know me. I'll prove that to you.*

"Guilty people keep secrets," Jane says.

The painting is now propped against the round, stuffed chair in Jane's guest bedroom. The rain pelts onto the roof. Isabelle is wearing a Bonnie Raitt concert T-shirt of Jane's and a pair of sweatpants that must have belonged to Jane's lover, Eva, because they're not Jane's size.

Isabelle has been up all night. After Jane finally went to bed, Isabelle stayed up on Jane's computer, which is set up on a corner desk in her kitchen. Isabelle's laptop is at Henry's house, whoever Henry is. When she types in his name, she sees who he is, or, at least, she sees an entirely different version of the man she knows. It's horrifying. His name is in news headlines, and he's there in photographs, too. He's walking down courthouse steps, and standing behind a lectern, wiping away tears. There is the name of the other woman, his girlfriend — no *fiancée* — from years and years ago, Virginia Arsenault, and her picture. She has a narrow pixie face, fragile cheekbones and poetic eyes, and she appears to be at a picnic; she sits at a wooden table with a checked cloth.

And there is Sarah, slightly more familiar. Isabelle knows only a little about her, because Henry doesn't like to talk about the past. Well, yeah! Of course not! Doesn't that make sense now! She previously had these facts (if they're facts at all, who knows, who can say?): Sarah, the perhaps cheating wife, left him, never to be heard from again. She worked at the university where they met. She had a master's degree in biology from Boston College, a doctorate in ornithology. He was attracted to her vivaciousness, her intelligence, but she was flirtatious and unpredictable. They fought. The relationship was tumultuous. They were married for just a few years. Aside from that, there was only a sprinkling of detail: She had money, she gardened, she liked jazz; the peach tart he still makes was her recipe.

But now here she is. She stands on the deck of a boat. Her hair is blowing; her smile is wide on her broad, confident face. Colleagues talk about her, their words in quotation marks in news articles: She increasingly kept to herself. She seemed withdrawn, secretive. There is a photo of the dinghy, washed ashore.

It is horrible. It is all so, so horrible. And there is more. There are video clips and interviews with relatives, and news updates, but it's all too much, and Isabelle finally flees the kitchen and heads to the guest room. She lies in bed. It's still raining. The wind still howls and whistles. Has this all been one day, really? Is it possible that so much can happen in just twenty-four hours? No. It is now the early hours of the next day, according to the red numbers of Jane's clock, but still.

Isabelle stares at the ceiling, and then at the rain racing down the window. The drops are made silvery by the moonlight. She gets up again, paces the room. She goes back to bed, stares more at the torturing clock. She is exhausted, but it feels possible that she might never sleep again. She'll just stay awake forever in this weird, nightmare world.

The women — Virginia and Sarah, they don't sleep, either. They are so alive in Isabelle's head. Virginia hikes on that trail with a lunch in her backpack. Henry hikes beside her. Isabelle plays the scene many ways — a slip and a fall. A sudden, despondent leap. Henry pushing — well, she just can't see this scenario. She wants to, she should, but she can't. He'd never.

But, then — Sarah. She sees her on the boat. She and Henry, on the deck, arguing. They struggle — no. They argue. Henry goes to bed. Sarah is pissed enough to leave.

She is unpredictable. She is flirtatious. Someone is waiting for her onshore. Or else she's drunk. She takes off. She falls in. She is never seen or heard from again.

Isabelle sits in bed, trembling. She clutches her pillow. No wonder he is drawn to the dark and misunderstood Poe, with all his own dead women, circling around him like spirits.

Isabelle runs to the bathroom and throws up.

She finally sleeps. There are vague sounds before she wakes in this strange place — a toilet flushing, a shower running, dog toenails *click-click*ing against wood floors. A bark, a shush. There's the lingering scent of coffee. She puts her crane robe on over the Bonnie Raitt concert T-shirt. There's a note from Jane on the coffeepot — *Eat something* — and a muffin on a plate covered in Saran Wrap. There are two sets of eager eyes peering up at her, a pair of muffin fans with wagging tails.

The horror of her now-life settles in her stomach. Of course she can't eat. Rosie and Button share the pastry. Her terrible luck has become their good fortune.

Isabelle is still in shock. It is a gray, immovable block. She is paralyzed and sickened. She has no idea what to do, none. Every task she'll now have to complete — it's more than she can take in. She'll have to find somewhere to live. Pack and unpack again. And she'll have to talk to Henry. She'll have to arrange to get her things. The idea terrifies her. She's scared of him, that man in the news articles from last night.

Guilty people keep secrets, Jane said.

Isabelle remembers a few times when she has kept secrets and told lies: in second grade, when she broke her thermos from her Spider-Man lunchbox, hid it under her bed, and fake-cried to her mother that it had been stolen. In junior high, when she bragged to Jeremy Knight that her father wasn't around because he was a roadie for Guns N' Roses. In high school, when she told her mother that she and her best friend Heather were going to Anacortes to go to the outlet malls, when they really went to Planned Parenthood to get birth-control pills. In the fall when she met Evan, when she altered the number of guys she slept with, because of his surprising jealous streak.

You could say she kept these secrets and told these lies because she was guilty. Or you could say she kept these secrets and told these lies because she was afraid, ashamed, and because there was a greater good involved.

Her own Henry, the one she knows — he would be waking up now on the mattress they'd just brought over from her house. He'd be making coffee on a morning that was supposed to be the first of their new life together. He would be crushed. He would be destroyed. He would be torn up and heartbroken.

This is how your good sense leaves you. In small bits of twisted reasoning at an early hour, when so much has been lost that you're wearing someone else's shirt. When so much is at stake that you can almost feel sorry for what terrifies you.

CHAPTER 14

It is dusk. Weary is watching Simone and Yves on the same branch of the same tree in their roost. They're a pair. A couple, if you will. Yves moves his head in, kisses Simone's slightly open beak with his. She stretches her neck, and he twirls feather upon feather of hers, preening. Strengthening their bond.

Weary knows, though, that all is not the Disney Channel in the world of *Corvus.* Yves has snuck off on more than one occasion to have extracurricular fun with Little Black and Corbie. The sneaking shows intent. Exceptionally intelligent animals like *Corvus,* like *Homo sapiens,* will use their exceptional intelligence to get what they need most. They'll scheme and lie for sex, and they'll recruit one of their own to conquer an enemy, and they'll perch over a lame animal, waiting for the kill they know is coming. When the kill doesn't happen soon enough, they'll lead a wolf or another predator to the ready mark, because sometimes you've got to be the one to get the job done.

They see the big picture, the possibilities. They watch. They act, when the time is right.

Weary shifts position, shakes a locked knee. He watches Simone, that sucker. He scritches a few notes in his pad. He wants to write *revenge, revenge, revenge* on every line on every page. Or else, *justice, justice, justice,* which is a less satisfying word, but perhaps a more technically correct one. He wants to rip out the pages and toss them in the air or burn them while shouting, *Got you, fucker!* He wants to pounce and gnash his teeth and tear and destroy and triumph. But he just crouches in the jungle, silent and careful, waiting, even though it kills him.

Darkness is falling, and Simone and Yves settle in for the night. Weary crunches and snaps his way back out of the forest. He tidies up the office, shuts off the lights. He locks the door. The top is down on the Jeep, as it's a warm evening. He's looking forward to the leftover green pawpaw curry from last night's dinner.

As he drives, he breathes to remain calm,

to quiet the thrum of drumbeats in his body. The drumbeats are there and this tumble and rush of feelings are there, because he's been carrying a kernel of information that's a seed beginning to sprout. Wow, such serene and unruffled wording! Kernel, seed, sprout? Explosive device, hand grenade, neutron bomb! He must keep his emotions in check. He must not move too fast.

The seed: a charge on the Visa after all this silence, from Flowers.com.

Yes, it could be many things, perhaps, but Weary knows it isn't. He remembers the huge bouquet that came to the university for Sarah after Henry first told her the tragic story of Virginia. The size of that bouquet! How much that thing must have cost! She loved it, too. After she'd found out about Virginia, she felt sick and stunned and full of doubt. She considered never seeing Henry again. Oh, Weary can practically see her now, trying to work. Staring off, unable, walking away with her lunch at the cafeteria and forgetting to pay. She was a mess.

But then those flowers came. The sweet words. The reassurances. It was Henry being Henry, the man she'd come to love; the man she *knew*. She felt sorry for him! He was practically a widower, and then he'd waited so long to love again. Virginia sounded like a whackjob, to be honest. Sarah wasn't like her, not one bit. Isn't that the way it goes? You're nothing like the one that came before, until you realize you're uncomfortably similar to the one that came before.

After that, there was a swift change to the other side. A fierce loyalty to Henry. She wouldn't hear a bad word against him. She shut out her own questioning voice. Weary gets it, but Jesus! It breaks his heart. There was the hastily planned wedding, the ceremony with only their nearest and dearest, and there weren't many of those. Henry's brothers. The few people from the university who loved her most. An old aunt. A self-involved nephew. She'd gotten too isolated. Before Henry, she'd had a few failed relationships with assholes, even a broken engagement, and that gets to be humiliating, doesn't it? Bad decisions become embarrassing to share, and friends drift off after no communication. The circle around them was small. But she looked beautiful. What's the bride-word? *Radiant.* She believed her whole life would open up after that, Weary remembers.

He also remembers the slightly sick feeling he had that day, though, the faint echoey dread he felt when North slipped the ring on Sarah's finger. It looked like a tiny noose on a little neck.

"Why, why, why?" he mourns loudly to the jungle bumping by him. He pounds the steering wheel of the Jeep with his fist. Why had she been so stupid? Yet why is anyone so stupid? Who can understand the sneaky way the past whispers in our ears and leads us toward catastrophe? Some dark piece crooks its wicked finger and you follow, because the finger looks familiar. Childhood is the far-off radio you're not sure if you hear, Weary knows. Childhood is the strong perfume you stopped smelling. But your trusty subconscious is never not on the job, no. It hears; it smells. You ignore its warnings. You follow its urgings.

Sarah, with her fuming father and trembling mother . . . She didn't have a chance! Of course Henry North looked like Prince Charming, riding in to the rescue. Sarah was a lost child, and there were poisoned apples and haunted trees. After Prince Charming kissed the princess, she awoke to find he had the eyes of the crone with the candy house, and the hands of the father that allowed his daughter to sweep ashes. Weary is not just angry at one man. He is angry at all the people who are somehow larger and make others smaller, who use

181

their power over those more powerless, whose dark psyches twist and ruin the small, bright spirits of others.

The Jeep bumbles and careens down the road, and Weary is whipped and lashed by foliage that he swears has grown overnight. It smells like rotting fruit and night falling out there, and the jungle feels suddenly hazardous. The worst dangers here are in the sea, but he still imagines snakes looping down from trees and scorpions skittering up pant legs and bad men with machetes. He must watch his mood, with the flowers on the Visa and all of these memories and thoughts crashing in. He's getting the creeps. He wishes the top were up on the Jeep.

He grips the gearshift, to remember his own command. He is not small and powerless! He can't change the past, but he can alter the future. The point is . . . He's driving. Downshifting. Making purposeful moves.

"Action, Jackson," he says to himself, cheerleading. He thinks of the real mob guy by that name, enforcer, debt collector. The time for tears and fears is done, Mister. No trembling violets in *this* Jeep!

Weary must focus on what happened after the ceremony. Most critical: remembering what *Virginia's* friends and relatives did after they heard about the wedding. Virginia's sister, Mary; Virginia's friends, Florence and Shelby from Chelsea — they were no Weary. They did not follow North's every move with Weary's studiousness and dedication. They read about Henry and Sarah in *the paper*. The morning paper (they still had those then, how quaint), the *local* morning paper! Without the news splashed smack in front of their noses, they'd have never known he married.

When they found out, though, they descended. They swooped in, black feathers raised and flapping, hooked feet gripping hard. Too hard. There was too much flapping, too much screeching. It looked unhinged. It looked crazy. The way they called and called, trying to tell Sarah things she didn't want to hear, trying to *warn* her . . . They had nothing on North, not really. Suspicions. All that noise and urging just looked like pain, trying to find a purpose. Weary thinks of his own father, with his endless paranoia and his battles with neighbors and electric companies and government offices. The focus on an enemy just made his father's empty, aching life bearable, that's what it seemed.

The crucial fact: Those women were easy

to dismiss because of their approach, and Sarah paid the price. Well, not *easy.* Weary remembers the way Sarah slammed file cabinet drawers and left her purse on the bus and stared down into her yogurt cup as the dire warnings spun around her. She fought with one of her last loyal friends, Hannah, and then stopped taking any calls with a Lexington area code. No one could talk sense into her after that. Sarah was stubborn. My God, she was stubborn, and while it can be a fabulous trait, a trait that brings loyalty and dedication to a goal, it can also be a terrible one. A blind and narcissistic one, leading down a road to snowballing ruin.

Oh, Sarah.

He misses her so much. He loved her, he really did. But he should have loved her more, and he should have looked out for her. That's the kind of love she deserved — solid, clear, steadfast. His love is a lost love. A too-little-too-late love.

He won't make these same mistakes again, any of them. He won't love too little, and he won't panic or act in a way that will make Isabelle shut her eyes and clap her hands over her ears. One should never swoop. One should never screech. One should never flap and fly around in pain and anxiety.

One should move carefully and slowly. One should watch from the tree branch until the time is right. One should lead *Homo sapiens* to their own conclusions, same as *Corvus* leads the wolf to the lame animal. The wolf will save face and then make a powerful choice.

The best predictor of future behavior is past behavior. This all might be folly. It might be very dangerous folly. Weary may be that crow out on a limb, but with her small, delicate hands, Isabelle is no wolf.

Overhead, the sky is immense and dark. Foreboding. But Weary forces himself to notice that it is brilliant, also. There are voracious, venomous centipedes, but the lovely nocturnal kagus, too, with their gray plumage and red legs. He takes in a big lungful of New Caledonia night air, which is not just dank and rotting, but sweet with ripening coconuts and leaves folding into sleep. This has been a healing place, a lush and welcoming one. It's a sheltering haven of palm fronds and clear waters and good people. He misses being near what Sarah loved, what might bring her closer — that coffee shop, Très Largo, where he can still imagine her with her own hands around one of their big cups, and her own home, where he can envision her in her athletic attire, chattering away, sipping a cold drink after a hard run.

She is gone, though. He must relish his life; cherish the bounty. The stars shine like mad. The crickets and the giant coconut grasshoppers thrum and chirp. He is almost home. It's good, so good, to be alive, and he tries to tell himself that this joy is a truer truth than the terror brushing up the soft hairs of his arms.

CHAPTER 15

Before Isabelle heads to Island Air, she dumps the bouquet into Jane's trash can. The roses have gone crunchy and the water has turned into a smelly, murky brew. She slams the lid. The arrangement was so large, the flowers took up much of the dresser in Jane's guest room. Jane herself glared in their direction whenever she passed.

Isabelle couldn't throw them away, though, until now. The roses were small artworks of nature in every color, beautiful, velvety, innocent of wrongdoing. Isabelle felt some duty toward them. Not to Henry, but to them — to the growing and traveling they'd done to get here. Now her duty is done. Farewell, good riddance.

Today, Isabelle will leave work early to look at an apartment above Randall and Stein Booksellers. After a few weeks at Jane's, it's time to find a permanent place to live. Jane has been more than generous, but in spite of her repeated reassurances that Isabelle is welcome to stay as long as she needs, Isabelle is starting to see the strain as she bumps into Jane in the kitchen, and as her late-night television watching awakens Jane, even with the sound turned low. She is disrupting Rosie and Button's usual schedule, too. They don't go to bed until she does, when their job of watching her is finished, and in the morning, they straggle around like hungover partygoers. It seems like Isabelle is exhausting everyone. Probably, she's just very tired of herself.

The place above Randall and Stein Booksellers may be Isabelle's only option. There's not much available, rental-wise, on Parrish. Joe offered his pullout couch, and Eddie said his buddy might be moving, but these are both temporary and uncertain solutions. On top of everything else, it's the tourist season. It kills her that her own house is lost to her, that she is basically homeless, that she'll have to move again and pull stuff out of storage and buy some of the same things she's just sold or given away. She's mad about this. It's not Henry-anger, though, or other-anger, something finally mobilizing and powerful. It's self-anger, which is a short slide into self-hatred. When she had to downsize to her place in Queen

Anne after Evan left, she swore she'd never move in with a man again unless it was going to be permanent. This speaks to how much she believed in Henry, which is why she is so furious at herself now.

Stupid, stupid, dead mother Maggie says.

Will she ever shut up? Probably not. She's in the ground, and louder than ever.

Now that the stinking flowers are in the trash, Isabelle hauls the can to the curb. It's garbage day, and the least she can do for Jane is wrestle the waste bin to the end of the road, which has been swallowed by the morning fog. It's some flower-trash-garbage-day metaphor, but she's too depressed to care about anything clever. Hey, Henry could write a pathetic poem about it! Dead beauty with curlicues, and prim, forgotten words, whatever whatever. Talk about the King of Horror.

There it is: that glimmer of fury that appeared after her mother died. It skipped off like a schoolgirl when love blossomed between her and Henry. And it has been hiding in professional deference to the self-hatred and blame that's been consuming her lately.

It's there, and then it's gone.

That morning, the fog lies low over the

whole island. When Isabelle brushes off her hands and walks back up the drive to her car, she can't see the crows overhead, but she can hear them. There are hundreds of birds up there somewhere, leaving their roost and heading to their feeding ground for the day. They *kawkawkawkaw*, navigating through the blindness.

The main road has disappeared, too, and the street signs have turned into spirits. As Isabelle drives, there are only two beams of headlights disappearing into white. Isabelle fears she'll see Jane's truck upended in a ditch, wheels spinning. She and Jane both make it to work in one piece, though, because there's Jane's truck parked safely in a spot in the Island Air lot when Isabelle finally arrives.

Inside, pilots Eddie, Joe, Liz, Kit, and Louise are all business. There's none of the usual joking and sharing of last night's movie or what Louise's cat did, or Kit's usual bullshit big talk, which is just as common on the company's radio frequency as it is on land. The conversation is all about reports and route recommendations, and whether Joe should take a plane up to scout and radio back his yay, nay, or maybe. Eddie, a former bush pilot, who often starts his opinions with, "Hell, in Alaska, we'd

. . . ," thinks it doesn't look bad at all, but Maggie's presence hovers here, too. She'd always been unimpressed by anyone wanting to shoulder their way through a fog delay. Maggie's mother, the intrepid Agnes, used to let pilots decide for themselves, but this frustrated dispatchers, who ended up with a mess on their hands, and it confused the passengers who were left waiting while others departed. Federal weather minimums applied to everyone, Maggie always said, and they'd take off as a team or be grounded as a team. It pissed off veteran pilots like Eddie and Kit, but Maggie was boss.

This morning, they're all a bunch of junior high kids with the substitute teacher, seeing what they can get away with.

"Let me just go take a look," Joe says. "Worse that can happen is I crash into the side of a mountain and the business tanks." He chuckles like a sicko.

"In Alaska, we'd have been outta here an hour ago," Eddie says. He always has a story about a bear encounter, a vomiting passenger, or a damaged plane in an isolated location.

"We're holding," Jane declares.

Kit, who's nearing sixty and has seen plenty of fog in his days, makes a disgusted noise.

191

There's nothing to do but make more coffee until better weather arrives, so that's what Isabelle does. She brings a cup to the small customs trailer, where the officer, Ray, waits for the Air Canada plane from Victoria. Back outside, she can hear the slosh of the waves against the dock. A few seagulls cry, the sound of abandoned babies, and in this grim gray-white, a foghorn moans. The fog is thick enough that it's wet against Isabelle's face.

Her phone vibrates in her pocket. The ringer has been off since the pilot meeting earlier. But she's kept it off before that, too, because she didn't want to hear Henry calling or not calling. For the first two days, he phoned repeatedly, but lately he's stopped. Henry hasn't called; no one has, really. Only Thomas Sedgewick, who's rung her up from her childhood home, wondering if there was a key somewhere to the back door. It makes Isabelle realize how small her world has gotten.

Now Isabelle checks her messages. It's just Bonnie Randall, owner of Randall and Stein Booksellers, needing to delay their meeting until tomorrow. Fine. Moving into a small apartment in town after all the space of her mother's house with those views and the comforts of familiarity . . . The thought of it fills her with dread.

When her phone immediately vibrates a second time, she expects to see Bonnie's number again. But this time, *Oh, shit,* it's him. It's Henry. Something clutches her heart — fear, longing, unfinished business, who knows what. She doesn't answer.

She's seen him since that horrible night with Ricky Beaker. She had to go back there, to get her laptop and a suitcase full of clothes, since most of her stuff was at his place. He promised he'd be away and would leave the door unlocked, but he was there, and he followed her around and pleaded with her to look at him and listen.

But when she looked at him and listened, it was strange, because weird words about a dead woman and a missing wife were coming from Henry's mouth, the mouth she kissed. He looked oddly like the Henry she knew. She shoved these thoughts away. She was sure that Henry was gone forever.

She also saw him once in town, pumping gas at Eugene's. Strangely, he was not surrounded by police cars or news media helicopters. He was just putting his wallet into his back pocket. She saw him once more, out at Point Perpetua Park. At least, she glimpsed the flash of his jacket, his familiar gait, as she drove past. She slowed and then parked and watched him for a while. He didn't look like a killer or a maniac. He looked like a man with a lot on his mind. He looked like a brokenhearted man, actually.

Now here's Henry's voice, coming out of her phone and into her ear as she stands at the end of the Island Air dock, which looks out into a sea of white and more white. She used to swim in these waters, out by Maggie's house, out by Remy/Louella's/ the musician/Henry's house. She'd practice for her high school swim meets, slicing through the choppy, cold waves. It made her feel strong. She hasn't felt strong like that in a long while.

Someone I want you to meet. Dinner. Just that. If tonight doesn't convince you . . . The Bayshore. Our favorite, right? Please. I deserve that, I think. We *do.*

She sighs. She rubs her head. It is suddenly aching. She feels slightly sick. What's odd is that Henry just sounds like himself.

He's a liar! Maggie reminds.

But Isabelle lacks the energy required to either agree or not. The moving, the loss of her mother and her home, the shock of Henry's past and the way she found out — plus Evan, God, Evan, the loss of him and their life in Seattle, and the vast question of what she should do now — it's all exhausted her. She's so weary. She could almost slip off her clothes and edge into that fog and swim out to the far place where the whales slumber. She could almost just let the waves take her.

The weather finally clears, and the company takes off, looking like a friendly toy fleet off to happily conquer in the play war. Joe is returning a couple to Seattle; Liz has two sisters who've just sprinkled their father's ashes. Eddie is island-hopping with a businessman and his camera. In the late afternoon, there are arrivals. Joe brings a family that needs restaurant recommendations and a babysitter. Kit's hipster couple has a Visa that's declined. Liz returns with a doctor and his wife who are visiting family. Louise brings a "VIP" who turns out to be an aging child star from the old *Eight Is Enough* show. No one can remember her until Liz caves in and googles.

Isabelle ties down planes and hauls luggage and completes payments and arranges for a car service for the celebrity and the doctor. "Car service" — ha. It's Jason Meadows with his father's black Buick with the tinted windows. When the day is done, she heads back to Jane's. She has not made a decision about Henry's invitation and the mysterious person he wants her to meet. She thinks maybe she'll just read in her room with Button and Rosie. But when she gets back to the house, she gets a clean, plump towel from Jane's cupboard. She strips off her clothes and gets in the shower. She chooses something nice, the least wrinkly thing in her suitcase, and before she knows it, she's wearing lipstick.

Lipstick has its own ideas.

Isabelle leaves a note for Jane, who's having drinks and burgers with Kit and their pal Terry at Bud's Tavern. Isabelle lies. *Going to see old friends,* she writes. *Might be late.*

People who lie have secrets, Maggie now reminds. *You're a fool.*

She doesn't even care. Her mother never trusted anyone.

Henry and his guests stand when she arrives. Isabelle is surprised to find that they've already met — it's Dr. Mark and his wife, Jerry Kennedy. Ms. Kennedy made the Island Air reservation and paid with her own card, so Isabelle did not see the North name. Pilot Liz just dropped this couple off three hours ago, and Isabelle shook their hands and rolled Jerry's expensive metal suitcase up the dock, while they chatted about the fog delay and waited for Jason Meadows in the Buick.

"Isabelle, I'd like you to meet my brother Mark. And his wife, Jerry," Henry says. He's wearing that blue linen shirt, the one she's unbuttoned many times. Henry looks nervous. Also, exhausted. He's aged since she's seen him, if that's possible. Or else he's just lost weight, and the skin of his face hugs his cheekbones.

"We've already met!" Dr. Mark says, taking her hand. "This is *the* Isabelle?"

"The one and only," she says. She remembers Mark from Henry's family stories, the brothers playing lacrosse, making forts, Mark as Batman to Henry's Joker, while their youngest brother, Jack, had to be the audience. She can see the resemblance now. Mark is younger than Henry, but they have the same forehead, the same something around the eyes.

"I'm an idiot," Henry says. "It didn't even occur to me — your flight coming in . . ."

"Well, we changed our plans at the last minute. You were likely thinking of all that talk about ferry schedules. I couldn't stomach the thought of that boat," Jerry says. Jerry is a marketing consultant for a "major corporation," a fact that she worked into the conversation earlier that day, as if providing her résumé at the outset would settle any pesky questions about social hierarchy. Isabelle has no idea what a marketing consultant even does, though the words *major corporation* make it sound like Jerry is keeping state secrets for government leaders. Jerry wears a buttoned suit jacket and has the sort of aggressive manicure that suggests she returned her original engagement ring for the larger one she now wears. The diamond is big enough to have crashed on earth and caused the extinction of the dinosaurs.

"I'm confused," Mark says. "Henry said you were an editor."

"I can't remember what I told you and what I didn't . . ." Henry says.

"He tells us nothing." Jerry waves a hand, a casual demonstration of their superior intimacy.

"I *was* an editor. When I lived in Seattle." Isabelle sits in the empty seat next to Henry. Now they're a couple across from another couple at dinner. What's strange is that Mark has sweet eyes, and he's wearing the sort of cartoon tie favored by pediatricians; when Isabelle's vision adjusts to the dim light of the restaurant, she sees that the pattern is a parade of tiny Tweety Birds.

"Of course you forgot! This guy walks around with his head in the clouds half the time," Mark says, in an affectionate, arm-socking tone. "Mom always said, if she asked him to go get his coat, she'd find him in his room, building a rocket out of LEGOs."

"I haven't seen calamari as an appetizer since 1999," Jerry says as she peruses the menu.

They order drinks. If anyone seems capable of committing a crime, it's Jerry, who asks for sparkling water with a small lime cut in quarters, two pieces squeezed in, two left whole on the side. Isabelle wrestles with that disorienting sense of unreality that results when facts collide. They are in a regular restaurant and talking about regular things. The waitress comes by to take their orders. Water slides from a silver pitcher into their glasses, and ice cubes clink.

Sitting beside Isabelle, Henry looks like his once-beloved self. There's his same profile, the one she's used to seeing in the car seat beside her, or on the couch, or in bed. At one moment, his knee touches hers, and she almost grabs it playfully, forgetting completely about what's happened and all that she subsequently read online.

After everything in those articles, after his

lies, she'd stuck him in a box labeled *bad* — evil, fraud, deceiver, maybe even murderer — and she'd taped it shut. But now he's somehow out of that box and mildly passing her a basket of dinner rolls. It is true, it is very true, that he may be completely innocent, the victim of bad luck and terrible heartache, and this is now seeming not just possible but likely, with his familiar right hand around a silver knife, spreading a chilled square of butter. The articles about Sarah's disappearance, the story of how they'd gone boating in Rockport and had tied up for the night and how they'd been drinking and were heard arguing, and then how he went to bed only to wake and find her gone . . . It all seems a horrible tragedy that he's somehow survived.

And yet hands are deceiving, aren't they? They tuck you in and wrap thoughtful gifts and make a meal and they slap and hit and grab your hair and yank your head back. How do you read their guilt or innocence or their whole history as they turn a key or plink a keyboard or set down a knife at an angle against the plate? She can't forget all of those articles and video clips she saw in Jane's kitchen that awful night and in the following days, as she searched on her own laptop set against her knees. After Sarah disappeared, there was the breaking news of the long-ago death of Henry's previous girlfriend, Virginia Arsenault, a presumed accident, and a flurry of accompanying outrage. There were Virginia's friends, talking to a reporter about how they never believed Virginia had jumped. There was an incensed leader of a Stop Violence Against Women group. There was Henry, with his bent head, walking into the station to be questioned. There was Henry's lawyer, protesting innocence, claiming victimization and suffering. There were the words *open investigation* and *remains a suspect* and then a dwindling of reports.

There was that horrible clip of Henry himself; it was a little over two years ago, and he looked so much younger, wearing a suit she'd never seen before, and a gold wedding band she'd never seen before, either, but it was still undeniably Henry. And it was dreadful, too, because he was sobbing and choking through his words, turning his head to blow his nose, begging Sarah to come back. Isabelle's heart cracked at his grief. Weirdly, she wanted to hold that crying man whom she suddenly remembered she loved. He was clearly devastated.

There was a quieter feeling, though, as she watched that clip, perhaps brought on

201

by all that she read, or by the fact that he'd lied to her, or maybe it was something else, something about Henry on that tape, although it was impossible to tell which of these it was. The feeling was *doubt.*

Is he faking it?

So she'd made him evil. She set him in a clear, tidy place in her mind labeled *No More.* But now here he is, or, rather, here she is, and dishes of food have arrived, and this kind man, this brother, this pediatrician, is reaching toward Isabelle's hand, setting his on top of hers.

"Henry asked us to come to talk about the elephant in the room," Dr. Mark says.

The words sock her in the gut. She has no idea how she got here and how this has become her life. If Evan hadn't finally pressed for divorce because she *felt more like a sister* and because they *were two different people,* she'd be ordering Pagliacci Pizza at their old apartment and opening a bottle of wine. It seems like proof of some sort. Proof that life can have its own current, speeding you past the scenery of its choice, snagging you on one particular overhanging branch. A branch that — for whatever messed-up reason — is *meant.*

"It's an outrage," Jerry says, sawing her steak with coldhearted efficiency. "What this poor guy has been through . . ."

Henry stares at his plate.

"I know, I *know,* this is shocking," Dr. Mark says, and the funny thing is, he's taken the tone of a doctor. He's being the firm physician, relaying the sad news of the tumor and the reasons to be hopeful. "I know a person asks oneself how there can be such a coincidence. I asked it myself. I can only tell you that there can be and that there was."

"I didn't know Virginia, but Sarah was *nuts,* trust me." Jerry pops the steak into her mouth, dabs her lips with the napkin.

"Henry wouldn't hurt a fly. This man" — Dr. Mark points his finger across the table at his brother — "has been through hell. I wouldn't wish the past years on my worst enemy, let alone on Henry. He has a heart of gold. You wouldn't believe how strong he's been during this unimaginable ordeal. I could never have been as strong. Henry, I couldn't."

There's a noise beside her. An *ah* of pain, cut off before it becomes a sob. Henry is trying not to cry. He has his fingertips pressed hard to his eyes. God, it's awful.

"There is no evidence, no reason to think anything happened except what did happen. Henry has never once deviated from his story. Not once. Virginia was a sad, frail, despairing young woman, and Sarah was an unhappy, dramatic one. She stirred up trouble."

She didn't sound like she stirred up trouble, though, not from what Isabelle read. "People said, people who worked with her, that she was conscientious. Devoted. Extremely intelligent," Isabelle says. And somewhat wealthy. Isabelle doesn't mention this, but people in the articles do. This fact is always attached to the word *motive*. Isabelle hasn't eaten a thing. Her shrimp lie on her plate, looking suddenly like a very wrong choice, the most wrong, with their pink, bare flesh, and the way they curl into themselves as if in protection.

"Oh, she was smart, all right," Jerry says. "Driven like you wouldn't believe. She's probably married some millionaire and is living on a fabulous ranch in Montana. I never liked her. She was calculating."

"Jerry," Mark says.

"And, my God, are we saying anything tonight about the one we really wonder about? That professor? The bird guy? We saw it with our own eyes at that holiday party." Jerry leans in toward Isabelle. "Henry and Sarah had this big festive event for their university friends . . . We brought the kids for Christmas. Swear to God, this man . . . Was he her *boss*? I can't quite recall, but he was *completely* leering, and she wasn't doing anything to discourage it, that's for sure."

"Can you incompletely leer?" Mark asks.

"You saw it. She *loved* it."

"Jerry, come on. Stop."

Henry is right. It feels shameful to bash her.

"The guy was good-looking, I admit. He had some sort of charisma, but *Jesus*. And you know what else? She was cold. Total disinterest in the children. The girls did everything to get her attention, and zero. Zilch. Nothing. Like they didn't exist."

"Not everyone is maternal," Dr. Mark says.

"Complicated," Henry says. "She was complicated."

"We don't know what happened, all right? We only know what *didn't* happen," Dr. Mark says.

"She was drinking. We argued. She was upset. She was there, and then she wasn't. That boat was gone . . . The water was rough that night," Henry says. He hasn't eaten anything, either. His slab of halibut is untouched, and so are those glistening summer vegetables. His roll is missing one small bite. "But I'll never know for sure, do you see? I will never know."

"She probably had a plan. She probably had someone waiting for her. That guy . . . A plan that went very wrong."

"We don't know," Dr. Mark says. "I don't think it's helpful to go all conspiracy theory, Jerry. You know how I feel about that. It's not where the evidence points. Drinking, anger, a boat? It seems clear. And, Henry, you'd probably rather think she's alive somewhere, but that's just not likely. You *do* know, Henry. We've never heard a word. Not a peep. Maybe it's time to finally accept the truth."

"It's awful. It's just awful," Jerry says. "If she went overboard, this man never even had a chance to mourn, the way they were after him. Can you imagine?" She looks at Isabelle hard.

Isabelle shakes her head. She can't imagine. Actually, she can't at all.

"Our whole family has been broken by this. Devastated. I feel so sad for my brother."

Mark does look broken and devastated. He quietly leans back in his chair, away from Isabelle, as if he doesn't know what else to say. He sighs. And it's a true and honest sigh, an exhale of painful years and sleepless nights.

What else is there to say? Because, if Henry really hasn't harmed anyone, then this is the worst nightmare. He is the most tragic kind of victim, one who has lost loved ones *and* his own life. If Henry is an innocent man, Isabelle herself is just one more person in a line of people who has wrongly persecuted him.

Her heart squeezes. It feels like — she doesn't have any idea. Maybe grief? Grief for the women and Henry and herself and all humans, up against the awful shit life brings?

No one speaks. There is just restaurant noise — the din of conversation and the clink of silverware and glass. The weight of the silence is immense. The weight of the loss is.

"Does anyone else need another drink? Because I sure as hell do," Dr. Mark says. They all relief-laugh. All of them, even Isabelle. Because who doesn't need a drink after this? They order aperitifs and a dessert to share. Jerry chooses the peach tart. It's another deplorable choice, Sarah's specialty, but no one corrects her.

The drinks arrive. "This is crazy, but I want to make a toast," Dr. Mark says. They lift their tiny glasses. "To the future."

They clink. They empty their glasses and Henry orders another round. Isabelle loves aperitifs. She loves the miniature vessels and the liquid, thick as a potion, and she loves the word itself. Maybe it's just the alcohol softening her heart and nerves, but something feels cleared away. Her spirit has ever so slightly lifted. There is this doctor, a pediatrician, a man who is trusted with what's most precious in our world, and there is that doctor's own trust, placed in Henry. There's a family, and a brother. Henry is an uncle to their two daughters. There is, she can see it between them, love.

There is *belief.*

She is pleasantly intoxicated. She should've eaten something if she was going to down these drinks. But, God, the fuzz and warmth feel so good. It feels like such a relief.

Under the table, Henry takes the tips of her fingers in his hand.

The peach tart arrives. Mark and Jerry dive in. *Like crows on a carcass,* she thinks.

Her mind is being dramatic. Stirring up trouble. Acting complicated. *Stop it,* she tells herself. *It's just a dessert!*

Jesus, Isabelle. I can't leave you alone for five minutes, Maggie says.

But they're in The Bayshore, where Isabelle went to dinner before homecoming in her junior year. She suddenly remembers her date in his awkward suit, the boutonniere with its stem wrapped in green tape, and the pin with a fake pearl on the end. Now, there is some argument over the bill. Henry wins and pays. He helps her with her sweater. There are no evil men with shoving hands here. No demons with glowing eyes.

Outside, the fog has come back. They stand under the restaurant's red awning. Jerry blows into her hands as if the summer night has turned frigid. The fog has swooped low, hovers thick over the water and the docks so that only the red wharf lamps and a few haloed streetlights can be seen. The sailboats clank and groan in the mist.

Mark and Jerry hug Isabelle goodbye.

"He's a sweetheart," Jerry says. "For God's sake, he's a *poet.*"

"He needs you," Mark whispers to Isabelle, squeezing her shoulder.

Mark takes Jerry's arm and they head to Maggie's old car, parked across the street. Unlike Maggie, the car, a dim, mystical outline, is keeping its opinions to itself. Mark and Jerry disappear like apparitions, giving Isabelle and Henry a moment alone.

"I'm starving," he says.

They both laugh. It is such a normal thing to say.

"Me, too."

"You met my brother."

"I like your brother."

"Jerry takes some getting used to."

"I think this is probably true."

"I want to take you out again. Soon. Can I reintroduce myself? Start over, since I fucked this up so bad?"

"I don't know, Henry. I have some thinking to do. You lied to me. That doesn't just go away. None of this can just go away that easily."

"I lied to you, and I'll never forgive myself for it. God, I hope you can understand why I did. How do you handle something like this? I don't know, Isabelle. Clearly, I didn't handle it well. It just felt so good to be ordinary, if you can understand that. Please say we'll at least have dinner."

"Jesus, Henry. This is a lot. It's all a lot to take in."

"Please. Dinner! Just that."

His face, his blue shirt, the glowing yellow windows of The Bayshore, they are the only thing she can see clearly in this fog. She smells his familiar scent, and the boozy warmth from their breath.

"All right."

Isabelle! You fucking fool! Maggie says. Isabelle's friend Anne would say it, too, and Jane will when she hears about it, Eddie will, any sensible person who is told the story will. She can hear the chorus: *What an idiot! How pathetic! How stupid! Who would do that? I would never believe him! I would never do something that insane! I would never, I would never, I would never,* say the righteous.

And why is it that her fury blooms so full and magnificently bitter there, in her own mind? She can box and punch in that barbed garden, spread poison at the roots, fling bolts that singe every little shrub in sight. She can fight with herself, because her opponent is weak. *You never once placed your trust somewhere questionable?* Isabelle silently shouts back to the choir. *You never once made a dubious choice in the name of love? You have never decided to maybe forgive a lie? Well, congrat-u-fuckinglations. You are incredible! You deserve a medal! Judge away! Sit high up on that throne of righteousness. Just be careful you don't fall.*

She should have stopped at aperitif number one.

The ceiling swirls in Jane's guest room. It's

been a night of bad idea upon bad idea, because, back at Jane's, she remembers a bottle of Baileys in the high cupboard of Jane's kitchen. Why not have another? Now, the cream-and-alcohol spin, and she's on a teacup ride on that bed. *Life is a teacup ride,* Isabelle thinks, but she's drunk.

Some reasonable part of her lays out a calm plan: She'll take her time to decide. She'll wait and see what she feels about this horrible situation with Henry. She can walk away anytime she likes.

But another piece of her, a quiet, dangerous piece, the piece she wouldn't admit to having in a million years, just watches Jane's ceiling make another revolution around her sun, knowing Henry may be her fate. She desires things — she doesn't even know what, just large things. Fast rides on motorcycles, careless sex, foreign lands, *something.* Something *not this.* Something not Isabelle Austen, self. Her drunk head plus the darkest parts of her soul decide. It's your worst nightmare of an election, where the crazy write-in wins. Anne and the sensible people in her head groan. But Isabelle believes that even Anne and the sensible people have secret longings for wild open air and speeding scenery, for the fear and hope in unfamiliar skin.

Well, she'll end up with either the love or the punishment she deserves, for sure.

CHAPTER 16

Matias's eyebrows are like two magnets, attracting, repelling. "Visually restricting string tests . . . horizontal mirror . . . green dog toy," he says, sitting across the desk from Weary. These are the words that zip out, anyway, from the hum and drone of the rest. They buzz in front of Weary's face like an annoying fly that he wishes he could swat away. Matias is a nice young man with sincere eyes, a nest of black hair, and one of those beards that takes itself too seriously. Weary forgets what those beards are called. Only men over forty wear them in the States, but that news hasn't made it to New Caledonia yet.

"I think it's potentially an important discovery, Dr. Weary. It's early yet, but —"

"I'm sorry?"

"These clusters of perineuronal satellite oligodendroglia in the telencephala of healthy NC crows."

"Yes, yes. That's very exciting. Thrilling, Matias. Thrilling."

"In humans, low numbers are linked to —"

The window is open, and a warm breeze drifts through, but so does laughter. It's Lotto and Yann.

"Mieux surveiller, ourson . . ." Yann says, in a teasing, singsong voice. Better watch out, bear cub. He sounds drunk.

"Tais-toi. Tais-toi cr . . . tin!" Shut up. Shut up, moron.

"Pauvre, professeur solitaire. L'admettre, tu crois qu'il est sexy." Poor, lonely professor. Admit it, you think he's sexy.

Terrific. Wonderful. Just great. Weary understands immediately that he is the butt of this joke. He is the lonely professor, hot for a "bear cub," which is French slang for a young and hairy gay man.

Matias blushes. He is crimson. For God's sake. Get with the times! But these things are not spoken about in this region, let alone accepted. The people here are traditional and private. This behavior of Yann's will have to be addressed, even if Weary has heard the whispers about himself before. He knows what a lot of people call him. *Discret.* A reserved and closeted homosexual.

Well, so what, there are rumors. Of course

there are. Weary knows he must seem like an odd, solitary bachelor who keeps to himself. They will talk and guess, because he *is* keeping secrets. They don't know about Sarah. Gossip all you want. He knows who he is, and what he wants, though lately what he wants most is interfering with regular life.

Those new photos — they are the cause of his current problems. He can't focus on his work. He can barely concentrate on anything. He is so, so close to his heart's desire that his mind can only hold this single thought, which everything else swirls around like a cyclone: *Soon.* He left the water running in his bathroom sink at home. He locked himself out of his house and had to climb in through the kitchen window. *Soon, soon, soon.*

Right now, the file folder with Matias's study information sits open before him. *This research aims to challenge the previous claims that cognition of NC crows is linked to enlargement of associative regions such as the mesopallium or increased foliation . . .*

It looks like Chinese. Weary can't make sense of it. It's so much *blah blah blah* that it makes his head throb. Yann is still laughing loudly outside, but he's moved on to sexy-sexy comments about Aimée now.

Weary hates assholes like that. Yann's days are numbered.

"Are you all right, Professor?"

Matias's eyebrows now huddle in concern, two fuzzy family members at an intervention. Weary realizes he's snapped a pencil in half. The two pieces are gripped in his palm. "Of course, Matias. Perfectly fine. Fine."

"Perhaps we should wrap up? Maybe, uh, we can speak more another day —"

"Yes, yes. Onward! Excellent work. Until Monday, then. You know where you can find me, should the NC's start using the string to knit sweaters, ha-ha."

"Ha-ha," Matias chuckles politely. He looks nervous. He hurries out of there. This Henry North business better resolve quickly before Weary loses his job.

Goatee. That's the word for Matias's beard.

Back at home that evening, a real insect buzzes. A mosquito, his abdomen fat with blood. Dengue fever exists in New Caledonia, so Weary does not want to take chances. He chases the brute with his slipper. It *zzz*'s in front of his face, taunting, then scoots to a high corner. Weary stands on a chair and waves a broom, but no luck.

Fine. It's a distraction, anyway, from the

lure of the computer. He tells himself not to do it, but he can't seem to stop. Isn't it strange, all this time spent looking at other people's lives instead of living our own? Peering and lurking and comparing? He doesn't know why other people do it. He doubts their goals are similar to his. He checks again. His old pal, ShutR. Surprise, surprise. There have been no new photos in the last day, no new photos in the last twelve hours, six hours, one hour, ten minutes, five minutes, two, since Weary last looked. He has no idea how many times he's refreshed that page today alone.

A hundred? That sounds crazy. It sounds insane.

Could anyone blame him, though? Weary's plan has been two years, almost three now in the making. He's ready for his next move, by God! No wonder he clicks and clicks on his variable interval schedule, waiting for the reinforcement he is dreaming of, the *yes–go–it's time*! While he still clicks and waits, clicks and waits, though, it's weird, it truly is, how day by day, events seem to follow right along the path he assumed they would, step by tragic step, much to his delight, dread, and utter terror. Isabelle knows about Henry, Weary is sure, and she is with him regardless, and those photos are proof. You can start to feel a little like a magician or like God, big hands on the keyboard, imagining the storyline that then comes alive.

He glares at that mosquito, clinging now to a lampshade. A roach (so many of them here) scurries under the desk and disappears, but who cares. It won't kill anyone like that mosquito might. "You think so, do you?" he says aloud. He grabs his nightshirt, whacks. The mosquito flits off, and the shade tilts.

The words *plan, plot, scheme* make him feel evil, even when he just thinks them. He is not evil. He's not crazy or obsessed. Okay, he's obsessed. But he reminds himself that this whole . . . what? Thing, situation, mess, reason for living . . . It did not begin as a *plan.* Not *this* plan. He was only coping with the terrible and shocking loss of Sarah, the shaking horror, making his way moment to moment through the slow recuperation to a time when he could even sleep again.

And then one night, he finally did sleep, but he woke with a start as if he'd been slapped from a dream. His eyes popped open and he suddenly had an understanding, a dawn of realization. A midnight strike of genius.

He knew what had to be done. He knew

what *could* be done, *if.*

After that, the long watch began. And Henry North helped everything along, just by being Henry North, and doing what Henry North does. First came the migration, his move to Parrish. Then came the courtship displays. Henry faced the female and fluffed his feathers. He spread his wings and tail and proceeded to bow repeatedly while uttering a brief rattling song. Interrupted by a frightening predator, the female took flight. But now there's more fluffing and bowing, and the mating resumes.

There is no guarantee, none, that any of Weary's efforts will even pay off. In spite of the way the storyline ticks along, it's all a long shot. Weary tries not to think about how long of a shot it actually is. Instead, he must focus on what he understands about human and animal behavior. He must use his critical eye to study the images for the smallest detail, the tiny indication that it's time. Past behavior is the best indicator of future behavior, but where is that moment where the two intersect? Where is that point in the center of the X, where *past* and *future* is *now*?

His house has grown dark and he hasn't even noticed. He doesn't bother turning on the lights even when he goes to the kitchen to refill his wineglass. He's back again. Refresh. Nothing. It's still that last image that appeared a few days ago.

It's so compelling, though. He leans forward, studies it once more. It's the two of them, Isabelle and Henry, hiking.

Hiking, of all things! Before these images appeared, the expensive dinners started up again on the Visa, along with the big grocery bills. There were gas purchases on the mainland, too, with two nights at the W hotel in Seattle (resulting in a few romantic-weekend, standard-tourist-fare shots on ShutR — the Space Needle, the Pike Place Market, et cetera). But these images are the most disturbing thing to appear. This pair of boots next to another pair of boots. This overhang on a gravel trail with, sure, a lovely spread of sea below. A lovely spread of sea below, below, below . . .

The boots are the largest cause of his recent distraction; they trouble him and refuse to leave his mind, because what is Isabelle thinking and feeling right then inside of them, knowing what Weary is sure she now knows? What questions haunt her as she stands at that ledge? It is not difficult to imagine what she might think and feel. It would be impossible to go on that hike without your heart aching, without a small trickle of fear rolling down your spine. Her boots would crunch a rhythm of *did he, didn't he, did he, didn't he.* She would notice that Henry was strangely unaffected by the trail and its height, unblinking at the fact of hiking itself. This lack — it would wiggle and creep under her skin.

She would keep the mood cheerful. She'd avoid any argument. She would wonder, not for the first time, why this man spends his life studying another man who had very complicated relationships with women.

Empathy is as easy for Weary as it appears to be for *Corvus frugilegus,* who will console a friend after that friend has been in a fight, setting beak to beak, body to body. The boots distress Weary, the same as *Corvus* will become distressed when a close member of his flock is, fearful when a beloved is fearful. Weary grieves for Isabelle and the way her old life is gone, as *Corvus* appears to grieve when coming upon a dead comrade. He will call out to the others, and they will all poke and prod the corpse, cawing with emotion. Seemingly, they will reflect on the scene and attempt to understand the manner of demise. They will bury the body with grass or twigs. They will gather, even, for what appears to be a funeral.

A healthy *Corvus* will aid a crippled one,

and this is also what he tries to remember when he looks at those boots. He feels *all* those things as he leans forward and studies that image: distress and fear and grief and compassion. And, more. More, because, like *Corvus,* too, he is not just a kind and generous animal. When crows circle that dead body and determine that foul play was involved, they never fly over that area again. If they know the perpetrator, they will scold and mob. The birds, on occasion, murder one of their own for reasons that mystify scientists.

When Weary looks at that other pair of boots next to Isabelle's, he is not mystified.

He is sure, very sure, those crows have their reasons.

The mosquito is back. It buzzes and flits across the light of the computer screen and then lands. It is heedless, but Weary smacks that bastard hard with his palm. Blood splats everywhere. It's all over Isabelle and all over Henry. Blood actually smears down their pixel faces, down to their pixel footwear, as he tries to clean the screen with a wad of tissue. God, it's gruesome. Honestly, it's hard to look at.

CHAPTER 17

Isabelle finds a single boot, but then needs to hunt for the other one under the bed. There it is, a bit dusty, and lying next to one of Henry's dress shoes. It's fall, and the tourists are gone, and it's an orangey crisp autumn day, all pumpkin-spice and knit sweaters and wood smoke and burning leaves in the air. A month has passed since that night at The Bayshore, a month of nights with the rod of Joe's pullout couch across her back, since she couldn't bear Jane's concerned, confused eyes on a full-time basis. In those weeks, she raided the Coronas and handmade mac and cheese in Joe's fridge, and stayed up late talking to him about her conflict over returning to Henry, and Joe's recent breakup with the entitled Danielle. They caught up on Joe's family, and on Maggie's passing; he reminded her of the time when she was seventeen, when in a moment of teen rebellion she called Maggie a bitch, and Maggie grabbed her and hit her, and she went to Joe's house to stay for the night. She'd forgotten all about this. How is it possible, this forgetting? It just is. But he reminded her of good things, too. Maggie running the food drive. Maggie yelling louder than anyone at the high school football games.

Joe had been sweet, warming up burritos for her in the microwave, leaving the light on when she was out with Henry, giving her space when they were on the phone at all hours. Joe said stuff like *He seems like a nice guy,* and patiently listened to all the ways Henry was being Henry again, but even better — contrite, sincere, believable, open. Finally, though, Joe booted her out of the nest.

If you're going to do it, do it a hundred percent, he said. It was something Mr. Hopper, his old wrestling coach at Parrish High, might have told him, and Joe is as overly generous as Isabelle by nature, but she listened to him anyway, and here she is now, snagging that boot with her fingertips and she lays sprawled on the floor. Joe or no Joe, she is a believer in a hundred percent.

When Henry suggested this hike last night, Isabelle pushed Virginia's name out of her head. *Pushed:* Oh, God. That sounds awful. Isabelle pretended a hike up a mountain was just a hike up a mountain, and that nothing bad had crossed her mind. Henry is so sensitive, he's like a decaying tooth that recoils at the slightest hint of cold.

Which means there is a lot of pretending that a lot of things don't cross her mind. She admits things have been difficult since she moved in with both Henry and his past. It's difficult to untangle what's her and what's him and what's his strange history, pressing in on all sides. Dr. Mark's *elephant in the room* is not so much an elephant as two once-breathing women. Isabelle can almost smell their perfume following her as she goes about her day. As she and Henry make dinner, Virginia sets the table. As she and Henry drive to a restaurant, Sarah sits in the back. On a beach walk, Virginia follows without making prints in the sand, and while they make love, Henry uses some technique, something just a bit too rough for her own liking, that she wonders if Sarah liked.

When there's this weird space that comes up between them, Isabelle is sure that it *is* her, failing at this. She doesn't want to fail, because he's trying so hard. She doesn't want to fail for a million of her own reasons, too, some practical, some buried so far down she has no idea they're even there. She has decided to trust and commit, and those are not fifty or sixty percent words to her. Those are a hundred percent words.

Henry is being kind and supportive, loving. He tries to be lighthearted, even when his fat legal bill arrives in the mail. *I want to make your life easier,* he told her, and so, in spite of her protests, he insisted on looking over Island Air's finances and made a suggestion list of mutual funds for her mother's house money, since he's invested like a pro in the past. He also gave her a joint credit card, so that they might feel a further sense of a combined future. Isabelle appreciates all this, but it feels a little like he's jamming right up into her, rooting around in her private family business, even demonstrating a lack of confidence in her choices. Admittedly, it's also been helpful. The boy that built rocket ships with LEGOs has a mind for numbers, along with a love of words. His investment plan sounds like a wise one. She's tucked the credit card in her purse and they use it when they go out to dinner together.

Also challenging? Jane and Eddie, who are acting like the protective parents she never had. Jane's on high alert since Isabelle returned to Henry. *Why is he with you every minute now? Are you ever alone? Why does he hover in the background every time I call?* Eddie says goodbye to her on Fridays with a *Watch your back.* He's not joking, either. *I don't like the guy,* he says. He gave her a printout of one of the articles she already read, one that appeared after Sarah died. It features Virginia's sister Mary and a few of Virginia's other friends reminding the public that she, too, met an uncertain end. This is almost like love coming from Eddie, who still needs help turning on the computer.

They are an enmeshed family. Joe plays the unflinching sibling and tells them to lay off. When Henry comes to pick her up from work one day, Jane stares him right in the eyes. It's an animal move. It's a beast of nature making a statement to another beast of nature. Henry would not go back there after that. When Isabelle confronted her, Jane apologized. *I'm sorry,* she said. *I get it. I do. I can see why you'd want to be with him, after everything you've been through.* But it was a laden concession, based on a desire to be supportive, not on true support. *We just worry about you, is all.*

Fly as a team, grounded as team — sometimes a team stood too solidly behind you. Sometimes you wish your team would just butt out. She gets it — Eddie and Jane have known her since she was a child, they care about her, but they don't know Henry.

And then, too, there was the day when a detective, Ray Prince, flew in from Boston and came to their house. Ricky Beaker was like the hostess with the company VP, chest puffed out as he stood on their doorstep next to Detective Prince. Detective Prince and Tiny weren't there to talk to Henry, which was the most horrifying thing. They wanted to speak with *her.* The nearest Isabelle had ever gotten to a life of crime was her appearance in traffic court for a speeding ticket. This happened in Seattle, and she was driving too fast only because Evan crashed his bike and broke his ankle.

"We won't take much of your time," Detective Prince said. "We just have a few questions."

"I told Detective Prince, here, you might live with the guy, but you got a strong moral code," Ricky Beaker said. "Remember how your mother used to report speeders on the loop? And didn't she start that local amnesty chapter, in the early eighti—"

Isabelle was so shocked and horrified that the police were on her porch that she slammed the door on Ricky Beaker and Detective Prince, nothing she'd have ever thought was in her good-citizen repertoire. In elementary school, she'd been taught that police officers were your friends. They'd even gotten a coloring book featuring a policeman reaching toward a cat in a tree and a policewoman helping an old lady cross a busy street.

When Henry got home and heard what happened, they threw some things into a bag and went to Seattle for an impromptu "romantic" weekend, much of which was spent with Henry in their room at the W hotel, on the phone to his attorney.

It's strange the way a life can turn. She'd been shocked when she first found out Evan had once been arrested for marijuana possession. Now pot is legal in their state and she's living with a man that some people believe is a murderer.

Jesus. It's best to not think it straight out like that.

"Ready?" Henry calls.

"Just a sec!"

Henry appears in the doorway as she tosses on her sweatshirt.

"Are you going to be warm enough in that?" he asks.

"It's breathtaking."

"Literally, for me," Isabelle says, puffing

on the incline. Henry was wrong about needing more than a sweatshirt, which she now has tied around her waist, but he is right about the beauty. As they make their way up the trail of Mount Independence, every tree that's able is bursting color. It's early morning, so a few sparse wisps of fog still linger like second thoughts in the valley below.

"The mist . . . 'How it hangs upon the trees. A mystery of mysteries!' "

He is cheerful. The poem sounds almost cheerful, too, for that creepy, morose Poe. She wishes that of all the poets in the world, he'd have chosen someone else to be fascinated by. Poe is another specter that whispers from the corners.

Now Isabelle concentrates hard on the burn in her chest and the pull of her thighs and the orange fire of the leaves. She tries to focus on her protesting hamstrings. Because, when her concentration slips, there is Virginia. How else could it be, on a hike like this? Isabelle pictures the photo that's in all the newspapers, the photo Virginia's friends released to the press after Sarah disappeared. Virginia, with her narrow pixie face and fragile cheekbones. She looks tragic, but maybe this is only because you know her fate.

"Wait. Look at this! Stop a sec, I've got to take a picture."

"No complaints on this end."

Below, the world is spread out like a Thanksgiving feast; it's all fall bounty. There is the great, shimmering sea, and little humps of islands, and the swish-strokes of deep green and orange from the trees. Admittedly, it's hard to focus on the feast amid the fact of *below*. It is far down. There are big, rough rocks the whole way to the bottom. Isabelle considers what those jagged boulders might do to your soft head and to your fragile construction of bones. She's been up here plenty of times, plenty. With friends and boyfriends, when there was fried chicken someone's generous mother made, when there was beer and sun lotion, bare shoulders and even a small boom box. It's never been a place she thought of as dangerous. Only fun, only beautiful. But, look — it's all of those things.

Henry is twisting that long lens, and there is the *shakunk* of the shutter. Now he aims it down. How can he bear it? He has told her the story of that horrible day, how Virginia seemed to toss herself off out of nowhere, how he desperately tried to climb down to save her. The CPR, the calls to mountain rescue — the wait, and then the way she stopped breathing before they arrived . . . The investigation by the park service, the grief of her friends and family . . . How can he not look at every slope for the rest of his life and see Virginia tumbling, banging, crashing, screaming? Yes, it was years and years ago, but how is this possible?

Move away from the ledge, Isabelle! Jesus! Maggie says, and this time Isabelle listens.

"I like you there. It gives perspective," Henry says.

Too bad. She steps back, away. Henry is not doing anything wrong. He is not hovering around behind her with his hands raised, ready to shove. His eyes are not narrowed with evil. There is not some black cloud over his head. But it's what he isn't doing that turns some unsettled earth inside her. He isn't keeping Isabelle away from the edge. He isn't aware of what she might be feeling right now. He's just taking pictures, like a cliff is just a cliff.

Isabelle starts to sweat. She feels like she could be sick, although it's probably just the heat and exercise. They are the only two people on the trail. It would be so easy, she understands. No one would even hear you as you fell. What was in Virginia's mind, when both feet were suddenly no longer on the ground?

Henry looks happy, snapping away. And then he turns and sees her.

"What?" His voice is terse.

"What do you mean?"

"What's wrong?"

"Nothing."

"Nothing?"

"Yes! Nothing. I'm fine."

"Why are you over there?"

"Over here? There's no over here. We're on this tiny little path. There's only here and more here —"

"Fuck."

His whole face changes. He turns right around and stomps back down the trail. They haven't even gotten to the top yet. His lens cap still sits on a rock. His boots spit gravel like furious tires on a dirt road.

Isabelle doesn't follow. She just stands there. She turns hiding-mouse quiet. Stunned-deer still. This is her learned response with perhaps dangerous humans, and certainly with angry ones. Her heart thumps. She waits until it seems safe. Then she takes Henry's lens cap and puts it in her pocket.

She follows him down, keeping several paces behind. She feels that tiptoey guilt, too, the shame that says his anger is somehow her fault. She's turned five, trying to hide in her room after she has done bad things she can no longer remember. What can a child do to make an adult get that frightening? No idea. And while she cannot recall the bad thing, she vividly remembers the frightening adult. She remembers the hot sting of the slap, the yank of her hair as her head was pulled back, the large, twisted face, the fear that she'd be small and alone in the world forever unless she could make her mother like her again.

There is no closet to hide in on Mount Independence. She's a grown woman, but try telling that to her stubborn psyche. Knowing these things and changing these things are on different orbits. She doesn't even truly believe she can rid herself of certain responses, even with a hundred years of therapy. Guilt and paralysis in the face of other people's anger is now set into the folds of her brain, as fixed as her eye color. She can't mobilize an aggressive defense because that arsenal is boarded up and locked.

Her own anger, God, what would that even look like? She pictures a mushroom cloud, atomic, cinematic fury. What a joke, though. She's been furious and people haven't even noticed. After Evan, friends said, *God, you must be livid,* and she'd agree that she was. She wanted to be livid. She *must* have been, but she also guessed that *livid* did not feel like being the last human in a ruined landscape.

Midway down the trail, Henry stops. He shakes his head, runs his hand through his hair. His eyes catch hers and plead.

"Fuck," he says again, but this time the word is a sigh, not an arrow. What a useful, multipurpose word *fuck* is. It doesn't deserve its bad reputation, Isabelle decides. It's practically friendly. Look, now it's saying, *This is hard, this place we're both in.*

Henry holds out his hand. She takes it. She doesn't want to, actually; she doesn't even want to get back into the car with him right then. She wants to be an entirely different person living in another country. But she also wants things to be okay. The need for *okay* — Jesus, it gets a person into the worst and most long-lasting messes. Henry also wants things to be okay right then, she's sure, because he says, "Isabelle, I'm sorry."

And then his face softens. The worst has passed. The child her would have chanced coming out of her room then, would have sat at the dinner table and eaten the peas even if her stomach was still full of dread.

"Henry, come on . . . What do you expect?

It's going to cross my mind. Of course it is. Look where we are!"

"It's fine."

"It doesn't mean I think you actually did something. It's just, *wow.* It's high, up here."

"Let's just drop it."

"I'm sorry."

"No, no . . ."

"I'm doing the best I can. I'm human, Henry. We're hiking. You guys were hiking. Anyone would have the thought."

"Well, my darling, for your information, I'm not going to shove you off this cliff. You have the car keys."

"Shit." She laughs.

And he laughs, too. He squeezes her hand.

"Let's go home," he says.

"Let's."

The mood is shaky as they head down. *I don't know if I can do this,* she thinks. And he's so sensitive to any withdrawal on her part that she knows he's just read her mind. She feels it in their clasped hands. She feels it in the thick, weird energy between them. She might as well have spoken her doubts aloud, by the tightness that appears in his jawline. It's hard to know what's him, and what's him in this situation, but it's like he's poised, watching and listening for rejection. It's all quarter-inch moves and undercurrents; he reads paragraphs into her averted eyes or the slightest insincerity in her tone. But he's right, isn't he? Her laugh wasn't entirely a laugh, and he knows it. She swears she can lie awake at night with a doubt or a question, and he'll awaken and curve his body against hers to answer. He's right, so no wonder.

After what he's been through, it's understandable that he needs her loyalty above all else. She forgives him things because of it. She slips her hand free.

"Race you down," she says.

When they get home, the air between them has lightened. They got burgers at The Dive on the way back. Isabelle believes in the power of burgers plus onion rings to make most any day better. Now Henry is writing. This means he is locked away in his office, typing on his laptop in rapid bursts, long pauses in between.

Sometimes, Isabelle thinks of this as "writing," quote-unquote. It's disrespectful, really, but she allows it of herself, because Henry takes himself so seriously. He doesn't want to be interrupted and he needs utter silence, as if he's involved in delicate negotiations to prevent global catastrophe. He emerges a while later, satisfied but secretive.

Still, she keeps her mouth shut. It's his creative path. People get to express themselves any way they want. He loves the writing in some weird tormented way, same as all writers, and that's what's most important. His ego about it — maybe it just jabs at hers. Her past publishing job, as insignificant as it was, is the one place where she's the competent one, the more experienced one. Maybe people in love shouldn't have these small, unspoken competitions, but she's pretty sure that most couples do. There will always be little splinters.

Night is coming earlier now that it's fall, and outside the big windows of Remy's house, it's dusk. Isabelle stands at the glass; she's in her socks, and her hands are tucked into the sleeves of her sweatshirt. She watches the sky, because she sees them — the few small dots of black coming, growing in numbers. Now the crows are overhead, and the long line of them stretches over the water. It's been a while since she's really taken them in, stood underneath them and listened to the *puff-puff* of wings. It's wrong, to let something that majestic and strange become just another overlooked event.

She opens the sliding door, which screeches along its track.

"Don't go out there, Isabelle! That deck!"

239

Henry calls from down the hall.

He's right. They really need to talk to Remy about replacing those rotting boards. She sticks her head outside instead. Sometimes the crows are high, high up, and sometimes lower, like tonight, low enough that you can see the ribs in their wings and their thick, round bodies, shiny and satin-black. They seem especially eerie but also especially right in this fall evening sky. You could see this hundreds of times and it would still give you a little shiver.

Mystery of mysteries!

When the crows are gone, Isabelle takes her phone into the bathroom. She locks the door. She looks up the *mystery* line. She's been looking up everything lately — all furtive, clandestine searches for reassurance. It's the sort of hunting for information that's actually hope that you won't find what you fear you'll find. She locates the poem. It bothers her that it's called "Spirits of the Dead."

You are hiding in your own bathroom, Maggie points out.

Why is she even here with him? She can't do this. She is not generous and trusting enough to handle any of this. What if she is not generous and trusting enough to handle any relationship? Her mother wasn't.

Henry is reading her mind again, through the walls of his office this time, because there he is. He's coming out of one door and she's coming out of another, and he takes her in his arms in the hall.

"Writing is like exercise, isn't it? You always feel so much better after you've done it. Thanks for your understanding, love." He kisses her neck. He's told her a million times that this, this phase right now, is an adjustment period. Learning to accept his past, forgiving him for lying, even moving in together at all. There will be rocky patches. It will take time. They'll get through it together.

The word *phase* — listen, it's a warning sign.

When the sun drops, it gets cold fast. He brings her one of her own blankets and wraps it around her shoulders where she sits on the couch. He's attentive this way. Her mother would have said *smothering*. Clearly, she likes smothering. He makes a beautiful fettuccine. There is chewy sourdough and a lovely salad with a tart vinaigrette. She is seduced with butter. She shoves away that stupid poem as they eat — that poem with its spirits who never go away, whose red orbs are like a burning and a fever that will cling to you forever.

They do something unusual. They leave the dishes. Henry hates to have a messy kitchen in the morning. But this night, he takes her hand, and they drop clothes along the way to their bedroom. Her worries drop away, too, and her incessant thoughts quiet. It's just her naked self and his, animals in their den, mates. His eyes catch hers in the dark and hold. She sees who he really is in there, thank goodness. That's Henry, and God, Henry feels so good.

"I love you," he whispers.

"I love you, too," she says. He can tell she means it because she *does* mean it. She means it thoroughly and completely. She's crazy about that man, even if people might say she's just plain crazy. She's sick and tired of people and what they say. All people — the sensible voices in her head, and her mother, and Virginia and Sarah, and newspapers, and Jane and Eddie, and detectives. All of this worry and weirdness is worth it. He's right. It's an adjustment period. It's hard, but in the end what matters is that it's the two of them getting through this together.

There will come a day when this strange time is in the past. Isabelle forgets, though, that both strange times and the past are a burning and a fever that can cling to you forever.

While both Isabelle and Henry are more likely to be reading than watching sports, Henry occasionally likes to catch a game on TV, especially now that the New England Patriots are playing the Seattle Seahawks, meaning Henry's brothers are texting him various bets and taunts and he is texting them back bigger ones and so forth and so on. Before this day, Isabelle would not know a Patriot from a Bruin, but Henry has appointed Isabelle his Seattle rival, surprising her with her first-ever sports jersey. While Evan would watch sports alone or with his friends (including Heather the Snowboarder, probably), Henry has made it all good, American fun. He wraps tiny sausages in biscuits, and he has made a three-layer dip. There are hot wings coming.

Midway, Isabelle wishes she had a book, even if Henry is explaining all the parts that make it entertaining — one player's sad childhood, another's inspirational comeback after an injury. There is lining up and crashing and more lining up and crashing and that announcer voice and shrill crowd hum that make her brain feel like it's a blinking fluorescent light.

Henry looks adorable in his Patriots shirt, though, and she jabs his ribs with her feet from her end of the couch. He grabs her ankles and scoots her on her butt as she shrieks.

"Looking for trouble, Missy?"

"Your players are losers." She knows nothing about it. He yanks her ponytail and then tickles her madly and she tries to get him back and then they start kissing, and then he flips her around so that she's on his lap.

"I make football better, right?" It's the perfect Sunday.

"You are the official pain in my ass."

She gets him again, with her elbows and fingertips, and the crowd cheers and they miss a big play.

"Aw, shit, what'd we miss?" he asks, but it doesn't matter. In two seconds, his pants are down, and her new jersey is off, and her mouth is on him, and no one cares about any game. It's over fast, the great kind of fast, hard and physical, same as smashing players. He collapses on her. Oh, they are sweaty.

"Look at us," she says. She feels so happy. They're half on the couch, half off, and there are napkins dotted orange from wings tossed on the floor, and strewn pillows and clothes. Her hair is bunching from the band.

"We win this game," he says. He strokes her face, but then suddenly he lifts off of her. "Stay right here. Hell with it. I was going to wait until some big, important moment, but why? This is perfect. This is what I most love about us." This last part he shouts from the far-off land of the inside of their closet.

He's back. He's naked. She's sitting up, panties back on, clutching her shirt. "Just a sec," he says. He shoves on his pants, belt dangling. Of course, she sees what's in his hand.

"Be my wife," he says.

My. Something Evan never said. Maybe something nobody ever said, certainly not her own disappearing father, or even her mother, whose *my* was more *mine,* or even *me,* indicating ownership, and giving her the sense that she was a Christmas tree laden with ornaments and tinsel and popcorn strings and blinking lights and non-blinking lights, still required to be merry in spite of the weight and the fire hazard.

But Henry's *my* feels — right then, anyway — like the softest, most safe version of *my.* A longed-for version. The coziest belonging, the big dream fulfilled, a merging without suffocation.

My, though. *My* at all . . . *Well, never mind*

that right now, she thinks.

He slips the ring on her finger. They admire it and smile at each other. The smile is an answer, Henry knows. Look at her, with a diamond ring! She and Evan bought plain gold bands at an online store. He'd take his off to shower and leave it on the sink for days. How strange and old-fashioned this ring feels, like she's completed something in a way she never had with Evan. It's beautiful. She's never been a jewelry person, but she loves how it glints like the tips of waves do on a sunny day. And, you know, she has time, she tells herself. She has time to let her questions resolve themselves. Right now, she can just enjoy this strange, new weight on her finger. Right now, she can just sink into this relieving feeling of her uncertain future, settled.

"It looks a little big for you, actually," he says.

CHAPTER 18

Sometimes, it seems there really is a tiny cartoon devil and a tiny cartoon angel on his shoulders, like in those bad movies. Probably, Weary would have two identical ravens instead. The birds would be messengers from heaven and hell, and you couldn't tell which was which, same as in Poe's most famous poem. In spite of the complicated mess of his actions, though, the point is — Weary believes in goodness and in justice. He believes in making things right, even his own wrongdoings.

He sometimes has guilt, in other words.

He sometimes has misgivings.

A beautiful word, really, *misgivings*. He imagines the strange gifts crows bestow on humans they come to have affection for — screws and bottle caps and dead bugs, shiny, sharp glass, fishing lures, and small Matchbox cars plucked from yards. They are misgivings, but special givings, too.

Well, crows do love their shiny things.

Shiny things like diamond rings, he sings to himself. It's both a cheerful and sickening song. Weary saw the Visa bill. Tiffany's, wow. Spare no expense, Mr. Marvelous. Sarah's ring was some vintage thing. No sense getting jealous on Sarah's behalf, but still.

Weary walks up the many, many steps into the Cathédrale St. Joseph Nouméa. He crosses the doorway, with its two rectangular spires on either side. Each has a clock set high up in their stone, and the Virgin Mary holds infant Jesus in a lofty cupola between them. Weary chooses this large, busy place over the smaller mission church for privacy. Services are over. It's nearing late afternoon. Inside, it is smaller than it looks from out, just two rows of wood pews and one chandelier, which resembles a double-tiered wedding cake made from iron. It's quiet, except for the click of his sandals on the floor and the whispers of tourists, who snap photos. It smells all warm wood and wax in there. Above Weary's head, the structure of the dome looks like a splayed bird wing.

Weary kneels on a padded bench. What he says is between him and God, but the basics are: He asks for forgiveness. He has done much wrong, that's for sure. He most definitely requires an understanding God.

Weary has always tried hard at religion, ever since he was a child. He used to kneel by his bed with his little hands folded and his eyes clamped shut, even when his parents didn't require it. You can be a scientist who does not strictly believe, yet you can still hope there is some being in the world who will comprehend your muddled motivations, see past your criminal turns, who knows your heart.

He lights a candle for Virginia and for Sarah. Then he lights a third for Isabelle.

Back outside, Weary winds his way through the streets. He hurries past the large hotels out near the marina where the cruise ships come in, and the stacked apartments with their overhanging balconies, and pastel-colored shops. He rushes around tourists in their shorts and tank tops, who stroll and pluck in the outdoor Le Marché de Nouméa. He passes that hideous McDonald's. See? He lacks for nothing if he goes into the city, even Quarter Pounders. The lush quiet of the mountain and his tucked-away home is good, but big and busy is good, too.

Especially today. This city visit is for prayers and practical needs and tending to a generalized passion with no usual outlet. In an enterprise like this, one requires people who lend a hand and keep your confidences, a single person you can trust, either because they care about you, like Weary's dear Gavin Gray, or because they are maybe without conscience, like Jean-Marie. Weary calls Jean-Marie *petit chief,* because he acts like a little chief, the way he can get anyone to do anything.

Weary waits for Jean-Marie outside Le Bilboquet, at one of the tables under the green striped awning. Weary orders a shot of liquor. It's too early, but he needs the courage. The alcohol spirals with the heat of the day, though, and makes Weary's head feel strange. He watches the building. Watches, watches, until — there. Yes, finally. Jean-Marie has appeared on his balcony. He is smoking a cigarette. He has a movie-star profile.

It's the signal. The last thing Weary needs is to be seen with someone like that in public. He slips a few francs under the bill and crosses the busy street. A taxi honks at him. The lobby of the apartment building is sweltering. You'd think Jean-Marie could afford a place with air-conditioning.

Weary rides the elevator up. Then he is at Jean-Marie's door. It's open just a crack, and Weary pushes inside.

"Cela fait longtemps," Jean-Marie says. It's

been a while.

"I have —" Weary removes the folded sheet from his pocket. It's a list. The things he'll need next, and the things he'll eventually need. Now that a ring is in the picture, he has to get a move on. These matters take time, even if Jean-Marie can get anybody anything.

"Put it there."

Weary sets the list on a table. There is a large Kanak print hanging over it, a woodcut image of an octopus, white and black, with tentacles reaching. What is creature and what is water is unclear.

"Venez ici." Come here.

In the States, one might call this one-stop shopping. Jean-Marie is likely a sociopath, but he is a handsome one. What's a person to do? And Jean-Marie keeps his mouth shut. They have . . . *an alliance,* Weary might call it.

In seconds, Weary's tunic is off, and so are his shorts. God, it's hot. They are on Jean-Marie's bed, under the ceiling fan, which *whir-whir-whir*s and wobbles unnervingly. It's quick, but after so long, that's how it works. Weary still has needs. In spite of his preoccupation with justice, his body still hums and then hums louder until the hum must be addressed. *Addressed,* dear Jesus,

Jean-Marie is gorgeous and incredible, a psycho-God.

And Weary . . . Well, yes, there are the small vanities, the physical truths: the gray streaks appearing in his hair, the imperfect parts of his body in spite of the laps in the pool, but so what. He is beautiful enough. He still has a pulse; he still feels the pulse deep within him. In spite of all the heartache over Sarah . . . Well, come on. He's not dead yet.

CHAPTER 19

The season shifts again. The leaves drop, clog up drainpipes. Torrents of rain whoosh down, forming small rivers in the gutters and big splashy pools around the street corners. Those months in the Northwest soak everything — lawns and socks and tree limbs, which drip drops on your head. Big windstorms pass through, shedding pine needles and tossing branches like angry cavemen throwing their clubs. They lose power for a few days, and while Isabelle is used to this and gathers the candles and flashlights and blankets, Henry is not. Every time he hits the light switch out of habit and only gets the impotent flick, he swears.

This season of gray is hard for new residents. Everyone else is accustomed to the monotone curtain that falls sometime in October and stays down until spring. Locals welcome it. Sure, it's an endless wetness across the spectrum from drizzle to downpour, but it's the tucking-in season. You put on your sweater and you get stuff done. Who would do anything if it were sunny all the time? Who would ever get down to business? Sun in the Northwest means play. This gray means head-down productivity, plus the best, most cozy weekends of books and movies and pajamas worn at all hours. Maybe breakfast in a café with windows dribbling rain. Because who wants to hike and sail and climb and road trip in *this*? Ah, fall. Locals drudge through the drops, happy to have their months of complaining back again. The birds look miserable, and everything is back as it should be after that brief, wild sun-party.

Meanwhile, the folks who've just moved here flirt with suicide.

"How can you stand it?" Henry asks. "Will it ever be anything but gray?"

"Look, there are a hundred shades of gray. It has its own beauty."

"Will it ever stop raining?"

"Maybe in June. You knew about this when you moved here."

"Yeah, but . . . *Jesus*. It's so *depressing*."

Isabelle fears that Northwest weather is like the holidays or a sudden illness — it brings out who you most are. If you are easygoing and industrious you'll learn to knit, and if you are moody, you'll only see despair in the stark branches set against the sky. And this sodden time makes Henry turn his collar up and hunch. He drags the trash cans to the street like a disgruntled employee, and when the wind howls through the trees, he paces and eyes the limbs suspiciously to see what might fall next. He stares out to the waters of the sound, watching them crash and roar, like the fretful wife of a sea captain.

It makes him feel some sense of impending doom, a lack of safety, Isabel guesses. A metaphorical something blasting through his roof. She catches him on the computer, looking up his own name. Searching for any new development that might mean he'll be hearing a knock at their door. His uneasiness makes her uneasy. The windows rattle and thunder rumbles as it does, as is usual. This year, though, it makes her jumpy, too.

This evening after dinner, he is wrapped in a quilt, and he is wearing puffy down slippers on his feet as he watches TV. It feels like an overreaction. It feels like pouting and drama. It's cold in Boston, too, after all. Henry's arms are folded. It's the adjustment period, maybe. Or just the weather, or this island, which doesn't suit him after all, or else his life catching up to him again, now that their romance is turning to relationship. She thinks of Clyde Belle in this house, what he did out there on those rocks with that gun.

Henry can be hard to talk to. At least, anything that appears to be rejection has to be handled with care. You could say most anything to Evan. Probably, because he didn't much care what you thought. Isabelle sits down next to Henry. She sets a hand on his quilt-thick leg.

"Henry?"

"Mmm?"

"I was thinking . . ."

"What?"

"You know lately, this gloom . . . Maybe it would help if you, I don't know, got a job or volunteered somewhere, or took up a new hobby. I think most people find that if they just stay locked up inside they feel worse . . ."

"Isabelle, I've been working all my life. I have another job now. I have a book to write."

Every time he says this, she inwardly groans. First of all, Henry did not leave his life in Boston to merely follow a creative urge. Second, she's met plenty of people who quit their jobs to write, and they're always like this, indulgently imagining that they're Hemingway hanging out at Les Deux Magots, when they're just themselves in a Starbucks, racking up debt on their Visas. Quitting a job to linger in casinos and play the nickel slots is a saner option.

Underneath her eye rolling and inward groaning, though, there's a quieter and more important question. It's been bothering her. She doesn't understand what he's doing with this book, and what he hopes to accomplish. Does he really envision publishing a volume of poetry as anyone else might? Is it some vast self-deception, some fervent wish that his public past will just be *overlooked*?

She can't ask. It's a prettily wrapped package with a bomb in it, sitting on their living room floor. Those packages seem to be stacking up.

"Well, maybe you shouldn't stay here all day, then. Can you go to the library? You know, like you did when we first met? You need to get out."

"Out of the house, there's a target on my back. People know about me. People talk. I feel it. I'm sick and tired of it. I need a rest from that misery. There's nothing you need to solve here."

But he doesn't take his arms out of the quilt or make a move of any kind. He stays

257

wrapped up in that cocoon. It seems like someone ought to solve something.

"You're not yourself."

"I'm fine. Maybe we should set a wedding date. *That* would help."

"Henry." It's an ongoing dispute.

"You ask what will help, and when I tell you what will help, you don't want to do it."

"I *do* want to, just not yet. I told you. It's too soon. I can't rush into it."

"Maybe rushing would be good for a change. How long did you date Evan before you finally married?"

"That was his doing, and you know it. If we're going to be married forever, it doesn't hurt to take our time now."

"And you wonder why I'm depressed?"

"I'm sorry, Henry."

"It's not your fault. It's my fault. It's me. If I hadn't come with all of this . . . baggage. We'd be riding off into the sunset. You'd think I was a good catch. You'd think you were lucky to have me."

"Henry, stop."

He looks at her, raises an eyebrow. He looks mad. Maybe furious. She can't tell what's sadness or depression or anger or need. She can't tell what's the burden of his old life, or the weather, or the way she's not measuring up. Before now, she thought he was just sensitive and depressed about his past, but she wonders if maybe he's just sensitive and depressed.

She unwraps the blanket.

"Don't," he says.

She does anyway. She has to solve and worry and charm and make right. Her heart pumps guilt to the different parts of her body. The guilt travels to her organs and muscles and to her nervous system. It's part of her structure. It's the message that travels among the other essential messages of hunger and fear and safety. She folds herself up in the blanket with him. When she glances at his face, his cheek muscles are tense and his eyes distant.

Quiet works, too. Soft steps. As a child, Isabelle would just wait out the storm. She stayed still. She made herself as small as possible. Fear and stress hunched down with her. They wriggled inside, snipped the pathways of her brain that said *run,* messed with the control board. They turned the anxiety dials all the way to the right, shut down the switches for memory and survival, and settled in for the long haul.

With her head on Henry's chest, she can hear the thump and squall inside of him. It sounds like a storm in there, too. The rush of his own blood and the gust of emotions sound terrible enough to name, same as a hurricane. It could be named *Depression* or *Confusion* or *Post-traumatic Stress*. It should maybe just be called *Tempest*.

It should maybe be called indigestion, *Isabelle. Stop making people so much larger than yourself.*

She ignores the Maggie in her head. The big thing she knows about storms is that they always pass. They always come back, though, too. Somehow, down in the storm cellar, she always forgets that part.

The gray of fall transforms into the deeper gray of winter. Every now and then, just to keep everyone on their toes, a blue-sky day appears, and everything is covered with the white glitter of frost. On Main Street, the Christmas decorations go up — loops of fake evergreen boughs, wreaths hanging on the lampposts. The tree in front of the library gets adorned with strings of colored lights, and big gold and red ornaments the size of grapefruits. Jane knits Isabelle a scarf. It's a gesture of love. It's four feet of woolen mutual forgiveness. It's an expression of reluctant acceptance of Henry, which means Isabelle really can't confess the truth now, about Henry's troubling moods and her own strange bouts of unease. She hasn't said a word about any of that, and so it looks like those secrets will stay secrets. Still, every one of those stitches say that Jane is in her corner, no matter what.

"It's beautiful," Isabelle says, and winds it around her neck.

"Just how I imagined. That blue with your eyes," Jane says. She plucks and adjusts the scarf, stands back and nods her approval.

"I didn't know you could knit," Eddie says.

"I learned. Margaret MacKenzie gave a class at the library."

"I guess you *can* teach an old dyke new tricks." Eddie chuckles.

"Where's mine?" Joe says. "I want one."

Pilots Louise and Liz meet eyes, and Liz rolls hers. They are hoping they don't get invited to the family Christmas dinner.

"Thank you." Isabelle kisses Jane's cheek.

And maybe, *maybe,* there won't even be any more unsettling moments that she should be divulging to the people who care about her. Maybe it all *has* been a phase. Because, shortly after, Henry cheers up. Sarah's life insurance company, New Haven Providence, has informed him that after nearly three years, they've completed their investigation. Sarah has been declared dead in absentia, her death ruled accidental, and they will be sending him a check. It is not the anticipation of the money that lifts his spirit, he says again and again. It's the evidence of redemption. *Accidental* confirms Henry's story, that they had been arguing and drinking and that later that night, Sarah drowned while taking the dinghy ashore. *If an insurance company can't find a way* not *to pay, well, then . . .* he says. They celebrate. The celebration feels wrong to Isabelle. Sarah is still dead. The pop of the champagne cork startles Isabelle like a gunshot.

Isabelle has retrieved her winter coats from the storage box at Island Air, and they now hang on the guitar hooks in the closet. It makes the coats look strange, like an imposing army of men, shoulders up to threaten their enemies. It's an illusion. She grabs the black wool one, then her purse and keys.

"Heading to work!" she calls.

Henry is just out of the shower. His hair is wet and he smells all soapy clean and toothpasty mint. His towel is wrapped around his bottom half, a sweatshirt hastily thrown on top.

"Kiss goodbye!" he commands playfully.

He tastes good. She loves his ass in that towel, and gives it a grab. He looks into her eyes. "Let me see you," he says.

"I'm late."

"They'll go on without you. You should really just sell that place and we could travel. You're always talking about wanting to do that."

"I am?"

"You are."

"I'd be bored without a job. I'd get cranky."

"You're still beautiful when cranky."

He's trying to start something. He kisses her more slowly, trickles one hand into her white blouse, runs the other down the back of her black jeans. She doesn't know why he's doing this now. He knows she's meeting Jane early to go over the winter schedule, vacations, and the hiring of extra contract pilots. It's almost a test, she thinks. One of those horrible loyalty tests you can never win because they're not meant to be won. They're meant to demonstrate how a person is victimized, how they never get what they want, not from you, the withholding daughter-friend-lover, who is letting them down. *Me or them,* the kiss asks, the hand demands.

"Henry."

"Just come here."

"I've got to *go.*"

He pulls away. There's that slight exhale, the *whff* from the side of the mouth, a succinct report on the extent of one's flaws.

"Tonight," she says. "Rain check."

He reaches up and fastens the next highest button of her blouse. "Showing off for Joe?"

"Silly. You know Joe's practically a brother to me."

"I wonder if he acted like a brother when you lived with him for that month."

She gives him a little shove before she leaves, because he's joking. She's sure he is. Mostly sure. Virginia had male friends in her life, after all. At least, Isabelle heard the story of how she and Henry met, two groups of pals canoeing. But Sarah had that professor, the ornithologist, who Henry suspected was more than a friend. Whenever he comes up in conversation, Henry's tone turns sarcastic and spiteful. *He was probably in love with her,* Henry once said, *while she likely just admired his birdbrain.* According to Jerry, there was more than that to admire, since he was attractive and charismatic. Who can say? The point is, Henry seemed to honestly believe in some relationship between them, which is likely why he's so watchful about Joe.

Evan could not have cared less about any

other men in her midst, at least after his early flare of jealousy flamed out. She could have walked around naked, sitting on the laps of rivals, and he wouldn't have even noticed. It's kind of nice to be powerful enough to spark a little possessiveness.

What's weird, though, is that she doesn't feel powerful. Henry's hand buttoning up her shirt like that — it gives her a funny squeezing in her chest. What is it? Something bad. A strange, small dread. Her spirit shrinks, as if it's in one of those plastic bags you connect to your vacuum to suck the air out.

Isabelle drives down Main Street. The wreaths and the boughs seem to tilt strangely. Maybe it's because Nathan the artist and Roddy Jones hung them after the Beer and Books club meeting. Or maybe it's because her personal ground has shifted.

On this Saturday morning, Henry fries eggs. There is the crackle and spit of hot butter as Isabelle sits on a counter stool, blabbing on about Kit and the passenger he had, the one who brought so much luggage a second plane had to be hired. It's stupid, she knows. Why is she even doing this? But since Henry's comment, she's careful to avoid mentioning poor, innocent Joe. Joe was the pilot of the second plane, but she lies. Or, rather, she edits. In the telling, she changes the identity of the pilot, turns Joe into Liz. Now she starts to tell another story about Maggie, how one time she got pissed at a rude passenger and tacked a "handling fee" onto her credit card, when Henry, who is sliding eggs onto two plates, suddenly stops. He's caught sight of something out their kitchen window.

"Sarah, look," he says.

He doesn't even realize what he's done, because he's so intent on the small wood-pecker right outside on their tree. The bird is a stunner, all right, a real showstopper, with his fluffy black-and-white-striped head with its swath of red, and those black-and-white-spotted wings. Isabelle has frozen there, holding the forks. Henry turns, sees her, realizes.

"Oh, crap."

"It's okay."

"I'm sorry. I can't believe I just said that. I saw the bird, and . . ."

"It's all right. I understand."

She does, sort of. Birds were Sarah's passion. Isabelle holds those forks as the eggs, shiny with grease, get cold. The bird *bam-bam-bam*s the tree. Sarah's name hangs there in the air.

"Open mouth, insert foot," Henry says.

It's more than just a casual blunder, because her name immediately exhumes the body disappeared at sea. It shouts the fact that Sarah was a real, living woman, who once sat in a kitchen with Henry, about to eat eggs. It's a slap of a reminder. She was a woman to whom he would say *Sarah, look!* A woman who then might stand beside him to watch a woodpecker. Her lungs were full, and her heart was beating.

The woodpecker drills for insects buried deep in the trunk of that tree. Isabelle feels sick. She doesn't want those eggs. She just wishes buried things would stay buried.

They huff and stomp in the cold. There's a light layer of snow on the ground at Andresen's Tree Farm, a forty-five-minute drive outside of Anacortes. Okay, fifty-sixty minutes, after the ferry ride, and then there was the trek up the mountain, and the walk out into the forest with the saw. It was farther than she remembered. Well, she'd done this back in high school with a group of friends. A group of friends that included Joe, which is something she doesn't say. This is getting really silly, because Joe has no idea he's become a bit player in her homelife drama. When she sees Joe, he's the one who

says, *So, hey, how's it going with the prof?*
He's the supportive friend who even suggests they all go get a beer together sometime. Meanwhile, Henry bristles when after-work gatherings are mentioned, and he drops little questions about Joe as if he suspects they've reignited their high school romance and have embarked on a torrid affair.

Lately, too, Evan has been getting slings and arrows, derisive comments about jocks and salesmen, to the point she's becoming slightly protective of Evan, who didn't have a Ph.D. and who couldn't cook fine foods or speak eloquently about American literature. And like she also did with Evan, Isabelle has cut the number of men she's had sex with by half when recounting her history. Henry doesn't need to know about that artist, either. It's her business. Maybe all men have a jealous streak. Do they? She has no idea. Jealous streak — it sounds almost fashionable, like those people with black hair with a swath of white in front.

Lies! One of the ten signs of a healthy relationship! Maggie says, up there on the mountain.

"It's beautiful, isn't it?" Isabelle says.

From where they stand, they can see the Andresens' barn, set picturesquely on the far hill, which is surrounded by next year's baby trees. They are walking among the larger, taller ones, which grow larger and taller still the farther they walk. In the distance, she can hear children laughing and shouting. A dog barks and barks. She cups her mittened hands around her nose and breathes in and out to warm it.

"It's beautiful, yeah," Henry agrees. "It's far. Is everyone here opposed to just getting a tree in a grocery store parking lot?"

"Don't be so stingy." Isabelle puts her arms around him from behind, and they step like a puffy-coat-plus-a-puffy-coat giant.

"Hypothermia doesn't make me feel generous."

"Get in the spirit."

They walk a little, holding hands. "This one," he says.

"This one?" They've barely looked at all. She would like to hunt around a bit, debating the pros and cons.

"It's freezing." He stomps his feet to keep warm. "Plus, it's great. It looks just like a postcard of a Christmas tree."

He's right, and so she says, "Let's do it."

He kneels. Of course, the knees of his jeans get immediately wet. He leans under the dripping branches, sets saw against wood. It's like taking a plastic knife to a pork roast. Not much happens.

He wipes his brow. He tries again, as Isabelle feels the tension build. This was all a bad idea, and the degree of badness grows. First, there was the too-long car ride, and then the wait in line for the saw as Mrs. Andresen chatted merrily with a family of five, and then the hard hike up, and now this — this academic, this professor, kneeling on snowy ground and attempting to fell a tree. She had imagined something else — something holiday-magic-ish. Something fun — new romance, their first tree. She hadn't pictured the way the elbows of his nice down coat are muddying and how the slit he's made in the trunk is still only as thick as an envelope.

Now she says something bad. At least, something that only makes everything worse. "Can I help?"

"I can cut down a fucking tree, Isabelle."

She is silent. In the silence, her mother perks up, irritating as a wind chime.

This is your dream man, this insecure asshole with two dead women in his past?

Shut up, shut up, shut up! Isabelle thinks. It's nothing she'd have ever said to Maggie in real life. *And shut up to everyone else with a comment, too! This is one, small event. One story.*

Should she name every kindness now? Every soft and loving word? Every conversation about Sarah and Virginia, where he's cried and poured out his heart? Should she enumerate every time he's been patient and generous and humorous? If there were some accounting sheet, some log of this versus that, some way to measure the whole, he'd come out shining.

He'd better rack up forty-fifty sweet nothings after the way he just talked to you, Iz.

Her mother is right. Damn it! She is. And Isabelle *wants* to storm and fume at Henry, kneeling and sweating in the snow. She wants to rail, because she's only trying hard here, trying to make a fun holiday, trying to lighten their lives and bring joy and create new memories. He doesn't have to snap. He doesn't have to ruin everything.

She doesn't fume, though. She doesn't hurl a retort or return to the car without either him or the fucking tree. But in that junk pile where her anger is buried, an old bicycle settles and a paint can shifts, and there's a little shimmer of something. She remembers another Christmas, when she was just a child and she tried to make cookies in their kitchen. She wanted to make the ones she saw in magazines, but there was flour everywhere and she'd spilled the red sugar she'd found way back in the cabinet, and Maggie was yelling, screaming, her face contorted. One day, in that junk pile, piece will connect with piece and the monster will be built and he will be fierce. She will fume and snap and rail, and fucking weenie men with fancy Ph.D.s and lame poems and bully mothers and bully everyones will step back and tremble at the flames coming from her mouth.

But now she says nothing. There's only the grunt and exhale of Henry's effort, and her own breath still hovering in the cold air. The fix they are in grows along with the badness of this idea, because he *can't* cut down a fucking tree. Or maybe he could, but it might take until next month around this same time. By then, they'd be half dead and starving and frozen and Christmas would be over, but the thing would finally come crashing down. So he *can't,* basically, and she feels a laugh, a gleeful, spiteful *ha-ha* dancing around somewhere in there, in the vindictive recesses of her mind. It stays there, of course, with all the other dangerous things.

He flings his coat off. "This isn't helping." It's the jacket's fault, for sure.

Isabelle doesn't know what to do. She watches, she looks away, she frets inwardly. There is so much trunk left, it's like they were never here. "Let's just forget it," she says.

Well, that's wrong, too, of course. What isn't, at this point?

"Jesus, Isabelle, really? And don't tell me, because I don't want to hear it, how that asshole Evan could probably cut this down in two seconds."

Of course, she would never say something like that. She had never in her life said something like that. Honestly, it's a weird thing to even come out of his mouth. It's almost . . . She doesn't want to think the word, so she doesn't, not outright. Instead, the word drifts around her mind like a ghoul: *disturbing.* She feels that word in her chest, and it sits alongside the other one she felt the day he buttoned up her blouse: *dread.* They are bad words, paired up. Henry is still trying to saw and his armpits are ringing with sweat and his hair is falling over his face. No one is around. Not one person. There are no sounds of children or dogs anymore. They're on a mountainside, alone.

Before she thinks what she is going to think, she takes off. She starts running.

"Isabelle! What are you doing?"

"Getting help!"

"Fine!" he shouts. "Whatever!"

Now her chest really hurts, but from cold, from slicing blades of frigid air plus the physical exertion of sprinting down the trail. They'd gone pretty far, after all. She's glad to be back at the shingled shed, where Mrs. Andresen rings up purchases and hands out candy canes. Mrs. Andresen's son, Drew, follows Isabelle back up. He's jovial, with cheeks like round, red apples. He knows his way around the mountain, and knows his way around those trees and the egos of men from the city.

"Some of those trunks are hard as rock," he says, when they arrive.

"I'm glad it's not just me," Henry says.

"Nah," Drew says.

Drew hauls the tree back down as if it's a bag of oranges. He tosses it up on Maggie's old car and ties it down, rodeo style. "There you are, folks."

Henry soothes his bruised self-esteem with a fat tip. But he scootches and squirms the entire drive home, making a point about the discomfort of his wet clothes. Isabelle keeps her eye on the tree. The last thing they need is to lose it on the freeway.

"What's the problem?" he asks, when

they're finally on the ferry heading home. They don't even get out of the car. They just sit in Maggie's Acura with the tree on top, packed among the other cars. The ferry deck rumbles as the scenery speeds past.

"Honestly?" she says.

They fight. It feels dangerous, fighting in that car with nowhere to go. She could get out, but she'd only be on a moving boat in the middle of the icy sound.

Are they fighting too much? All couples fight. Is he too insecure? Everyone has faults. Is he *guilty,* after all? No! No, of course not. He is a victim of tragic circumstances, and even New Haven Providence agrees. Look, there it is in the mail when they arrive home — that check, finally. New Haven Providence has done much to quiet any doubts, because Henry's right. If an insurance company actually pays . . . And when he opens that envelope, she can see that he is a man who has been under much stress. He has been through *hell.* They make up. Today, he has simply been a struggling human being with elbows and knees now muddied like a child's, a man who wants to be big in the eyes of the woman he loves.

She understands this, but bigness is beginning to be a strange concept. Because . . . Something is happening. Amid the loudness and largeness of the holiday — the clamorous bell ringing and looming, lit trees and gigantic candy canes in yards; the colossal blow-up Santas and mammoth reindeer on roofs and the supersized manger with the huge baby Jesus and the enormous, can't-miss-it, tinsel-glitter guiding star on the church lawn — Isabelle is shrinking.

CHAPTER 20

Weary is angry. He is raging, stomping, furious. It's a beautiful, blooming anger. It opens like a flower, or like the jawed pod, the carnivorous clamshell mouth of the Nepenthes pitcher plant. Maybe he should be furious with New Haven Providence instead of with Henry North. No! Since he opened his bedroom computer on this balmy winter night and saw the check deposited into Henry's account, he's raging at both of them and at everything in general. He wants to light things on fire or start an earthquake.

How was Weary able to see this deposit? None of your business. Let's just say people should change their passwords. Let's just say even people who are supposedly so smart are stupid, the way they keep a favorite word for years on end, the way they choose something utterly predictable (*Nevermore?* Please), the way they use the same password on every account from their old university email to phone companies to banks to online stores. Let's just say that if you think he's only been snooping in ShutR and a single Visa bill all this time (his best sources, granted), you're kidding yourself.

What the hell is up with New Haven Providence? Police, insurance investigators — it all could have stopped there. It *should* have stopped — finis! *Complète!* — if people were doing their jobs. Weary could have folded up shop right then, went back to his quiet life among the *Corvus.*

Idiots! Losers in leisure suits, fat men in uniforms! He knew this would happen, too. He *knew it*! And nothing, *nothing,* makes you more furious than being proven correct. Just as he suspected when Sarah disappeared, after news reports started dwindling, after there were no more revelations of late-night fights or drunk arguments on boats, after Virginia's relatives retreated back into their lives, after detectives made only one measly phone call to the New Caledonia Corvus Research Facility and Sanctuary to ask questions — it's essentially over, from an official standpoint. The insurance check is written, and the police and DAs have pretty much moved on to cases they can solve and prosecute. His last hope for a legitimate solution is gone. Henry North escapes punishment! Twice! And he goes on his merry way with a fat wad of cash!

No one will care about Sarah anymore. No one's cared about Virginia for a long time.

It's up to Weary now.

And it's up to Isabelle. Poor Isabelle.

It's time, anyway. The ring, plus the passage of a few months, means Henry North has started the peck, peck, peck at Isabelle's spirit, Weary is sure. This is what happened with Sarah as soon as commitment entered the picture, and Henry North will keep on being his insecure and narcissistic self, sure as corvid Yves will be sneaky and Little Black will be gentle and Corbie will be aggressive when thwarted.

After the ring and the wedding, the slide was swift for Sarah. Why did she stay? Why does any woman (or man, for that matter) stay? The swiftness of the slide is part of it, that's what people don't understand. You're down, down, down in the pit before you know it, and the walls are high and slick and there are no toeholds. You are so small and your voice is tiny while you're there at the bottom. No one would hear you, anyway. Something feels a little familiar about the darkness, too.

And, yes, Sarah lacked "self-esteem" certainly, that magical potion people seem to have either too much or too little of. She had to summon it and fight for it, he knows. She left home and got an education and established herself at the university. But her strength was fragile, wasn't it? Contingent on the external, and Henry North flipped the switch hidden way down inside. He was something recognized, something that compelled her. He was a remembered voice, calling. Henry North took her love and he smothered it, broke its neck. She was old, familiar prey. He was an old, familiar predator. You succumb, that's what you do, if you haven't ever learned to fight.

Where is Weary now? What is he even doing, as these thoughts roil and rumble and gather steam? He is in his closet (ha) at his home on the hill. It is night. It is dark, except for the moon and the yellow light of his room blazing. Crickets and insects chirp and bleep and party. Birds sleep. The bamboo doors of Weary's closet are flung open. You should see all the stuff in there. Clothes of various sorts, books, trinkets. Everything he acquired here in New Caledonia to fill and fill the hole of loss. He shoves all the shit he buys into that closet so he doesn't have to face his lame desire for it. His other rooms are Zen, clean-lined and simple. Inside, outside. How things look, how things are.

He hunts, but it's not truly necessary. He knows where the box is. As he pulls that box down, he thinks of the crows and their protective rage. Like something out of a horror movie, those birds will dive-bomb anyone near their young. It happens every year from June until July, when the fledglings leave the nest. The older crows will menace anyone near their vulnerable offspring, wage a vicious attack to the back of a person's head. How do you prevent it, when it's the season of fury? Wave a tennis racket, or carry an umbrella. Wear a hat; walk backward. Face them. Look at them. They will only come at you from behind.

If you harm their young, if you threaten the new, budding confidence of what is fragile in the world, well, maybe you deserve what's coming. You deserve a surprising, vicious attack that you don't see coming.

Weary sets the box on his bed. There are treasures inside. Each is the glass or the fishing lure or the Matchbox car or the tiny skull or the bottle cap that is a crow's riches. *Corvus* will gather these private gems, and they will turn them over and over again, gazing at their beauty. They will bury these treasures, to keep them away from others. And then, sometimes, as a gift, they'll offer them.

Weary is lucky to have Jean-Marie, who is not only an excellent lover and a superb procurer of documents, but also the *petit chief* of a first-rate courier service, which promises expediency and anonymity. The first package will arrive when Isabelle is alone, while Henry is away on his little trip back home, according to the ticket purchase on the Visa bill.

Weary holds the watch to his ear. It's silly — he knows it has stopped ticking. There's nothing he can do about that now. He just has an irrational wish to hear the sound and see the tiny hands move again. It reminds him of the history books he likes to read sometimes, stories of war and disasters, torpedoed ships and murdered leaders. He always hopes they'll turn out differently somehow, even though, of course, they won't. They are stories that have already happened, with the fates of the doomed determined long ago.

CHAPTER 21

On New Year's Day, Henry flies out to visit his brother Mark, Jerry, and their two daughters. He missed his family over the holidays. Isabelle stays behind. She's a believer that absence makes the heart grow fonder, or maybe she just needs some time alone. Missing a person is good for love. Longing for them is.

But after Henry leaves, it's not longing she indulges in. The first half of the day, she's full of get-it-done energy. She jumps into the sort of industriousness meant to keep oneself out of trouble and one's mind quiet. The ornaments come off the tree. She drags the dry behemoth to the curb for the Boy Scouts to pick up. She sweeps and vacuums all those needles, plucks the pointy spikes from her sweatshirt, wonders why humans put themselves through such misery every year. But just after half the lights around the windows are down, right as she picks off a piece of tape from the ceiling molding, she stops. She gets down from the stepladder. She gives in to a strange restlessness, the urge to search, which has been insistently bugging her, like a high-pitched frequency she can only somewhat hear.

She looks in their closet, full of their clothes hanging on their hangers, same as they are every day. She smells one of Henry's shirts. Ahh. Notice: It's love she mostly feels. Then why this, now? Why is she fishing in these pockets? Pants, jackets. She finds a foil-wrapped stick of gum, some coins, some lint. She looks in their dresser drawer, in the wood box he keeps there. Older coins, some cuff links, a teeny tiny key, a watch with a slinky metal band. His old wedding ring. She already knew these things were here. She places the ring on her left index finger, same as Sarah once did to Henry.

Get that creepy thing off! Maggie snaps.

Isabelle moves on to Henry's office. The musician left a sleek teak desk with two drawers, a modern swivel chair, a huge painting with yellow and black misshapen ovals that look like the routes of two drunk racecar drivers. The art isn't what you notice anyway. In that house, laid out horizontally along the cliff side, it's all about the windows, and the huge views from every room. Even this small office boasts wide vistas of the gray sound and the gray rocks and the gray inlet where the gray whales sleep. From here, she can see the squiggle of the trail down to the beach that hugs the bluff.

She sits in the chair, swivels a bit. This used be the Greggory girls' bedroom, she remembers, from when she babysat all those years ago. You'd never recognize it, as contemporary as it looks now. If she looks closely at the walls, though, Isabelle bets, she'll still be able to find the thumbtack holes from their puppy posters.

There's a cup of pens on the desk, and a blank notepad, and Henry's laptop. She takes a pen and gazes out the window like Henry might, scribbles a pretend spiral of inspiration, rips off the page and crumples it up. The house is so quiet that she can hear the *tick-tick*ing of the oven clock in the kitchen. She opens the window above the desk and inhales the sea air. A seagull screeches. The waves crash. Rain pitters against the deck and drips down the drain-pipe. She misses Henry, she thinks. At least, the house is so quiet without him that she feels its emptiness. Now that her busyness has stilled, the stark gray out those windows is almost spooky. She listens for the creak of footsteps, or the slow turn of a doorknob. No. She's fine. No one is there. It's just her and all those ghosts in her head.

Isabelle pictures Henry in his airplane seat, his earbuds playing classical, his eyes closed. She wishes she were sitting beside him holding his hand, about to visit his family and the city he spent so many years in. And she's glad she's not there. Really glad. She's happy she's not squished into the seat beside him, holding his hand, about to visit Jerry and Dr. Mark, staying in their guest room. Maybe she's meant to be alone. Unmarried. Deliciously free of people's expectations. It sort of sounds like heaven, actually.

She opens the top drawer of the desk. There's a stapler, a box of paperclips, a bottle of Wite-Out, index cards, office stuff. She moves on to the next drawer.

But, wait. Locked?

Locked! She unfolds a paperclip, jabs it in the tiny hole until she hears a mouse-sized click. This may be all the evidence she needs that Henry is not a criminal. The drawer opens easily, and she suddenly realizes that the tiny key in his dresser drawer box would have been easier yet. No criminal would be this sloppy or exert so little effort to cover up his crimes.

And there are no crimes here. Just poems, most of which she'd already seen that time on his desk, poems of ringing bells and windswept beaches and empty rooms with fluttering curtains, poems echoing the voice of his greatest, long-dead influence, Mr. Poe, with the same swirls and flourishes of language. Perhaps there's some cryptic message of guilt in them, but Isabelle doesn't think so. He is guilty of impersonating the voice of his favorite author, and he's guilty of getting a whole lot less writing done than he's implied, but the same things are true for most beginning writers.

Open me, says his laptop.

Or maybe that's Maggie again. No, because *here's* Maggie. Maggie is saying, *Snooping on his computer? Wow, true love! Why are you with this guy, if you are pushing that power button right now?*

I just need . . . Isabelle tries to explain, but she has no idea how. What does she need? Love? Safety? Or does she just need to try and try to get love and safety from a place she'll never, ever get love and safety?

Reassurance, she says to the Maggie-ghost. *I'm just looking for a little reassurance.*

Nice diamond, Maggie says.

Isabelle takes off her ring, sets it on the

notepad. Is it really snooping when he's told her all his passwords? See how transparent he is? See how open? He didn't even bring his laptop with him! It's sitting right here! What is she expecting to find, anyway? A written confession?

Nevermore, she types.

If anything, his laptop is too clean. There are a bunch of photos, but only recent ones. There's only a small amount of music. Desktop icons for his bank, his credit card, his investment company. There's a bill-paying app. A document file labeled *Poems.* He bought this laptop after he arrived here, she thinks. It's new. No wonder. She draws the line at his email. She won't find anything there, anyway, she suspects. He barely communicates with anyone. She shuts the machine down.

Half-assed detective work! What about search history? What about hidden files? Maggie says.

Isabelle hates herself.

When Henry calls later that night, she is sitting in the middle of a mess in their living room. He'd be shocked at what a disaster it is. There are old moving boxes, which she's using to pack away the Christmas decorations, open and spilling their contents. The lights still hang halfway down from the window. The screen of her own laptop is frozen on a scene midway into a bad Christmas-wedding movie. An empty Marie Callender's plastic tub, with smears of red spaghetti sauce, sits on the coffee table with a fork dropping from it. A half-empty bottle of wine is there, too, accompanied by a juice glass ringed in burgundy. The musician who used to live there would have been proud. It looks like the hotel room after the concert. She just needs to fling her panties and crash a lamp or two.

"I am sleeping in a pink bed in a pink room with a faux zebra rug," Henry says.

"You're a diva."

"Oh, and a stuffed panda where you should be."

"That sounds like good company."

"You'd be so much better. I was wrong not to insist you come. The girls want to meet their new aunt. I miss you."

"I miss you, too."

"We went for Mexican. What'd you have for dinner?"

He'd be horrified. "I had Thai Ginger delivery."

"Nice."

"The Christmas decorations are almost down."

"You're a saint."

Isabelle hears the shriek and stomping of little girls in the distance. The phone rustles and clunks. "Help, help," she hears him call from far off. "It's a princess attack!"

He's back. "Iz, they're corralling me for another round of Candyland. Talk tomorrow? I love you and miss you."

"I love you and miss you, too."

"Keep my spot warm."

"Will do."

She eats some semi-defrosted Sara Lee cheesecake straight from the tinfoil pan. She is repulsive. Also drunk. It is possible that he's too good for her. She doesn't deserve him.

She sleeps with his shirt. She wakes at 2:00 A.M. because the wind is howling and that house is too empty. All of that glass shakes in the storm. She is holding a fistful of cotton stripe, so no wonder she was having strange dreams about trying to catch a man, a delirious, unkempt man, who paced sepia-toned streets in rumpled clothing from another century.

The wind and the waves roar, and rain splatters the windows. The house trembles. She knows who the man was, the one in her dream — tortured poet, creator of detective fiction, writer of horror stories. She's hit with one of those sudden, middle-of-the-night truths, helped along by nightmares. Henry is likely more drawn to the man than to the melancholy waters and golden towers and valleys of unrest. Just the man, Poe, who longs for his mother and grieves for all the dead young women in his life. The man who was clever and brilliant and immature and a plagiarist. Isabelle remembers a professor of hers, arguing against the general theory of the lonely and misunderstood Poe, saying instead that he was small-minded and mean, with an ego so fragile that he couldn't stand to be embarrassed or diminished. Poe was generous and stingy both, the professor had said. But he wanted to be admired. He demanded pity. And he got it, especially from women, because what a tortured soul he was, and how sad it would be to be that tortured, even if he was sometimes intolerable.

Isabelle understands this, as the moon slowly slides into view in their window: the man recognizing the other man. The same personalities have existed over time, haven't they? The same weaknesses, whether in a human being wearing a waistcoat or a down jacket from REI. The pit and the pendulum, the tell-tale heart, the maelstrom, they all happen inside of a person. What tumbles around a human mind is the truly terrifying and dangerous thing. And the scared, lost child in a human being could either stay a scared, lost child or become a reactive, threatening monster.

Isabelle shoves the pillow over her head. The truth is too loud, and so is Maggie. *When are* you *going to stop being a trembling little girl, Iz? Rise up, Muchacha. How about a little* nevermore *of your own?*

It will all feel overly dramatic in the morning.

She is in her robe and barely has the coffee made when the doorbell rings. Maybe it's Remy, finally. Remy has been avoiding them, ever since Henry began nagging her about fixing the deck. Or maybe it's Officer Ricky Beaker again (Please, God, no), ready to barge in and question her. Either way, it's early, people. She hasn't even brushed her teeth yet, so she's still her disgusting single self, with old wine and now coffee breath. She notices her bare hands. She forgot to put her ring back on. It's still sitting on that pad in Henry's office.

She peeks out the front window and sees the big, brown UPS truck rumbling off. She opens the door, and she's hit with fresh, winter cold. That's right — there's life going on outside. You can forget that. She breathes in a nice, big lungful of morning. There's a padded envelope on the front step.

Curious.

And, wait. What is this? It's addressed to her. No one sends her anything, except Amazon and Nordstrom and DSW, when requested.

From who? Okay, weird, there's no return address. She's momentarily unnerved. Actually, all alone out there, she feels uneasy. Maybe this is like that pair of handcuffs that was left on their porch a few weeks after they moved in. Henry said to ignore it, because shit like that happened to him sometimes. You had to grow a thick skin and forget it.

But this has lovely, foreign stamps. The package has been sent from . . . She peers. Rochefort-en-Terre, Bretagne, France.

She doesn't know anyone from France, but her friend Anne travels a lot. She hasn't heard from her in months and months, but maybe this is why. Maybe she hasn't just disappeared because Isabelle pushed her away, her last friend, because she can't bear to be honest about her most recent romantic situation. Exotic world tour, it would be just like Anne. Isabelle feels a pang of longing for all the adventures she herself hasn't yet had. And *Rochefort-en-Terre* sounds completely harmless. It sounds like a place where cows would wear little bells.

She hopes Anne sent her a fun bracelet or something. She squishes the package, trying to guess. Maybe a bracelet. A small, long lump.

She takes it into the kitchen, opens the top with a pair of scissors. She leans against the kitchen counter, reaches in. There is no card. Just something wrapped in tissue.

She unrolls it.

Her heart flips. She feels suddenly sick. It's a watch. A woman's watch — small, oval, old. It has a brown leather band, and the band is ripped. The last few holes are torn straight down, so that there are two, tiny strips of leather. The little prong of the buckle is bent sideways. It has stopped at ten seconds after 2:40.

Isabelle shoves her hand in the envelope again, but there is nothing, no note of explanation, nothing but the watch.

The glass and metal of the watch face is cold. Isabelle turns it over.

Oh, dear God. Oh please, no. It's engraved.

Virginia Arsenault. ARHS.

She flings it in horror. It lands with a clunk under the counter, where there are cereal crumbs and spilled bits of sugar. She eyes it like it's a coiled snake, or a deadly insect.

Who sent this? What's it supposed to mean? Is it some message from Virginia's family? One of those friends in the articles, who pleaded for justice for her death? But what message is there in an old watch?

She should call the police. Then she remembers — the police won't exactly be jumping to protect her or Henry from senders of broken watches.

The house is still a wreck. She does something that underscores the general downward direction of things — takes a swig of what's left in the wine bottle along with her coffee.

She paces around. Back in the kitchen, she picks up the watch again. She sets it beside her on the couch, sits with crossed legs with her laptop. She clicks off the frozen holiday wedding movie. *Virginia Arsenault, ARHS,* she types.

Algonquin Regional High School. Virginia graduated twenty-six years ago, eight years before Isabelle herself. There's a photo of Virginia, in a small group of teenagers wearing tracksuits. She's the smallest of them, standing in the center of the front row. She's beautiful and young, with dark hair and those elfin features Isabelle recalls from the other photograph she saw. Virginia is a tiny doll.

The watch must have come from one of Virginia's sisters or her friends. Isabelle remembers their anger in those interviews after Sarah's disappearance. She looks up their names again. Mary Youngers. Florence Watanabe. Shelby Frey. With addresses in Boston, Lexington, Chelsea. Shelby's Facebook page has a profile picture of a cat, wall posts from a vacation in Hawaii. None of them has any obvious connection to Rochefort-en-Terre in Brittany, France. Maybe one of them went on a trip. Maybe they used the opportunity to hide their mailing address and their identity. Maybe they want to remind her that Virginia was a real person. Her watch is a real object, which belonged to a real human being whom they loved.

This must be it. It feels like the most logical explanation. But something is off about it, too. The watch is intimate — too treasured, one would think, to stick in the mail and send to a stranger. It has import. An eerie, distressing import. She feels shaken and disturbed. She takes the watch and shoves it deep down into one of her boots in her closet.

She can't do anything the rest of the day.

She's frozen; she sits in a chair and stares out the window, thinking. The surf breaks against the rocks again and again. She checks the locks and the windows. She feels watched.

She tells herself that she's acting crazy. She is still in her robe, the one from her mother with the crane on the back. She forces herself to put on some clothes, brush her teeth. Staying around the house in this state is not good for anyone; just ask Clyde Belle or Henry himself.

She goes out, buys some groceries. She will cook something, just to prove she can be on her own without falling to pieces. She sticks stuff in her cart and then puts it all back. She checks out the alluring array of green Marie Callender's boxes, chooses the family-size macaroni and cheese.

When she comes out of the store, she sees Kale Kramer, resident thug, smoking a cigarette over by Randall and Stein Booksellers. Who knew people even smoked anymore. But Kale Kramer is only a harmless visual distraction compared to what's disturbingly right in front of her. Officer Ricky Beaker is parked at the curb. He just sits there in his cruiser, his eyes on her. Maybe she is feeling watched because she is being watched. He follows her when she pulls out. She takes the curves of Deception Loop fast and hard to lose him, until her mind supplies images of princesses and movie stars plunging to their death from speeding cars on high cliffs. She ducks into Point Perpetua Park. It looks like Ricky Beaker has given up on her. She gets out, glances over her shoulder, but she's alone. She walks the stormy beach with her hands shoved in her pockets.

An awful thought occurs to her. What if Ricky Beaker is not hunting her, but protecting her? Somehow, this feels more terrifying. She files through her memory. Has she seen him more than usual? Driving just behind her, or parked outside of wherever she is? She doesn't know! Damn it! She's got to stop this. She tries to concentrate on her feet on that hard sand, the surf rolling in and the surf rolling out. Walking against the strong wind feels good. If she looks up, she can see both her mother's old house and the house she lives in now. She picks up some beautiful, smooth rocks from that perfect spot where water meets shore, where all the stuff both good and bad collects, and she puts them in her pocket and brings them home.

When Henry calls that night, she does not tell him about the watch. She listens to his stories about the nieces and Jerry and how Mark has a lot of patience, putting up with that bitch. The family all went out to lunch and to a movie. He bought the girls baseball caps with the restaurant's rooster on it. Tomorrow, his other brother, Jack, is expected to fly in.

She listens to his voice on the phone, and notices how those beach rocks look entirely different now that they're out of water. They've lost their magic. They're plain and dull since they're no longer where they belong. It always goes like this. Still, people just can't seem to let things be. *She* can't. She can't resist picking them up, even though this happens every time.

That night, it's impossible to sleep. Isabelle swears she can hear that dead watch ticking from inside her boot. She is sure that if she looks out her window, she'll see Officer Ricky Beaker's squad car parked under the streetlight in front of her house. She wills herself not to look.

Willing herself not to look is something she's good at.

CHAPTER 22

The New Caledonia Corvus Research Facility and Sanctuary has visitors from the Auckland Zoo. Two women and two men are there to catch the Coconut Lorikeet (*Trichoglossus haematodus massena*), so that they can study the prevalence, origin, and locations of Parrot Beak and Feather Disease in the New Caledonian parrots. Weary is with them out in the jungle now, helping with the mist net. Lotto is there, too, as is Hector, the new assistant. Yann is gone, fired. Good riddance, loser!

Maybe Weary was too hard on him. After all, even *Corvus* will tease another creature just because it's funny to do so. The thing about being Weary's age, though, and living through what Weary has lived through — you don't put up with shit. People will treat you the way you allow them to treat you. This can be a hard-earned lesson, one that takes years and years to get through one's slow, stupid head, but once it's in, it's in.

Yann begged for his job. Heh. Too little, too late, buddy. On top of making fun of Weary within earshot, Yann had made comments about the female students, their fuckability, their weight, their general worthiness. Weary hates a misogynist.

See you later, asshole.

So Hector is here as of today, tromping around the jungle with the Australians, climbing trees with Lotto to place the rope lines. God forbid the visiting researchers would have to climb a tree. Two long lines now fall from a pair of widely separated Niaoulis, dropping from the branches like the ropes from an old swing. Hector and Lotto are getting along fine, and Hector is hard working and amiable, even with all of the teasing he's gotten this morning. Teasing, because Hector is also the name of the notorious saltwater crocodile who turned up on the beach at Mu in 1993 and has never left, the island's only croc, a famous creature who still gets the occasional media attention of an aging star athlete. Poor Hector the human — he's been putting up with the fallout. He must get it everywhere he goes, the giggles and jaw-snapping gestures.

"Croco!" Lotto calls. "Pull it up! Is it twisted? Hook it to that side rigging there."

"Green side up. It'll go up half-cocked like that," Weary calls. Honestly, visitors make Weary a little unhinged, with their demands on his time and their prying eyes.

The net scritch-scratches up. In the often-dull work of researching birds in the field, this is a big event. "Brilliant. Just brilliant," Callum says. He's the alpha of the Aussie group. Now they all crane their necks and gaze at a sky full of black mesh. They admire their trap. It's funny, the bounty of choices a person can make with a life. You can work at a tire store or become a banker or a deep-sea diver. You can live in a city, or way out here in the jungle with the birds. You can live with a creep or a sweetheart or all alone. Choices are beautiful, when you think about it.

Not one hour later, a Lorikeet flies right in. *Right in!* There is much excitement over one little Lorikeet. The researchers are thumping one another on the back. "Look! Look at the tiny thing!" one of the women says.

The bird twitches and flaps in shock and Callum trots over with his cage to retrieve it. As he watches, Weary can't help but think of Isabelle and his own beloved *Corvus. Corvus* would never be so easily and quickly captured, and neither will Isabelle. You have small-brained birds and then you have the willful, determined, incredibly intelligent crows. Creatures like that, like Isabelle — they'll remain cautious even if those nets are set up to save their life.

Why couldn't she have been so cautious right from the start? Why couldn't Sarah? It kills him. Undoing things is so much harder than doing them. Some handsome guy with a good job recites a little poetry, and bam. Smooth hotshots like Mr. Marvelous who pick up the check can be their own mist nets. Good character rarely shows off. It's quiet.

What're you going to do? You're a creature, a fish, who glimpses the shiny red globes of the salmon eggs when you are searching and hungry. You bite down. They taste like heaven; there is a satisfying and salty pop. Just before the fiery pain of the hook sets in your flesh.

And yes, the hook has set, because Isabelle is still appearing in photos on ShutR. Even after receiving the package with Virginia's watch. At least, there's the bump of bone at Isabelle's wrist on a handrail, and there's a wisp of her hair blowing into the frame as they ride a ferry. There is the cuff of her sleeve during the spectacular show of a rainbow across the water.

Weary knew Isabelle wouldn't leave Henry after one mailed accessory. He expected that, and in some ways, he respects it. Well, he understands it. She's loyal. If anyone is loyal, it's Weary. It's all right, too, it's more than all right, because the great payoff, the big bells-and-whistles jackpot, will only happen if Isabelle comes to her own conclusions in her own time. He can't rush her. He must provide rewarding lures only, no sudden, punishing hooks. In a full-on attack, a creature will only attack back.

But now, his next package waits in his office, locked in the file cabinet. Weary looks at the sky and the sun, gauges the time. He doesn't want to be late. Jean-Marie doesn't wait for anyone.

"Let's try again," Callum says.

"Lift it back up, Croco," Lotto yells.

Weary is pretty sure that even though Isabelle stands beside Henry North in those photos, witnessing a rainbow, the watch isn't far from her mind. Does she guess what it means yet? The rip and tear? Sarah didn't at first when she found it in that wooden box that Henry had in his dresser. For months, she thought it was an old keepsake. But then she discovered that photo in the garage, in the box marked *Electrical,* and she snuck the watch out of the house, brought it to Officer McNealy, the detective who investigated Virginia's case all those years ago. He was unimpressed. The old watch meant nothing. Virginia meant nothing by then to the Boston Police Department.

It is so much more than an old watch.

It is *proof.*

After that, Sarah kept the watch in her desk at work. She only told one other person about that watch and that photograph. *One* person.

It pains Weary. His throat tightens. He might cry. His own culpability. Losses upon losses. He should have done more. He should have done more *sooner.* He worried at first, sending Isabelle that watch. It felt like a risk, sending the real thing, but only the real thing hummed and throbbed with life. Or, rather, hummed and throbbed with death. There'd be no more chances after this, regardless.

"It can't possibly be as easy as the first time," Callum says.

But it is. The minute the net is up again, another Lorikeet flies right in, and the researchers cheer and hoot and hop around like their team is on a winning streak.

He leaves them to it. He has his own business to attend to.

"Professor!" Lotto calls, as if Weary's missing the exciting part. He only waves his hand and heads off into the brush. He's in a hurry, and Lot can take it from here. He doesn't want to chance them spotting his watering eyes, either. All of these thoughts of capture and memories of the past have made his heart constrict. He realizes that he must have bitten his tongue in his rush out of the jungle, too. There is the sudden metallic taste of blood and a throb of pain, and it's an old taste and an old throb, like his mouth remembers long-ago hooks setting into his own unsuspecting flesh.

CHAPTER 23

Before she heads to work, Isabelle removes the watch from her boot and zips it into the pocket of her nylon jacket. She does this every time she leaves the house. When she goes on an errand, she tucks it into the pocket of her jeans or the pouch of her purse, and it rides along with her to the Front Street Market, or the library. Every now and then, she'll feel around to make sure it's still there. She's uneasy leaving it in that boot. She listens for Henry in the shower or the kitchen or on the phone and then she hurries to retrieve it, her heart thumping madly. She returns it to the boot every night, so that it doesn't drop from a pocket or he doesn't find it in her purse while looking for her keys. Of course, this is all asking for trouble.

Now, on the dock at Island Air, she pats the pocket of her jacket, checks for the reassuring bump of metal. Then, she tosses

Joe his bag. He's heading to Nanaimo, B.C., to pick up a group of businessmen who'd recklessly gone up the Inside Passage to do some winter fishing.

"We shouldn't risk your neck to save theirs," she says. There's been word of bad weather, too.

"No worries. I'll take off out of Departure Bay. If the waters are too rough, the fishermen get to have another beer."

"Be safe. That's all I ask."

Joe smiles. He's got a head of curls and eyes dark as ink. He's the kind of friend who is family, especially after the month on his couch, but she hasn't forgotten what those eyes once meant to her. She gazed into them most of her senior year, sometimes as they lay in the twin bed of his room when his parents were away, and she longed for those eyes when he went on a family trip to Chicago for three weeks. They'd sent each other lengthy letters then, real letters on paper, the kind of sweet, romantic gesture Isabelle can't even imagine now after love has gotten as brutal and chaotic as a prison riot.

Was it wrong of her to think that life with a man like Joe seemed limited? She'd wanted more, more, more, even if she didn't know what *more* looked like. Just *not this.*

She wanted to live somewhere foreign, maybe, somewhere large, do something interesting. But, look, she hardly had great big adventures in the city with Evan, and before him, with Adam or Michael. She and Evan saw a few plays, went on a trip to Belize. Now she is back on Parrish, and this relationship with Henry is the large, confusing *more*. Henry's life has been so tragic and complicated that she's been spun and spun in a dizzying circle trying to understand both it and her own choices that have led her here. Your own choices can be so utterly baffling sometimes.

A limited life looks beautiful next to this, Maggie says. *A philandering pharmaceutical salesman and a professor with two dead lovers? Some intense relationship where you can't feel safe is your idea of* excitement? *What, you can't find your own life adventure? Fucking A. Get a map! Point your finger. Go,* Maggie says.

Maggie is getting louder and louder. She just won't shut up lately. She's the raven at the window of the chamber now, cawing and squawking. The dead don't stay dead, that's one thing that's clear.

I'm involved in some intense relationship where I can't feel safe because of you, mother dear. Plus, where did you ever go? You owned an airline! You never left here!

Peace Corps. 1963, Maggie says.

"Shit," Isabelle says.

"Everything okay?" Joe calls.

"Oh, yeah. Just something I forgot. Have a good flight!"

Joe slips into the cockpit. Buckles up. He flips on the master switch, then the fuel pump; next, the ignition and starter switches. The propeller starts to turn, and the engine builds from a whine to a roar.

Joe signals with a wave, and Isabelle unties first the mooring line then the tail line. The Beaver glides away. As it skirts along the water, Isabelle unzips her coat pocket, fishes inside the nylon.

She rubs the back of the watch with her thumb. It's oddly comforting, same as the bit of blue beach glass she used to carry when she was a child. She used to make wishes on that glass, though she's far past knowing what to wish for anymore. Maybe clarity. Maybe just peace, so that she and Henry can move forward in their life together. She doesn't believe Henry would have or even could have harmed Virginia or Sarah. He's a gentle person who expresses sadness every time there's the terrible smack of another bird crashing into their glass windows. She can't imagine any reason he'd have for doing something so horrific, either. There isn't a reason. Virginia was just a girl. Any talk of an affair on Sarah's part seems like mostly halfhearted speculation, and money from New Haven Providence would never be worth what Henry's gone through. Henry — this is what a person must understand — he just *wouldn't*.

Still, she's been uneasy since Henry's come home. It's because of that watch. She hasn't told Henry about it, and now it's a lie that sits between them. They are all in a relationship — her and Henry and Virginia and Sarah. They are all a part of a story, one she doesn't fully understand, and one that disturbs her.

"Hey!"

There's a shout, and the *thump thump* of running feet, and Isabelle startles because her first thought is that it's Henry, and she's been caught. Her guilt — for the watch, for her thoughts about Joe, for her wish for a different and far-away life — makes her jump, and the watch flies from her fingers and skitters across the wet dock. She falls to her knees, reaches and grabs it before it plunges into the water.

"Damn, I missed him," Eddie says, as the engine of the Beaver churns to full throttle and the plane rises. "What'd you drop, Izzy?

My God, you flung yourself down there like your newborn fell in." He offers a hand and she takes it.

"I almost lost . . ."

"Probably that big diamond."

"Yeah."

"Good, I'd say. Sorry if I surprised you. I was hoping to catch Joe." He lifts a small cooler. "Heart, for a transplant."

"Oh, my God!"

"Kidding! It's his lunch."

"Jesus, Eddie."

"Are you all right? You're white as a sheet."

"Fine."

"You don't seem fine. You're a nervous wreck. When Jane came up behind you this morning, you'd have thought she was an ax murderer."

He realizes what he's said. "Oh, hell. I'm sorry." He takes her arm, grips it. "Isabelle, Christ. Look at me."

She does. His old eyes are gentle. He's got a grizzly, unshaven face, the kind of face that's been through things.

"I'm okay, Eddie."

He stares at her, hard. "Are you scared of that fucker?"

"Of course not."

"The way you just jumped . . . If you're scared even for one second . . ."

"I'm not scared, Eddie. Of course I'm not."

"I would beat that asshole to a pulp, and don't think I wouldn't. Don't think I *couldn't.* Jane and I would take turns. If anything happened to you, your mother would haunt us from her grave. What are you doing with a guy like that? How about someone you can trust, huh? How about someone without suspicions like that all around him."

"I do trust him."

Eddie makes a face. "Two women, Isabelle. *Two.*"

"If I had any doubt . . ."

"What's it take? You? Number *three*?"

"Don't."

"Come on."

He doesn't say anything more. He shakes his head. His bluntness is unnerving. It is the voice of a reasonable person, calling out to her in her unreasonable world. It's unwelcome, honestly.

"Come here." Eddie hugs her. He takes her in his big bear arms and just hugs. He smells like evergreen boughs and motor oil. She thinks she might cry. "I mean it . . ."

"I'm fine." Her words are muffled against his big coat.

"Jesus Christ, kid."

313

■ ■ ■ ■

She feels the tension the moment she walks in the door. Henry is in the kitchen, unloading groceries from two brown bags. The way he reaches inside them, though — it's slightly aggressive, and he sets down that can of tomatoes with a *bamp.* There's a rigid set to his shoulders.

He doesn't need to say a word. Isabelle is skilled at reading mood and temperature. You might say it's one of the things she does best. She's had a lot of training. From the time she was small, she could sense the shift in a profile and feel vibrations of trouble in the slightest downturn of a mouth. Words are easy; anyone can read those. Big deal. Isabelle can intuit the rising pressure in the atmosphere long before anyone speaks. She can read every silence.

"Henry?"

"Mmm-hmm?"

Now, there's tone to factor in. The *Mmm-hmm* is a clean blade against her skin. It's sharp with purpose. He has not just simply had a bad day, or gotten some upsetting news.

"What's the matter?" Of course, he has two choices now. He can calmly tell her what's bothering him or he can make her work for it, like her mother always did. Maggie would give you two days of silence frigid enough that you'd confess to treason and beg for forgiveness even if you never knew what you actually did wrong.

"Nothing's the matter."

It could make a person scream. It could make a person throw things and slam doors. Still, Isabelle wants to be calm and powerful; mature enough to take him at his word. She refuses to play this particular game. She hangs up her jacket. She leaves the watch in the pocket, where it's safest right now. She intends to go about her night as usual, because if he can't just talk to her like an adult, she doesn't need to beg.

By the time she's changed out of her work clothes, though, the *nothing* has gotten under her skin, where it now wriggles and grows. It is a mystery. A nameless accusation. The urge to scream and throw and slam is speedily vanishing, as is her vow not to get pulled in. It's all replaced with a vapor of worry. What has she done? She scrolls through her possible wrongdoings. There are always lots of them. Which one? Not knowing the *nothing* can drive a person nuts. Trying and trying to figure out the *nothing* is how you start to pay for your crime. It's the proof of love and loyalty the accuser is looking for.

She is a master of giving proof. *Fine! You want me to grovel, I'll grovel! See how good I am and how much I love you?* she thinks. Her fury is fighting for its freedom, but the old, habitual fear shuts it up. Her thoughts are going rogue. A tiny rage clangs and bangs and tries to rise. What would happen if the lid came off her anger? Best not to find out.

"Tell me, Henry."

"Do you even trust me?"

"Yes, Henry. Of course."

God, sometimes you hate your own self. He is still unloading two measly bags of groceries. *Look at what I do for you,* the carton of butter says. *I deserve so much better,* the container of mixed greens whines. The refrigerator slaps shut. Isabelle stops Henry. She places a gentle hand on his arm. What she feels mostly is *Please. Please* be reasonable. *Please* stop. Her whole life she's been pleading for unreasonable people to be reasonable. From her mother to Evan and now Henry. Please and pleasing — she knows lots of tricks for this part of an argument, too. Soft voice. A little joking. A lot of apologizing. Never blaming. Gentle steps. Have a little compassion, those who judge!

If you can say *Back off,* it's because you were allowed. Maggie was a force of nature and an excellent trainer, and all it takes is a harsh tone, and Isabelle will sit up and beg.

"Henry. What's going on?"

"Were you in my office?"

"When?"

"When I was away. Were you looking through my stuff?"

Oh, no. No!

Any anger that was there is now entirely gone. Poof! There's not a single trace of it. Any compassion has run for the hills. Her heart feels dark with dread. She is strangely terrified, as terrified as when she thought Maggie had found her journal, or her birth-control pills, or that college application essay she never sent, the one where she wrote about her desperate need to leave home, all proof of treachery. She had betrayed Henry, too, and now he knows. Isabelle tries to think what evidence she left behind. *How* did he know? Did she leave coffee rings on a poem? Forget to lock the desk back up? Oh, my God. What if she left that paperclip lock pick on the desk? Shit!

"What do you mean?"

"Clearly, you were in my office."

Now, she sees it — the pad of yellow-lined paper on the counter. He picks it up and

317

waves it at her.

"A pad of paper?"

She is losing her mind. She has a flash of fear that she wrote something on it that day, some confession of her true doubts, some blast of vitriol about the way he lied to her. Honest and awful words that she completely forgot about.

"I see the swirls. The impression left by the pen."

"What? I don't understand."

"The *swirls*."

It's quiet. There's only the *tick-tick* of the kitchen clock. The barely visible phantom loops on that pad look innocent, almost merry. But the way he waves that pad is strange and upsetting. She feels sick. Something bad is happening, that he can see those imprints as ominous. And yet, she *had* been in there. She *had* been snooping.

"I was just trying out a pen, Henry."

"A pen."

"You have all the good ones. Am I not allowed to go in there and get a pen? Are you implying that a room in our mutual home is off limits? Because that's just wrong."

"It's not that you were *in* the room. It's what you were *doing* in the room. I mean, you were there, weren't you? When I was gone? Sitting at my desk, trying to find some sort of *evidence,* taking notes for your interrogation of me . . ."

"No, Henry. No!" She flushes. It's uncanny, the way he knows things, the way he senses the slightest wrongdoing against him. He hears every unspoken rejection. And he is right. He is always right.

"Do you want to leave me?"

"Of course not. You know I love you."

"I just feel . . ."

His voice breaks, then.

"What?"

"I feel you stepping back. These little distant moments . . ."

"Every relationship has those, Henry. Every one. Evan's and mine did. I'm sure you and Sarah —"

"Oh, we had those, all right. We had plenty. Look what happened. She's gone."

"I'm here, Henry. I'm not going anywhere."

"You don't trust me. I've been nothing but honest since you found out. I've been an open book. You *know* you can ask me anything."

"I do trust you."

"You question . . ."

"It's just hard, Henry. I mean . . . This isn't a regular situation."

"Years ago, I dated an unstable woman.

319

That's my crime! Virginia was always making threats. Always! Crying . . . some big scene. I should have gotten her help. If I'm guilty of anything, it's that."

"I'm sorry."

"Do you know what that was like for me? Seeing her fall? Hearing her? Waiting for help to arrive? I will never recover from that. Never."

"I'm so sorry, Henry."

"Can you even begin to imagine, then, Sarah disappearing? That night, the wind, the rain . . . Her *gone*? Sarah, Jesus! You know, I could not handle her. I really couldn't. I should have just let her go. Long before that night. You know, sometimes I wonder. I really wonder."

"Let's just forget this for tonight, huh? This whole thing with the pad of paper . . . *A pen,* Henry. That's all. Let's just stop this right here, okay?"

"What do you mean, 'stop this'?"

"This! Tonight! This discussion. Let's just order a pizza. Open a bottle of wine . . ."

"Cooking relaxes me."

"Well, you can cook, then."

"I just can't stand it if you doubt me. I can't stand being *distrusted* . . ."

"Come here."

She puts her arms around him. His body

is as tight as if it were bound in ropes, like the wrists and ankles of mutinous sailors about to be tossed overboard. She pretends to squish his arm muscles, loosening him up. But it feels bad, touching him.

"I can't be perfect, Isabelle. I feel like I have to be perfect to make this worth it, considering everything else. I mean, are you going to stay with me when I've had this cloud of suspicion over me *and* I act like a bastard?"

"Don't act like a bastard, then."

He shakes her off.

"Kidding! I'm kidding."

"Don't leave me."

"Henry, stop."

He puts his face in his hands. She puts her arms around him. They are like that a long while, and then he kisses her. He unbuttons her blouse. Then he takes her hand and leads her down the hall to the bedroom. He can feel every disloyal thought, so she concentrates on his body, on wanting his body, wanting the body that is there, which could belong to anyone. She concentrates on want, and conveying want.

Afterward, they lay together. She is starving and she has to pee, but she senses she should let him get up first. Anything might be a rejection.

He is in a better mood now. Sex, the miracle cure. "Dinner? Are you hungry? I'm starving." He rises, tosses on his jeans.

"Dinner sounds great."

"Wait until you see what I'm making."

He leaves the bedroom. In a few moments, there's the clatter of pans and the smell of herbs in butter. Isabelle is just tying the sash of her robe when he calls to her.

"I forgot to tell you. You got a package."

She goes into the bathroom. She splashes and splashes her face with cold water. She tries to stay calm, but there is a rise of anxiety that makes her heart beat like a hummingbird's.

He has put on some music. Jazz. Jazz makes the anxiety worse. There's a glass of wine set out for her on the coffee table. The night is foggy, and out the window she can see the distant arc of the lighthouse beam.

She sees the package on the hall table. It's a small padded envelope. It screams and shouts.

"Who's sending you things from France?" Henry yells from over the pop and sizzle of chicken cutlets in oil.

"Anne!" she shouts back. "She's in . . ." She checks the postmark. "Lourmarin, on a tour. Feels like a silk scarf."

"Something paper, I thought."

"She loves those arty gift cards."

It is now official. Isabelle is colluding with the sender of the packages. It is the two of them (or more, who knows — she still imagines Virginia's girlfriends) against Henry. She takes the package and shoves it into the back of her closet.

"Something I'll never wear," she says when she returns. She puts her arms around Henry from behind. "That looks amazing." She concentrates hard on believing in the silk scarf and its ugliness.

"It better be amazing, since I'm such an asshole," he says.

In the night, that unopened envelope beats and thumps in the closet. It is the tell-tale heart under the floorboards, saying *Guilty, guilty, guilty.*

Who is guilty? Him? Her?

The sound of it is so loud. It thrums in her ears. And yet there is something louder. A realization from her own actions this night. The way she step-stepped around his need, the way she lay with her head on his chest until he rose. She remembers her father, tip-tip-tiptoeing, slipping out of doors, tending with the right gift or the soft word, digging the sneaky tunnel to freedom with a spoon.

It's plain old instinct, because betrayal, disloyalty, rejection . . . Sometimes it's dangerous, isn't it? Sometimes it means a golf club gets raised, or . . . A cliff, a boat . . .

Get the fuck out, Maggie says. *Now!*

A person can be mean *and* right.

Why aren't you leaving? Why aren't you getting out of there right this minute?

Why *doesn't* she leave? It's the million-dollar question. She doesn't leave because she's scared and doubts her own perceptions and her own reality. She doesn't leave because this is where she lives, and living elsewhere feels too hard. She doesn't leave because she's sure things will get better and that this is temporary and that the man she saw first is the real man she's with now. She doesn't leave because she has some dogged trust in the reasonable, some unmoving refusal to believe in her own peril. She has a persistent and against-all-evidence faith that those she loves won't harm her. No, not faith — something much more fragile: a wish.

She doesn't leave because she's stupid, stupid, stupid, Maggie says. *Anger saves you!*

What anger? Henry breathes softly next to her. She can see his chest rising and falling in the dark. She pulls the covers to her chin.

That's right. Get comfortable.

Who is *this*? It isn't Maggie, and it's not her own self, speaking this time. She hasn't heard this voice, him, her father, in years and years. She suddenly has a clear vision of the back of his head on long car rides, streetlights shooting flashes of light, the radio low.

Might as well settle in, Izzy, he says and sighs. *We're stuck in this tuna boat and miles from home. Not much else a person can do but make the best of it.*

She drifts off. She dreams of auto-bingo, and sprawling farmland, and fast-food drive-throughs. She dreams of a pulsing envelope, with a heart inside of it, ready for a transplant. She dreams that her own wrists and ankles are bound with rope. She's a mutinous sailor, about to be tossed overboard.

CHAPTER 24

It's early in the year, a good month early, for rains like this. Tropical storms don't usually arrive until March. But the water lashes and hammers down; it slants meanly from the sky and pummels the roof, the ground, and Weary's head as he hunches his shoulders and runs to the Jeep.

There is no telling who can get where. Roads will be washed away. The power is out. But Weary is the one in ultimate command (nice — he likes that), and so, come hell or literal high water, he must get to the research facility and make sure the captive crows are tended to.

The wipers flick-flick-flick-flick so fast, but still, he can barely see. The palms whip and sway like manic hula dancers. The Jeep sploshes and spluts in the deep water-filled ruts of the road. At one point up the mountain, he has to gun the accelerator and hope for the best, as there's a good two feet of floodwater blocking passage.

This would be the time when it would be nice to be back in Boston, tucked warmly into a Starbucks, reading *Behavioral Ecology* while sipping a peppermint mocha. Then again, that would mean he would not have just made it to the other side of that near-river by his own daring and valor. Anyone can order a double tall. Weary is here at the epic center of Woman-God-Mother-Nature, working with and against her. A palm branch hits the top of the vehicle with a crack, but he is unafraid.

It's glorious, really. Look around. He's *alive*!

The research facility looks brave, too, out here in this storm. With every light out, it's dim, though, and the overworked gutters pour and pour. Inside, Weary shakes off the wet. First things first — the stores of feed. With the power gone, the eggs are out of the question, same with the fish bait and snails. It's grains and cat food, shelled nuts and earthworms this week.

When Weary gets to the storage shed, he sees that Lotto is already there. Big, good, devoted Lot. Weary's heart swells with fondness for him. It lifts with love for fellow humans together in bad times.

"It's raining like a bastard," Lotto says.

"It's a typhoon!" Weary says. "How did you get here?"

"Bike," Lotto says.

"Bike?" Weary can't imagine it. There's no conceivable way. "Bike and a miracle?"

"This storm's not so bad." Lotto was born in Nouméa. He's used to these squalls. "Matias was here before me."

"Good, good," Weary says. But what he means is *Fantastic*. What he means is *Thank you for being fine people with fine characters, almost like family.* What he means is *People like you make a place home.*

"You should go back to your house now, Professor," Lotto says. "It'll take me and both my cousins to get your Jeep out if it gets stuck."

"*You* should go back, Lotto."

"I'm staying. Plus, Grandma'am is driving me crazy."

"I don't want you to be alone up here."

"How could I be alone, with all of them?" He hooks his thumb toward the corvid pens. "Matias is probably staying, too."

"Shame about the generator."

"Piece of shit. Anyway, a generator doesn't have a chance against this. You ever see a local with one?"

"They're expensive."

"Using your head is free and works better.

I'd get back down the mountain in a hurry, though, if I were you."

"I appreciate you, Lot."

"It's quieter here with all this wind than at home with Grandma'am and my sisters yapping at me."

The thing is, in spite of his unconventional situation, life is beautiful here. Life is large. Life is one hundred percent.

With no power, and only the glass of wine for company, Weary is cut off. No phone, no television, but, more important, no Internet. No *news.* He paces, tries to read. Paces some more. Think of all the things that could be happening with Henry North and Isabelle, during this big stretch of pummeling rain and nothingness.

Plus, he will admit it. He's become a little addicted to the click-click, the possibilities in the refresh. He's as bad as the crows with the levers and their hope for their favorite treats. He presses and presses, only he gets tidbits of information instead of tater tots and hard-boiled egg.

The shutters *bang-bang-bang.* Weary tries to eat what is still safe to eat in the fridge. Drinks more wine. (Well, anyone would.) He paces some more. Knowing that the birds are in good hands back at the center, he has only one worry, one obsessive thought, one question.

What is happening, Isabelle?

Weary thinks of the one-eyed, long-bearded, Norse God Odin, the Raven God, with his long, dark cloak and broad hat, with his two goddess crows, Hunnin and Munnin, who bring him the news from all over Midgard. The ravens fly through the nine worlds and then return to Odin's throne at dinnertime with their reports, mostly news from the battlefield, news about his female warriors, the Valkyries. Better yet, the raven goddesses could see into the future. They knew who would die, who would conquer, and they would whisper these knowings to him.

Weary could use those crows now.

He can only use the flight of his own imagination. He forces himself to settle into his desk chair, which sits in front of the dark, lifeless computer. The alcohol helps. He shuts his eyes. He raises his black satin wings. He lifts off. The wind through the palms sounds like the atmosphere zipping past his raven ears. The cliff is behind him, and now there's only sky. He crosses the sea. There is a glass house on a bluff on an island. He swoops past the window, peers inside. There is a man and a woman.

They fight. They make love. A padded envelope sits on a table.

Raven Weary perches on a deck rail. Watches.

Empathy. What is she feeling? What is he? The envelope, which was once in Weary's hands, is now in hers. He's seen the hands; he imagines the lovely fingers opening the package. He imagines the weight of the ring on the left hand. Rip, tear, and then the images spill.

Weary knows there's a good chance that Henry North will see the package this time. Perhaps he'll even open it, paranoid child that he is. Would it hasten things? Blow it all up? God forbid, draw them closer for a time? Weary can't control everything. But it seemed right to send the second envelope to their home where he might find it. It's a little shakeup. A little rattle to the nerves.

Weary tries and tries to stare with his small, black-marble raven eyes into those large glass windows. The best predictor of future behavior is past behavior. One might think that Henry North is only paranoid because he's been an unfairly and consistently hunted man. But no. Henry North is paranoid because he's paranoid. He's paranoid because he's insecure, and he's insecure because he's been made small by that

331

shitty, mean father of his. Weary is not unsympathetic on this point. He remembers his own father and the broken hinge on that violin case when he was a child, how scared he was to admit to it, because of what would happen. Still, you can blame and blame all you want; your actions are still your actions.

Crows are scavengers. They pick, pick at a body until only the skeleton is left. At first, for Isabelle, there will only be Henry North's confident solid self, his largeness in the world, his practiced largeness. But then, even without Raven Weary pecking away to expose the soul, Henry North will show what he's made of. Little by little, he will reveal the thin skin, and then the cruel heart, and then the fragile architecture beneath.

Raven Weary sits on the deck rail and watches. And then he lifts off again, to bring back the news to Norse God Weary, about who will win and who will lose this battle.

It's possible he's drunk.

CHAPTER 25

"Glad I caught you before you went home, Izzy. Can we talk for a sec?" Jane asks. *Caught you* sounds like an accidental meeting, but Jane just jogged to the parking lot from the office, and her big chest is heaving a little from the effort.

"If it's about the Quinces and Shorecrest Engineering, I'm sorry." Isabelle mixed up the reservations, and they ended up sending a small plane to pick up the large group.

"I don't care about that. It's fine. We'll eat the refund. But, you, Izzy . . . Are you all right? You don't seem well. You look awful. And you're so distracted lately, I'm worried you're going to walk off a cliff.

"Shit." Jane realizes what she's just said, shakes her head. It's been a problem, the unconscious slips of everyone around her. There have been many nervous twitters around too many words: *dead, missing, murder.*

"I'm okay. I've just been busy."

"Busy."

"Yes, busy. A lot, you know, on my mind. I appreciate your concern, I do. It's all good."

"I don't want to press you. Just, I'm here. If you ever need to talk. Bud's? Fried chicken? A little catching up?"

"Thanks for caring, but I promise, I'm fine. Really. You and Eddie can relax."

Jesus!

"Not dinner, just a beer? I've got a twenty burning a hole in my pocket."

"Sounds great, but another time? I've got to go."

She's got to go, because she has something important to do. She phoned Henry earlier. She'll be home late, she lied, because the gang is going out to eat after work.

Is Joe going to be there? he asked.

No. It's his sister's birthday.

My God, she's been lying a lot. The lies come so easily that she's starting to get worried about keeping track of them. She should maybe get a binder with colored tabs, like she used to have for her high school world history class. The lies are necessary for keeping the peace, she tells herself. *Keeping the peace* is not a red flag. It's a small city on fire before the war.

Like everything else, the lies are complicated. What is the situation, and what is merely her, being crazy, being unable to be in a relationship at all? Because she lies about Joe because Henry is jealous of Joe, and she lies about her doubts so she doesn't trip his insecurity, and she lies about things like this package now riding on the seat next to her in the car, because it would make him lose his mind with understandable upset. But she also lies about small, inexplicable things. Decisions she's made. Food she's eaten. Things he'll judge her for, but more than that. Things she just needs to keep for herself because she needs something that's away from his prying eyes. The cheeseburger becomes a turkey sandwich just to have a little room to breathe.

Confusion is so helpful, the way it makes a bunch of commotion and noise so you can't see the thing you don't want to see.

"Another time, then," Jane says.

Isabelle waves goodbye to Jane, who looks sad standing there in the parking lot. Isabelle misjudges the driveway and ends up bumping one tire down the curb as Jane watches. Damn it! The more Jane and Eddie worry, the more frazzled she gets, that's what she tells herself. On the way into town, she runs a stoplight she's been navigating since she learned to drive, and a Darigold truck narrowly misses her as the driver leans on his horn. Maybe she's the real danger to herself. Isabelle's phone buzzes from inside her purse. She pulls into the back lot of the library, parks next to the dumpster as if she's eluding the cops after the bank robbery. She checks her messages.

Just wanted to say I love you. Have fun tonight. I'll miss you.

Sweet, right? It's sweet. So why is she feeling the increasing need to flee? The more Henry worries she's about to leave him, the more he presses. And the more he presses, the more that she's about to leave him.

She hurries across the library lot, which is dark except for a few circles of streetlight. She has a flash of memory: walking across her high school parking lot on a night like this, a night under this same winter sky. There was the slam of car doors, and Joe's fingers in hers as they ran to the doors in their fancy clothes, and just ahead, in the gym, the sound of a band playing. Joe was laughing and joking, and the boutonniere Isabelle had just pinned on was hanging there by good fortune, but she did not feel good and excited about the dancing and kissing and fun to come. She felt guilty and bad. She felt sorry. When they left, she saw her mother alone in the window, watching them go.

The padded envelope is hidden in Isabelle's bag. She wants to open it here. She runs up the library stairs. Inside, the library is beautiful, with large windows and warm wood, and a domed ceiling with the sky painted on it. She looks up at the blue sphere with the puffy white clouds and, for the first time ever, notices a tiny black bird with spread, soaring wings.

Why the library? She feels safe here. She always has. It's a place of both escape and order, a sanctuary, her church. There are answers here, too, and quiet, sheltering corners, places to hide. She ducks past the desk to a tiny carrel in the back. It's next to natural sciences — dinosaurs and volcanoes — where only nine-year-olds doing school reports go. The nine-year-olds are all home having dinner, so there's no one there.

She slides the package out of her purse, same as a spy with state secrets. She has not opened it yet because the house felt too exposed, and so did her car, and so did anywhere else she could think of but the library.

Her heart is throbbing. Her stomach hurts. She's afraid of what she might find, but she knows she has to look. There's a trash can right there. If it's horrible, she can make a mad dash, shove the contents inside, and go back to seeing only what she wants to see.

All right already! Just fucking do it, Maggie says.

Isabelle rips it open. She reaches her hand down.

Photographs. She peeks. Nothing horrible, no dead bodies, no bleeding wounds or Henry wielding a knife. It's a place. Some outside place. It's beautiful, actually.

There's a stretch of purple wildflowers on a high, high hill. No, a mountain, because now look. There's a whole rocky ridge below.

There's a trail.

Oh, God.

Isabelle's heart plummets — it drops so suddenly, she's a diver who's gone too deep, too fast. Her lungs squeeze. She can't breathe, because she knows what this is. She knows where this is. There is no note, no anything else, but she doesn't need one. This is *that* trail. Virginia's trail.

The photos look recent. At least, they don't have the yellow haze of age. There's also a satellite image, something from Google Maps, an overview. There is a close-up of the ground itself, and of a lookout point, with hills that form a W in the background. *The* lookout point. She knows it is. Of course it is. The spot.

What strikes her — this isn't what she imagined. Not at all. *Skyfall Ridge* — you envision a narrow and winding trail. She always saw it one way in her mind, a path with only a small margin for error, plus a despondent woman, or maybe just one who slipped. Henry said he wasn't completely sure that her fall was purposeful, but that it seemed so. Virginia had been talking all the way up, about her unhappiness with her job and friends and family, how she never felt like she was enough. She was emotional. They stopped briefly. She was overwrought. *I don't even know what I want* is what she said, according to Henry. It could have been a split-second decision or an accident. Before he knew it, she was going down. Isabelle hiked plenty herself — she knew those spots where there were tight switchbacks or where the trail had eroded, where careful footing was the only thing that kept you from plummeting.

But this looks nothing like that. The trail is wide. The lookout point in these photos is large enough that you could stop there to take in the view. It's not a precarious ledge at all.

Which is exactly the point, she understands. It's the message of these photos. *Look,* they say. *Not so treacherous, right?*

"Oh, my God," Isabelle says out loud in the quiet library. She shoves the chair away from the desk. She's back to plan A. She jams the contents into the innocent library trash can. She feels bad about sticking that stuff in there. It's like she ditched the weapon and the bloody sheets in this friendly, helpful place.

She hurries past Librarian Larry in his denim shirt. She flees. She's as terrified as if someone were chasing her. By the time she's passed under that domed sky and pushed through the doors to the crisp night air, reason (she tells herself it's reason) has caught up. She has no idea what those photos are! She has no idea who has sent them. It's creepy! It's awful and horrifying. She's likely the target of something malicious, and she's lucky they didn't send her an envelope of that white powder, whatever it was, that people got after 9/11. What is she thinking, just opening stuff up from wacko strangers? Has she lost her mind? She needs to tell Henry. This is the man she loves, a man who has been good to her, a man (she reminds herself) that she *trusts.* He's her lover and her friend, and now that he's parted the curtains and stepped onto her stage, her life will never be the same again.

Jesus, she has to tell him about this. This crazy shit in the mail — it could be dangerous.

She doesn't tell him, though.

When she gets home, the timing doesn't feel right. He's sort of in a mood. At least, he's being aloof, meaning he's slightly injured about the whole evening. It's hard, because he's aware that he doesn't exactly get a warm reception at Island Air, and yet Island Air is Isabelle's weighty legacy.

"How'd it go?" he asks.

"Boring. I left early. I mean, you spend all day with people, so it's tough to want to spend your free time with them, too, you know?"

"Really."

"But it's good for us as a team."

"If those people aren't a team by now . . ." He's flicking through channels on the TV.

"You're right."

These are charmed words. He reaches out his hand, pulls her next to him. "I missed you," he says into her hair.

Why spoil the mood? Let sleeping dogs lie, don't upset the applecart, all that. As if she needs any encouragement to avoid conflict. In terms of avoiding conflict, she's her own personal SWAT team.

So she still has to tell him.

It's Saturday, and they take the ferry to Anacortes because Henry wants to buy some All-Clad Copper Core pans. Isabelle has no idea what All-Clad Copper Core pans are. All-Clad Copper Core sounds like something you might need if you're building a nuclear reactor.

Turns out they're expensive. Really expensive. Since he got that insurance check, Henry's been spending money like mad, which bothers her. It feels like dead-wife money. Still, he's been through so much, and anyone who's lost their spouse in such a horrible way and then is interrogated mercilessly afterward at least deserves the cookware of his dreams.

They have fun at the mall. They sit across from each other at a small plastic table and eat gourmet hot dogs. They get samples from See's Candies. Isabelle buys the lipstick she likes. Food plus new toys puts them in good spirits. They hold hands and smooch under mall palm trees. They tolerate screaming children and harsh lights with cheer and patience, and they point out stuff they'd never buy in windows. It's a great day. They're happy. Isabelle remembers why she wanted this. She and Henry are in love. She keeps admiring his profile beside her.

Heading home again, they wait in the car in the ferry line along with everyone else. A dog stares at them from the next car over. They're finally ushered on, and this time they get out; they edge between the cars and head up the stairwell to sit on a padded ferry bench. Henry wants a coffee, and Isabelle has one, too. She's still got to tell him about the packages, and this undone deed feels like it's growing larger and larger, like every undone deed, but worse. The more time that passes, the harder it's getting. She just needs to do it. Get it over with. She'll make it all sound casual and assuredly handled. But she can't keep a secret like this from the man she sleeps next to every night. And look at what a great day they had. This will be her life. His past, like every past, is an unavoidable part of the whole.

"Want to walk?" he says.

"Let's do it."

He's brought his camera. They stroll to the outside deck. It's freezing out there. Her eyes start to water. Below, the Puget Sound rushes past, gray waves and whitecaps, with a gray-white sky overhead.

"I can't feel my lips," she says.

He stops snapping photos. "Come here." He wraps his arms around her. It feels good, even with the bump of his camera between them. The coffee surges, shoots bolts of goodwill and confidence.

"Henry. There's something I have to tell you." She says this into his coat. She actually sort of shouts it, because they're outside and the wind is rushing past her ears.

"What, sweet?"

"I got a package."

"From your friend Anne?"

"No, a different one." Shit. Shit, shit! The aim is to be honest, and she's failing already. She didn't think this through. She can't tell him about the watch or the supposed silk scarf from Anne. He'd be upset at the lies, upset at the time that had passed since she confessed the truth. "I got it at work . . . It was strange. No return address . . ." This was the problem with lies, the way they tangled up worse than Christmas lights in a box. "Anyway, Henry, it was weird, okay? I just wanted to tell you. I don't want you to worry."

"What was in it?"

"Just some photos. Photos of like, a trail."

"A trail?"

"I think maybe, you know, where Virginia . . ."

"Oh, *fuck.*"

"I'm sorry."

"Why are you sorry? It's her fucking *sisters*. They're going to haunt me till I die! Fuck, fuck, fuck! Was it her sisters? Was there a note?"

"No note. No name."

"Cowards. They won't even claim the act? Terrorists at least do that! Jesus. Where was it from?"

"I couldn't tell . . . No return address."

"The postmark?"

"I didn't even look." Shit! "I was shocked. Anyway, it's not important. I just thought you should know."

"It's not important? Trust me, it's important. It's freezing out here. Let's go in."

The doors whoosh shut behind them. Isabelle's nose is dripping. She wishes she hadn't told him. The problem is, she's not thinking clearly. Every step is a possible misstep; thinking clearly feels like an impossible mission.

"You need to show me. I want to see what they sent."

"I tossed it."

"You tossed it? Why did you do that? I need to see! I've got to send that shit to my attorney! I won't be hounded . . ."

Around them, it's all normal life. People are reading paperbacks and tapping on their tablets and phones. The sun is setting outside the big ferry windows. Well, sun — there's been no actual evidence of it for days. It's just the gray of late Northwest winter, getting grayer before it turns dark.

"Henry, we don't need to give it more energy than —"

"Tell me what was in the photos. Tell me exactly."

"I don't even know. I don't even remember exactly. Some trail . . . An overlook —"

"An overlook. It could be anywhere, anything . . ."

"There was just this trail. A fairly wide . . . I mean, I was surprised."

"What are you saying? What do you mean, 'surprised'?"

"I mean, I'd just always pictured . . ."

"What the hell are you saying?"

This is going wrong. This is going really, really wrong. They are standing by the racks of island real estate magazines and pamphlets for whale-watching tours and fishing trips. They are right near the restrooms, and people are going in and out, looking in their direction because Henry's voice has risen.

"I'm not saying anything. I was just surprised when I saw that trail. I just always thought, I don't know . . ."

"I can't believe this."

"I'm not saying anything other than I didn't imagine it that way."

She knows she shouldn't say more. She knows she's dug herself so deep already, but she can't help it, because in spite of the carefulness and tiptoeing she's been doing, she has questions. The packages have made this worse. The questions pound like a surf inside her, and even if she tries to clap her hands over her ears, she can still hear them crashing on her eroding shore.

Don't be stupid, Maggie says. This could refer to a hundred things, but Isabelle takes it to mean *Be bold. Ask. Speak.*

"You want me to fucking act it out?" Henry spits. "You want me to show you how it happened on that trail? Is that what you want?"

"You said . . . You said if I ever wanted to know anything . . . I mean, I just wondered, how . . . You know, slipping! I just wondered! Because it wasn't some tight edge! You said I could ask you anything!"

"I told you. She was upset. A person who wants to slip can slip, whether it's on six inches of trail or six feet, all right, Isabelle?"

"I'm sorry. You just said —"

"How do you even know what those

pictures were? I've had enough of this shit. I don't need this from you, too."

He turns, shoves his coffee cup down into a trash can, and stalks down the aisle between the rows of seats. Heads turn. His camera bumps on his hip. He takes the turn toward the stairwell.

Couples meet each other's eyes. Isabelle feels the shame of a public spectacle. She is frozen in her spot next to those pamphlets. She feels the tip and sway of the boat. The scenery continues to rush past, and the passengers turn their attention back to books and phones. Isabelle briefly considers various options: Jane could pick her up at the ferry terminal; she could stay at the Cliffside B&B; she could ride the ferry back and forth, back and forth, until a plan forms. But she realizes she is stuck, so stuck, because this is her life now, and you can't just ditch a life, can you? Not without chaos and remorse and shame. No, she'll have to get back in that car and go home.

She waits for the announcement that they are docking. She joins the crowd moving down the stairwell. She wonders for a moment if she'll even find him there, or if he, like a despondent Virginia, will have flung himself out of a terrible life and into a bitter end. But, no, there he is, sitting in the driver's seat, staring forward as if he doesn't see her tapping at the window to be let in. He's locked the doors.

He makes her wait. Finally, there's the click of the latch.

She gets in but says nothing. The silence is awful. It is filled with arrows and spears and wounds gushing blood. She sits there in it, taking the unspoken hits.

Don't do it, Isabelle, Maggie says. *Don't you dare do it.*

What does Maggie know about relationships? Nothing. Nothing that allowed her to ever keep one alive. He's right, too. How *does* she even know what those photos were?

"I'm sorry, Henry," Isabelle says.

The apology doesn't do anything, anyway. He still sits there with his stone face. No, wrong. It does do one thing — it makes Isabelle feel like shit about herself. It takes her down another notch. The old freight elevator lurches, plummets to a lower level, where it's cold and musty, dark and damp. It's not a place for people of power. They sit at the top, where the sun shines and it smells so good, their lungs puff up with air.

She said she was sorry, but she isn't sorry. Not one bit.

They ride home without speaking. When

they arrive, Henry gets out of the car, walks ahead of her. She carries the small bag with the lipstick and the big bag with the All-Clad pans. He has left this in the car to demonstrate that it's not important to him anymore. The rustling of the bag sounds wrong and shameful as she dumps it in the hall.

He disappears into their bedroom. She hears the closet door open as he undresses, the bang of his belt hitting the floor. She hears him brush his teeth, which means no dinner. There is no slamming, only the heavy treads of gloom and depression that are her doing. He gets into bed and puts the covers up over himself, even though it's only seven.

She thinks of her father, hiding behind his newspaper and work-work-work. She thinks of him in Florida after he left them. He married a demanding woman with demanding children, continuing a life of sacrifice and hard emotional labor before he finally died, of pure exhaustion, probably. All of those years of pleasing and tiptoeing must have done him in, Isabelle thinks, as she tiptoes into her own room with the lump of Henry there under the covers.

She doesn't get into bed beside him, though. This is not because she's rehearsing a torrent of necessary words; she's just weighing which option keeps her safest from his fury. Anyone judging her now has been safe, she knows. Anyone judging has been able to look at a lump like that and say, *Knock that shit off, Mister,* or, *I won't take this anymore.*

Still, there's a flame, a small flickering inside of Isabelle. It is still doing its caveman-spirit, life-force best. She barely feels it there, her human pilot light, keeping on, keeping on, until the biggest, nastiest storm blows it out. It's trying its best to kick the shit away, though, so the oxygen can get in. The little flame is responsible for the smallest move Isabelle makes right then, a fashion choice, because Isabelle does not choose her big, thick old sweats to change into tonight. No, she slips on the crane robe her mother gave her. It's silky-satin and not warm, but it's sleek and beautiful and strong, like Isabelle herself might be in her right mind. She remembers the Greek story from her college literature class, too. How a flock of cranes hovered over a thief until he, racked with guilt, confessed his crimes. Maybe it was better not to think of that particular story. Maybe better to just imagine the awkward bird with the long legs and long neck who could actually fly.

She wants out. *Fuck you,* she mouths to the sleeping hump. And it's not Maggie, either. It's her. The pieces of her anger shudder and hum from where they lay.

She steps back out of the room and shuts the door. She makes herself a fried egg; also, some chocolate milk and toast, cut into triangles. She considers a glass of wine, but thinks perhaps her story, this story, has had a lot of wine already. She would like to change the direction of it. But she understands something else — this particular narrative must reach its end, just like a road, before she can turn around.

What a bunch of crap, Isabelle! Maggie says. *Get the fuck out of la-la land! Stop being an idiot! This particular road does not end at a tidy little cul-de-sac where you make a sweet little U-turn. Open your goddamn eyes. Look! Look where this road goes. It goes straight off a fucking cliff!*

Cliff. She imagines those photographs. She wonders again who sent them. She sits in the musician's black leather lounge chair, pivots so she can see the stretching waters of the sound, and the beam of the lighthouse making its slow arc. She sees a crow out there on the deck rail, peering in at her. She's never seen them at night before, but there he is, his black marble eyes glinting.

Silvery clouds speed across the sky. The tips of waves glow white in the moonlight. It starts to rain, little pit-pats. She thinks of Virginia, wonders how small a person has to get before she can no longer save herself. The way Isabelle feels right then, in that chair, wearing the too-thin armor of that robe, drinking chocolate milk, she can see Henry's version of things. His is the version that makes sense, actually. Because she can see how a person could be despairing enough to do the job herself — to jump, without any help from him. Even without any hands on her back, Virginia could have become small enough to disappear entirely, all by herself, with one last move. Isabelle is weary, too. Her personal glow has dimmed. The island feels like it's closing in on her. She can almost imagine the flameout: her spirit, drained of vitality, filled with despair and enough of Clyde Belle's misery to fling herself from the rocks just outside this deck.

Don't be dramatic, Maggie says. *Admit it, Isabelle. You can see a different story, thanks to those photographs. You can see a different story, thanks to Henry himself and his petulant ego. Hands shoving.*

Maggie is a know-it-all. Maggie should shut her bossy mouth. Maggie . . . Well, she might have been mean, but people respected her boundaries. Or, at least, they didn't tread over them. People may like Isabelle, but respect is a whole other thing.

It gets late. Isabelle watches the miracle that is the moon eek along the sky. Finally, she returns to her and Henry's room. She lets the robe fall to the floor. It drops into a silky puddle. It has no magic powers, unfortunately. It does not stop her trajectory or fill her with the full and necessary outrage. She gets into bed beside Henry.

But she lies awake for a long time just listening to the rain on the roof, and tossing, turning, turning, tossing, wide-eyed, restless, because something has changed. She does not know what has changed, or what the nature of the change exactly is. She does not know if the change has made her larger or smaller. She does not know if the change brings her closer to a ledge or closer to the ground. She only feels this strange flutter, the arc-flap of wings, as a bird either settles or takes flight.

The flutter and the flap, the flutter and the flap. The night goes on. The wind begins to howl. When Isabelle shuts her eyes, she sees only a wide, roomy trail.

You better be careful, Maggie says.

Isabelle tries to pull the covers around herself without disturbing Henry. It is long

354

after midnight when she realizes that the flutter is her heart, and that the change is a realization: *Out* may not be as easy as it seems.

CHAPTER 26

There are things like meetings. There are grants, and funding concerns, and there is talk of "community outreach" and "public programs," which Weary must fight off with words like *research facility* and *focus* and (when he brings in the linguistic big guns) *integrity.* Gavin Gray taught him well; he taught him what was necessary for the survival of *Corvus* and this place, but also what was critical for Weary's own survival. Every day, Weary thanks Gavin Gray. He sends love skyward, on the back of a bird.

There are all these phone calls. Emails. *Caw-caw*ing chatter. But at the heart of it, at the every-day center, there's Weary and the research; there's Little Black and Corbie and Rousse and Snap and Billy and Simone; Yves and BG and Fou-Fou and Petit, and the captives, like Mean Boy and Lovey and the injured Bobo, and the rest. There is Matias with his clipboard in the pens, and Aimée in the jungle, sitting on a stone, eyes up to a nest in the hidden V of a tree. There is the *bam-bam* of hammers as Hector and Lotto repair damage from the storm, a fallen drainpipe, the roof of one of the pens. They have already removed the X's of tape from the windows, which they'd tacked up after the typhoon warning came.

They are a smoothly functioning communal roost. Smaller in numbers than the hundred to two million crows in some roost locales, and more recently settled than the hundred years that many roosts have been in existence. But a communal roost just the same.

Weary leaves early, because all is ticking along and functioning beautifully without him. Also, he sneaks away right then because like many American crows, he leads a double life. There is the territory he lives in with his large extended family, and there are the places he flies solo, fields and dumps where he goes alone to scavenge and feed his hungers.

Today, it will be all business, though. Or, rather, this day is not about physical hungers but driving emotional ones. When Jean-Marie appears on the apartment balcony as Weary sits at the table at Le Bilboquet now, Weary only downs the last drop of an espresso. He does not need the shot of liquor this time, the tiny-glass courage required to disrobe in front of the gorgeous Jean-Marie. This will be a quick meeting. Weary races across the street. It's hot, the hottest month, humid. He wipes the sweat from his forehead before Jean-Marie opens the door, because vanity is still vanity. He hopes he still smells good after all that waiting in the humid shade under Bilboquet's striped awning.

Jean-Marie wears aviators on his head like a guest star on *Miami Vice.* He's dark and sexy enough for the television version of the underworld work he does, even if it's 1970s style, all unbuttoned shirts and tight jeans and sideburns. Weary considers his retro good looks a perk, a buy-one-get-one, a party favor. Jean-Marie takes the new envelope that Weary hands him. Weary packed the single photo most carefully. If Isabelle rips it up or trashes it, there's no replacement. It's a risk, but what isn't. He's counting on Isabelle. She's his last chance. She's the plan, one hundred percent, and if the plan goes south, there will not be another. At least, that's what Weary says now. He's too tired to do this again. Fury is exhausting. Worry is, too, and so is responsibility of this magnitude. If Isabelle fails him (or, please, please, no, if he fails her) he'll turn his eyes back to the birds and only the birds. Henry North will have gotten away with it — with all of it, murder and soul murder.

This exchange completes Weary and Jean-Marie's business for today. He's almost sorry to be going so quickly, because there's this fleeting relief with Jean-Marie, the freedom of being known. But, then — maybe they both aren't in such a hurry after all, because Jean-Marie's smile is slow.

"Regardez ce que je dois ici." Look what I have here. Jean-Marie waves a small package like a treat, raises his dark eyebrows enticingly.

"You did it," Weary said.

"Bien sûr."

"So soon! I thought I'd be waiting weeks."

"I aim to please," he says. Oh, and he does. He does. Jean-Marie's voice is low.

"Let me see."

"Où est ma merci premier?" Where is my "thank-you" first?

Heat radiates from Weary's face down through his whole body. Well. Well, why not? Is this moment not worth a celebration? It's perfect, really — no time for nerves or regret, only the fast sweep of passion. Jean-Marie leans in, and there is his warm tongue. There's the rough press of his cheek, and then a grind of hips. Weary thinks of the cloacal kiss, the rubbing of the male crow's cloaca against the female after she solicits sex. Quickly, though, crows and anything avian is gone, everything is gone, except bodies and their vibrating. Weary's hands undo Jean-Marie's shirt, his pants. Jean-Marie's skin burns hot; it's slippery with sweat, and they drop to the floor right there. Right there in the hallway of Jean-Marie's apartment.

Life is short. That's one thing Weary knows. There is joy in what has occurred. He is surprised with pleasure, with Jean-Marie's tongue; he is surprised by the waiting package. He cries out. It is over in seconds, same as with *Corvus.* Seconds are long enough. Jean-Marie politely kisses down Weary's neck, but then pulls on his pants.

"Ne pas oublier," he says. Don't forget.

As if. Weary could never forget that package; he could never forget any of this day and its unexpected delights. This is what it looks like when things go right. When things tick along according to plan, the whole day moves gratifyingly forward. He can feel so tired, and then be so invigorated. He can be ready to just let it all go, and then he can remember everything — the beauty of his life now, the relief of it, and the beauty of his anger, too.

Weary waits until he's back in the sweltering Jeep before he opens the envelope. In those shorts, the sun-hot seats sting the back of his legs. Oh, whatever. Who cares about the searing pain! He rips open the package to find the precious document inside, the handsome burgundy of the French passport.

He flips it open. There's the photo, and it's lovely.

CHAPTER 27

"Package for you, Isabelle. Under the front desk," Jane shouts.

The shock smacks her. For a second, Isabelle can't breathe. The degree of surprise is her own fault. She's allowed herself to believe that the package-sender had stopped. For two weeks, there have been no strange items in the mail, no furtive outreaches. She could almost tell herself that it had all been a creepy but brief interlude, something she needed to move through to get somewhere else.

And she could almost tell herself that those packages had merely messed with her head, except, packages or not, she has still been secretly feeling it — an agitated sense of a ticking clock. It's . . . She doesn't know. Just something *imminent.* Because, while there have been no watches belonging to dead women and no photographs of plunging cliffs, there has been Henry, pressing

362

about a wedding date. Henry, with his petty jealousies and small criticisms (*I can't even see you with some dumb jock like Evan* or *You lack sturdiness, Isabelle* or *Your flakiness is showing, Iz*). Henry, with his restless discontent, which could be — really it could, she's seen it a million times — the result of the endless Northwest winter.

And there has been Ricky Beaker in his squad car, parked under lampposts and across streets, lurking behind her a few lengths back. There is no longer any question, none at all. He is following her. He is watching her. Sometimes, he even gives a little wave, as if he's there by mutual agreement.

Now a package — here? *Here?* It frightens her. The sender knows where she works, and probably a lot more about her, too. *Who* are *you?* her thoughts shout. This mysterious sender scares her more than Henry ever would or could.

The sender, or what the sender sent? Maggie asks.

Shut up, shut up, shut up!

Isabelle unwraps Jane's scarf from around her neck. She takes off her hat. She's afraid to look. She edges toward the desk. Peeks. Yellow padded envelope, familiar foreign stamps. She feels sick. She feels dizzy.

"Australia!" Jane says. She's come out of her office to refill her cup; she's holding the glass carafe of the old Mr. Coffee machine they have on a little table in the main room. "Isabelle?"

"Australia?"

"Your package. Are you okay?"

Isabelle tries to examine the stamps from where she's standing. It's true. They look different from the ones before, the ones from France.

"Isabelle?"

"Um."

"What is going on?" Jane says. "I'm finished with the ducking and dodging. You need to talk to me." Eddie laughs loudly outside. He's with Bonnie Randall of Randall and Stein Booksellers and her new boyfriend, Dan Wykowski, the art teacher at Parrish High since Isabelle went there. They're heading into the city for the weekend. Dan has Bonnie's flowered overnight bag hanging from his shoulder.

"I, uh . . ."

"What is that? Who is that from?"

"I don't know, Jane."

"Let me see that. Hand that over."

"Jane, it might be . . ."

"Is someone sending you stuff?" Jane has the envelope in her hands.

someone with a message.

This is the part she doesn't say.

Because in that photo, Virginia wears a watch. Isabelle knows this watch very, very well. In fact, it's in her pocket right then, as she sits by the old Mr. Coffee machine, with its liquid turning acrid. She knows what's engraved on the back: *Virginia Arsenault. ARHS.* One of the most important things about this photo is the purple flowers at Virginia's feet, the same purple flowers as on the trail. Also, the double hump of mountains in the back that form a huge W.

But the most important thing is the watch. The unbroken watch. The watch without a ripped band.

It tells a story. At least, it is trying to. Watch on. Watch ripped, and off. Watch on, ripped, and off, the day of the hike. Piece plus piece.

She grasps the dilemma immediately. She grasps it because of the calculations her own mind makes. What does this photo say? Nothing! Not one thing. There is no proof of when it was taken, for starters. Even if these were the same clothes Virginia wore on that same day, it is still not proof. There is no date. The hike could be one of a hundred hikes. The ripped watch and the photo together wouldn't be considered evidence. Where was the watch even found? If it were with her body or on the trail, Isabelle assumes it would be packed away in a case file. If it were found somewhere else, *where* else? By whom?

It could be a trick. And why no note, no name? It's frightening, and it says nothing, even if it is trying to say everything.

"You stay here," Jane says.

This is not a difficult command to follow. Isabelle wouldn't mind staying by Mr. Coffee and Jane forever, protected by steady usefulness and dogged strength. She might sit there as long as a glacier.

"Little Ricky is right out front," Jane says. "I'm going to have a word with him." Jane is already putting on her big lumberjack coat, the denim one with the red plaid inside.

"He follows me. He's making me nervous, Jane. I can't stand it. I go get a latte, there he is. I buy a stamp, there he is."

"I'll take care of it."

Isabelle sits in that black padded chair and watches as Joe unties the lines and Eddie's plane lifts off. It's an office she's been in a million times since she was a tiny girl. Yet she experiences an odd displacement. Like she's waiting in some other room or office. A police station, maybe.

She is not feeling like herself. In fact, her *self,* whatever that strange thing is, hovers like a vapor. She is wispy and insubstantial. She can't put thoughts together, only *purple flowers, trail, watch,* as the plane crosses the sky like the crows on their commute.

Jane returns. She says nothing about her chat with Ricky Beaker, but Isabelle notices that he is not gone. Not at all. In fact, he's everywhere she is, even more.

Driving home that night, she thinks about the times she's been truly afraid. She isn't counting the times Northwest nature had been the one to do the frightening, with raging storms, a car sliding on ice, a huffing bear outside by the garbage cans, a bobcat crossing her path. She is thinking of the human-to-human sort of afraid. And not the sort of human-to-human stuff of empty parking garages, or approaching footsteps on silent streets, or the uneasy-for-no-apparent-reason first date, but the large and immediate kind. The fear that's raw and primal, because the cause is right there, shouting in your face. There was her mother with the golf club. And the times when she was a child, with her back against her bedroom door, while Maggie pounded on the other side. Later, when she was older, after that diary, and after small moments of rebellion. She can still feel her hair gripped tight in a fist, rug burns on her elbows, the burn of a smack. There was one boyfriend after Joe, too, who screamed at her in an enclosed car and grabbed her under her chin and squeezed, so very, very close to her throat. She stayed quiet and agreed with him until she could get back home. After that, she locked her door and never saw him again. Evan once got drunk and angry and chased her until she shut herself in their bedroom.

When your face is so near to a gnashing animal like that, a dangerous beast, what is petty fury about pen swirls on a page? What is a bashed ego at a Christmas tree farm? What is ferryboat fighting? Nothing. Nothing like golf clubs or upraised hands.

It's all *maybes* and *mights.* It's all some glimpse into a slightly opened door, but it isn't the door swung open, baring the ugly contents of a terrible room.

This supposed fear is just her, she thinks, as she takes the dark bends of Possession Loop. Her weakness, her scared-nervous self, her usual clouded vision. It's all coming from her own head, her overactive imagination, aided greatly by some creepy sender of packages who won't even say who he is. Some fear of fear is not actual fear. Some worry of danger is not danger. It is not being face to face with someone's rage. It is not true peril.

The problem she has with anger — it's large in scope, see? Because it's not just about *her* anger, but about everyone else's, too. Childhood fear smashes the original parts, leaving them either destroyed entirely or wonky and askew, no repairs available for that particular model. What is reasonable anger? What does it even look like? What is fair in the anger world? And what sort of anger should make you afraid? Gnashing teeth? Shouting? That horrible flashing in the eyes? Undercurrents? Do undercurrents even count? And what does one do with the "I'm not angry" angry people? They send the wonky parts into some terrible squeak and confused spin, an are-they-or-aren't-they muck. Every version of anger could make her afraid, was the problem, and not afraid enough.

Which means — action is difficult. It's impossible. Isabelle stands at the machine that measures tremors underground, she looks down at the squiggles and blips that say an earthquake is coming, and she sees only the unreadable but lovely-come-to-think-about-it design. Look at the red peaks and valleys! She hears a beeping, but what is that? It sounds far away. Maybe it's a truck backing up.

Something is broken, understand? When it comes to anger and danger and self-protection, there's just a general haze and a muffled sound. It'll take the earthquake itself; it'll take a piece of the roof actually falling on her head to truly grasp the danger.

She pulls up in front of her and Henry's house. She's arrived. She collects her purse and her jacket. She imagines all the people who would judge her for walking up to that door, turning the knob, going in; all those people who'd say *I would never do that! Not superior me, not fortunate me, not ever-knowing and evolved me!* Apparently, this part of her anger is working perfectly. This is where one right wire connects cleanly to the other, because, if you ask her, people who judge without knowing can go fuck themselves.

"I'm home," she calls.

The photo joins the watch in the hiking boot. Another problem is that Henry is mostly fine. She and Henry — they are. They do regular stuff — they talk about their days, they sift through the mail, and take the garbage to the curb. They make morning coffee, and pay bills. It rains. It rains and rains, and it storms. Henry writes, and he even briefly takes a painting class from old Jenny Sedgewick before dropping out. He feels stared at, he tells Isabelle. He feels restless. Will this winter last forever? (Yes, pretty much.) Will it always be this gray? (Uh-huh.) His restlessness makes her feel bad. The weather seems like her responsibility. The power goes out multiple times. There are candles and flashlights and cold, cold sheets and sudden bursts of light at midnight. He needs to find something else to do with his day. Writing isn't enough. He has too much time on his hands. He's climbing the walls, just waiting for her to come home. What does "climbing the walls, just waiting for her to come home" look like? His occasional irritation. Slightly suffocating attention. Discontent, which becomes a permanent boarder in their house. It also looks like great meals and warm welcomes. Suffocating attention can be sweet attentiveness. There is no roof beam smacking her head. There is only the sort-of-maybe fact of the watch and that photo and his history and her sense of something . . . What? Something *not good* about to happen. Foreboding, which feels like a permanent pressure in the chest.

Penny for your thoughts?

Oh, nothing! Just watching the sky.

Just watching the sky?

It's a . . . moving canvas, she lies.

You seem so far away, he says. *Don't go too far.*

They walk on the beach at Deception Point. They can see Officer Ricky Beaker's patrol car parked up on the cliff.

"Honestly, I'm going to strangle that asshole," Henry says. He kicks at a watery tube of seaweed on the beach.

The atmosphere feels tumultuous, plump with suppressed rage waiting for an outlet. The morning was already bad-electric and wrong because it was one of those restless Sundays where you stay in bed too long, where you force yourself to get up and go out, but find you've gone beyond the point of no return. All morning, no food was right and nothing was on TV and there was nothing good to read or do, in spite of so many options in the wide world. And then came the car ride and Ricky Beaker, and now Isabelle's ears feel funny, like before a storm. The palette outside is the same as it's been for months, gray with gray with gray, broken up with blue-tinged rocks and silver-white sky.

"Tiny has nothing else to do. There hasn't

been any real crime here since Vince Mac-
Kenzie offed his lover's ex."

" 'Crime here since.' "

"What?"

"Are you implying something?"

There's a bloated seal on the beach, flies buzzing around it. She and Henry step in a circle to avoid the corpse. By the time Isabelle's on the other side of the doomed animal's body, the atmosphere plus death plus Ricky Beaker plus the direction of life in general has spiraled her into a worse, reckless mood.

"I'm not implying anything. Jesus, Henry."

Her sharp tone is only a lob of the dullest spear, but to Henry it's a missile. It's always a missile! He drops her hand. His body goes rigid next to her. "Don't take it out on me," she says. "It's not my fault he follows us everywhere."

"You know, you're right. Life with me just sucks. Life with me is every awful thing."

Yeah. Sometimes, yeah! "Let's not fight."

"This place . . . I thought it was going to be a retreat! A sanctuary. A creative, restful sanctuary! But, Jesus! I don't know if I can take it. Small asshole cops plus depressing rain, rain, rain. This weather will drive a person mad."

"It's not that bad, Henry. It's cozy. You

can get a lot done."

"Cozy? Oppressive! That's what it is. We need to think about moving. Maybe back to the East Coast. Not Boston, not after that hell, but . . ."

"I have a business here."

"Sell it! Come on! Think of the freedom. Think of all the choices we'd have . . ."

He stops walking. In an instant he sees her face and what she is thinking. How, how, how does he do it? He can see that his idea is not *freedom* to her, before she even knows it herself. Leaving with him, leaving what little is hers and going to the east coast with only him to hold her aloft is perhaps more accurately . . . *captivity.* She has not even clarified this for herself. The words have not even formed. It is as substantial as that foam curving up to the shore, but he spots it.

"Isabelle," he whispers.

"Henry, I just . . ."

"Are you ever going to marry me? Are you ever going to *commit*?"

From where they stand, Isabelle can see the blip-shine of glass from their house, and the brown splotch of shingles from her childhood home just beyond. Two homes, one cliff. It's almost more than she can bear. They stand in the soft, sinking part of the sand, the metaphor part, where land meets water and your footprints fill up and then disappear. All at once, every hidden thing rises. Every tip and toe, every bit of care and every denial she's used while trying to build a good life — they show themselves and then crumble and sink, and something else shoulders in. *Out!* she thinks. *Done!* Suddenly, the scorecard of what she gets versus what she's given flashes, and the crowd boos. Suddenly, there's a glimpse of life alone, and as dim and dire as that might look, it's better than *this.* Suddenly, that solitary new maybe-life is a joy party in comparison, and *alone* is shininess beaming down, a relief. There are suddenlys upon suddenlys, because that's how it works with nice people like Isabelle, nice people with those particular broken parts. The *done, finished, enough* comes all at once, and when it does, it crashes down like a wave and makes things vanish. The tiny flame inside, the one that's been steady the whole time, it's hotter and more powerful than she knows.

"Am I ever going to *commit?*" her breath comes out in a sarcastic puff. It's cold out there.

"I mean, I wonder, okay? If this is about more than me and my past. You were with

Evan *five years.* Maybe, you just . . ."

"Maybe I just *what*? Have some issues about committing? I *do* have some issues about committing. To you! I need time to think . . . I have some issues about trusting this whole —"

He grabs her wrist. "Don't say anything you can't take back, Isabelle. Calm down! Stop right now."

He *grabs* her *wrist.* He grips it hard. His fingertips squeeze her veins; press her pulsing artery.

And now, with that . . . He's done it. He's crossed the ultimate boundary of hers. He's put a hand on her in anger, which brings up every hand on her in anger, and all those memories plus the right now smash together like a multiple car pileup. She twists her arm to get free. Calm down? They are standing by the shoreline, and as she pulls away hard, the woven bracelet she is wearing breaks and drops to the sand. A wave crawls in fast and snatches it and out it goes. It is a meaningless bracelet, something she bought at an art fair for a few dollars; she has others at home. But it suddenly (suddenly!) feels crucial. Beloved, even. She splashes in to retrieve it, even though the water is icy, even though the bracelet is already too far out.

"Isabelle, are you insane? Get out of there! What are you doing? This is nuts! Stop acting crazy!"

And suddenly, too, she sees it: The story that could be told of her. The unstable woman, the unhappy woman, the dramatic woman, the woman who couldn't commit. The crazy, deranged woman.

She is up to her knees. The water is so cold that her legs go numb. The waves play rough. The surf pulls hard. Her hands reach for the bracelet and for balance both, lurching upward like a toddler learning to walk. Her jacket is getting soaked.

His arm hooks around her, firmly yanks her back to shore. But not before she makes one desperate grab and snags the bracelet.

"Jesus Christ, Isabelle! What has gotten into you?"

Her jeans weigh a million pounds. Now sand adheres to the wet, adding a million more. Her shoes and socks are too sodden to walk in. She struggles with the wet laces, manages to haul off her shoes. Her crumpled, soaked socks look irrational and defeated.

"Is that silly bracelet worth hypothermia? Being pulled out to sea in this weather? What are you thinking! Come on. Let's get you home. My God, what a day. Let's just go make a fucking fire and get out of this gloom. Why are we even fighting when we love each other? I told you, this place! Makes you insane. Look at you!"

They trudge back up the beach, up the trail that hugs the cliff. Tiny Policeman still sits in his cruiser. Henry glares at Tiny. Where was Ricky Beaker when she needed him? Clearly, only she can look after herself. Isabelle tries to wipe the sand off of her clothes but it's sand on pants and coat and now sand on hands. Henry is disgusted with her, but he's also being oddly gentle. He takes her hand, which is freezing. He places his own coat over her shoulders. She knows why he's being gentle. That grab of her wrist. Oh, she knows that game, the way the nicey-nice gestures of unspoken apology come after someone's gone too far.

When Isabelle gets back home, she puts the bracelet in the boot with the watch. She understands that they are broken in the same way.

CHAPTER 28

On this warm day, Weary relaxes. His pool is private, protected by the isolation of his property and by the large bamboo gate and the palms. How peaceful it is. What an exhale.

He stretches on the teak lounger with the towel on top. It's a rare occasion, a day to just unwind and sip a cool drink and swim when the temperature rises. It's the hottest time of the year but also the rainiest, so when a shower passes overhead, briefly dropping warm, soft rain before moving on, it's an expected and welcome interlude, even if this month's copy of *Behavioral Ecology* gets soaked. Poor *Behavioral Ecology* — it's momentarily forgotten until too late only because of what hasn't been forgotten: Sarah's journal. Weary snatches it up fast when the first drop hits his cheek. He grabs it and wraps it in the towel and holds it close, safe and sheltered, as the cloud sprinkles the sweet holy water from the oceans over them both. *Both,* because the journal is what's left of Sarah. Her voice is there, her experiences. It's evidence that she existed.

It gets hot again, and so he swims, and he does something uncharacteristic then, maybe because he feels so good lately, so hopeful for the future, so reborn. He slips free of his suit. Well, all right, not slips. Getting out of a wet bathing suit is always more of a twisting, pulling battle. He drops the bundle of wet by the side of the pool. This is uncharacteristic, as Weary has always been somewhat modest regardless; it's his usual insecurity, he's had it his whole life, and he's made peace with that fact. He's in fine shape really, all that trudging on mountainsides, and as he swims, he feels good. Sleek as a moray eel (*Muraena* to the locals), smart as a tiger shark; hidden and rare and secretive as the nautilus, that rare mollusk of New Caledonia. He may — yes indeed, with a little luck — prove to be as poisonous as the tricot rayé, the striped sea snake of the region, whose venom is deadly and for which there is no serum. He has survived and endured, same as the Grande Terre reef itself. Life is good, in other words, in one of the most stunning places on earth. Even if he has worries, even if the clock ticks and so much is out of his hands, he must remember to take in the beautiful fact of being alive.

He towels off. He decides to stay naked. Why not? He sips his guava juice. Now there's the sun again, warming his whole body, loosening his mind. His thoughts drift in the manner of the pool's plastic chlorine dispenser, shaped like a space capsule, which always ends up bumping against the same corners by the stairs. He thinks of Isabelle and Sarah and Virginia, and he thinks of birds, of *Corvus*.

He thinks of the three species that look most alike to the common observer — the crows and the ravens and the rooks. And they *are* alike, but they are different, too. The ravens, for example, are larger than crows, while the rooks are slightly smaller. Raven feathers are somewhat pointed, whereas a crow's are rounder, and a rook's are particularly silky. Tail feathers vary, and so do calls, habitat, and such, and yet, Weary thinks . . . They are corvids, all three, family, with a shared fossil record dating to the mid-Miocene, seventeen million years ago.

Sarah, now she would be the raven, with her larger size and flatter chest and throaty voice, and Isabelle would be the crow, medium build, perfectly proportioned, with her neat, upright demeanor, and Virginia would be a young rook, with her small size and pale white face, a *young* rook, though, before they plump up and gain their baggy trousers. She never had the chance for that.

This is silliness, he knows, the worst sort of anthropomorphism, but it's his day off, and he doesn't need to be a scientist every minute. The recent photos on ShutR, and, now, rereading Sarah's journal — it's all made his mind swirl and knock. In a few of the new images that have appeared, Isabelle swims, too. She's in a pool, and she's in the sea. And she's strolling beneath palm trees, and sipping drinks at a bar on the beach. Weary knows exactly where they are.

The Visa card showed the purchase of the tickets to Riviera Maya, but even without that information, Weary would recognize La Casa Que Canta, where North and Sarah also went, just after Sarah found that photo in a box in their garage marked *Electrical.* At first, Sarah thought *Electrical* was just Henry's linguistic whimsy, because there were a few letters from his overbearing and critical father in there, too, and a running medal he earned in school, though he was humiliated by sports growing up. But then, as she riffled through, she saw that photograph of Virginia at the bottom, covered by everything else. And when she did, she immediately matched the watch in the photo to the ripped watch in the box in his underwear drawer, and that's when she knew. She *knew.* Well, maybe she always secretly knew, that's what Weary thinks, but the photo was proof. Enough proof for her, if not for any detective or prosecutor.

Because, well, by that time, she knew Henry, too. The watch meant nothing without the photo, and the watch and the photo meant nothing without knowing Henry. How does one explain the intricacies of a delicate ego? An ego like a piece of antique lace — if it's not handled carefully, then one little finger can poke through and rip and destroy.

After Sarah saw that photo, it was over. The truth was clear. God, what a wreck she was then. She didn't even look like the same person anymore. You can be doing something so simple, looking for an *adapter* in the garage, and life as you know it can end.

Weary wonders if Isabelle has any idea that Henry swam in that pool before, ordered that same drink on that same beach, with a different woman at his side. Weary flops to his stomach for an even tan. And those photos of Isabelle — it was shocking.

She has changed so much from that early image of her on the sailboat! She's so much thinner, and there are dark scoops under her eyes, little hollowed-out thumbprints. She looked pale, even in that sunny weather. Well, Henry would have insisted on sunscreen, Henry would have insisted on the right and exact SPF, because that's what he's like. Sarah could have told you that.

Honestly, the photos agitated Weary when he first saw them. Not just because of the unnerving echo of place and people (and, really, Mr. Marvelous — the same *restaurant*?), not out of some weird jealousy (how great, having such a lovely time), but because it propels him right back to those months before Sarah disappeared. She'd gotten thin, too. Her cheekbones were cliff angles in her broad face. She'd confessed that she'd gone inward. In fact, she'd confided in only one person. Yes, *one*. Oh, those long, intimate phone calls and secret meetings! Long distance? What long distance? A person is practically right there, when their breath is in your ear. Yet, still, Sarah grew smaller daily. Her physical body, her voice. She was slowly disappearing before the sailboat trip, until she actually disappeared for good.

Weary was glad when the next photo

popped up on ShutR, the one of the light-house with Isabelle out front, meaning she was back in the gray gloom of the North-west. She was wearing her hat with the pom-pom on it, which makes Weary think of a playful child on a snow day. He was relieved she was home again, safe and sound. You know, for now. Because those other photos disturbed Weary greatly. *Disturb.* Continue to.

It makes him lose sleep at night. No wonder he's practically drowsing off right here in the middle of the day. He had failed Sarah, and he has vowed not to fail Isabelle. Is he moving fast enough? The hollowed eyes and the weight loss, the damage of being picked at and constantly watched and measured — well, that's killing enough, but Henry's insecurity and his control can turn truly dangerous in a second. That cliff worries him. Where their house sits. That sea does.

It's hard, so hard, to watch from afar. Wouldn't it be nice not to be the only one doing a damn thing about Henry North? But, no, he can't go there, to that old place, he can't revisit his useless but fervent desire for aid and rescue. It is up to him, and the harder he grasps that fact, the better. His own heart must beat a steadfast *jus-tice, jus-*

tice, jus-tice under the floorboards, like the vital organ in the Poe story. His commitment must be equivalent to Montresor's in that other tale of revenge. There is no room for the weak here, only heroes, riding the backs of ravens. He must rise and fly fast and fight the currents. He must reach Isabelle before it's too late.

Weary sighs. He is supposed to be relaxing, but it's hard to relax. How can he? He dangles his arm down the side of the lounger, reaches for the journal. His fingers tap the cover. Does he really need to read it again to remember any of it? He practically has it memorized. Pick a passage, any one. The words unfurl in his head like familiar lyrics.

He reminds me about the lemon in my own peach tart, lectures about the spacing of bulbs in my own garden, even tells me where to hang the hummingbird feeder. Near the red flowers, *he says.* Since they see in ultraviolet. *Thanks so much for basic hummingbird fact number one! I can now toss my Ph.D.!*

Weary likes that part: *Thanks so much for basic hummingbird fact number one! I can now toss my Ph.D.!* But what comes next — it's painful to read. The entries were written before Sarah found that photo in the box marked *Electrical,* before things got dark

388

and darker still, and so the words bring a sick feeling, the desire to shout warnings from the future. *It's no big deal, really, right? He's just trying to help. That's what he says. So why do I feel like the box I exist in is shrinking and shrinking? Sometimes I imagine it — being out of the box. Breaking right through it. God, the light and space would be lovely. Still, he's a good man. He means well. He's just a wounded little boy inside.*

Weary can imagine Sarah, holding the feeder filled with sweet syrup. He can see a tiny bird, fluttering suddenly right next to her. He can hear, no, he can *feel,* her laugh of surprise. There is Henry's voice, breaking the joy. *Near the red flowers!* Weary sees it all so clearly.

He is drifting off. It's the sun and the swim and the restless nights. The swirl toward sleep is pleasant. It plucks him from reality, lifts him vaguely upward . . . Virginia is Sarah is Isabelle. Raven is crow is rook . . . There is some ringing, ringing, pounding, far off . . .

Holy shit!

He leaps up. There *is* ringing and pounding! He is wide-awake now, with terry-cloth bumps across his cheek and drool down his chin. He grabs the towel to cover himself. Who is at his door?

Jesus! What was he thinking, lying there naked?

He opens the front door as the truck rumbles off. His heart pounds at the scare. Everything is okay. It is only a package.

It is the router he ordered, in hopes of better Internet speed. The photos take forever to load, and there's no time to waste.

CHAPTER 29

The watch, the bracelet, broken things . . . Isabelle replays the words in every combination. *The bracelet, broken things, the watch . . .* She thinks of them while she showers, with her head tipped back to the warm water, and she thinks of them when she leaves for work and sees Tiny Policeman parked across the street, eating a maple bar and sipping coffee before he starts the cruiser's engine and pulls out behind her. She thinks of the words as she takes the hand of a tourist stepping out of the Beaver, a woman traveling alone, and she thinks of them as Eddie starts the propeller. She thinks of the words as the hundreds of crows fly silently overhead in the early hours in a pink sky, heading to who knows where.

Too, the words come to her as she swims in the Caribbean Sea off the Playa del Carmen, and while drinking margaritas with Henry and doing laps in the blue tile pool of La Casa Que Canta. The trip was a surprise. Henry gave her the tickets under her pillow with a note: *You said you needed time to think. Let's think together somewhere new and beautiful.*

After *broken things, the bracelet* on the beach in front of their own house that day, and even after a romantic vacation for two, the apologies keep coming. Or rather, versions of apologies because they are not, not this time, the actual words *I'm sorry.* There are small acts of kindness. Blankets pulled to cover shoulders, little cluckings and tendings. A special bar of chocolate, her favorite music played during dinner. Agreements and compromises.

And now, something even larger.

When she returns home from work, there's an offering: a stack of poems on the coffee table. Attached is a note that says *Read me,* with a smiley face. There's a sharpened pencil set on top.

The bracelet, the watch, broken things . . .

"Are you sure?" she calls to Henry, who is in the kitchen.

"Very."

It's an offering because he thinks they're good. He thinks they're a way to woo her, to bring her back to him, to think well of him. To admire him, and want him. The pencil is a little biscuit tossed to the puppy.

He wants to draw her to him again, because he knows she's far off. Even after the candlelit dinners on a Mexican beach, even with lovemaking and life going forward, she's absent. His hand grabbed her wrist in a moment of fury, and it broke something, and since then she is in this strange state of suspension. She is staying as quiet as possible, so that he does not glimpse the constant electrical impulse sending a repeating message. The message is not *Leave now.* The message is *Manage the beast. Manage the beast, until you can sneak away.* Probably because *Leave now* was not an option back in the early days of the broken machine. Only *Manage the beast* was.

Too late, she understands: If you are trying to manage a beast, it is already impossible to manage the beast.

"Do you want me to read these now, Henry?"

"Please. I need your professional input. I think I finally may have a collection on my hands."

It's a minefield. And she's maybe not in the best frame of mind to do this thing. *Frame of mind,* what a strange phrase. She wishes her mind had a frame, so it might stay contained in a reasonable rectangle. It has gone rogue. It is plotting secret escape at every turn. She does not want out because she's suddenly convinced he is guilty of something horrible. No. She doesn't believe that. She can't. She wants out because he's a difficult and temperamental man with a weighty history, a man she can no longer tolerate, a man who will not take this news well. She wants out because he grabbed her wrist and crossed her most cherished line, and because she can't handle any of it — *the watch, the bracelet, the broken things* — any longer.

She takes her hat off by the pom-pom ball, making her hair stand up with static. She unwraps the scarf Jane made her.

He brings her a glass of wine, sets it down next to the pages.

"I have to use the bathroom first," she says. She doesn't. What she has to actually do is move the watch and the photo and the bracelet back into the boot from their current place in her jacket pocket. She goes to their room, listens for the sounds of cooking — a fork against a bowl, the clatter of dishes. Safe. She shoves everything down into the boot, closes the door quietly. All day while she's at work, she worries that she's somehow forgotten to bring the stuff with her, that he'll find it, that she'll come home to a furious Henry. She checks her pocket repeatedly to make sure the objects are still there. When she feels the edge of the photo, the watch, the bracelet, she's relieved, but also . . . What? Properly disturbed. *Reminded.* She needs these reminders daily, multiple times a day. *This is your life now and don't forget it, even if this won't be your life forever.* She knows it's not forever, because there's this feeling, a feeling that something is about to happen. It follows her everywhere.

She removes her coat, hangs it on the guitar hook.

"Wow. You must have had to go badly."

"What?"

"Using the bathroom while wearing that big coat."

He misses nothing. It's become a part of living with him, the microscopic examinations, the little suspicions. She explains things she never had to explain before. She justifies, because he thinks something is strange, and he is right. "Couldn't wait," she says.

"I don't expect you to read the whole thing tonight, of course," Henry says. "You'll want to linger." He can't resist hovering. When she sits on the couch, he actually places the pages of the manuscript on her lap.

"I'm sure."

"You read. I'll finish dinner. Stroganoff sound good? I'm thinking of all the most rich and delicious things so you won't just move the food around on your plate."

It's true — she hasn't been eating. Nothing sounds good lately. Not the fancy meals at that hotel, not Henry's fine cheeses and meats dribbling bloody juice. Jane has been ordering in lunch for the crew, shoving roast beef sandwiches at her, and little igloos of potato salad. She can stomach Cream of Wheat and bananas. Her dream meal may be frozen dinners back at her childhood home. How could she have ever sold the place?

You've got the money. You're hardly stuck. Just go! Maggie says. Easy for her to say.

"Henry, if you keep looking over my shoulder, I can't read."

"Well, of course, I'm nervous. As a writer, you pour your heart and soul on the page."

"I understand."

"You should just experience it first, before you take the pencil to it. I'm sure that's what the real editors do."

She lets the comment sit — in part, because she doesn't want to fight. But there is another reason she says nothing. A sick feeling is overtaking her. Some sort of horror, because right away she sees that the poems she'd found in the desk were only castoffs, ruses, maybe; not *the* poems, not *these* poems. These are entirely different. As she glances quickly through the pages, her palms go cold and she feels that almost blue lack of oxygen in her head that means she might pass out. These are poems about women, lost women, lost loves.

The lines swarm and swirl, and words leap out, words like *tremulous* and *Heaven* with a capital *H*. There is "The Sea, To —," which she recognizes as an echo of Poe's "The Lake, To —," with a similar narrator finding solace in water, in spite of its treachery and danger. She sees "To the First Mrs. —" and "For Ginnie," with the echoes of Poe's own lost-love poems, "Annabel Lee," "Lenore." More words jump: *Luminous, Beauty, Taken, Alone. Mystery, Flight, Toll, Tomb*, and *Kingdom*. She glances through. There is grief and more grief. *Slumbering, Heartache, My Darling* . . .

"They're meant to be read in order."

"I am reading them in order."

"I heard you flipping pages. Which one are you on?"

She can barely speak. "Henry, I've only started . . ."

"I'm just wondering, because you're so quiet."

"I'm on . . ." It's hard to breathe. " 'Gone Before.' "

"That means you're on the third one already? You really shouldn't rush. Poetry shouldn't be rushed just because it's brief."

The ceiling seems to be lowering. The walls are coming in. "Henry, I can't read them if you're going to act like this."

"Like what? I thought you had experience working with writers."

"They weren't exactly in the same room with me, breathing down my neck."

"Well, of course you worked on books about hiking trails. And Northwest B&B's . . ."

"Maybe this isn't a good idea."

"I'm just saying, you aren't an expert in poetry."

"It sounds like you need to hire an expert."

"You don't need to get touchy, Isabelle. I'm only remarking on the fact . . ."

Her head hurts. Her wine is already gone. Something's burning.

"I smell charred —" she says.

"Shit!" he says. "Fuck!" There's a rattle and clang and he shoves the pans off the stove. "Well, scorched meatballs are nice.

How about that for dinner? Is my cooking as good as my writing?"

"I haven't said a word, Henry!"

"Exactly! That's exactly my point! You're just sitting there with your mouth in some disapproving line . . ." He's waving a towel at the smoke detector, which is shrilling.

"I'm taking it in . . ."

"Three poems already, and nothing? Not one peep? Not a simple sigh? I'm just looking for an overall impression . . . one kind utterance!"

"If I say something too soon, it's wrong. If I say something too late, it's wrong! I like them, Henry! They're . . . surprising. I'm a little . . . I can feel you . . . pouring your heart out!"

"Pouring my heart out? Jesus. You make me sound like a schoolboy. These were women I deeply *loved.*"

The poems are on her lap. The fourth one, "The Subsequent Lover," stares up at her. Isabelle puts her head in her hands. But then the weight of the manuscript is gone, whooshed away, snatched up. "Forget it. This was a bad idea."

"For God's sake!" she cries.

The smoke detector is silent. The darkness behind the windows makes Isabelle feel she's alone with Henry on their own solitary planet, spinning together in the vast, awful universe.

"This is just . . . I wanted to share my soul with you. My life . . . What this has all been like for me . . . The depth of my *devotion*. Never mind. Just, never mind. This is *worthless.*"

He shouts the word *worthless* in her face. She can feel the heat of his breath, even though her eyes are tightly shut. She starts to cry. It's all too much, too fast. There's so much failure and mess that despair takes over. Everyone is here, in this one room. She and Henry, Virginia and Sarah.

The front door slams.

Good. He's gone. Her heart cracks open, but she doesn't sob. She doesn't weep over where she's ended up. She doesn't snivel and blub and bawl about needing a plan and not having one. No, when her heart cracks open, she stops crying. There are no tears. She's frozen. Every part of her is frozen and stunned except that tiny flame, growing tinier.

She hopes he's gone for a long while, but she knows he won't be. *Now's your chance!* Maggie shouts. Isabelle could grab her purse and the hiking boot and just *go.*

She doesn't go, though, because she's a deer in the headlights, and there are a lot of headlights. A traffic jam of them. So many headlights, and all of them so bright that she's immobilized. The poems are shouting, too. Screaming warnings. What does it mean that he's written them, and what does it mean that he actually hopes they're published? He wants to live in peace; he wants his privacy. But does he also imagine the whole world reading his poems, seeing his genius, finally *understanding* him?

The poems tell a story of lost love and utter devotion. And they tell a story of a large and doomed ego. It scares her, that ego. For the first time, she's honestly frightened of who he might be. For the first time, her doubts seem real. She knows what happens when fragility and rage and thwarted desire mix. She has a childlike urge to run to her bedroom, hide in her closet; sit on her toy box with her ears plugged.

She peeks out the blinds by the front door. Tiny Policeman has not followed Henry. Instead, he's there, parked out front. He's talking on his phone. The dome light of the cruiser is on.

He is there, so she is safe, she tells herself. *Right.* Maggie scoffs. *Ricky Beaker keeping you from harm? Remember the Tostitos?* One time, while trying to apprehend a shoplifter at the Front Street Market, Ricky Beaker had a run-in with a display of potato chips and ended up breaking his arm. A deputy from Orcas had to come and run the police department until he got his cast off.

Right then, Isabelle misses her mother. In spite of the golf club memories, and her fear, she misses her mother so bad. She misses her voice on the phone, her humor, her roast with rosemary potatoes. She has some toddler desire to crawl on a lap and cry and have safe arms around her. Probably, she's just missing something she never had, but still.

And then, another package comes.

It arrives at her work again. She sees it before anyone else, because she's the first one there. She's been going to the community pool very early every morning to swim laps. She swims because there is no place for all her anxiety except exercise. And she swims because it's an approved way to get out of the house before Henry even wakes up. Swimming is a good thing, he thinks. The best form of exercise. A fine way to stay in shape. So she does her laps alongside old Cora Lee from the Theosophical Society, who, in her green suit, is thin and shriveled as an aging celery stalk. In the calm burble of underneath, Isabelle listens for some larger plan, something beyond the current one, which involves stepping quietly backward until Henry is so disgusted with her that leaving becomes his own idea.

That morning, her hair is still wet when she arrives at Island Air. The fog hasn't even lifted, and Tiny Policeman isn't on the job yet. But the package is there, shoved through their mail slot, stuck halfway in and halfway out. She knows it's for her, because of the stamps: images of a strangely patriotic kangaroo with a British flag in the background. Also, smaller ones of animals, candidates for an adorable children's book — koala, wombat, Tasmanian devil. They could all go on a journey together and find the real meaning of friendship.

She snatches the package. Now, she looks over her shoulder to see if Jane or anyone else is coming. Silly — it's too early. The doors are still locked, shop is closed; the seaplanes are tied down next to the dock, propellers silent. It's strangely quiet, without the usual rumble and roar of floatplanes leaving and floatplanes arriving.

Isabelle turns around. She heads over to the big storage center, where her old things are kept, and where Island Air's ancient Zenith is parked, too, waiting for repairs.

She crouches behind the far cement wall. A squirrel stops to stare at her from an evergreen tree. She rips open the envelope.

Photocopies, this time. Handwriting. Five pages of paragraphs, short and long. No dates, just messy, looped writing; the kind of writing meant only for your own self.

It's a journal.

She crouches there and reads. It's freezing outside, even though March is coming, even though Isabelle's wearing Jane's scarf and a hat over her wet hair. The morning has that cold smell of far-off snow and leaves burning.

He's just trying to help. That's what he says. So why do I feel like the box I exist in is shrinking and shrinking?

More, more: *I can't make a move without comment. Every clothing choice, every decision about food, or my body, or even which direction to go when I drive . . . I can't take it anymore . . . I am thinking a lot about Virginia.*

Sarah. Entries from Sarah's journal.

This could be Isabelle herself writing. All of those lines — hers.

"No," she says aloud. She *must* have said, because there's the puff of her own breath. The morning darkness lifts; the sky has a stripe of pink. And here they come — the crows on their morning commute. First, just a few black bodies, working hard against the sea draft, and now more and more, a wash of inky satin on pink. Isabelle holds those pages on her knees. She chooses one thick bird among the many, and imagines she is that creature, heading somewhere else.

They come and they come. And after the mass of them passes over, after there are only the few stragglers left, Isabelle rises. She peers around the corner of the storage building. No one has arrived yet. She walks out to the dock. She stands at the end. She rips and rips and rips the pages into tiny pieces. She lays them down into the water and lets them soak and sink and be carried away.

There are too many pages to keep, and there is enough in that boot already. She won't need those pages to remember the words, anyway. Especially those last words, the ones that tell her that the watch and the photo had once been Henry's, and that Sarah had seen them and doubted, the way Isabelle is doubting now. Sarah doubted, and then she was gone.

Today, I found a photograph, hidden in a box in the garage. Virginia, wearing that watch from Henry's drawer . . .

The sprinkles of white paper disappear

like snowflakes. Behind her, Isabelle hears a car approaching. It is just Jane, who waves. Isabelle waves back, thankful that the bits of journal have now vanished. She has some strange feeling that she is part of a plan, though this may just be her usual passivity, her urge for rescue, since she does not have a plan of her own. Still she feels it, an odd connection to the package-sender. It's almost a motion deep under the ground, a riffling in the air currents. It's disturbing, and yet it feels like propulsion. Of course, there's always a strange energy just before an earthquake, just before the plates shift, and everything trembles and wrecks.

CHAPTER 30

Right there in the New Delhi airport, Weary decides that the one-day conference he just attended will be his last. He is exhausted. There's the time difference, for starters. He can't handle it anymore. Five and a half hours for a trip that fast is enough for him to feel achy and spinning. He was awake all hours of the night, and now he is left with a strange pressure in his head. There was New Delhi itself, too, the mad crush of cars and strange little taxis and bicycles and people and jammed-together buildings and jammed-together languages and jammed-together smells.

And then there was the event, the International Conference on Animals. Even with his single fifty-minute talk, which came after Dr. Isaac Roseway's on "The Neuropsychological Issues in Australian Kangaroos" and just before Dr. Margaret Che's on "Wildlife Systems and the Epistemological Implications for Environmental Analysis," it was stressful. Gavin Gray had always underscored the need for a normal yet cautious face in the world, a public presence for the facility, but Weary thinks passing this particular hat to his best Ph.D. students might be wise now. Even Gavin Gray might feel differently if he were alive today — two years ago, there weren't so many phones, so much clicking and tapping and documenting of each and every moment. It's utterly nerveracking. In spite of the firm rules *No recordings! Turn phones off!* Weary swears he heard the *whoosh* that meant a photo was taken.

Must everything be shouted about and publicly demonstrated? Must every inane thought and minor occurrence be boringly proclaimed? Who really cares! If a tree falls in a forest and no one has taken a picture of it, did it really happen? What are we doing, watching everyone else eat and vacation and succeed, succeed, succeed? Document the forgotten lettuce leaf turned to liquid in the fridge, photograph the sore throat and the crushing failure! And how does anyone do anything surreptitiously anymore? How does anyone have a moment's privacy? We are witnessing the age of the secret coming to an end, he is sure.

Still, the conference went well, and there

was more than polite applause for his talk, "Intelligence in the Corvid Family." He heard the murmurs of appreciation for the facts he conveyed: that corvid brain size in relation to their bodies is equivalent to that of great apes and dolphins. That corvids use a part of the brain with no human counterpart. That, while all corvid brains are large, the brain of New Caledonia's *Corvus moneduloides* is largest of all. There were chuckles at Weary's story of the university crows in Japan, who wait patiently on the curb along with the pedestrians for the traffic lights to change. When the lights turn red, they hop out into the street with their walnuts, plucked from nearby trees, and set them under car tires. When the light turns green, they collect their newly cracked bounty.

And there was a hum and buzz at one other story in particular. That of the Clark crow of North America, who collects up to thirty thousand seeds in the winter and then buries them for safekeeping in a two hundred square mile area. Over the next year, they manage to locate ninety percent of those seeds or more, even when they disappear into deep, deep snow. Humans, he told the delighted crowd, often cannot locate their car keys from the day before.

That is the power of memory, Weary thinks, as he sits in one of the black vinyl seats set in a row on the gold patchwork rug of the Indira Gandhi International Airport, waiting to board his plane. That is the power of intelligence.

Intelligence is not something one usually ponders at the airport, not with the travelers baffled by shoe removal and metal bits in pockets, not with the balancing of too many things, like the man in shorts and a blaring blue graphic T-shirt coming Weary's way, wheeling luggage while impossibly clutching a foil-wrapped dosa and a lassi with a plastic straw. With the conference finished, though, Weary can mentally luxuriate. He can ponder and pray and dream about hidden bounty and the best way to crack a nut. All Weary must do now is wait for the boarding call, bustle inside the plane with the other cattle, and sit for the too-long ride home. And then it will be time. When he gets home, he'll send what he believes will be the last package. The package that completes the plan. That is, if Isabelle and her own intelligence can be counted on.

An ill-attended child with a Hello Kitty roller bag bumps his shoes, but he barely scowls. No, all the horrors of the airport fall away as Weary imagines it: He envisions himself flying to the very spot in the two hundred square miles where the document is buried. He imagines unearthing it, even though it is covered in layers of time and secrets. But he will not peck and consume and indulge. He'll set it in Isabelle's hands instead. He'll deliver it like a shiny treasure. The next move will be up to her.

Finally, they board. Well, eventually, Weary does. There is first class, and MVP this, and MVP that, and Gold this and Silver that, special this, special that, until it is practically just Weary and the man with the now half-consumed dosa.

He is filled with exquisite joy, though, when he finds his seat. He has struck the real traveler's gold, hit the mega jackpot, because there is an empty seat between him and the young Indian woman in her salwar kameez, the loose trousers and tunic in shades of orange. The woman has her book already open, and Weary is next to the window. He feels fortunate, because his thoughts need this extra room. He hopes the space between him and her, his fellow passenger, muffles the *ba-bamp* of his heart. Now that the conference has been ticked off the list, there is just Weary and his deepest desire, and he is terrified and buoyant and impatient.

Honestly, he can't wait.

Here comes the safety business, exit aisles and flotation devices, with the accompanying cheerleader gestures from the flight attendant and the nonsense about the whistle on the life jacket. The plane roars and lifts. Weary is already checking the time. There will be the cab ride home, the sleepless night, the next morning at work, the excuse and the escape to Jean-Marie's. He will leave Jean-Marie's sweltering apartment, knowing he has done all he can. Then he will wait to see what happens.

Brain size to body: There are the dolphins and the great apes and the corvids. But larger still is the human brain. Weary is counting on this. He cannot spell out the most important information in that document, not without putting himself in danger. It will be up to Isabelle to see what's really there.

Weary peers out of the plane window, which has tiny crystals forming at the edges. Clouds stretch to infinity. Here, it is too high even for birds. But Weary is soaring. He flaps to that glass house on that cliff. He imagines Isabelle with her brown hair and kind eyes. She's smart, because Henry wouldn't be with her otherwise.

Still, when she was with him, how smart was Sarah? How smart was Virginia?

God, it makes his stomach lurch with nerves, or maybe it's just the *chaat* he ate at the Hotel Delhi.

Come on, Isabelle, he says to those stretching clouds. *Come on,* he pleads, as the woman in orange turns another page.

CHAPTER 31

Managing the beast looks like this: One is soft and sweet when the beast is in a stormy mood. One jokes when he is sullen. One avoids certain topics — past loves, neglected needs, anything else that might trip the circuits of insecurity. One makes promises that won't be kept, about cross-country moves and wedding dates and future plans. One secretly continues to plot escape, even if so far this still only includes vague, mental packing, and quietly but purposefully disappointing him until he leaves of his own accord.

To keep her anxiety down, to keep from jumping out of her own skin while she waits for him to leave her, Isabelle swims. And she swims. Her hair lightens from the chlorine in the pool. The muscles in her arms turn hard as baseballs. The rains lessen, too, finally — the temperature rises. Tiny daffodils pop up along Main Street.

Driving past, Isabelle sees the usual corner of her mother's yard filled with purple crocus. At Remy's, the trees begin to blossom. Outside, it smells warm and pastel when the sun comes out.

She could probably swim in the cove now, like she used to in high school. One day, she hunts around in the storage unit until she finds her old wetsuit. Henry thinks it's a crazy idea, but she hangs it in her closet, where it droops like a rubber woman.

Henry buys an almanac. He pinpoints two days in July with the least rainfall. "Twenty-one or twenty-seven?" he asks Isabelle.

She knows the right answer. The earlier date, not the latter. Choosing the latter equals rejection. "Twenty-one?"

Their wedding date.

Something else happens, just after the first green leaves unfurl and the clouds part, showing kaleidoscope blue: Tiny Policeman gives up his mission. One night, Isabelle looks outside their front window to find the street empty. There's just a lamppost shining its circle of light, and the neighbor's cat slinking around. Officer Ricky Beaker is gone in the day, too. It was probably those early hours at the pool that got him, plus just plain boredom. He apparently came to the conclusion that he had a better chance of making some big bust with his old punk nemesis, Kale Kramer, than with Henry, who drives the speed limit and always goes to bed before eleven.

One warm Friday, Isabelle sees Tiny P. coming out of the Front Street Market, dipping the spoon end of the straw into a Slushee.

"Good afternoon, Isabelle," he says.

"Good afternoon," she says.

"Beautiful day, isn't it?" His teeth are stained a light purple from the grape liquid, making him look like an overgrown child. Still, he watches her face. It's strange, but in spite of the Tostitos debacle of the past and the Slushee of today, she can feel him reading her, taking in the possible facts. The question is not about blue skies and summer.

"Yes," Isabelle says. "It is."

"All right. Good. Well, turn your tires to the curb when you're parked downhill. You don't want to risk rolling into traffic."

"Thank you, Officer. I'll do that."

Tiny Policeman goes on his way. She never realized how reassuring it was to have him there, until he was not.

It's pure luck that she hears the rumble of

the truck. It happens to drive up in the time between Eddie's next departure (with a pair of couples who've just spent the week at Asher House B&B) and Liz's arrival (the first load of employees from the Binyon Optical annual retreat). The point is, no seaplane engines are roaring. Usually, she can barely hear herself think, which is convenient. But now, there's only the sound of the truck heaving up the road, grumbling to a stop: Big Jim Roberts from UPS, bringing a package. A padded envelope.

Isabelle runs. She runs up the dock *to* Big Jim Roberts, not *away* from Big Jim Roberts. She knows the package is for her. She doesn't want to see what's in it, but she also *has* to see what's in it. That day — more luck — there's a problem with the credit card machine, and Jane's on the phone in her office, distracted. No one else in sight cares one bit about what she gets in the mail. Or, at least, if Ray in the customs trailer sees her rushing to accept a package, he'll think she's excited about a delivery from Amazon. When she reaches Big Jim, she's out of breath.

"For me?"

"Yup. Where the hell is Nouméa?" Big Jim asks.

"Nouméa?"

"Never heard of it, either?"

"My friend is on a trip around the world."

"Trip around the world. I may never get off this island. Signature required."

"Really?"

"Your friend wants to know it arrived."

Oh, wow. It's a new development, and the uneasiness starts back up again, that giant, restless creature who stirs in the pit of her stomach. Big Jim hands her the machine and the stylus.

She signs. "Have a good one," Big Jim says.

Now, bad luck. No purse, no coat. As soon as Big Jim drives off in the brown truck, she shoves the package inside her sweater. It's practically a living thing against her skin; she feels its pulse and its will.

Where to go? She sneaks around the back of the building, past the ailing Zenith, which she's sure eyes her with disapproval. More good luck, though — her keys are in her pocket, after a trip back to her car earlier for her forgotten lunch. One of these keys fits the storage unit, but which? Her hands tremble. It's like she's got the kilos of cocaine and must now start the getaway car. It's tricky business for someone who gets nervous parking for fifteen minutes in a ten-minute zone.

There. She opens the storage unit, closes the door behind her. It's cold inside, echoey. There's her mother's dining room table, and boxes with her mother's handwriting on them. *Holiday Decorations. Isabelle — Childhood.* There are boxes with Isabelle's own quick, upside-down scrawl, too: *Books. Misc. Living.* There's a floor lamp from her and Evan's place. A propped-up headboard from her mother's bed. There's that leather chair she used to read in when she was a child and couldn't bear to give away. She's forgotten about this stuff. It's been hidden away in this frigid place, but it's still here.

This is a mistake. There are much better places to open this package, places less haunted. Her mother roars to life. Even with the large, dusty-warehouse-ness of this building, Isabelle smells her. She sees her, propped against that headboard. She sees her, bent over that box, putting an ornament that Isabelle made in elementary school on the tree — a clay angel, a broken wing hot-glued back on by Maggie herself. A tender gesture, because, of course, there were those, too.

Remember yourself? Maggie says.

Yes.

Open the fucking thing.

Isabelle sits in the leather chair. The

leather is freezing at first. She takes the package out from under her sweater.

Postmark: *Nouméa.* She examines the stamps. *Nouvelle Caledonie.* Three kinds of exotic birds, plus one large fish with a concerned expression. *Zone Du Grand Lagon Nord.*

She feels it, squishes. Another fat clump. Letters, maybe? A document? Something grips her heart, tight, tighter. She rips open the envelope.

It's a stack of paper, folded in half. It's long, legal-sized.

Last Will and Testament of Sarah Banks North.

Isabelle takes the hit, which is a solid punch in her gut. Is she even breathing? Barely. She lays the will open on her knees, because her hands are shaking so badly. She thinks she hears the rattle of the doorknob, but it's just her nerves.

I, Sarah Banks North, of the City of Boston, County of Suffolk and State of Massachusetts, being of full age and of sound mind and memory, do hereby make, publish, and declare this to be my Last Will and Testament . . .

Isabelle reads quickly. She can't hide in here long, as Liz will be arriving at any moment with the opticians. She scans the pages. Clothing, personal effects, automobiles, the house, bought in her name — it all goes to Henry, of course, her husband. Now, her personal trust fund. Forty-five percent to Henry. Five percent to the Archdiocese of Boston College, her alma mater. Twenty-five percent divided amongst Alice Reynolds, Jared Reynolds, and Janice Reynolds. Twenty-five percent to the New Caledonia Corvus Research Facility and Sanctuary.

What does this mean? Isabelle already knew the house was in Sarah's name; she knew about the trust fund, and Sarah's money. She knew Henry received a large portion of it, plus more when the New Haven Providence policy kicked in. She already understood this. Everyone did. The police did. None of this is shocking. What is she being told here? Who are these Reynolds people? No idea. Sarah was an ornithologist, and so money to a bird sanctuary does not seem surprising or revelatory. Isabelle doesn't know *what* the will is trying to tell her, but perhaps she finally knows *who* is trying to tell her? Someone from the New Caledonia Corvus Research Facility and Sanctuary. Because *New Caledonia.* Those stamps. Then again, why be this obvious and not leave a name? It's a trick, she's sure.

She feels unwell. She is shivering, from the cold in there, and from holding this horrific document. She leaves the storage unit, locks it up. The package is in her sweater again. She heads to her car; hides the envelope in the wheel well in the trunk, under the tarp that covers the spare tire and the jack. She locks everything up. By the time she is halfway to the Island Air office, she's convinced herself she left it unlocked, and heads back to do it again.

She isn't sure of anything. Not the locking of the car or her own intentions or even who she is. *You are so sensitive,* Henry tells her. *Here, let me help you with that before you hurt yourself,* Henry says. *Well, there isn't much point doing nice things for you, is there?* Henry says.

In the sky, the Beaver roars, and the body of the plane grows larger and flies lower as it approaches, ready to splash down. Jane has noticed her absence. Isabelle can see the angry huff of Jane's shoulders as she stalks out to the dock to do the job of the missing lineman. The Beaver lands, neat as a dragonfly on a pond, and Jane gets the ropes. Isabelle is halfway down the dock when Jane spots her.

"What the hell!" Jane is too old to be hunched on her knees like that. Tying those lines will test her cranky finger joints.

"I'm sorry, I —"

"Where've you been?"

"I don't — I've got some —"

"What's wrong?" Jane has to shout. The propeller still spins, a blurred and dangerous circle.

"Fever. I've got some fever."

She does. A fever or something, because she is hot and cold at the same time, and she's shaking all over. It feels like fever and like panic, and like standing close, too close, to that propeller.

"For God's sake, go home, Isabelle. Go home and rest and eat and —"

"I'm sorry."

"Go."

She does. Who is this person, stumbling down the dock? It's a ghost woman. *Remember yourself?* Yes. No — that person on the dock is so tiny, Isabelle can barely see her. She is a memory, that's all. Wait. Can you have a memory for something that never was? Maybe that figure is a specter of lost potential.

Isabelle unlocks her car again, locks the doors when she's in. The *thunk-thunk* is reassuring, but it makes her think of the sound of locks, all locks, the pointlessness of them, like the time she tried to lock her bedroom door against her mother's rage and she shoved through anyway. The pointlessness of locks, and the need for them — big locks, mighty ones, the permanent kind that come on prison cells.

Her head throbs. Of course, she doesn't go home. The sky is spring blue, but she drives in a blind, gray fog to the library. Her fever-palms are clammy, and her shaky legs make her foot press too hard on the accelerator. She's a dangerous driver now, and Remy, who Isabelle spots drinking coffee in the window of Java Java Java, is watching her intently. Remy — she's one to talk, driving five miles an hour on the blind corners of Deception Loop.

Isabelle almost expects the document to have vanished when she opens her trunk. She questions her own sanity. Did she really just hide a will in her wheel well? Did she really just get a package from the other side of the world? Does she live with a man with two dead lovers? Is her mother really gone, or is Isabelle just here at home, visiting on spring break, heading to the library to stock up on a few good novels?

Wake up, wake up! Maggie sings, same as she used to when Isabelle was going to be late for school.

■ ■ ■ ■

She finds a computer at one of the back tables. She takes the will out of her purse. She hunches over it, like a prissy schoolgirl protective of her test answers. She was actually kind of like that in elementary school, if she's being truthful. If she's taking a hard look at her failed self. My God, she's made so many bad choices.

She types: *Alice Reynolds.* Too many hits. She types *Alice Reynolds, Boston.* Nothing. Then, *Alice Reynolds, Sarah Banks North.*

An article about Sarah's disappearance, from *The Boston Herald.* A quote: *Alice Reynolds, the missing woman's aunt, said, "I always thought Henry was a fine man. They always seemed happy. As a Christian, I won't leap to judgment." Reynolds lives with her son in Yorba Linda, California.*

Son. Jared? Jared and Janice, cousins?

She types: *Sarah Banks North. Will.* Too many hits. *Sarah Banks, of Staten Island, will marry . . . Junior champion, Sarah Banks, will compete . . .*

She types: *Sarah Banks and Henry North. Money. Trust fund.*

Disappearance of Local Woman Stirs Debate. The Boston Globe, this time. *Police are*

425

still seeking answers in the disappearance of Sarah Banks North. Close friend Hannah Fallahi calls yesterday's press conference held by husband Henry North and Police Chief Ross Buckley "a total sham." "One only needs to understand the amount of money involved to seriously question Mr. North's claim that Sarah 'ran off.' I can state unequivocally that her trust fund was significant," Fallahi stated.

No. Isabelle doesn't believe this. If Henry had a role in Sarah's disappearance, money wasn't the reason. She rejects this idea outright. Henry may like his fine things on occasion, but he's not motivated by a driving force for *more.* In spite of the money he has, there are holes in his socks. His favorite sweater is an ancient brown cardigan from the Gap. He tells her she spends too much after seeing the new swimsuit on her Visa bill — her private card, not the shared one he insisted on giving her for dinners out.

She types: *Nouméa.* She types: *New Caledonia.* She looks at images of a remote island. She types: *New Caledonia Corvus Research Facility and Sanctuary.* It's a bad, out-of-date website, featuring a map of the area with a big red star marking the location of Mount Khogi. There are images of crows in trees and crows in cages. There are only three tabs: Contact, About Us, and

Research. She clicks Contact, sees an email address, *Director@corvusRF.com,* and a phone number. She tries the About Us tab. *The personal vision of Dr. Gavin Gray, the New Caledonia Corvus Research Facility's mission is to preserve the earth's biodiversity and to secure the future of the corvid species in its natural habitat. We work to fulfill that mission through research, field and captive studies of corvids, particularly Grande Terre's* Corvus moneduloides . . .

The library computers are slow. It takes minutes upon minutes for a page to load. Jesus, she could run home, she could do some errand, do impossible shopping for another *bathing suit* even, come back, and still be waiting. She hears a clock ticking, but it's possible the sound is in her own head. Isabelle looks over her shoulder, but only sees librarian Sasha with her spiky Mohawk and her *Smashing the Patriarchy Is My Cardio* T-shirt, shelving in the biographies.

Dr. Gavin Gray.

The name is familiar, but she can't remember why. This speaks to the state of her mind, because the name is *very* familiar. It's an important name. It has a bad feeling around it, but what? The library has become noisy and she can't concentrate. There's the scurrying and chatter of little children, the motion and rearrangement of stuff, strollers and bags and jackets. A baby wails. A kid whines. Story time, she guesses. She types it in the search box: *Dr. Gavin Gray.* The results go for pages and pages. She could be here for weeks. She types: *Sarah Banks North* and *The New Caledonia Corvus Research Facility.*

Nothing.

She types: *Sarah North. Dr. Gavin Gray.*

An article. "Corvid Survey Techniques Through the Measurement of Biotic and Abiotic Features," and all at once Isabelle remembers.

Oh, shit. Of course. Of course! Dr. Gavin Gray, Sarah's friend, focus of Henry's jealousy. It always seemed silly, this idea of an affair. At least, more ridiculous the longer she knew Henry and understood the depth of his insecurity.

Dr. Gavin Gray, she types again. Could he be the one sending these packages? From various, what, lecture circuits, or something? What do ornithologists even do? Are there universities in the French countryside? *Dr. Gavin Gray, Rochefort-en-Terre, Bretagne,* she adds.

Nothing.

Lourmarin. Dr. Gavin Gray.

Nothing.

Dr. Gavin Gray, Australia.

Surveys and Research and Yookamurra Sanctuary, Australian Wildlife Conservancy. Industry Group Seminar, La Trobe University, Featuring Drs. Kenneth Rich, Genevieve Rich, Dr. Gavin Gray . . . LaTrobe University Graduate Research Group adviser, Dr. Gavin Gray . . . Spontaneous Metatool Use by New Caledonian Crows ". . . differs from Torresian crows (Corvus oruu) . . ."

Isabelle's neck aches. The throb in her head has become something more solid, an iron wedge, hot-cold and pressing. She does not understand what she is being told, and it seems that Gavin Gray is a busy man. Too busy to be sending her mysterious packages with the personal effects of a dead colleague.

There is a smattering of applause and the sounds of bodies in motion again. Story time is over. A toddler in a denim jacket peeks around a corner at her and then disappears.

Isabelle does that thing frustrated searchers do — she hits a random number on the line of search results. It will be a last pull of the slot machine before she gets out of here. She can't stand even one more slow-loading page.

But, then . . . Wait. Maybe she *can* stand another slow loading page, because what is *this*? Is this the same Dr. Gavin Gray? Because if it is, Dr. Gavin Gray is not nearly so busy as she just thought.

If this is the same Dr. Gavin Gray, he is not busy at all. He's *dead.*

Famed Researcher Loses Cancer Battle. The Boston Herald this time. Famed ornithologist Dr. Gavin Gray, best known for his research on tool use in crows, lost his battle with cancer on Tuesday. Gray, 47, a longtime Boston resident and professor at Boston University, founded The New Caledonia Corvus Research Facility, in the Pacific, and was instrumental in the discovery that crows manufacture hook tools to aid prey capture. University President Shauna Vicars said, "Gray's contribution to the scientific community and to the greater understanding of animal intelligence is one that Boston University is very proud of. He will be missed by family, friends, and colleagues." M. Weary, who will continue Gray's work at the facility, said, "It's a loss. A great loss." In lieu of flowers, sister Denise Fredericks of Needham asks that donations be made to the New Caledonia Corvus Research Facility, BP 8145, Nouméa, New Caledonia, 98846.

Isabelle leans back in the library chair,

ends her session on the computer. Her best lead, Dr. Gavin Gray, could not be sending her packages, unless he's sending them from the grave. Certainly, he would need more stamps for that. She feels a hit of disappointment. She's back to the same large and empty unknowing she was at before.

She can't go home yet. It's early, and she feels too disturbed, too unwell. She can't bring this into the house — this strange chill and heat and headache. She makes another dangerous drive back down Deception Loop; she loses speed and then picks up speed from distraction. There's a swerve around a dead opossum carcass on the road, the near miss of gore and guts on her tires. She spots the moon in the sky, weird and white in daytime. She knows this road so well, but it's like she's somewhere she's never been before, which of course is true.

She heads for the other side of the island, the Straits, where the Hotel Delgado sits, and where the entrance to that trail is, the one that heads to the McKinnon family plot. She parks in the hotel lot. Hardly anyone's out there, just the employees of the restaurant setting up for dinner inside, a man staining his boat, a solo tourist on a bike ride.

She sits on the bench overlooking the marina. She stays for a very long time. She's forgotten all the body stuff, the hunger and the need to pee, the usual functions of a human in a day. All of that has shut right down, and there's only the pumping of her heart on some sort of invisible life support. She is thinking too much about Clyde Belle and his blood on that rock, that's for sure. Clyde Belle was likely this exhausted.

The sky dims, and the horizon earns a crown of gold. The crows come. Here they are, and she must be still alive after all, must be wanting life, because there's that awe. Awe lifts in her, a sunrise. She watches the birds fly in their endless black line, looking like a forever swath of smoke. She listens to the *whiff-whiff* of wings. She thinks of other crows in a far-off place, New Caledonia, crows in a jungle, carefully fashioning their hooks. Here, she watches the swerve and dip of certain individual birds. Most flap with seriousness and steady industry, but a few veer and drop and rise again before resuming.

She has veered and dropped, but has no idea how to rise again. She watches, hoping to learn. It looks so easy. But she can only imagine what it takes to make this trek every day. When the fog is thick, they caw and caw and fly low to make their way through it, and when the wind is strong, they beat hard against it, and when it snows, they still go forward, white flakes melting on black satin. What it takes to keep on like that — Isabelle has no idea. Right then, she has no clue.

"Isabelle, thank God! Where have you been?"

"Just, late. I had to stay late."

"How could you do this to me? You couldn't call? You know what it's like for me! After Sarah, how can I not go mad with worry? I rang and rang . . ."

He did. On that bench, the phone buzzed and buzzed like a dutiful but despised alarm clock until she turned it off. "I'm sorry."

"I was scared to death!"

"I'm an hour late, Henry. I got caught up at work . . ."

"Is that what they call it now?"

Her coat is still on. Her purse is still over her shoulder. Her head hurts so bad, lopping it off sounds all right as an option.

"Isabelle?"

She's dizzy. The floor tilts, and the walls shimmer. It might be her own body, attempting to shake some sense into her.

"Are you all right?"

"I don't feel well."

"Oh, darling. You poor thing. You look awful."

"Maybe it's the flu," Isabelle says.

"Who have you been kissing?"

"No one, Henry. No one." She is so tired.

"Only kidding, my sweet! It's a joke. I'm just so relieved you're here. I thought . . . Oh, never mind. Get in your pajamas. Get into bed. I'll bring you soup," Henry says.

She does what he tells her to do. She gets into her pajamas and climbs under the covers. Every part of her aches. It aches because the fog is heavy and the wind is hard and because there is only cold. Henry sits beside her on the bed. He gazes into her eyes. He rubs her arm. She can barely stand his touch. There is a watch in a boot in her closet, and a will in her trunk. She has to get out of here. Right now, she's not sure which one of them has more secrets.

CHAPTER 32

So many dangers, that's the problem. So many ways things can go badly wrong. The clasp of talons, the swoop of a river, *mortality* just lurking around, waiting for an opportunity. Last year, the crows they followed had eleven new chicks. Of the eleven, there are only four left — Chouchou, Bijou, Bébé Noir, and Poli, short for *Polisson,* rascal.

The owls and the torrential rains don't help. A goshawk got Coco as Lotto watched. Poor Lot can barely share the news. His big face squinches up, and he rubs his eyes to keep from crying.

"I can't stand it," Aimée says. "This is awful."

"Life in the jungle," Weary says. "Best not to get attached."

Listen to him! What a fraud. What a poser and a liar. Weary's own throat is tight with tears. They were all so fond of Coco, that funny little bird. He wants that hawk dead, honestly. He wants to hunt him with an arrow, shoot him right through the heart. *Best not to get attached.* Right! So coolheaded and in command! So *not* the true Weary, who is carefully hidden. Inside, he is scared and unsteady — he's very, *very* attached. He has not heard anything from Isabelle and he is going crazy. Inside, he is cawing and flapping and pacing, same as Lotto said Simone did after Coco was snatched. Lotto said that hawk ripped Coco open right there as he watched.

"Onward. Today is a new day."

And they do go onward, and it is a new day. An astonishing one. He and Aimée trudge into the deep heart of the banyans. They hunch, and then sit. Neither speaks, because their eyes are on Bébé Noir their youngest, six months old. Bébé has been hacking at a Pandanus, and leaves fly every which way. But then, Bébé does something different. Look! It is happening! She is tearing a strip from one jagged-edge leaf. She is pecking and forming it into a perfect spear. It's a spear she'll use to capture insects and grubs and slugs deep inside trees or far down in the ground.

Aimée grins like crazy, scritches on her pad. It takes six months of apprenticeship, they are finding, before a young bird can make the hook or the spear. Before that, they are all thrashing and bumbling, inept to the point of comedy. Poor things, they must learn from the ones that came before.

Aimée's eyes meet Weary's. What he sees in hers is familiar. Pride, affection — love, even. For months they've been watching their chicks. Silently (and sometimes not — some researchers talk much too much in the field) urging. Hoping their little charges stay out of the danger that is everywhere around them. Hoping they conquer the challenges of the wild, and avoid the tragedies of their peers. But then comes a moment like this. *Look at Bébé now,* Aimée's face says.

See? They are parents. Loving parents, *attached.* Weary lacked these in his own life, and he never had a particular desire for children of his own, yet it's something he still feels stirring in him, the respect and longing for the bond. Why are New Caledonian crows so smart? The same reason many children are. Unlike most crows elsewhere who live together but separate, guests at the same party, New Caledonian crows live as family. Offspring stay with their parents for a very long two years, and sometimes longer, as if they still need dad slipping them a twenty for gas money long after college. The family forages together. They chat. They *play,* making toys from sticks and pinecones. The parents groom, patiently teach, patiently demonstrate by example.

They invest, as Weary has invested in Isabelle. And while Weary is only a handful of years older than Isabelle, not old enough to be her parent, he is trying, is he not, to patiently teach, to show by example? He urges his own slowly developing charge; he leads, demonstrating what he knows from his experience as the senior, wiser one.

And he worries. He frets. God, how he frets and how his mind tosses. With no photos on ShutR and no useful new information on the credit cards (Front Street Market, gas, Ace Hardware, mundane stuff), he feels a tumble of fear. It's like every long night in New Caledonia, wondering who in the flock will be alive when you get back to Mount Khogi.

He knows fear. For others, for himself. He knows what it's like to be so terrified that you separate from your own body; so terrified that when you return, you say, *Yes. Yes, there I am.*

Still, Weary smiles and nods at Aimée. It's a sweet moment, this victory for little Bébé.

He only hopes that an owl will not pluck Bébé from his roost as he sleeps helplessly.

Those owls — they are one of the reasons the crows are black. Black helps them blend in with nighttime shadows. But an owl does not rely only on sight to hunt. Hiding in shadows is nothing. The owl listens for the slightest sound in the night. He'll locate his prey by their softest breath. He's all camouflage and quick capture; his talons will crush a skull and knead a body. His bill will scissor and tear flesh.

As any parent knows, you agonize. So much is out of your control. You can teach and warn and suggest, but the baby is still in the woods. You try not to think about the worst, but the worst always hovers out there, because it's the truth, too. It's as much the truth as the surviving.

As far as Weary can tell, Isabelle still sleeps beside Henry in that glass house. He would never judge, though. Sometimes you don't wake up until the owl sinks its beak into your chest, right before he stops your heart.

CHAPTER 33

And then something bad happens to Isabelle. Something worse. She is sleeping restlessly beside Henry when her phone rings. And rings.

It's Jane. There's been an accident. Joe, socked in by fog overnight in Seattle, took his four fishermen up to Nanaimo at first light and then hit a submerged shipping container when he attempted to land.

"It's all that shit from the tsunami. It's a minefield," Jane says.

"I'm coming."

"There's nothing we can do but wait for news. Dear God. Joe . . ."

"We'll wait together. It might sound worse than it is. We don't know . . ." Isabelle says as she reaches for her jeans.

"Let him be okay. Please. Just let him be okay."

He is okay. He and the four fishermen are

at Nanaimo Regional General Hospital, and Joe may have broken a few ribs. One of the fishermen is being observed for heart attack–like symptoms, which later prove to be only the shooting pains of a bad scare. His heart is fine. They are lucky. Joe was water taxiing slowly, treating the area as if it were chock full of objects after reports of fifty-five-gallon drums, lawn furniture, and even a drowned motorcycle in the area. Only the de Havilland was seriously injured. It punctured a pontoon, necessitating their rescue by a crab boat.

"Thank God," Jane says. "Thank God, thank God, thank God." Jane is an atheist, but these are pesky details in a crisis.

"When I was in Alaska . . ." Eddie says.

It is lunchtime before Isabelle realizes.

In her hurry to get here, she left the stuff — the watch, the photo, the bracelet — in her boot at home with Henry.

The sick feeling starts as soon as she remembers. Then comes the terror. She tries to calm herself with reason. Henry is busy. He's been working on his poems again. He's also begun the repair of Remy's rotting deck. The day before, he'd made two trips to Ace Hardware — to buy lumber, a new skill saw, other tools. She is not sure he

441

knows what to do with the tools, and neither is he. But he was happy with his new toys, and he was in his office all evening, watching online videos featuring home-repair guys.

See? He won't be snooping around, looking for evidence that she's slipping away from him. He won't find it and utterly lose his mind. He has things to do. Even if he went into her closet, he wouldn't see that watch! He's probably been in there a hundred times already. She's even had near misses while she was home, and it was fine. Why would he even reach his hand inside her boot? He wouldn't.

There are a lot of reasons a seaplane might crash. Lots of ways flight can go wrong. Improper techniques and procedures, landing on water with the wheels extended instead of raised, bad weather, gusty winds, rough water pitching the plane, and, perhaps most dangerous of all, glassy water messing up perceptions of height and depth. But how often is there an actual accident? It's a rarity, she reminds herself.

Then again, all of a sudden there's a storm, Maggie says. *Out of nowhere.*

All of a sudden, there's a half-submerged Harley-Davidson that'll kill everyone on board.

Isabelle tries to keep the panic down. She

can barely focus as Jane discusses the plans to get the de Havilland repaired and Joe back to Parrish and the fishermen up to Alaska to resume their trip, minus the heart-attack man who wants a shuttle home immediately. (*Like there's a shuttle? What kind of shuttle?* Jane says. *Sure, I'll just call him a taxi.*) She wonders if Evan felt like this during his affairs; if he worried she might pick up his phone or see some hotel bill or spot a fallen earring in his car. The package-sender is almost like a lover, with the hiding involved — with the secrets and the fear of being found out. But also like a lover for the need of connection, regardless of the risks.

Henry could look right in that closet and not see a thing, she tells herself for the hundredth time that day.

And then she gets a text.

Sorry to bother u at work . . . Don't we have heavy gloves here? Looking everywhere.

During the drive home, she imagines it: the way she'll feel the negative electrical charge from down the street. She'll stand outside the front door, the briny, something-dead smell of the sea wafting past, and she'll do what she shouldn't and turn the doorknob. He will be in bed again, his shoulders turned away —

No. He'll be standing right there as she comes in, face red with rage. He will grab her wrist again. She will try to twist free. More things will break, big ones.

Maybe he'll just be gone, she tells herself.

Maybe you'll be number three, Maggie says.

She should have worked harder and faster to find a way to leave, and now it's too late. Instead of managing the beast and hoping for some magic resolution, hoping he'd leave her after all the distances she'd too gently and politely set around like dishes of candy, she should have just bought a ticket to somewhere and got the hell away. Why did she feel she owed him? Why does she feel she owes everyone? The worse the human, the more she tries. Nothing feels safe, that's the problem. No plan does.

He won't hurt me, she tells herself. She still questions if he's done actual, physical harm to Sarah or Virginia. She knows she must placate him, and she can see his fury sitting just past his insecurity. But she can also now understand the despair that would lead Virginia to her death, and she can understand the anger and alcohol that would lead Sarah to hers. And, well, it's awful to think it, but if something ever happened to her, his life would be over. She could fall off a cliff of her own accord, and he'd be in prison for good. No one would ever believe a third accident. He would never let that happen.

Like rage is rational? Maggie says. *Stupid girl. You must really miss me. Can't wait to see me again, huh? Hope kills. Naïveté does.*

She heads home. Riding along with her is her utter refusal to believe in the truth of her own peril. Peril is for strangers on true crime TV. Peril is not for regular people like her, people who wear flannel pajamas and who eat Grape-Nuts and who get their oil changed when the little sticker tells them to. She knows from the journal that she and Sarah shared the same doubts from the same watch and photo, and that they shared the same demeaning moments, and the desire to flee, but that is all she knows for sure. She and Sarah also both understood Henry. *He's just a wounded little boy inside,* Sarah had written.

Stupid, says Maggie.

I know how to handle him, Isabelle thinks.

Arrogance, her mother says. *Omnipotent narcissism.*

Isabelle keeps her keys in the pocket of her jeans, though. She leaves the car doors unlocked. Just in case. In case she needs to be out of there, fast.

Her chest feels hollow. She is sick with dread. She opens their front door.

"Hi, sweetie!" Henry calls. "Hope you're hungry, because these potatoes I just made are fabulous."

The potatoes *are* fabulous, and so is the roast chicken. Her relief has helped her appetite. Henry bought some chocolates at Sweet Violet's, which he sets on the coffee table, alongside two tiny glasses of amaretto. He is talking animatedly, about two-by-fours and joists, about the call he'd gotten from his brother, about Jerry's promotion and his niece's gymnastics meet.

"Maybe you'll actually like it," he says.

After the words *uneven bars* her mind wandered, and she's lost the thread. She has no idea what he's talking about. She's been watching Henry, remembering the reasons she fell for him. Such a handsome man. So smart. So organized and confident. What a wonderful life it would be, sitting on this couch, eating chocolates and drinking a cordial after a meal like they just had, made by this man, with his gorgeous hair and beautiful grin, and his command and wit.

"Like it?"

"The new poem? 'Renewal'? Are you even

listening?"

"Of course I'm listening. I'm sure I'll love it."

"Like you loved the others."

"Henry, no words would be enough for you."

"Are you saying I'm needy?" he says, but his voice is light. "I am needy. I need you."

He leans in, kisses her. His tongue is a distant thing to her, an invading, poisonous creature she wants to fend off. His hands are over her, and now he's on top of her. It's dark out, but the lights are on; anyone taking a dark solitary walk on the beach will see them. "God, it feels like forever," he says.

It has been a while. She's used every excuse, from fatigue to periods. She's tried all the tricks, from falling asleep to staying up late.

He unbuttons her jeans, works them down her hips. The keys in her pocket clank to the floor. He doesn't notice. She tries to concentrate, tells herself this is the Henry she first met, the innocent Henry, the one she couldn't get enough of. It doesn't work, and so he becomes Evan, and that's bad, too, so he becomes some stranger, and that's no good, so he becomes Joe, the early Joe from high school, not the one of today, cherished pal, still thankfully alive but with broken ribs and, after today, with a story to rival any of Eddie's.

Nothing is working, but no matter, because Henry sits up suddenly.

"Do you hear that?"

"What?"

"Is that rain?"

She listens. Yes. There's the *pit-pit, pat-pat* of drops on the roof and the garbage can lids and the decking.

"Oh, shit! I left all the tools out there."

He pops up off her. He pulls his jeans back up, leaving the belt hanging loose.

She sits up, too. Yanks her bra back down.

He opens the sliding door to the deck, lets in the delicious night smell of wood smoke and damp earth. "Hell, I should cover them, at least."

He hurries off toward the garage, and she gathers her jeans, those keys. In the bedroom, she changes into her robe. She feels down inside the boot and finds the watch and the bracelet and the photo still there. Close call, but everything is fine.

A chocolate sounds nice.

She is choosing. She thinks the square ones are caramel, but she's not sure. You never can tell, until you poke the bottom, or just go for it and pop it into your mouth. That's the trouble. Even chocolates are a risk. She knows that round one has the potential for being a revolting cherry, so —

"What the *fuck,* Isabelle?"

There he is, standing right there, and she goes from chocolates to shock in two flat seconds. She's in utter disbelief, because after all the worrying and all the imagining of every bad thing, she never imagined this. She didn't ever foresee him standing there with the tarp from her car in one hand, and the will in the other.

"What. The. *Fuck.*"

"Henry. Henry . . . I didn't —"

"Where did you get this?"

"It came in the mail, Henry. I'm sorry. I should have told you . . ."

"Oh, you think? You think you maybe should have told me that asshole was sending stuff to you? Instead of *hiding* it in your *trunk*?"

"I'm sorry. I'm so sorry. I don't even know who it came from!"

"I know who it came from! New Caledonia? That fucking sanctuary? It came from that asshole Gavin Gray! The fabulous Gavin Gray! Who was fucking my *wife.*"

So fast, it happens. The slide from peace to fright. From potatoes and chicken to red rage. Of course it's fast, though, if it's always been there, sitting off the coast, waiting for the right drop in atmospheric pressure.

"Henry. I'm sure —"

"You're sure *what*? What are you sure about, huh? I told the police, you want to find Sarah? She's probably there, with him! They went! They looked! They said no way. The prick was too sick to get it up. Wow, look who's had a miraculous recovery. Look who's still trying to ruin my life."

No. No miraculous recovery, but she doesn't say this. Honestly, she's too stunned to say anything real or right. She's too shocked to do anything but *ward off.*

"It doesn't mean anything, Henry. He's just trying to, I don't know! Tell me something about you, and Sarah's money . . . But I already know —"

"It doesn't mean anything?" He flings down that tarp. His face is right in hers. "I don't give a fuck about the will. You want to see the will? I got a copy here! I'll show you! Just ask me! I'll show you anything, I told you! I don't care about all those people. Virginia's friends, Sarah's people . . . I don't even care about *him.* But you? You! You hid this, Isabelle! You fucking hid this!"

She backs up, bumps the coffee table. She thinks of her keys, now back on her night-stand in the bedroom where she keeps them. His face is huge in hers, and his mouth contorts. She feels his breath on her cheek.

"I didn't —"

"You did. You *did.*" He presses forward, and she moves back, and he still comes at her, everything large — voice and body. There is nowhere to go. She is almost over the ledge of that open door, where just beyond, the rain pours and the rotting boards have been yanked off in spots. "You hid this in your trunk, like a suspicious *coward.*"

"I knew it would upset you. I didn't want you to see —"

"You didn't want me to see, because you *hide,* and you *sneak,* like a little —"

He grabs a handful of her robe. The satin is in his fist and he is shaking it, and he hates her then, she sees that clearly in his eyes and in his clenched teeth. And then he does it. He shoves. That fist with the robe in it — he pushes her, hard. She stumbles backward, clutches for the doorframe. She is outside, on that deck, and suddenly she is down, one leg falling and cracking through the decaying lumber. There's a pain as wood rips skin, slashes up her calf, and the splinter and crash of chunks of things dropping, something sliding, some tool, which rolls and tumbles.

She's down on the deck with one leg dangling where it's only down, down, down below and it's raining hard now, drenching her hair and her satin-clad shoulders, and when she looks up, she sees him, the man who shoved Virginia down that cliff.

"Oh, shit," he says. "Goddamn it. Oh, Isabelle. Sweet Izzy . . ."

"Get out," she says.

"I'm sorry. Jesus, I'm sorry." He reaches his hand out to help her up, but she only grapples for bearings, gets on her knees. She struggles to her feet.

"Get *out.*"

He turns. There's the fierce whistle of his exhale as he storms off. She hears his keys, swiped from the counter. The door slams and the house shudders.

Inside, Isabelle shudders, too, when her mother's car spits gravel and screams down the street. She slides the door shut, locks it. The room is cold from the night and the storm and the anger. The will and the tarp are tossed on the ground, and her leg is bleeding. Her leg is a *mess.*

She limps to the front door and locks that, too.

She dab-dabs the blood with a washcloth, but it keeps coming. She cleans out the splinters, runs water over her leg as the slash in her skin gushes. She's made a trek of blood drops like breadcrumbs to the bathroom. The cut is right there on the shin, where the skin is thin. The washcloth looks like a leopard pelt with spots of blood, so she gets a towel, holds it there until it soaks and finally stops.

The washcloth, the towel, they are disturbing to look at. Without them, and without the will and the tarp and trek of drops, it could almost be any other night. Look, there are the glasses of amaretto with their milky residue, and the chocolates on a plate. She could trick herself into thinking he's in the other room, looking at home-repair videos, or deciding which movie to watch. But she can't trick herself anymore. She can't unsee what she saw so clearly.

She knows. She knows without question. There could be some mysterious watch and a photo and his own petty jealousies and God, even that shove — but then there was his face. And his face changes everything.

The hatred in his eyes. A jury could never see that, could they? But she did. She did, and the regret pours in, and the remorse, and the knowing, and the fear. Jesus, she has been so stupid, and careless, and she is so sorry, to everyone, to herself, to Virginia and Sarah. She is so, so sorry, and, now, so afraid.

She shoves the towel and the washcloth in the back of her closet, into her zippered-open suitcase. She can't bear to look at them. There. Gone.

She peeks out the front door. She takes the will and the tarp out into the rain. She opens the garbage can lid, and drops them in. Not good enough. She covers them with the last bag of kitchen garbage. She is scared out there — she looks up and down the street, which is empty, shiny black with rain. The dark, dewy trees loom overhead. They tell her what a fool she's been. They tell her she's in much, much trouble now. She hurries back inside.

She locks the door again. Her phone is vibrating. *Buzz, buzz. Buzz, buzz.* A text. God, she doesn't even want to touch that phone.

Staying at Bayshore Inn for the night. Talk tomorrow.

Bayshore Inn — just above the restaurant where she and Henry and Dr. Mark and Jerry had dinner. It could have all been over then.

For the night.

Talk tomorrow.

The beast she must manage is much larger

454

than she ever thought, and much more dangerous. But she'll never spend another night with him under the same roof again.

She calculates. She doesn't want to respond at all, but if she doesn't answer, he might return. If she says too much or too little the beast might pace and stomp and drive her mother's car back into the night and come into this house.

Okay, she types. It's such a strange little word. So small. What word would be big enough for what she knows now?

She sits wide awake on their bed. She is sure she hears things. Cars driving up, doorknobs rattling. She remembers the key hidden under a flowerpot, set there in case they got locked out. Oh, God! She runs outside in her nightgown, retrieves it. So many ways we aren't safe! She goes back to her bed. Gets up again. She shoves the entry table against the front door like they do in bad movies. The kind of movies where women get punished with violence for stupid decisions like staying in a creepy house with a monster in it, or leaving a creepy house with a monster in it. Either way, she's stupid, because the monster is waiting, and either way it's her fault because she doesn't keep him away.

Her thoughts replay: He grips her robe,

he shoves; she's down. He grips Virginia's T-shirt, the one with the winged heart, and he shoves, and then Virginia's body smacks and bumps against rocks, and her arms flail, and her hands grab. *Virginia, Sarah, Virginia, Sarah,* her mind urges. It is trying to speak to her, to give her answers, but fear makes it too loud to hear anything else.

Isabelle doesn't know what will happen next. So she just sits there in the dark with her eyes wide open until she finally sleeps.

What happens next is a phone call. Just after she finally dozes, sometime after five in the morning, her phone rings. Oh, it's awful, that moment when you wake and the reality of your life rushes in. Is it true? Is this what's happened? Is this her life? It is, it is. The whole disastrous mess, because it's him calling, and it's her calculating again.

She answers. There's his voice, and he's crying. She can almost imagine the smell of bacon coming up into Henry's room from the Bayshore restaurant.

"I'm sorry, Isabelle. I'm so sorry I lost my temper. That will — I mean, wow. You didn't tell me you got this thing in the mail . . . You hid it . . . You kept secrets from me. I mean, I thought you *trusted* me. We love each other! Don't we? I love you. I mean, you're going to be my wife! It's understandable I lost my temper, isn't it?"

She doesn't know what to say, so she says nothing.

"Don't you think it's understandable?" he cries. "You can't just hide something like that . . ."

"I need some time, Henry. To sort this through . . ."

He starts to sob.

She's buying time.

"You can stay in the house," he says. "I'll stay here for a while. Until we can figure this out. Whatever you need. I'll come by in the morning and get some things while you're at work. Don't give up on us. Please, Iz."

"Henry, maybe it's best if I went to a hotel. It's your house . . ."

"No! It's *our* house. And if you leave, you might never come back. You stay there. *Please,* Izzy."

"All right."

"I'm sorry, Iz. I'm sorry for losing my temper. Try to understand. Don't leave me. I don't know if I could go on if you leave me. Just stay there, at home. *Our* home. Until we sort this out. We can get counseling or something. Couples counseling."

"All right."

"Just don't leave. Take your time. We'll figure this out."

This is the plan for now. At least, this is what he thinks is the plan.

Maggie is silent. Maybe from fear or shock, or because Isabelle is finally seeing clearly. Or maybe Maggie's just holding her breath.

Joe is back on Parrish, but he can't fly with those ribs. Things are a mess minus him and one plane, and Jane's going nuts with schedule changes and calls to contract pilots. Tourist season is starting to pick up. Still, Isabelle calls in sick.

"It's fine, Isabelle. It's fine," Jane says. Jane just wants her off the phone. At this point, Isabelle is more hindrance than help.

Isabelle heads into town, but it's all sneaking and spy moves. When she drives down these familiar streets, she's looking left and right, left and right, fearing she'll glimpse her mother's old car. There's a creepy city park in the center of town — at least, it's dark from the shade of its large evergreens, and there are park bathrooms with wet floors and the lingering smell of cigarettes. In high school, they had end-of-the-year parties here, and the moss-thick lawn would fill up with parents and food on picnic tables, columns of smoke rolling up from the small grills set into concrete squares. Kids would sneak beer, and some band that would break up two weeks later would play on the top of the hill. But now Isabelle drives into the lot, parks near the volleyball pit, empty save for a drooping net and a rectangle of damp sand. No one will see her car here.

She makes a lurking rush for it, the police station. She's been here only once before when she was maybe ten years old. Then, she was with her mother after they'd had a break-in at Island Air, back in the day when they had an actual cash register with actual money in it.

Inside the station, there's a water cooler set next to two chairs, and one of those machines with old weird candy from the late 1970s. Rosemary Milligan, Jed Milligan's mom, is at the front desk.

"Isabelle! How great to see you! What can I do for you?"

Rosemary Milligan, with her big cushy breasts and her blunt gray hair — she stares Isabelle right in the eyes. She knows.

"I was wondering if I could speak with Officer Beaker."

"You're in luck. He'll be here any minute."

Isabelle waits beside his desk. On it,

there's only a single file folder, and a neat stack of paper napkins, and a photo of a cat under a Christmas tree. In the trash is a burger box from Pirate's Plunder and a soda cup with a plastic lid and a straw, fiercely crushed. Ricky Beaker actually hitches his waistband when he sees her, as if he's the sheriff in an old western. He smells like he's just come from a shower. There's the tart waft of that green Irish soap. She stands a good three inches above him.

"Well, look who's here," he says.

She tells him about the shove. She tells him about the will and the jealousy. She shows him the watch and the photo.

It's nothing they don't already know. He looks at her as if she'd gone to a party and was somehow shocked to find that people were drunk. He taps a pen, waiting for something significant.

"Well, I'll tell the Boston folks, but I doubt it'll change anything."

"He shoved me, Officer. Like he shoved her."

"You should get a restraining order," he says. "Want me to take those?" He's referring to the watch and the photo.

"Will they help?"

"You got them from some stranger in the mail."

"Never mind, then. I'll keep them." He shrugs. Virginia's life seems to have come to that: a shrug.

"What's going to happen?" she asks.

"He'll get away with it. He already has."

"That's all you have to say?"

"He'll get away with it, unless he does it again."

Henry said he'd come by in the morning when she wouldn't be there, but she's nervous going back to the house. It's late afternoon, and there's no car in the drive, but still. She unlocks the door, looks for signs that he's been home. The kitchen's been cleaned. The counter is shiny, and the coffee cup that she left in the sink that morning has been put away. The bed has been made.

It's a silly thought, but there regardless: If she wanted to put her dirty cup away, she would have put her dirty cup away. Okay? Thank you.

She opens his closet. She can't tell what's missing, so not much is. In the office, his laptop is gone.

With the precious poems! Little ego glories! Florid eulogies for dead lovers!

Her anger is stretching out, like it's suddenly gotten more closet space. God, she's pissed. That shrug . . . She wants to only use the word *murderer* when she thinks of Henry, but his humanity makes the truth more complicated than that, makes his wrongdoings both larger and smaller. He is a coward and a bully, a soul thief, a spirit robber. But Ricky Beaker's shrug says Henry has won, that he's bigger than everyone. That he's a murderer who has gotten away with it. Henry has diminished and destroyed in order to feel larger, and he *is* larger. She's here, still scared of him. She is terrified. And the law shrugs.

This isn't her house. It's Henry's. No, it's Remy's, and before that, it was Clyde Belle's. Powerless Clyde Belle — how these walls must have closed in on him, too. How tormented he must have been by that gray sea, forever stretching outside these windows. Waves going in, waves going out, paying his misery no mind.

She can't stay in here. It's only late afternoon, and the long evening is ahead of her. She puts on her swimsuit, takes her wetsuit out of the closet. She hikes the steep trail down to the cove, with the rubber suit a soulless body over her arm. Down at the beach, she puts it on.

She plunges in. Dear God, the water is icy on her face. It is arctic and blasting. It is the elements of survival in remote places, smacking her a good one. She strokes. The waves push and shove and she shoves against them. Here, this is who is boss, the shoves say. She kicks, because this is who can kick back.

She has to stop for air and a rest. She floats there in the sea. She can see the lighthouse at the tip of Deception Point. The light looks small, but it's large enough to save sailors from drowning.

No more.

Funny, it's not Maggie's voice but her own. It's loud. It comes out of her like a serpent, a hydra, a devil whale. She could rise from that sea and breathe fire. She could wrap herself around evil ships and crush them with her body. *No more, you asshole. You bitch. You tyrant.*

She bobs there. Bobs — such a friendly word, a little party of a word, but this is not what she feels inside. Oh, finally, the pieces have shifted and shown themselves, recognized each other; connected to form one creature. It's anger, and more anger. It's fed-fucking-up. The sun will set soon, and the crows will come home en masse. But, look. There is one now, flying away. He's going the wrong direction. He's leaving this place, fighting against the high current with his wings and his will. Maybe no one will ever see him again.

She beats the water currents back to shore with her own will. The cold has brought fury and some mobilizing energy. Henry is *more powerful,* as all the more powerful people in her life have been. Larger, stronger, more in the ways that make badness win, but fine. *Bring me down fighting, at least. At least, I can kick and scream on my own behalf.*

What makes the monster finally emerge? What finally gives him life? No idea, but once he's there, he's there. He is gloriously, viciously, permanently there.

Take that, you bully, says Isabelle, a long-ago age three. *You can't make me,* says Isabelle, a long-ago age six. *You don't scare me,* says Isabelle, a long-ago age ten. *You're not the boss of me,* says Isabelle, a long-ago age fifteen. *Fuck you,* says Isabelle, age now.

She almost reaches shore, when a new word appears. Oh, it shines like steel in the heat of the sun.

Hate.

She tries it out. *I hate you.*

She is on the beach now. She should be breathless, but — surprise — all that swimming has made her strong after all. She screams, yells. Her voice fights the wind but is louder than the wind.

Again: *I hate you!* And *You will not ruin me!*

It's almost beautiful. Frightening, but powerful. Wow, how it shimmers, how it throws bolts.

How it makes her see the picture, stunningly clear all at once.

The watch, the photo, the journal.

The will.

The hate.

Take that, you bully.

Can it be?

Giddiness rises. It *can* be.

It *is,* she's sure of it.

Oh, wow. Oh, beautiful strength and triumph. Beautiful retribution. Yes. Take that, and that!

Dear God, the joy fills her along with the realization, no, the *hope* does — the hope of the underdog, who might actually pull off the win. Not alone, though. She has to be the one to help. Her will, joining another's will; her final act joining another's actions, because she knows who sent those packages, yes she does. *Yes!* she thinks. *Yes! Yes! Yes!*

She is flying when she reaches the trail. There are a lot of steps, and it is a long way up after that, but she's got this. Her muscles pull and remind: A body is a force. Her own is small and it's been both harmed and ill-used, but just because something was doesn't mean it always will be.

Back home, she sheds her suit. She changes into dry clothes and gets back into her car. She heads to the Front Street Market, checking over her shoulder. She buys a disposable phone, because she sees the whole story. She has always been good at seeing the whole story — she's a reader and an English major and an editor. But more than that, she's smart. She remembers how smart.

At the house again, with the locks clicked shut and the table shoved against the front door, she pours herself a glass of wine for the last of the necessary courage. Maybe soon she won't need the wine, but not yet. Maybe she'll always need a little support when she must be this brave, but who cares? Who wouldn't? She calculates the time difference. She makes a call.

That night, Ricky Beaker is back out on her street, and between him and that swim in the sea and the rise of the underdogs, she sleeps like the dead.

CHAPTER 34

There are so many different kinds of calls. There's the noisy outcry of rival crows before a fight, and the continuous cawing of a murder of crows as they mob the source of their thrill and peril. There are the short bursts of caws followed by silence, which make up the companion calls; and the sub-song mixtures involving coos, rattles, and clicks. There is the *car-car-cockle-cockle gargle,* often from a young bird begging for food, as Bébé Noir is doing now. Tahlia scritches on her clipboard, and Weary watches, listens.

Of course, there is the liquid *coi-ou* of courtship. And the far, far quieter call: the hidden sound of passion called the whisper song.

But one should never forget the most intriguing *Corvus* call of all — the ones in which the birds pretend to be other birds. The crows are such good mimics, they can even pretend to be humans speaking human words.

"Professor!" Lotto appears. "Phone for you. A woman. She says it's urgent."

Weary rises quickly. He hurries out of the jungle, runs to the office.

A woman. Urgent.

It has to be her. It has to be Isabelle, making her own call from her own jungle. She's done it! Oh, he hopes, hopes, hopes she has. He can't wait to hear her voice. He can't wait to say, *Yes, I know.* Finally! He can't get there fast enough. He is huffing and puffing. His muscles flame from effort and speed. Right then, if he were a corvid, the call rising from his own chest would be one never heard from *Corvus* before — the pure joy of song.

CHAPTER 35

Every day, Isabelle swims and swims in the cove. She swims at the same time each morning. People see her. Ricky Beaker does, and so do the new neighbors, John and Rock, from way down the beach, the couple with the dog. They are always out when she is. The dog's name is Cordelia. Isabelle pets her. She sniffs the rubber of Isabelle's wet-suit. Even though it is summer, it's still too cold to swim in the sound without it. She tells the couple how much she loves the water, even if her fiancé thinks it's danger-ous to swim out there.

She meets Jane. At Jane's house. When she drives down the gravel road to Little Cranberry Farm, she thinks about the last time she was here, and how she could have saved herself a lot of trouble. Then again, she wouldn't be here now, doing something this large. Crows fly, planes do, and so do superheroes. All right, of course, she is not one of those. But she lately feels ready to take on every past and future villain, from cheating husbands and controlling, violent boyfriends to frightening mothers and righteous hair stylists and rage-filled drivers and superior dentists. Every dismissive, entitled, sadistic asshole, watch out. There are things you can't unsee, and feelings you can't unfeel, and once anger is out of the box, it ain't going back in. Even if she can't fix it all, even if she can't force every bully to cower, she can make one thing turn out right.

And isn't this, strangely enough, the adventure, the large life, the bold move she has always longed for?

Isabelle is happy to see Rosie and Button, and they are happy to see her. They remember her. It's nice to know you're not easily forgotten.

"Are you sure?" Jane asks.

"Very. Are *you*?"

"Better believe it."

"Even if you'll be —"

"I know what I'll be. Eddie knows what he'll be. We're a couple of old hippies. We do whatever the fuck we want, if we think it's right."

"And Joe?"

"We're a family. We protect our own."

"Am I crazy?"

"Indeed you are."

"Let's toast," Isabelle says. They are nervous, even with the brave words. The right toast is complicated.

"To flight," Isabelle says.

"Safe flight," Jane amends.

The contracts arrive a few days later. Isabelle signs without even reading them. All she needs is a lump sum, some of which she'll make disappear, some of which will appear elsewhere in a few weeks time, when everything's ready.

She talks to Henry, too. She *caw-caw*s, coos, rattles, clicks. She murmurs a liquid *coi-ou*.

They talk every night. She paces while they do. She steps carefully, measures her words. He coerces. She stalls.

Should she feel bad? After all, he is still Henry. He is still a man she fell for and kissed and lay naked with, still a man she once saw a future with, even if it was always a complicated one. She *could* feel bad, because he's not some unformed image of a criminal. He has real wrinkles at his eyes, and a laugh that makes you laugh, and real insecurities, and real dreams and fears. But Isabelle doesn't feel bad, because Virginia

471

had those things, too. Real dreams and fears. Isabelle doesn't feel bad because she imagines that winged heart on Virginia's T-shirt, momentarily in flight, and then crashing.

"I want to come home, Isabelle. Haven't I been punished enough? It's been almost six weeks. Summer is almost over already. I'm sick of this. We can't let this go on too long."

"This has been good, Henry," she says. "The distance has been important. I was getting all wrapped up in my own head. Wedding, marriage, those packages in the mail . . ."

"Let me come home."

"Henry, I've told you a million times. You *should* be here at home. I should be in the hotel. I want to be."

"With you! I want to be home with you. And I won't allow it. I've told *you* a million times, if you move out, you may never move back in. I'm not taking that chance. I'll stay if I have to. I'll do whatever it takes."

"I just want to be in the right frame of mind."

"Committed, a hundred percent?"

"Right."

"Let me see you at least. I miss you."

"Oh, Henry. The separation helps me remember why I want this."

"I need to at least see you, Isabelle. At the least let's have dinner together. Sit at a table and hold hands. I can't bear staying in this room . . ."

"Are you getting out?"

"Yes, of course. I don't mean I've locked myself in here. I mean, God, I'm lonely. Please, Isabelle. Please. You have no idea what a torment this has been. Come on. Dinner."

"Dinner, then."

"Tomorrow?"

"All right."

What is she thinking! How can she see him, knowing what she knows? She is thinking of the greater good. She is still *managing the beast.*

Be careful, Maggie says.

Maggie's been so quiet. It's as if she stepped away, same as any good parent when their child is pedaling, pedaling on their own two wheels. But now the hand is back on the seat, because the bike is wobbling. There's been so much bravery and big talk, and then there's the truth of the tiny bike and the big hill.

I can handle him.

But of course Isabelle is wrong.

It's surprising, all the ways anger looks.

Viewed mostly from a frozen, crouched place, it seems like one animal. From down there, you think fury is in-your-face shouting; that it has a twisted mouth; that it has a hand on you, ready to harm. When it becomes yours to scrutinize and even own, though, it *is* like that — yes, it's furious, but it's other things, too. It's so quiet sometimes. It simmers. It plots and plans. It manipulates and lies. But it's not only ugly things. It's a force. It draws the line. It's not just an enemy.

And, look at all the things to be angry at. The biggest injustices, like murder. Like any violence, but lesser cruelties, too: being picked at, like a bad piece of fruit. Being made small. Being made frightened. *Being made* most things, because *being made* means someone more powerful has your arm twisted behind your back. It means that someone larger has used that largeness to do harm. Isabelle is angry at sarcasm. She is angry at names she's been called, and at unfair criticisms. She is angry at *the right way,* when what she does is *the wrong way.* She is angry at all the jobs she's foolishly taken on: the caregiver, the nurse, the listener, the self-esteem builder. She is angry at moods, and sullen, silent expectations, meanness. She is angry at ego and narcissism and the uncharitable stance; dismissiveness and using and demand, stupid ego-poems needing glorifying.

She is angry at her own self, for allowing. For acting like a scared child when she is a grown woman.

She is angry at her own self for managing and placating, which is what she does now, as she stares inside her closet, trying to make a fast decision because she's nearly late. Should she wear the same clothes she wore to work today? No. He'll feel she hasn't made an effort. Skirt? No. Inviting more than dinner, somehow, because he loves her in a skirt. Another thing to be angry at. He loves her in a skirt and heels, because he loves all women in skirts and heels, and so this makes her simply an image, an object.

Enough.

He'll read her mind.

She chooses a plain sundress and sandals. She quickly dabs perfume at her wrists and behind her ears as if she's a movie star from the golden age of film. Anger looks like this, a trick before the pounce.

He insists on picking her up. Like an old-fashioned date, he says, but she's sure it's because he'll also have to drop her off. He'll try to come in — into the house, into the bed. She can handle him! She can't stand the thought of him crossing a threshold to where she sleeps at night. She runs outside when she hears the car.

It's funny that he looks familiar, like the same old Henry, a man she bought a Christmas tree with. A man she bought cough medicine for, when he had a cold. She watches his profile as they drive; she remembers their first ride together after his car broke down, which seems like so long ago now. They head to The Bayshore again. It's Friday night, but it's still early, and there's only a smattering of diners sitting at the candlelit tables. Oh, he looks handsome, he does. It's wrong, how handsome he looks. His eyes glitter in that light.

She sits on the padded bench seat behind the table, and he sits across. Then he changes his mind. "Forget this," he says. "You're too far away. Scoot."

She does. Her purse is now on his other side. She leaves it there. This is the one wrong move, the thing that'll do her in. Or, rather, it's one of many wrong moves, but maybe the last.

She isn't thinking straight. And who can blame her? His hand holds hers, and she is imagining that hand in Virginia's. She is thinking about inky black prints on each fingertip. Anger, well, too, it can make you feel big and bold enough to be untouchable. Bigger than you are, and that can be a problem.

He is chatting. The drinks arrive, and then the appetizers. He has ordered two martinis, and the calamari Jerry was so disdainful of. More things to be angry at: presumption, disdain, superiority. He stabs a fried ring and dunks it in red sauce, pops it into his mouth. He dabs his lips with his napkin.

"Wait until you hear my surprising but wonderful news."

"Your poems?" Dear God, say it isn't true.

"No, no. My heart is broken! I can't write a thing lately, let alone wade in the publishing seas. *Other* news. Something else. Something for *us*." He lifts her hand, kisses it. Acid burns through her flesh, fury knocks against her bones.

"Whatever it is, it's made you happy."

"I'm happy to be here with *you*. But yes, happy about this, too." He pauses for dramatic effect. "I bought a boat today."

Jesus. Her heart drops. "A boat?"

She thinks of Sarah, of course. Sarah, and what Isabelle now knows happened to her on her last night. Isabelle thinks of Sarah thrashing in that cold, rough water, trying

477

to untie the knot of that dinghy as he watched. Sarah, disappearing into that blackness.

"I couldn't stand being cooped up all day, so I went down to the docks. And there it was! I bought it on a whim. A thirty-four-foot Sea Ray, with three berths! Master, queen, guest . . ."

"Wow, Henry."

"I said, to hell with it! I have the money. Can you imagine the fun we can have? We'll cruise the islands. It's a shame we've lost this whole summer. Still, we can go out in any weather, really. With that kind of ceiling height, you won't feel cramped if you're out for days. I haven't had a boat since . . ."

"Sarah."

"Let's not, Isabelle. Okay? I was going to say, 'Since I lived in Boston.' Let's keep the focus on the future. Wait until you see it! It's a beauty."

"That's great, Henry. That's fantastic."

And as horrible as she feels right now about a boat and Sarah and Henry wanting her on a boat, too, it *is* fantastic. It's a stroke of luck. A big, expensive purchase is *motive*. Money, the desire for it, greed — it's a motive people can easily understand. The real reason he pushed Virginia off that ledge — how could you even explain it, without seeing the hatred in his eyes? Rejection makes Henry feel so small and so furious that any woman who makes him feel that bad deserves to be punished. The *How dare you* of a fragile ego ignites a tantrum of rage and destruction that's so incomprehensibly primal, we must blame the victim and hunt for the big life insurance policy.

They order dinner. Plates arrive. A bottle of wine is opened, emptied. Henry is all lovey-crooney. He stares into her eyes. Isabelle forces softness into her own gaze, but truly, as she looks at him, she thinks about what makes such a man. Or any person. You can feel sorry for tyrants because they never got what they needed as children, either. You can feel sorry, or even forgive, but you shouldn't, because they've had the same choices as everyone else, and because that degree of empathy and kindheartedness only leaves you with your throat exposed right in the sightline of the hawk.

"This is why I need to see you. So I don't forget how beautiful you are."

Go ahead, she thinks. *Forget.* "Oh, you're sweet."

"Speaking of sweet, we must have dessert."

"It's getting late, Henry. We've had so much wine on top of that martini."

"I want to get you drunk so I can take advantage of you."

"I told you! We're just having dinner . . ." What a delicate lady she's being, there in her pretty little dress! She's making herself sick.

"Well, then, we're definitely ordering dessert. I want this night to last as long as possible."

He lingers over the menu. The waitress takes his order and then returns. She brings one plate with two forks. It's a slice of cheesecake, with a gory drizzle of raspberry sauce. He feeds her the triangle tip; he knows that's her favorite part of any dessert. She opens her mouth and takes it like a baby bird. He strokes her arm, up and down, up and down, and then her thigh.

Even though her skin recoils, even though she is counting each second until she's out of there, she stays calm. She's got this. She's had a little too much to drink, but still, she's the one in command now, how about that, Henry North? She is sitting there for the greater good. She is the one with the plan, even as he brushes her cheek.

"You have a little something right here," he says.

God forbid she be imperfect!

The largeness of anger can be such a

problem, if you're not careful. It makes you sloppy. It inspires big, impulsive acts like shoving someone off a cliff, and it makes you forget the details that keep you safe.

The check arrives. He reaches into his jacket pocket, feels for his wallet.

"Oh, shit," he says. "I must have left it in the room. Do you mind? We'll use the card."

The card he gave her months and months ago, the card she hates to use, because it was just another way he forced their togetherness. "Oh, sure," she says. She reaches for her purse, but it's right there next to him, and in a moment, his hand is inside.

Her wallet is in the center section, where she puts the things she most wants to keep safe. It's where she always puts the watch and the photo, too, and where they still are, after her visit to the police station. Since Henry left, she has not been diligently moving those objects from her purse to the boot in the closet, and she remembers this just as his fingers are down there inside. The realization flies to her gut with the speed of a fatal collision. She grabs for the purse, but it's too late. After all this, after everything, it is right then, at that moment, too late.

"What's this?" he says.

He lifts the watch out of the bag. He sees what it is immediately. The watch dangles between them as he holds it in his fingers. He stares at her in shocked silence and she is too stunned to move, and, besides, her heart has stopped.

He doesn't say anything, and neither does she. But his eyes go cold and it's clear, it's very clear: He knows that *she* knows. Virginia's watch, that photo — he may not know where she got them, but he understands that she has no doubts, none, about what happened that day on the trail.

He stares at her silently, but the loving gaze is gone. There's the clink and clatter of silverware and dishes, glasses and ice, the loud hum of conversation around them.

"Goddamn you," he says finally.

"Henry . . ."

"Now you've ruined everything."

His words are cold, too, so cold, and she thinks again of Sarah in the frigid water and she edges out of that seat. He grabs her arm. He grips tightly.

She yanks free.

"Wait —" Henry North calls, but she doesn't wait.

She pushes past servers and the hostess seating a party of four. She shoves and elbows her way to the doors, thrusts them open. She's outside in the dark night, without her purse, without a car. Where to go? She'll run if she has to. But she remembers suddenly that Tiny Policeman will be there, parked outside The Bayshore. She just needs to find Officer Ricky Beaker, waiting in his patrol car.

She madly scans up and down the street. Where is he?

It can't be.

He's not there.

He's not there!

She sees the packed parking lot full of Bayshore Inn diners, and she sees a Franz Bakery truck, and a pair of motorcycles across the way, but there is no cruiser. Tiny Policeman is nowhere in sight. Her own car is back at home.

She's stranded.

"Isabelle!"

He's outside now. He's there, holding her purse. Isabelle is in her pretty little sundress and her sandals, but she runs. The night has gotten chilly. You can feel fall coming. Dear God, yes, fall is coming, for sure — fall, a fall, falling.

She runs, who knows where. Past the marina by The Bayshore. She turns the corner. It won't take him long to reach his car. She searches for something, someone who might help. Her mind spins, crazy. The stores of

Main Street are closed. Only the pharmacy is open.

And then, oh *Thank God!* She sees her — Remy, coming out of the store, holding a small, white pharmacy bag. She's a tiny, bent figure on the street, lit by streetlight.

One wrong move — a watch in a purse, and she has messed up the plan so bad. There is no time for regrets, though, because the plan is something different now. The plan has changed to making it out alive.

"Remy! Can you help me? I need a ride!"

"Isabelle! What a pleasure. Well, sure. Of course, sweetie. As long as you aren't going to California, heh-heh."

Before Remy agrees, Isabelle is in that Volkswagen. She slams the door. Her heart pounds like crazy. She looks around, but there is no sign of Henry yet.

"I just had to get my blood-pressure medication," Remy says. She settles in. She hunts in her purse for her keys. *Come on!* Remy's old hand trembles as she gets the key into the ignition. "I'd run out of blue pills and almost didn't realize. You heading back to the house, sweetie?"

Isabelle frantically plays out the scenarios in her head. She shouldn't go back to that house. She should forget all about the plan. She should forget anything but her own safety. She should shout and scream, tell Remy what is happening. They should head for the police station. But then she realizes: This is what he'll expect her to do. This is where he'll go first. She still has time. There is still a chance to make this come out all right, if she hurries.

She forces her voice to be calm. "Yes. Yes, thank you. The house. My car engine . . ."

Remy's Volkswagen chugs down the street. Isabelle cranes her neck as they pass the waterfront. She can see Henry by the Acura, hurrying to unlock the door.

"They don't make them like they used to, do they?" Remy says, patting her dash. "Good thing I happened along! You look flushed, sweetie, are you all right? What's that on your arm?" Remy's right. Henry's fingers have left long red tracks where he grabbed her. She notices the way they burn now. "You weren't part of the big chase, were you?"

"Chase?"

Jesus, Remy is going two miles an hour! Isabelle looks in the side mirror as they head toward the loop. It's so dark out there, she'd see the pair of headlights behind them, but there's nothing. Just darkness and more darkness.

"That Kale Kramer. Finally caught in the

485

act! I just heard from Betty at the pharmacy. Bud called it in. That creep was hot-wiring in plain sight, right in front of the tavern. He was halfway down the block when little Ricky took chase. My, my, Tiny Asshole has finally had his day."

Isabelle can imagine it — Ricky Beaker, the law, the copper, The Man, hitting that accelerator, flipping that siren on, screeching in a sweet arc right in front of some rattled tourist's Ford Focus with Oregon plates. The highlight of Tiny Policeman's life! Until he hears that he missed the true action. Until what happens to Isabelle hits the news.

"Remy, can we . . . Um, we're driving a little slow."

"My car, my speed. Plus, I can't see a thing out here. Better safe than sorry."

Shit, shit, shit!

Think.

Be calm, Isabelle tells herself, but she is anything but calm. She has turned to ice, and her knees tremble. She needs to call . . . She can't call anyone. Her phone is in her bag.

They're at the house. It's as dark as this night is, so dark. In her haste, she forgot to leave a light on. "Here you are, sweetie. It's pitch-black! Aren't you worried about someone jumping out at you when you can't see? Someone could be hiding right there with a knife, for all you know. Well, good luck with your car. I'd wait to make sure you get in okay, but I've got to hurry and let Missy out. She craps all over from nerves if I'm gone too long."

"I'll be fine, Remy. Thanks. Thanks so much."

Now Remy screeches out of there. She reverses the car and is down the street before Isabelle realizes: no keys.

Her keys are in her purse. Shit. Shit! She isn't thinking clearly. She doesn't need much from that house, but she does need a few things. And she has to make a call, two calls, on that disposable phone that is thankfully still inside.

The hidden key under the flowerpot, she remembers.

But no. It's no longer there. She brought it in that night Henry shoved her.

The flowerpot is still there, though.

She saw this in a movie once, right? She carries the flowerpot to the side of the house. She lifts her dress over her head, removes it, wraps it around her hand to protect it against breaking glass. The Isabelle who cowered from her mother, who tiptoed around Evan and then Henry, the pleasing, law-abiding woman, she's gone. Isabelle stands there in her bra and underwear in the black of night. She listens for Henry driving up the street in her mother's car, but she hears only the crash of surf. Now another crash, as she bashes that pot through the glass with the force of her fear and fury.

Take that, you asshole.

Her fist is through. She has made a clean break, ha. She reaches in, unlocks the kitchen door.

Think, think, think.

Isabelle tells herself this. *She* does, not Maggie. Maggie's voice has vanished. Isabelle is riding that bike by herself now, but she is terrified. She is terrified and flying downhill, and her hair whips in her face. What can Maggie do? What can her mother's voice — the one she's been summoning for a year and a half — do now, anyway?

She puts the dress back on. She finds the disposable phone in her dresser drawer. Her fingers shake and it's all wrong-number dialing and then trying again, just like in those bad dreams. And then, thank God, *ring ring ring.*

Please answer!

Ring, ring, ring.

"Hello?"

Thank God, thank God, thank God! There are things that need to happen. Things she thought she had time for.

Isabelle's words come out in a rush. When she hangs up, she puts the phone in her small bag, newly bought. The phone is one of the things she must take with her. So is the small pack of documents and the Travelex cash card sent to her a week ago, and so is her laptop, with all the hunting and searching she's done on it. There's not much else she can take, except for the change of clothes she's also recently purchased.

There are two other things she wants to bring, though. Both are worth the risk. First, she stuffs Jane's scarf into the bag. And then, the robe with the crane on the back, the one from her mother. With everything she must now leave behind, she needs that robe. It's the thing she'll carry forward, satin-soft, the color of fire. The thing that will always remind her of who she is and where she came from.

The trail down to the water is steep, and even in these shoes, her feet slip from loose gravel. Her bag bumps against her hip. The wetsuit slaps against her arm. She hurries. She is trying to save the plan, even if it may be impossible now.

Her feet hit sand. The waves glow white in the moonlight. She will not put on that wetsuit and swim out into that water, though. The water has already done its job. It's made her strong — her muscles, her will. Instead, she sets the wetsuit by a rock for it to be discovered in the morning by her neighbors, John and Rock, and their dog, Cordelia. Overnight, the wind will scatter that rubber suit with a fine layer of sand. She sets it right near the rock where Clyde Belle put the gun to his head, but she is not despairing like Clyde was. No, she is terrified but determined. It smells so good out there, this place, this beautiful, tragic home of hers. She tries to make that smell a memory.

She hears it, then.

"Isabelle? Isabelllle . . ." Her name rides on a night breeze, winds down to the beach. He's up there, calling her, searching for her.

And then it comes — something worse. Something awful and bone chilling, but also strangely, deliciously satisfying. He's seen the broken glass. She is nowhere in sight. He suddenly understands everything, not just the watch and the photo, but who the watch and the photo came from. He knows who sent her those things, and so of course he suddenly sees his own future, he sees what is about to happen, because he shouts again, and his voice crashes and bashes down that cliff, same as Virginia's body crashed down that mountain.

"You *bitches*!"

Oh, it would be beautiful, wouldn't it, to scream back and rage in his face, to be the furious beast with the contorted mouth? But Isabelle understands so much more about anger now, and triumph, too. How quiet it can be. How sure.

A person like Henry could make you feel so small, you could practically disappear. It could seem like you had vanished. Yet you aren't gone. No, you aren't. You are still here, still vital. You have a secret energy burning inside, and when you unleash it, you are more powerful than you could have ever imagined.

She slips that ring, that big diamond, off her finger. She tosses it into the sea.

Victorious bitches, she thinks.

And then she hurries. She climbs the rocks, hugs the cliff. She darts from shadow to shadow so no one will see her. It's a difficult hike, but she's scouted this path. She's up that trail so fast, she barely feels the burn. Her blood surges. Still, in the deep dark, she almost misses the last, flat rocks up to the street.

At the top, there's a car waiting. The engine idles, headlights off.

Isabelle gets in. Her heart is beating so hard, she could be sick. Isabelle does something very Isabelle then. "Are you all right?" she asks.

"Fuck no," Jane says. "We've got to get out of here. I saw his car. He's right here. Are you all right? That's the real question."

"Fuck no," Isabelle says.

Jane drives with the lights off. "I did it. Ten thousand into his account. Jesus, we're Thelma and Louise here."

"Better ending, I hope." Jane's hair is wild, and she's wearing pajama bottoms and a Grateful Dead concert T-shirt. Her hands shake, too. "Oh, shit. Stay down," Jane says. "His car is there. Your mother's Acura."

"I heard him. He was calling for me."

Isabelle feels terror — at least, she feels a cold stone in her chest. Nothing pounds or stirs now; she's as still as a creature hiding in a jungle shadow. They are silent when they pass that glass house. Isabelle thinks of Sarah, how scared she must have been on that boat, when Henry realized that she knew what happened to Virginia. It's as terrified as she is now, with Henry hunting for her. How could you possibly swim in that cold and rough water? How could you possibly climb into that boat to save yourself?

At the dock, the Beaver is already there. The engine roars, the propeller spins. Joe has fueled the plane and is untying the ropes. There's no time for long goodbyes. The flight plan has been filed, and the box *Number Aboard* has been filled with the numeral *One.* She has to hurry. No one can see her.

"Be well, Isabelle."

"Thank you for everything, Jane."

"Your mother would be oddly proud, I think."

"I think so, too."

"Go. Go! We love you. Stay safe." Isabelle kisses Jane's old cheek, and they hug hard before Isabelle steps off that dock for the last time.

She takes her seat. Joe pops his head in. "Buckled in? Ready?"

"Ready. Thank you, my friend."

He takes her hand. Gives it a kiss. "Do it one hundred percent," he says, before he slams the door shut.

Outside, Joe unties the last lines. Eddie taxis across the water before finally rising. The engine roars, but Isabelle is silent, as Parrish Island grows small below her.

"In Alaska, I once gave the Barefoot

Bandit a ride from Ketchikan to Seattle," Eddie shouts.

"Your secret is safe with me."

Flying low over Lake Washington, just before landing, Isabelle ditches her laptop out the door. It spirals and spins before hitting the choppy waves. She can see it sinking. Fifty minutes have passed since she stepped off that dock. In those fifty minutes, she's become a new person. They land at Kenmore Air, which is staffed only from dawn to dusk. Night landings are allowed but not recommended due to small watercraft. Usually, a pilot must call two hours ahead to arrange the hundred-and-fifty-dollar docking fee when a landing is unattended. Well, they know Eddie. An hour is no problem at all. He does this all the time.

What's going to happen? Isabelle had asked Ricky Beaker.

He'll get away with it.

That's all you have to say?

He'll get away with it, unless he does it again.

He's done it again, because Isabelle is gone.

CHAPTER 36

Professor M. Weary showers and dresses. He can barely contain his excitement, but he must try. He knows it will take some time for Isabelle to adjust, and so he must give her adequate space and calm. That first night in her hotel room, Isabelle will fear every rumble from the ice machine and bolt upright at the footsteps of traveling salesmen. In the morning, the shock will hit. The disbelief will. She will question her own sanity. She'll circle her reasoning again and again. She will marvel at how little she has with her. She'll cry with regret and grow giddy with possibility.

He knows this.

He knows that she will look at herself in the mirror, at any alterations she makes in her appearance, and she'll feel a jolt, and a sense of marvel. But she'll look over her shoulder and weigh every word from every stranger. She will read every expression and gesture as she has done since she was small, but even more so, for a long while. It takes a long while to stop being afraid after you've been that afraid. It takes a long while to trust your own self when you've been so questioned.

Another thing she'll do? Replay that night again and again, same as Professor Weary did. *Does.* He remembers it all. It will never leave him. How, on the boat trip, Henry had caught Sarah writing that email to Virginia's sister, Mary. How Henry's face twisted in rage. How the hatred burned in his eyes. She'd been so careful, to hide the watch and the photo and her journal in Gavin Gray's safety deposit box, but she'd gotten nervous, cooped up with Henry like that on the boat. Scared, as his paranoia about Gavin Gray got crazy. Someone else needed to know what was going on, in case something bad happened to her.

And then it did. The worst possible thing happened. Henry flung open the cabin door, because he always, always knew when you were betraying him. He caught her with the laptop, wrested it away. He saw the name *Mary.* He saw the words *If any harm should come to me.* It was as far in the email as she'd gotten, but it was far enough. The professor still has nightmares about that argument, about pushing past Henry in that cabin, running across the deck, and realizing there was no escape. There was only dark water, and more dark water. Rough, cold water, slapping the sides of the boat.

In his dreams, the professor can hear Henry's screaming voice. *You know nothing!* And he can feel Sarah's voice rising in her chest, unleashing, because what did it matter now, now that this was the end of her? *I know* everything. *I know what you did.* In his dreams and even in his waking moments, the professor feels Henry's hands shoving, feels the shock and cold of being suddenly submerged. He feels himself kick toward the surface, gasping for air. Again and again, he tries and tries to untie that dinghy. He feels the thick wet rope, the fist of a knot, and then, dear God, the miracle of loosening. It loosens, the dinghy is free, and he grips its edge as waves smack his face, as he swallows water, and chokes and holds on. Sometimes, when night falls on Mount Khogi, when the jungle is all around him, pulsing and dangerous, he sees Henry standing on the deck of that boat, looming above with his arms folded calmly, because Sarah's fate was certain.

And sometimes in his dreams, he cannot untie that dinghy. He cannot keep his head above the waves as the dinghy bucks and drifts, as he thrashes and fights to stay alive. He does not finally summon the impossible strength to pull himself over the side. He does not make it to shore by his own will, letting go of that boat so that it will look like Sarah has drowned. He does not watch that boat disappear over the horizon, knowing he must disappear now, too, for his own safety. And he does not stumble to an old phone booth to make the call to Gavin Gray that will save him. He thrashes, he goes under. He wakes up, trembling and panic-stricken, just as the sea wins and swallows him.

He wakes up, and his heart pounds in fear, and he must assure himself that he is alive. That *she* is. Sarah, even if the old Sarah is gone forever.

Isabelle, too, will quiz herself on her new identity, as she hides for a short time in the busy anonymity of the city. She will say her name again and again until she believes it. Weary remembers Gavin Gray's eyes showing a mix of worry and glee when Sarah told him the name she chose.

M. Weary? Are you sure? Gavin Gray said.

Am weary? Am exhausted, Sarah said. *M. Fed Up.*

And Isabelle will be glad to be alive. So

glad, because she has been so frightened, and now she is not. She's free. This feeling will never leave her. She may forget it momentarily in the busyness of the day, in the heat or the demands of the jungle, but then it will come again: the rush of relief, the gratitude for her life and its splendor, and the sheer fact that it *is.* She is not Virginia. She's not one of the many, many Virginias.

Some things will be easier for her, thanks to Weary. The same way it's always easier for the younger sister, because the older one leads the way. There will be no need for chopped hair and bound breasts, something Isabelle, with her fine features and lilting voice and small hands, couldn't have convincingly pulled off, regardless. There won't be the scrutiny, either. She won't need to stay here, as Sarah has; after a while, she can go wherever she wishes. There won't be agents making a visit, trying to locate a maybe-missing person. She will not need Gavin Gray to hide her, bless his sweet soul. Gavin Gray, who loved Sarah beyond measure, who loved her better than anyone ever had, who rescued her and kept her safe, even if her own love remained only devoted and platonic. None of this will be necessary for Isabelle. Not when she is number three.

Not with the work already done.

Such a shame number two was not enough. But, look! An arrest, in twenty-four hours! The wetsuit was found right away, and so much more, too. What a field day for the media! Isabelle has done an astounding job, and so has he. Weary couldn't have hoped for better. Isabelle is a champion. Isabelle has done an amazing job, plus.

"She only swims in the morning, never at night," said neighbor John Cardinali, 42, who found her abandoned wetsuit at the scene. *"No one would swim in that cove after dark."* Remy Wilson, the last to see Austen alive, said, *"She was nervous. She practically jumped in my car. She was in a big hurry, all right. Terrified. And marks! She had marks on her arm."* Officer Ricky Beaker, of the Parrish Island Police Department, said there were signs of forced entry, and that North had Austen's purse in his possession.

And more, more, more! Oh, Isabelle, you beauty! You fellow seeker of shelter and justice! *Police say that two bloody towels were found in an initial search of the house, as well as a trail of dried blood on the floor. Investigation is ongoing.* She recently sold her business, and only that day deposited a large sum into his account! He just bought a boat! *The rest of her funds are unaccounted for . . .*

Nevermore, Mr. Marvelous.

It's a heyday.

It's *the last word.*

Weary likes to imagine that winged heart of Virginia's, at peace at last. He needs to get to the airport, but before he leaves, he kneels by his bed. He folds his hands. He says a prayer for Virginia. And he says a prayer for Isabelle, too, that she may be happy here, that she may feel the glory that safety gives. *Dear God,* he prays, with his little religious soul. *Please.*

What can you do? He went to Catholic school! It will never leave him. Weary believes that Catholics are like alcoholics. You can stop partaking, but you'll always be one.

He loves God, and life, and rightness and goodness. He feels utterly heady. Today, he will finally meet Isabelle, at long last. The professor has filled the tank of his Jeep for the ride to the airport. He has tidied his home. He has put fresh *Amborella trichopoda* in the guest room where she'll stay until they find her a place of her own. The creamy white, delicate flowers are endemic to New Caledonia. But more important, they bloom on the longest branch of the oldest tree, the first plant to ever flower.

Professor Weary has also made a dessert. His kitchen still smells warm and sweet from the baking fruit. Everyone loves his special peach tart. The fabulous, satisfying scent makes him think of his favorite news report yet, a video, one he has watched and watched again, because he still loves, loves, loves the Internet. It's Henry North, being hustled into a squad car. He is hunched, hurrying away from judging eyes. Quite clearly, you can hear him say, *They framed me!* But the most lovely part of this video is what comes next. The way the clip cuts to the news anchor, who quite clearly smirks. Her mouth goes up ever so slightly in the corner. Her eyes don't roll, but they don't have to. *Framed? Uh-huh. Right,* her face says.

What must Henry feel now, knowing that Sarah is alive somewhere, and Isabelle, too? What must he feel, understanding that they have finally and successfully avenged Virginia's murder? Well, what did Poe say, about old Fortunato? A wrong is unredressed until the avenger makes himself felt to him who had done the wrong. At long last, Weary can sleep like a baby.

Flight is a mystery and a miracle. Did it evolve when small dinosaurs went from trees to the ground, or from the ground up to the trees? No one knows. Only *Archaepteryx,* first bird, original bird, 150 million years ago, might have an answer. There are the scientific principles involved: the shape of the wing, the strength of the breast, the thrust and swim against air currents. There is the pressing down and the pressing against.

But, too, there is the simple beauty of the act. The impossibility of it. In a flock, there is a strength, endurance. There is a sense of purpose. There is *will.* They cross over the earth, going from where they began to somewhere else. It's survival; it's majestic. So light in feather, so hollow of bone, so small in a huge sky, and yet: They rise.

CHAPTER 37

She is not Grande Terre's *Corvus monedu-loides,* or the Northwest's *Corvus caurinus.* But she is flying. She is Isabelle Austen, on United Airlines flight 272 to Nouméa. No. She is Katherine Wiley, flying United Airlines flight 272 to Nouméa. Flight says, you can leave whenever you're in danger, whenever you need to be better fed, whenever you just plain wish. Flight says, you can change direction, with your own muscle and desire.

Her seat is in the upright position, and all carry-ons have been stowed, because they are about to land. God, she's nervous. It's like she's had six cups of coffee. Even after this long trip, she's awake as a newborn at some wrong, early hour.

Now, as the old man in his zipped sweatshirt and athletic shoes rouses from sleep beside her, she thinks of her father, running away from home. She is like him, she understands. She is someone who has a too-soft step, who's had to learn about anger. She is someone who reaches the end of tolerance with sudden finality and swiftness and totality, someone who flees, for worse or for better. But she is like her mother, too. She is fierce, a force, full of rage, full of determination.

She is the fusion of both. Fight *and* flight. From here on out, she'll have to claim the messy whole, and she'll have to fight for the messy whole. She'll hold her kindness close and wield it; she'll hold her anger close and wield it. See that woman, the one in the next row who clutches the armrest as the plane's wheels hit and screech on the runway? See her grip? That's how hard Isabelle will have to hold both father and mother, both the girl on the toy box and the woman who says *Fuck you.*

Oh, she can hear the chorus now. *Forgive all the injustices against you! Let go of your anger!*

She can hear her own voice, clearly, though. *Nope. Uh-uh. No way. Anger is necessary, and don't you forget it.*

She has such a small bag in the overhead bin, and a new purse, tucked under the seat. She bustles and shoves with the rest. Out the row of tiny airplane windows, there are palm trees swaying. The door is lifted. They walk down the steps onto the tarmac. Heat hits, the surprise of a new climate.

She waits in the customs line, with her heart galloping. But the officer only glances at her and then at her photo on the passport. He stamps the blank page with a decisive *ca-shunk.*

The airport is small, and only a few people wait there for the new arrivals. Even if the crowd were large, though, Isabelle would know her. Even with her gray hair pulled back, even with no makeup and cargo shorts and a man's summer shirt, Isabelle would recognize the face she's seen so many times in photos and news stories.

"Sarah," Isabelle whispers, as they embrace.

"Isabelle."

When they separate, Isabelle is surprised and touched to see that the professor's eyes are wet with tears.

"Welcome home," Sarah says.

They ride in her Jeep. *Professor M. Weary*'s Jeep. The professor is talkative. He's way more animated and cheerful than Isabelle expected. Way more joyful than she'd been led to believe. It's the chatter and glee and caw-caw-caw of a *Corvus* reunion, but Isabelle doesn't know that yet. She has no idea. Not a clue. It'd be easy, if you could read the future, but then you'd miss all the surprises and delightful discoveries: a corvid, sliding down a roof for the sheer fun of it, a corvid, dropping a stone on a predator's head, a corvid, waving a stick to get a friend's attention.

"Thank God you're all right," the professor says again.

"And you."

The top of the Jeep is off, and there's a small splatter of rain. It's not the cold, slanted downpour of the Northwest; it's a warm drizzle, with a soft touchdown. They pass a pastel-colored city and curved beaches. They take a rough road that leads up a lush mountain. Isabelle stares at Sarah's profile. She can't stop staring. The professor is so familiar, yet not. His story is Isabelle's own, yet not.

It feels like she could tell the story a thousand times, and it wouldn't be enough. "I was so scared," Isabelle says.

The face that turns to look at her is all Sarah's face. "I know."

"I'm having a strange sense of unreality."

"You will. You will for a while. Fear does that. Flight, too."

"Then what?"

"You land. You realize you landed safely.

You realize your wings are trusty after all."

"I have no idea what to do next."

Around them are banyans and coconuts and palms whispering in a breeze. Not whispering: the birds. They click and twitter and sing and shout, and it sounds like every bird in the world, including *Corvus moneduloides,* has gathered there to speak their mind about the state of the world. Isabelle reaches a hand out from the moving Jeep, and it brushes against a vibrant red frond.

"This jungle?" the professor says. "It looks pretty much like it did sixty million years ago. Right there? That's a giant tree fern, a species that's been on earth so long it's survived every mass extinction. You have time, Isabelle. To catch your breath. To figure out what you want. You have all the time in the world."

"Maybe I'll stay right here. Look at this place."

The professor smiles. "I love it here. I love this life. Now, I wouldn't go back if I could."

"Maybe I'll get a little house. Maybe I'll travel . . ."

The Jeep strains up, up that road. The professor presses the clutch and shifts, looks over at Isabelle in the passenger seat. "Maybe you'll never have to hear another fucking line of a fucking Poe poem as long as you live."

They laugh. God, they laugh so hard. Isabelle could ride like this forever, with the beauty stretching to infinity, with the rain falling like an elixir. But she can tell their destination is not far off. There is the sense of a clearing, a widening road, a larger expanse above. In another slow and bumpy mile or two, they'll reach the professor's compound, with its welcoming wood shutters and blue-tiled pool.

It smells like paradise out there. Isabelle is still off-balance, both excited and exhausted from the trip, but she feels something else, too. Something indefinable. A small shift. It's close to rest, but not quite rest. It's relief, maybe, the kind that may one day grow into a true sense of safety and gratitude. But right now, it's just a triangle of light; the same kind that comes when it's night and a door is opened a little.

Isabelle exhales. And what a fine thing it is, she realizes. An exhale like that is worth fighting for.

The Jeep jostles forward. The professor is chattering again. Flight says, you can brave the tumult of the upper atmosphere. Flight says, the view from above will transform you. Isabelle tilts her chin. She lets the warm rain fall on her face as overhead, a bird calls to another bird, and the palm trees swish, and the sky pours riches.

ACKNOWLEDGMENTS

A big debt of gratitude and deepest affection goes to Ben Camardi, for this one, our fourteenth book together. Much heartfelt thanks, too, to my editor, Shauna Summers, whose talent, support, and friendship are appreciated beyond words. I am a lucky writer indeed to have you in my corner. Also, gratitude to the team behind the book: Kara Welsh, Kim Hovey, Jennifer Hershey, Catherine Mikula, the unfailingly kind Maggie Oberrender, Hanna Gibeau, Marietta Anastassatos, Virginia Norey, and Nancy Delia. Counting my blessings, Random House. A shout-out, as well, to my team at S&S, who contribute to a seamless whole.

Closer to home — much love and thanks to my Seattle7Writers friends and the Seattle literary community. Being a writer is a whole lot less lonely and a whole lot more fun with people around you who understand

and who share the passion. Love, too, to my oldest friend, Renata Moran, who I appreciate even more as the years go by. Yurich clan — what a bonus it is to have you in my life. And, well, it could go without saying but should never go without saying — big love and endless gratitude to you, my family: Paul Caletti; Evie Caletti; Jan Caletti; Sue Rath; Mitch Rath; Ty Rath; Hunter Rath; my sweetest sweetheart husband, John Yurich; and my children, Samantha Bannon and Nick Bannon, who have given me nothing but joy since I first laid eyes on them.

■ ■ ■ ■

WHAT'S BECOME
OF HER:
A NOVEL

DEB CALETTI

■ ■ ■ ■

A READER'S GUIDE

A CONVERSATION WITH
DEB CALETTI

Random House Reader's Circle: Crows play a huge role in the overall imagery and underlying themes of the book. Do crows have any personal meaning to you outside the book? What inspired you to use them here?

Deb Caletti: Recently, we moved from the heart of the city of Seattle to a quieter spot near Lake Washington. We live in a house that is nearly all glass in the front (sound familiar?), which faces out to the wide lake and the big sky. It is an ever-changing show out there, from storm clouds and lightning to eagles and blue-blue-blue and boats of every kind. More relevant to the book — and just like in its opening scene — every morning at sunrise and every evening at sunset, the wave of crows passes by. Some-times they are down low near the lake, and sometimes right overhead, and sometimes they make a racket, and sometimes there is only the quiet puff of wings. And, just like in the book, too, they coincide with the arrivals and departures of the seaplanes, which are also here in my regular view (I am watching one land as I write). So, my very own setting inspired me. I wanted to know more about those crows. I wanted to research and learn about their lives, and to think more about flight in general. I wanted to share the mystery and awe of their mass commute. Like Isabelle, I have seen those crows hundreds of times now — through white fog and windstorms and against the sherbet colors of sunset — and I never fail to feel the wonder.

RHRC: In many ways, *What's Become of Her* is a story about returning to the past, and eventually moving beyond it. For Isabelle, it's coming home to take over the family business; for Henry, trying, and failing, to outrun his dark past. While writing, did you find yourself returning to your past as well?

DC: *What's Become of Her* is definitely a story about understanding and moving beyond the past. Isn't that what we all must do? No matter our situation, we grapple with where we came from and what that means and how it still continues to affect us. Isabelle does not just return to the family business, but to *all* of the family business in the largest sense — her relationships with her mother and father, and how those dynamics have affected her self-esteem, her partner choices, her sense of personal power, and her relationship to anger.

Most definitely I returned to my own past while writing the book. For me, if you don't make a personal and deep connection to what you're writing, the book won't be very honest or meaningful, to either write or to read. Every time I begin a book, I ask myself what is on my mind, what is bothering me, what I might want to think more about or understand better. With this book, it was my own relationship to anger, which is, of course, rooted in my own past. I'd been thinking a lot about that, how I often felt cut off from my anger, how I didn't really understand it at all, and how it seemed a useful and beautiful thing out of my reach. Like Isabelle, I'd had adults in my childhood whose anger had been large, and like Isabelle, I had grown into someone who stepped carefully around others' aggression and my own. But how could I, or Isabelle, make sense of anger and wield it? How does one embrace it as a part of the self-protective arsenal given all humans and animals? As a writer, returning to your past is where the good stuff is, for both the book and for you as an evolving human being. You roll back the rock from the cave door, and skeletons are in there, but there is also treasure. And writing about anger and fury and wrath and rage, especially when you haven't allowed yourself to get very near those things — well, it felt pretty great. Glorious, actually.

RHRC: Though Isabelle's mother died before the story begins, she is still the driving force behind many of Isabelle's actions. Can you discuss the challenges in creating and developing a character who lives only in memory but reaches so far beyond the grave?

DC: When someone dies or even just exits your life, they can still be very, very much alive in your own mind, and the more complicated the relationship, I think, the more likely this is true. I knew, then, that Maggie could naturally become a fully developed character just from her appearance in Isabelle's thoughts, especially if we also heard Maggie "speak" in those thoughts. Maggie would be less clear and wouldn't work as well as an off-screen character, if we didn't have a way of actually hearing her voice. Dialogue is so critical to a character coming alive for a reader.

Still, Isabelle's relationship and views of Maggie are only Isabelle's own, and readers would likely know that one daughter's take on her difficult mother will be both biased and limited. Rounding Maggie out, letting the reader see that Isabelle's experience with her mom was trustworthy, this required supporting evidence from others. With this in mind, I was careful to include Jane's own complex relationship to Maggie, as well as brief insights from the people in the Parrish community, from Remy and Jan, owner of the *Red Pearl,* to Joe, and even Officer Ricky Beaker.

RHRC: Weary is a very mysterious character throughout much of the book, and it's often unclear whether or not he is trustworthy. What inspired you to create him this way?

DC: The most obvious answer is that not knowing Weary's motivations — whether he is out to harm or hurt Isabelle — builds suspense. But I also love the idea that we are all unreliable narrators of our own story;

I love that every person brings their own history and temperament and a million other things to their view of their life experiences. I am intrigued by the way people can present themselves one way, but how, after learning the events of their past, you gain a deeper understanding of that individual. Weary is a complex character, with a traumatic backstory. He is full of rage and fury, but also full of love and regret. He is sometimes cocky, sometimes insecure; he is sometimes fearless and sometimes very afraid. He confuses and unsettles us, until the pieces come together and we finally see who he truly is and what has happened to him — and then, hopefully, every mystifying emotion and behavior makes perfect sense.

RHRC: Edgar Allan Poe has a strong presence in the book and heavy influence over many characters. What inspired you to weave the poet into a modern story, and what were some of the challenges you faced in putting a fresh spin on his classic work? How did this alter your writing process?

DC: I knew I wanted to write something with contemporary gothic shadings. With both the crow-raven element and the revenge theme, Poe was a natural consideration in terms of a tie-in. My mother had a book of Poe's poetry and stories that I read as a teen, and back then, I loved the melodramatic horrors and florid language of his work. I was an avid reader of Hitchcock stories and Agatha Christie, haunted anything, gloomy-castle-plus-heroine paperbacks on up to Du Maurier's *Rebecca,* and the southern gothic classics of Faulkner, Capote, Eudora Welty, and Flannery O'Connor.

When I started thinking about *What's Become of Her,* I returned to my mother's book of Poe (with its pink cover and raven on the front), which I still have on my shelf. In rereading these poems in light of the book, I was most struck by Poe's complex relationship with women. What leapt out at me was the lost woman, the idealized woman, the attractive yet passive and helpless damsel, the dead beauty on a pedestal, the woman-as-object. Reading once again about Poe, the man, was also enlightening. His vast, unrelenting ego and his terrible, tormenting insecurity jumped out at me, too, because, while I remembered these things about him and his work, all of this looked different to me now. As someone who, like Isabelle, followed the siren call of the past right smack into an abusive relationship, I felt quite certain that I knew what I was seeing. Although I am not a Poe scholar, I at least recognized warning signs — idealization, objectification, controlling criticism, rigidity, and possessiveness. Poe seemed to share these traits with Henry (and with most abusive men), and this was my "fresh spin." It did not alter my writing process so much as enhance it. That the same personalities (and personality disorders) have existed over time — it was a piece that added layers, I felt, to the idea that people from the past can go on haunting us.

RHRC: While reading, there were many times when our predictions about the ending were totally upended by new plot twists, which made the actual ending even more satisfying. Can you discuss why you chose the ending you did, and how you imagine Isabelle's life will unfold after the final page?

DC: In spite of all the heartbreak and horrors and tough stuff and too-real plot twists a life can bring, I guess I am still an optimist. I want to believe that we can summon the power to go from victim to hero, from tragedy to triumph, in our own stories. I chose this ending because I think it's the ending Isabelle earned and Weary earned and that they both deserved.

And while that might be lofty and novelistic, I do more realistically believe in our own personal evolution, in our ability to learn from our past, even if true change remains a bit of a daily struggle. I am a believer in one-step-back, two-steps-forward toward peace and joy. So, I guess I imagine Isabelle doing just this, but in her new environment now: evolving, learning, still in the daily struggle. One-step-back, two-steps-forward, in that beautiful place where she can finally exhale.

QUESTIONS AND TOPICS
FOR DISCUSSION

1. Even though Isabelle's mother is dead before the story starts, she still maintains a strong presence as a character in the book. How did her presence affect your perception of Isabelle in the present?

2. At what point in the book did you start to distrust Henry, and what were the biggest "red flags"? What advice would you have given to Isabelle in that circumstance?

3. The raven is a commonly used archetype throughout literature and folklore; discuss any potential impact that had on your reading experience.

4. Discuss the main themes of the novel. Which did you find most thought provoking?

5. Weary's motives are often unclear; at what

point did you know Weary was a trustworthy character? At what point did you have the most doubt?

6. Discuss the significance of the title as it relates to both Isabelle and Weary.

7. Though he is not a fully developed character, Edgar Allan Poe is referenced many times throughout the story, and his work adds layers of depth to Henry and Weary. How do you think the story would be different if Poe was replaced by Robert Louis Stevenson or H. G. Wells?

8. Who is your favorite character? Why?

9. *What's Become of Her* alternates between Isabelle's and Weary's points of view; in your opinion, how did this enhance the story? How would the story have differed with only one narrator?

10. Isabelle processes anger in many different ways throughout the novel; discuss which ways were effective, and which were destructive.

11. Discuss the significance of the closing scene. What were your primary emotions as

you turned the final page?

12. In chapter 16, Weary discusses how he is perceived by the people in his neighborhood in New Caledonia; did their perceptions match yours? How did these rumors alter your opinion of Weary?

13. As Isabelle and Henry's relationship progresses, his jealous side becomes more and more apparent. Isabelle reflects, "Maybe all men have a jealous streak. Do they? She has no idea. Jealous streak — it sounds almost fashionable, like those people with black hair with a swath of white in front." What does this line of thinking tell us about Isabelle? About Henry?

14. In the final chapter, Isabelle "feels like she could tell the story a thousand times, and it wouldn't be enough." What do you think she means?

15. Who would you cast to play each character in a movie of *What's Become of Her*? Why?

ABOUT THE AUTHOR

Deb Caletti is an award-winning author and National Book Award finalist. Her many books for young adults include *The Nature of Jade, Stay, The Last Forever,* and *Honey, Baby, Sweetheart,* winner of the Washington State Book Award, the PNBA Best Book Award, and a finalist for the California Young Reader Medal and the PEN USA Award. Her first book for adults, *He's Gone,* was released by Random House in 2013, followed by *The Secrets She Keeps.* Caletti lives with her family in Seattle.

debcaletti.com
Facebook.com/DebCaletti
@debcaletti

The employees of Thorndike Press hope you have enjoyed this Large Print book. All our Thorndike, Wheeler, and Kennebec Large Print titles are designed for easy reading, and all our books are made to last. Other Thorndike Press Large Print books are available at your library, through selected bookstores, or directly from us.

For information about titles, please call:
(800) 223-1244

or visit our website at:
gale.com/thorndike

To share your comments, please write:
Publisher
Thorndike Press
10 Water St., Suite 310
Waterville, ME 04901